YESTERWORLD

YESTER WORLD

DOWN WORLD, BOOK 2

Rebecca Phelps

wattpad books **w**

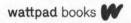

An imprint of Wattpad WEBTOON Book Group

Published in Canada by Wattpad WEBTOON Book Group, a division of
Wattpad Corp.

36 Wellington Street E., Suite 200, Toronto, ON M5E 1C7 Canada

www.wattpad.com
First Wattpad Books edition: December 2022

ISBN 978-1-99025-926-5 (Trade Paperback original)
ISBN 978-1-99025-927-2 (eBook edition)

Library and Archives Canada Cataloguing in Publication information is
available upon request.

Printed and bound in Canada

1 3 5 7 9 10 8 6 4 2

Cover design by Amanda Hudson
Images © Delveny, © getgg, © faestock via Shutterstock
Typesetting by Greg Tabor

For Steffen, who found me.

PREFACE

Time after time after time, I come back to this cold bricked-up door. Sealed, as it has been for over a year now, as I know it must remain forever. I don't know why I keep doing this to myself. I know I can never open the door to Yesterday again. I can never have Kieren back. Never talk to Brady about the things we saw under the lake all those months ago. And never tell my brother, Robbie, how my heart broke every day that he was trapped in the abyss lurking behind these immovable bricks.

Maybe I come to this room the way some people visit gravestones. The three doors are all I have left of my loved ones now. The rough, hard rectangles and their merciless mortar staring back at me. *Yesterday. Today. Tomorrow.* And me in the waiting room.

To open any of these doors is to open a pathway to death. I know this. And yet, it's as if they call to me.

No, I made my choice that night—my sacrifice. Can I undo it all just to have a moment back with my friends? What kind of monster would that make me?

PART ONE

CHAPTER ONE

"Marina, come back to earth," Christy said.

"Hmm?"

"You're doing it again, staring into space."

I straightened up and pushed away my lunch tray, the untouched macaroni and cheese having congealed into a yellow science experiment gone awry. "Sorry. I'm listening, go on."

"You sure?"

"Totally."

Christy glanced around the cafeteria at the hordes of teenagers stuffing their faces. We were sitting together at the edge of the stage rather than at the tables, a privilege reserved solely for seniors who were "academically excelling and consistently not absent," as Miss Farghasian was fond of reminding us. We were now at the start of the second semester, and those of us who qualified had dwindled from roughly forty to just seventeen.

"Okay, let's do this," Christy continued. "Which of the following is the correct formula for the ratio of cosecant? Opp over hyp, hyp over opp, hyp over adj . . . Macy Traper is pregnant, by the way."

"Hmm?" I brought my attention back to Christy from where it had landed: a spot on the stage that used to contain the words *Going down, down, down, to DW* but that now sported a brand-new floorboard, its shiny goldenrod color not quite matching its neighbors. "Oh, hyp over opp."

Christy slammed the book shut.

"What?"

"You're not listening."

"I am. It's hyp over opp. Wait, did you say something else?"

Christy just laughed, plopping the book back in her bag and shoving another bite of spinach salad into her mouth from a perfectly proportioned bento box, lovingly prepared with a real cloth napkin. "Never mind, it was a joke."

"Oh." I felt embarrassed by Christy's tone. She was right, I never seemed to be able to pay attention to anything for more than a few minutes anymore. I figured a change of subject was in order.

"What's today's note?" I asked.

Christy hummed a sort of "I don't know" tone and dug into her flowered lunch bag for the note her mother included every day. She straightened her neck and assumed a deep, rhythmic voice that I'm sure was meant to emulate her mother's. "'If you don't like something, change it. If you can't change it, change your attitude. Maya Angelou.'"

"I like that one," I said, as always feeling a vicarious surge of affection by hearing Mrs. Allen's motivational notes and imagining, if only briefly, that they were intended for me.

"We'll see if she changes her attitude when I tell her I'm not applying to Harvard."

"Berklee's an amazing college."

"It's a music conservatory. She'll disown me."

"Tell her Quincy Jones went there."

"Yeah, well, Michelle Obama went to Harvard, and that's all that matters. Did I tell you what my mom did at Christmas?"

"What?"

Christy gritted her teeth. "The woman printed out the Harvard application and left it under the damn tree like it was a shiny new bicycle."

I couldn't help but laugh. "She's proud of you."

But Christy just shook her head. We'd had this conversation almost every day for two months now, and it always ended the same way: a dead end.

"Hey, have you seen the new history teacher?" she asked.

"No, I don't have history till seventh," I reminded her, as though we didn't have each other's schedules memorized. But there had been buzz about the new teacher throughout the school.

Mrs. Appalitz, who had been teaching AP World History for about eight gazillion years, had abruptly retired in the fall after her husband had had a heart attack. The class had been tossed around from sub to sub ever since like a dirty napkin, nobody wanting to hold it for more than a couple of days.

But over Christmas break, the position had apparently been filled.

"Why do you ask?"

Christy laughed silently to herself in response, a coy smile spreading over her cheeks. "You'll see."

"What?"

"You'll see! Listen, I'm so sick of this salad. I'm going to get pie. You want?"

"No thanks."

"Be right back."

I pushed up against the wall on the side of the stage as Christy hopped down and headed to the dessert line, my eyes betraying me by falling back onto that shiny yellow plank of wood laid out before me, indecently bare.

o o o

I understood what Christy had been getting at the moment I stepped into the history classroom. A few months ago, we had been having a movie night at her place, and she'd insisted I watch the original Indiana Jones movie, as I'd never seen it.

About the time the movie made it to the Cairo scenes (when I was well into the extralarge tub of popcorn), Christy had leaned over and said, "You know, I don't usually go for white guys, but young Harrison Ford was *fine*."

"Agreed," I'd said. "It's something in his eyes."

"Like he knows a secret," she'd added.

The words *young Harrison Ford* had become a bit of a code to us ever since, as in, "He's not quite young Harrison Ford, but I'd let him buy me a coffee."

So here I was, sauntering into seventh-period AP World History, and there was a young man at the whiteboard writing out his name in bloodred ink: "Mr. Martel."

When he turned around, I saw the resemblance immediately, and I had to cover my face a moment to hide a smile.

It was something about the crinkle of his eyes or the way his dusty blond hair flopped a bit over his forehead. Maybe it was the fact that his tight khakis revealed he hadn't skipped the gym in a while. In any event, he was a more welcome sight than most of the teachers at this school, who all seemed to share the same predominant physical attribute: looking really, really tired.

I found my desk and busied myself with taking out pens and notebooks, trying to hide the smirk that still sat on my face over Christy's apparent teacher crush.

"So, that's the third time I've written out my name today," Mr. Martel announced out of nowhere, causing the general hum of commotion in the room to instantly die down.

"The first time it was defaced with a lovely arrangement of blue hearts."

Some of the girls chuckled at this.

"The second time it was a unicorn pooping out a rainbow onto the *M*. "

I glanced around the room to find that even the toughest of the crowd—the football players who sat in the back—were laughing now.

"I have to say, I'm a little disappointed in the effort. When I went to this school, we would have already hazed the new teacher with an open stamp pad on the desk chair or maybe a superglued filing cabinet."

Some general groans and laughter emerged from the peanut gallery, everyone instantly awkward at an adult trying to crack jokes.

"When'd you go here?" asked Angela Peirnot, her eyes falling to his feet and slowly making their way back up to the top of his head in the most obvious way possible.

"Oh, it was a fascinating part of ancient history known as six years ago."

Mr. Martel turned back towards his desk, and I heard Jackson Spartam, the biggest of the football players, whisper slyly to Adrian Washington, "How old is this guy?"

"Twenty-three," Mr. Martel answered from the whiteboard, apparently using his supersonic hearing abilities. "Which means that either I'm a total genius or the school was just super desperate for someone to fill the position. I'll let you guys decide. Now . . ."

He picked up the mammoth textbook we'd all gotten at the beginning of the year and waved it in front of him, indicating that we should take it out. "Who wants to talk about Alexander the Great?"

A grand total of nobody raised their hands.

"Oh, you're gonna make me call on you? That would be super embarrassing, for . . ." His eyes scanned the room, and I felt myself shrink into the official *not me, not me* position. Those crinkly Harrison Ford eyes, which I could now see were actually a rather striking green, landed directly on . . . "You." *Damn it.* "Your name?"

"Marina," I answered in a voice that came out squeakier than I would have liked. Getting called on in class was the sort of thing that used to make me wither into a self-imposed cocoon, but I had come a long way since starting at this school two years ago.

"It's your lucky day, Marina." The green eyes twinkled at me. "You get to read us pages one-forty through one-forty-four."

A general chorus of sympathetic groans rose up around me as I opened the imposing tome and began reading.

The text was pretty standard-issue world history: entitled white guy murdering millions of strangers in a quest to take over the world. I had trouble reading it with much enthusiasm.

AP World History had not been not my idea, it had been my guidance counselor's. "It would balance the AP Trigonometry and AP Physics beautifully!" she'd declared when I'd had my obligatory meeting with her at the end of junior year. She'd then fluffed her already poofy beehive of graying hair and popped a stick of minty gum into her red-lined mouth. "Gum?" she'd asked, offering me a piece.

"No, thank you," I had answered. "It's just that I'm going to be really busy with trig and physics, and I'm starting an after-school job teaching kids coding, so—"

"Perfect, perfect," she had choked out, coughing a bit on a glob of spit that had formed from chewing the gum too quickly. "MIT will love that!"

"I think I'm going to state school," I had meekly interjected, knowing that anything else would be out of my father's budget.

"Marina, you're a Latina engineering major! Schools are dying for you!"

"I want to be close to home."

"Will you fill out the scholarship form, at least?" she'd asked. I'd cleared my throat, realizing she wouldn't consider the meeting done until she'd convinced me to pack my bags for Boston.

I had nodded in a half-committed way before grabbing my backpack and clearing the seat as another girl, head buried in her phone, entered and took my place.

Reading aloud now from the textbook, I was really beginning to regret that I'd let the woman talk me into it. History repeats itself, they say (and the story of Alexander the Great and his supersized ego was proving no exception), but science, at least, always offered something new. Maybe that's why I loved it.

"'By the time Alexander was twenty-three,'" I droned on, wishing Mr. Martel hadn't assigned me such a large chunk to read, "'he had already conquered the known lands of Macedonia, Northern Egypt, and Persia.'"

I looked up at Mr. Martel, expecting to find him zoned out at his desk, the primary directive of most teachers who still force kids to read aloud to the class because they clearly didn't prepare a lesson plan long enough to fill the period. But instead, he stood front and center, his eyes trained directly on mine.

I cleared my throat to indicate that I was done, looking around sheepishly for someone else to have a turn.

"And what do you think of Alexander the Great, Marina?" Mr. Martel asked.

"Honestly," I sighed, not wanting to insult Mr. Martel but also not terribly interested in the subject matter, "pretty typical white dude, if you ask me."

I heard Adrian Washington laugh behind me, whispering loudly enough for me to hear, "Nice one."

I blushed a bit, but Mr. Martel's face was unreadable as he looked around the class. It occurred to me that he was the same age as Alexander the Great. Was he mad that I'd dissed his hero or something?

Thankfully, I didn't have to figure out the answer to that question. Mr. Martel turned away and began writing some homework on the board, providing a view in so doing that elicited an audible "Mmm" out of the mouth of Angela Peirnot.

o o o

Okay, I see it, I texted Christy as I left the school after the final bell and headed to the bike rack. I'd had my driver's license for months, but my after-school job didn't pay enough to buy even the humblest of used cars. Honestly, I didn't mind. I still preferred biking, even now that it was January and the air would bite at my cheeks as I rode. It made me feel alive.

There's a resemblance to Indiana, for sure, I added to the text before pressing Send. I put the phone away and slipped my hands into my winter gloves for the ride. As it was Tuesday, I didn't have work, so I headed home. By the time I'd made the fifteen-minute trek to my housing development and started punching in the garage code to put the bike away, she had already written me back six times.

More than a resemblance, said the first text. *Like a clone*, said the second. The third through fifth texts were just extra adjectives describing the new history teacher's assets, as Christy tends to send a new text for each individual thought that pops into her head.

The sixth text, however, was simply: *I'm telling Mom tonight. Wish me luck.*

Good luck!!! I immediately replied, followed by a heart emoji, a winking emoji, and finally the blowing-a-heart-kiss emoji. I was still typing when I made it into the kitchen and found my stepmother, Laura, sitting at the dinner table in front of her open laptop.

"Hey," she greeted me in her warm-honey voice, distracted temporarily by something on her screen before shutting the computer and giving me her full attention. "How was school?"

"Good," I said, smiling, always conscious of letting her know I appreciated how kind she was to me. Even after more than a year of living in this reality, a plane in which my real mother was living in Oregon with my brother, Robbie, and I was here with Laura and my dad, it still sent a small shock wave through my system to see her at the kitchen table.

She worked from home, copy editing websites for a couple of different legal firms, and this was her favorite place to sit, probably because the light was the best. It had been my mother's favorite too, when she had been here.

"You want a snack? I made butterscotch cookies."

I didn't really like butterscotch, to be honest, but I knew she had only made them for me. Laura was a thin, willowy blond woman with a nervous habit of skipping meals when she felt stressed. "Not an eating disorder," she had insisted once when I'd asked her about it, "just nerves." I'd nodded in agreement. But privately, I was pretty sure not eating was the definition of an eating disorder.

Laura had never had any children of her own. She'd tried when she was younger, with her ex-boyfriend Jonathan. But it just didn't happen. She had told me once, in confidence, that the infertility was part of what had caused the breakup. Each of them silently resented the other; each wondered whose flawed biology was to blame.

"Thank you," I said through a mouthful of butterscotch. "It's delicious."

Later, in my room, I lay on the bed before my own computer, my trig textbook open by its side. I found my mind wandering. Trig wasn't really my thing. I knew it was a prerequisite to the physics I would want to take in college, but it felt like a pit stop on the way to the city I actually wanted to visit.

My finger lingered on the keyboard, itching to toggle over to the site I had promised myself I wouldn't go to anymore. The ruby ring my parents had given me for my tenth birthday glistened against the caramel-colored skin of my pinkie—the only finger it could still fit on.

I glanced up from my computer and caught my reflection in the vanity mirror across the room. A face that looked more and more like my mother's every day stared back at me—her thin nose, her full lips. My half-Irish skin wasn't quite the same shade as her Mexican complexion, and my eyes were more hazel than brown, but other than that, it was like I had become her.

I still wasn't sure how I felt about that, just like I wasn't sure how I felt about my mother in general these days. Had I forgiven her for leaving? Had I really moved on at all?

I rolled my neck and took my fingers away from the keyboard, chiding myself to focus on the work before me.

But then my fingers found their way back.

Just once, I thought. *Just one more time. Then I'll stop. I know I have to stop.*

All I had to do was type *I* into the search window, and Instagram was the first suggested location. *Screw it*, I figured and hit Enter.

Kieren didn't post much, but his girlfriend did, and she would tag him in the pics. Her name was Stephanie, and she worked with him at his dad's cell phone store in town—the one I had strategically avoided going to the last time I needed a new phone.

She was very tall, ethnic in a way I couldn't quite place. Maybe Armenian? Very athletic. She ran half-marathons several times a year and posted pictures of herself and Kieren at the finish line. Once or twice, she'd even gotten him to run with her, and from those pictures I could see how much he'd filled out in the fifteen months since I'd last seen him—or rather, since he'd last known who I was.

He was tan in the pictures, proudly displaying his running bib, bulking out his now fuller chest so it rubbed against hers in a way that still killed me. Why did I keep looking at these pictures?

There was a new one since the last time I'd allowed myself to check the site: the two of them kissing over a small chocolate torte at what seemed to be a nice Italian restaurant. On the cake, in white icing: "Happy One-Year Anniversary!"

I slammed the computer closed.

Stop doing this to yourself, Marina, I repeated in my head like a mantra. *Let him go. Just let him go. You have to let him go.*

And yet, the following morning, as I biked to school in the chill morning air a full half hour before the first bell, I knew there was no stopping myself.

Just for a minute, I told myself. *I'll just do it for a minute. No one will have to know.*

I made my way through the labyrinthine hallways, once so shockingly foreign to me, now so familiar. The school was devoid at this early hour of the throngs of teenagers who would soon fill it. I weaved this way and that until I got to the boiler room door, remembering, as I did every time, how nervous I had been the first time Brady had led me here.

I checked over both shoulders to make sure the coast was clear and then slipped through the door, closing it silently behind me again.

Down I went, past the long-gestating furnace, past the termite-eaten workbenches covered in long-abandoned tools, now all interred in ancient shrouds of dust. I took the wooden key from above the door and let myself in to the most secret part of the school: the twisting, turning hallways left over from when East Township High was still Fort Pryman Shard, a military base decommissioned after World War II.

Through those dimly lit corridors I made my way, finally reaching the science room with the small army tent. I climbed down through the tent, spiraling down farther still on the corkscrew stairs, the darkness near total until the comforting faint purple light met my anxious eyes at the bottom.

As I strained to focus, searching out the three doors that had come to represent for me the final resting place of the girl I had once been, of the people I had once loved, of the dream I had once had of rescuing my lost brother, Robbie, I froze in shock.

Because the room was not empty.

And the doors were not all closed.

Slumped on the floor before the slightly ajar door to Yesterday, from which emerged a buzzing yellow light that told me it had recently been used, was Kieren. He looked up when I entered, not seeming nearly as shocked to see me as I was to see him.

Dear God, what did he do?

I couldn't speak. I found myself swallowing repeatedly, trying to wet my bone-dry throat.

"Kieren," I said, not sure why he seemed to be looking at me as though he knew me. As though he was overcome by seeing me.

"Were we in love once?" he asked.

And though my heart was pounding, flipping, breaking, though my voice felt a million miles away, I found myself staring into Kieren's searing gray eyes, my mind landing on the word it had been dying to scream for the last year and a half.

"Yes."

CHAPTER TWO

I ran up to the door to Yesterday, sidestepping Kieren's hunched body, and slammed the heavy barrier closed. But I knew it was futile. The door had been unlocked with the only key capable of doing so: a flattened penny crushed by the long-distance train as it barreled into the local station and created a momentary rift between the dimensions.

Once opened, only another such key could reseal it.

"How did you know?" I asked Kieren, who continued to watch me from the ground for a moment before standing to his full height, almost a foot taller than me. "How did you know about the key?"

He peered down at me now as if trying to make out a form emerging from shadows. "I learned how to open these doors when I was a freshman here," he said, his voice tentative, questioning. I let that sink in for a moment. In my reality, *I* had been the one to discover the power of the flattened coins. But I guess in Kieren's world, things had been different.

"And now I think it's your turn to talk," he said.

I felt flustered at being so close to Kieren. I had managed to keep my sanity over the last year, as much as possible anyway, by avoiding him completely. As he had graduated almost two years ago and didn't live in my neighborhood, that hadn't been too difficult.

But now he was so close I could feel his warm breath land on top of my head. I took a step back, trying to find my voice. But he took an equal step to meet me, and I found myself backed against the wall in the small chamber that held the three doors.

Kieren broke away from me then and put another flattened penny into the coin slot of Yesterday, sealing it back up again. He knew better than to leave any evidence of his visit or to create an opening for anyone else who might follow.

"What's your name?" he demanded.

"Marina."

"How do you know me?"

"We were friends once," I stammered, not sure how much I could possibly share without breaking the promise I had made myself: none of my friends could ever know what had happened. What if they tried to change something, alter the past? Robbie was safe now. I needed it to stay that way.

"We were never friends," Kieren said, his voice betraying no feeling at all, and the words hit me like a shower of ice.

"I don't know what to say."

Kieren glared at me for another moment before stepping back. "Wait a minute," he muttered. "Weren't you that kid Brady was talking to in the darkroom that day? Like two years ago?"

I gulped and nodded.

"You were the one who followed him to the train station and saw Piper leave."

"Yes," I admitted. It made sense that Kieren would remember that, for in this reality, Piper McMahon had still gotten on that train. She had still taken her DW parents through the portal, and they had later gone back on their own.

But seeing me confront Brady that day in the darkroom was probably the only memory he would have of me. Everything else had evaporated for him.

Kieren surprised me then by reaching into his pocket and pulling out a deck of playing cards. I couldn't help but inhale sharply when I saw them. They were a special deck we used to play with when we were kids. Every card had a picture of a different city on the back with a map of where in the world to find it. Robbie and Kieren and I had played with that deck so many times, I could still point to any place on a map from Albuquerque to Amsterdam.

"You've seen this before," he stated—a fact, not a question.

I could only nod in response.

"Did you put some sort of spell on this deck or something?" he asked.

I shook my head, not sure what he was talking about. "Like a witch?" I tried to joke, but it came out sounding angry.

"The deck . . . it's like it called out to me. I was asleep. One of those dreams where you know you're asleep, but you can't wake up. The deck of cards was . . . I don't even know. Vibrating. I knew there was something it was trying to tell me, but—"

"What did you see in the portal, Kieren?"

He flinched momentarily, hearing his name float off my tongue so easily, then turned to eye the Yesterday door again. Its faint yellow light was now beginning to fade behind the cracks at the top and bottom.

"I saw myself on the floor in my rec room. I was maybe eight, nine."

"You saw yourself or you *were* yourself?" I clarified, assuming he had just misspoken.

It seemed to surprise Kieren that I knew this particular fact about DW: when you go to the other side, if the other you is present, you become them.

"No. It doesn't work that way with little kids."

"What do you mean?"

"The molecular structure has to be identical. That's why you become your other self. But if you're a little kid or a baby or something, your structure is too different. So you can just watch it like a movie."

"Oh," I said, realizing something in the moment that I had long wondered about. Just over a year ago, when I had gone into Yesterday to undo the building of the lake portal, my brother, Robbie, was supposed to come with me. All my friends were supposed to come—Robbie, Kieren, and Robbie's new girlfriend, Piper. Then we were all supposed to return together when it was done, meaning we would all remember everything—we would all remember each other.

But at the last minute, my mother had stopped them, which was why I had had to go in alone. Inside the door, I had found myself in Portland a decade before, and the little-kid version of my brother had been there. I had long wondered what would have happened if Robbie had made it through the door with me. Would he have become his younger self? And if so, how the hell would I ever have gotten him out again?

I had resigned myself to the fact that it was for the best they hadn't made it. But with what Kieren was now telling me, I had to acknowledge that it wouldn't have been a problem.

The plan would have worked, I realized, both relieved and devastated at the thought. *It really would have worked.*

"You were there with me," Kieren continued.

"Hmm?" I asked, coming out of my reverie.

"You were there with me on the floor in my rec room. You were young. Like six. And there was another boy who looked like you."

"Robbie. He's . . . he's my brother."

Kieren paused and thought about the name, which of course meant nothing to him since in this plane Robbie had been raised thousands of miles away in Portland. Kieren eventually just shook his head. "I don't understand," he finally said.

I knew I had to somehow explain this to Kieren without telling him the truth. "It's a different plane is all. You know how DW is." I smiled, trying to sound casual. "I guess we were friends in another life."

Far in the distance, I heard the first school bell of the day chiming. I waited a few seconds for it to be over, then turned back to Kieren. "I have to go."

"That was the first time I went in." He stopped me with his voice. "That was two weeks ago."

"You've gone in more than once?"

"The second time, the three of us were playing Twister and laughing. We were laughing so hard I couldn't breathe. You fell on top of me."

I must've blushed, remembering how embarrassed I had been falling onto Kieren that day. God, I must have been nine. He had grabbed me and tickled my sides before I could stand, and his hands had been warm on my skin . . .

"And then I went in again this morning," he continued.

I held my breath. *What did he see? How will I explain it?*

"Your brother wasn't there this time."

"Okay," I said, calming myself as a wave of excitement turned my stomach to acid.

"We were older, teenagers. And so I did become my other self, I guess 'cause the molecular structure was similar enough by then."

Kieren walked back up to me, closer than two strangers should ever really stand.

"I was on the couch with you. Your hair was soaking wet. I guess you'd been in the rain. You were wearing my sweatshirt."

I knew which night he meant. It was the night I had remembered hundreds of times since: the night he'd first kissed me.

"And I was telling you it was going to be all right," he continued, close enough that I could feel heat emanating from his warm chest, almost brushing against me. "And I kissed the top of your head. And then your cheek."

I yearned to take his hand, to touch his chin, rougher now than it had been that night with a manly stubble he hadn't been capable of before.

"And then—"

"I really should get back," I suddenly stammered, knowing that I couldn't let him go any further. I would be too tempted to tell him everything in a moment. I had to think clearly. I had to protect Robbie.

"Wait—"

I turned to head up the spiral staircase. I could feel him grab at my backpack, but I didn't stop, even when I felt something snap off it. I kept running until I was back in the science room and then through the corridor leading up to the school.

It wasn't until I made it to my first-period trig class that I realized what Kieren had snagged off my backpack: my ID tag.

Would he come looking for me now? And if he did, how could I keep myself from telling him everything?

o   o   o

Mr. Martel appeared to be having a terrible day. Gone were the bad jokes, the sparkle in his eye. He looked tired, unshaven, and pissed off.

"That's East Township for you," I overheard Angela Peirnot whispering behind me to Adrian Washington, whom she was now sitting next to, her foot casually draped over his. "This place ages teachers *fast*."

I looked over my shoulder in time to see Adrian rub a hand up her thigh. Apparently they were a thing now. I wondered if Christy knew. She had been really into Adrian for a while there.

My eyes drifted away from the new couple, landing on nothing in particular while the recurring thought that had been gnawing at me all day continued to swirl.

Kieren made a key. He knows about the keys.

Angela giggled behind me, whispering to Adrian to stop tickling her. But I tuned them out, my body shrinking in on itself. As I did so, a new question sprang into my brain.

Did he discover them himself? Or did someone show him?

"Marina O'Connell," Mr. Martel almost spat in my direction, causing me to whip my head back around to the front.

"Yes?" I asked, sensing I was in trouble but having no idea why.

"What is this?" he asked, holding up a loose-leaf sheet of paper I had turned in to a substitute before winter break.

"Um, my notes?"

"Your notes? Surely not your essay notes?"

"Yes," I offered meekly, starting to sense where he was going with this.

"One sheet of paper? Your five-part essay on Genghis Khan that accounts for over half your grade, and, as of a couple weeks ago, you had one sheet of paper done? Did you work on it over Christmas, at least?"

I cleared my throat, looking around for backup. There must be someone else who had also blown it off?

"Well, it was assigned by one sub, but then the next sub didn't seem to know about it, so . . ." I let the sentence trail off. I was only digging the hole deeper, I now realized.

"So, you figured you didn't have to do it?" Mr. Martel demanded.

"I wasn't sure." Again I looked around, but everyone had their faces buried in their hands or were covertly scrolling through contraband phones under their desks. *Thanks a lot, gang.*

"You realize this is due in a week?"

"I'm . . ." *Think, Marina, think.* "I'm still doing research. I mean, I've read a lot about him since then."

"Where?" he demanded.

Wikipedia. "The library."

Mr. Martel's unrelenting green eyes bored into me for another moment, then he abruptly turned away. I felt sweat forming under my armpits. I took deep breaths to calm myself—a technique I had taught myself in the past year. When I was younger, being embarrassed would always make me cry. But I was too old for that now. I had to swallow it down, one way or another.

"Break up into small groups and compare notes. I hope the rest of you are further along."

The desks immediately began shuffling around me, and I was grateful for the noise. I spent the rest of the period sitting silently next to Jackson Spartam and Holland Pfeffer, who luckily for me was such a loudmouth it didn't seem odd that I wasn't contributing anything.

I was relieved when the bell rang, and I grabbed my bag to beeline for the door.

"Miss O'Connell," I heard Mr. Martel say before I could get there. It was like being harpooned with a large hook—wanting desperately to escape but knowing I was trapped.

The rest of the class filed out in seconds, and I found myself alone in the room with Mr. Martel, who perched owl-like on the edge of his desk.

"Please tell me you're going to rectify this situation."

"I am."

"Good."

He looked down for a moment, seeming somehow about ten years older than he had looked the previous day. Maybe it was the five-o'clock shadow or the crumpled shirt. What the hell had happened to this guy in the last twenty-four hours?

"Is that all?"

He cleared his throat as if coming back into the room from a faraway thought. "Yeah," he finally said.

I started to back away, grateful to get the hell out of there. Kieren's face was flashing before me, and all I could think about was what had happened that morning. Had it been real? I had imagined talking to him again so many times. It was hard to believe—

But before I could finish the thought, Mr. Martel stood up from his desk, and everything fell out of his pocket. "Shit," he muttered to himself.

I almost turned to leave, but I didn't want to be rude to the guy who held my GPA in his hands.

"Here," I offered, crouching down to help him pick up his dropped change.

He patted his empty pocket and seemed to remember suddenly what had been in there. Then he panicked, reaching out to stop my hand from retrieving what had fallen. "Wait, don't! Don't!"

I flinched away from him, something sharp cutting into my palm. I cried out from the pain and opened my hand to see what it was.

My eyes grew wide, and I stared up at Mr. Martel. He looked back at me, sheer horror in his expression. We were at an impasse, frozen, each waiting for the other to move as we crouched down together on the floor.

The bell rang, and several students began filing in. Mr. Martel stood, and I did the same. His eyes were plastered to mine, terrified once he realized that I had really seen it, that it was too late to pretend it was nothing.

I handed back what was in my hand, feeling how it had gouged a slash into my skin. I didn't even have to look at it again to be sure of what it was. I would know the feel of it anywhere. After all, I'd carried one in my pocket for months before I'd understood the power it possessed.

It was a penny, flattened by a passing train.

And the look that passed now between Mr. Martel's anxious eyes and mine told me one thing for certain: we both knew exactly what that meant.

CHAPTER THREE

"She freaked out!" Christy shouted over the blaring radio of her Subaru. She was giving me a ride to work after school as an icy rain had started to fall, my bike wedged awkwardly into her hatchback.

"But she must've known you wanted to apply to Berklee." I struggled to focus on the conversation as the events of the day continued to haunt me. Would Kieren come back again? Would he demand to know more? And what the hell would I say to Mr. Martel the next time I saw him? I had managed to make it out of his classroom without saying a word about what had been in his pocket, disappearing into the wave of students entering.

But I'd see him tomorrow. *Why did he have that penny?*

For the thousandth time, I fought back an impulse to confide in Christy, to just tell her everything. But, as always, it was impossible. It wouldn't be fair to her, I reminded myself, to dump something on her she couldn't possibly understand. I turned to her instead to hear more about her mother's reaction to the college news.

"Yeah, but she didn't think I was serious about it," she continued. "This is the psychological mindfuck my mom pulls on you—she lets you go just so far in one direction, just enough to make you think you have free will, and then she pulls this reverse psychology crap on you, seeding doubts, making you second-guess yourself, until you 'decide' to change your mind and do what she wanted you to do the whole time. She thinks I don't know she's doing it, but I do."

I was nodding solemnly as Christy spoke, trying to keep up with her train of thought but realizing that she was really just finishing up a private argument with her mother that I happened to be the audience for.

Still, I knew what it meant to her that I was at least listening. Maybe I couldn't talk to Christy—not really—but I told myself that being there to listen to her was still being a good friend.

The rain had turned to sleet, and it was pelting down on the car now, causing a thick cloud of white to obscure our view. I watched as it hammered away at the dirty snowbanks at the side of the road, turning them to pulp. After a minute more, the car in front of us was visible only when it got within five feet, and the traffic slowed to almost a crawl.

"Maybe we should pull over for a minute?"

"You'll be late for work."

"Better late than dead."

Christy thought about it for a second, then noticed her gas gauge. "I'm out of gas anyway. Let's pull into this station."

She maneuvered the car out of the congested lane and through a puddle the size of a small lake, coming to a stop under the overhang by the pump. But as soon as she opened the door, it was clear the sleet was coming in at an angle and smashing into the side of the car. There was no way to avoid getting pounded.

Christy and I just stared at each other. Usually, when she gave me a ride, we'd take turns pumping the gas. But neither of us seemed to want to volunteer this time.

"Rock, paper, scissors?" she asked.

"You pump, and I'll get us snacks," I offered instead.

"Deal."

I darted through the driving pellets into the mini-mart, shaking off the water from my flimsy sweater and deeply regretting that I had chosen today of all days to wear white. My birthday had been a few days before, and it seemed my newly eighteen-year-old body had finally decided that it was time to grow boobs. And now everyone in the gas station would be privy to that fact.

I discreetly shook the sweater out, trying to determine to what extent my white bra was visible beneath it as I headed to the chip aisle and picked out a couple bags—ranch for me, extra-spicy for Christy. I snagged a couple lemonades from the fridge and headed up to the checkout.

It wasn't until the very heavyset woman before me finished paying and moved out of the way that I saw him at the register. I didn't even recognize him at first, even though he basically looked exactly the same. For some reason, I remembered him being taller, but of course that was a ridiculous thought. People don't shrink in two years.

His hair was shorter, though, and his lips were drawn tight. He looked . . . he looked sad. That was the word. I don't know how long I stared, trying to make sense of why on earth Brady Picelli was standing in front of me at the A & P and not in Boulder where he belonged.

"Can I help you?" he asked automatically before he registered my face. Brady and I hadn't seen each other since the night I went back into Yesterday. I knew that he remembered me because we'd exchanged a few emails. But as far as he was aware, I was just some kid he'd helped navigate the halls of the school one day who had later followed him to the train station when his girlfriend, Piper McMahon, had gone to see the Mystics. He remembered showing me the doors beyond the boiler room and convincing me not to tell the authorities what had become of Piper.

But in this reality, that was the end of our connection. Brady and I hadn't gone to Portland together. I'd had no reason to go since my brother had never been sucked into DW. Instead, Brady had followed his original plan: waiting for Piper to return on her own. As the portal under the lake didn't exist anymore (thanks to my trip into Yesterday), Piper had never disappeared into it.

And so, in this plane, Piper had come back to Brady just a couple weeks after she had left. She had never fallen in love with my brother; in fact, she had never even met him.

She and Brady had stayed together and settled in Boulder, Colorado, just as they had always planned. And they were happy there; at least, that was what I'd thought.

"Holy shit," was all Brady said when it finally dawned on him who I was.

"Hi," I choked out, droplets of frozen rain trickling from the top of my head down my nose. I instinctively fluffed my white sweater, regretting the wardrobe choice more than ever. "What are you—"

"Look at you," he said, cutting me off. "You look amazing."

His eyes darted momentarily down to my chest, and I could feel myself blush, an old habit that died hard.

"What are you doing here?" I blurted out.

Instead of answering, he turned to an older Indian woman sitting on a stool behind him, counting out bills and wrapping them in rubber bands. "I'm gonna take my five, okay?"

She nodded, not looking up from the bills, her lips silently moving with the sums she was doing in her head.

Brady motioned at me to follow him. I looked anxiously towards the front door instead. "Hold on," I said as I popped my head outside, still balancing the unpaid-for chips and lemonades in my suddenly sweating palms.

Christy had pulled the car over to a parking spot and was having an animated conversation on her cell phone. From her body language, I could tell it was with her mother. I held up one finger to let her know I needed a minute, and she waved back that it was fine, obviously needing the privacy anyway.

I followed Brady through the store and into a small back office roughly the size of a minivan. He closed the door behind me and immediately cracked open a window. The onslaught of rain echoed against what sounded like a tin awning overhead, and the cold, heavy air filled the room with a whoosh.

Brady took out a pack of cigarettes, plopped one in his mouth, and lit it with a metal Zippo that he then clicked closed with an upward thrust of the wrist and shoved back in his pocket. He waited until he'd had the first drag before turning to me.

"I thought you quit?" I asked.

He looked at me, his eyebrows twisting in question.

"I mean, you told me once—"

"Yeah, I quit. Then I quit again. And again. You know how it is. I tried vaping for, like, a second, but then I heard that vapes have nine times as much nicotine as a cigarette, so, yeah."

He took a deep drag and blew the smoke out the window. Small lines had formed around his mouth, and his fingertips were yellow from the filters. He looked miserable and tired, and I couldn't help but feel that it was somehow my fault. I hesitated to find my voice before asking the question that I suspected I already knew the answer to.

"Where's Piper?"

He smiled and nodded, not at me necessarily but just at the question. He stared at the burning cigarette in his hand for a moment and then uttered one word, drawing out the hiss of the opening consonant: "Split."

I sat down in a desk chair and realized I was still holding the snacks. "I think I have to pay for these."

"Nah, they're on me. Go ahead."

"Thanks." I opened up the ranch chips and offered him one, but he shook his head.

"You know what sucks? She was happy. I know she was happy."

I nodded, letting him talk. His skin looked blue against the white mist in the window, his hair black. The mad crush I had had on him once came rushing back to me suddenly. God, I'd been crazy about him. Would I still be if I'd met him today?

"She really was," he continued. "When we first got to Boulder she was anyway. We got this little one-bedroom, and she decorated it. Got these colorful baskets at the dollar store. Everything went in a basket. Her books, her makeup."

"What about *your* stuff?"

"I didn't have any stuff. I just had Piper."

"And she didn't fit in a basket?" I asked, testing the waters to see if I could make him laugh. It took him a moment to realize it was a joke, but then he chuckled to himself.

"Did you ever meet Piper?" he asked. I had to think for a split second about what the truth was, or at least, what it was for Brady.

"No, not really."

"Mmm. She, um . . . she said she wanted to see the ocean. Felt like she was missing something, she said. I'd wake up in the night, and she'd be pacing, looking for something. And I'd say, 'Babe, what're you looking for,' right? And she'd just keep walking around. Wouldn't answer me. Didn't know."

I stared at my feet. Had I done this to Brady? To Piper? She'd told me once that she loved the ocean. She wanted to live there with Robbie someday. And she wanted me to come out and live with them. She had it all planned out in her mind—her life, mine, and Robbie's, organized into color-coded boxes.

And now what had I left her? The remnants of a dream I knew she no longer wanted.

"I don't know what I did wrong," Brady continued, stamping out his cigarette against the windowsill. "She never said. She just wasn't there one day when I got back from work. Left a note saying she couldn't pretend anymore. Whatever that means."

I cleared my throat, having no idea what I could possibly say to make any of this better. Guilt and sadness seemed to drown me. What I wouldn't give to shout my story out loud now, to tell Brady the truth. Piper was missing a love she'd never even met. How could he ever understand that?

"I don't know why I'm telling you this. You just . . . did I ever tell you that you remind me of Piper?"

I smiled through the pain of it. He had told me that once, right before he took me down to the boiler room for the first time. If I closed my eyes, I could still feel my hand nestled securely in his.

For the second time today, my past was staring me in the face, and I couldn't say a damn word about it. I knew I needed to leave the room before the strain of it started to choke me from the inside out.

"I'm sorry, Brady," I whispered as I stood to go. I made it to the door, resting my hand on the knob, but I couldn't look at him. The tears were stinging behind my eyes. "I'm so sorry."

"Wait, Marina, don't go—"

But I was already gone.

I ran out of the room, through the small store and into the pelting rain, slamming the door to Christy's car shut behind me.

She had ended her phone call and was listening to an Adele song on the radio, singing along in perfect harmony as the rain cast a steady beat on her windshield.

"Where are the snacks?" she asked.

I looked down at my empty hands, shaking from the wet and the cold. "They didn't have anything good."

Apparently accepting my answer, she backed the car up and headed for the road. I turned to watch the gas station disappear, straining to see the last blurry image of it before it was eaten up by the nebulous mist.

CHAPTER FOUR

"What do you want to make the robot do?" I asked my star student, Alyssa. At just nine years old, Alyssa was already showing an aptitude for robotics that made me wildly proud of her.

The gig at Kids' Science Lab was originally supposed to end after the summer, but when school started in the fall, I couldn't bring myself to leave it. Mr. Chu, the owner, said I could teach just two classes a week if I wanted, and I immediately laid claim to the Wednesday night "Little Tinkerers" class. I loved watching the looks on the kids' faces the first time they realized they could make their Lego robot do whatever they wanted simply by programming the actions into a tablet.

I also worked with some junior-high kids on Saturdays, but they honestly weren't as much fun. By that age, the kids didn't have the same sense of wonder watching a robot walk three steps and take a bow. They mostly just wanted me to help them with algebra and show them how to make stink bombs by exposing ammonium sulfide to oxygen. It got old pretty fast.

My Wednesday night class usually had six kids in it, but on this stormy evening, only Alyssa and young Diego had made it. And Alyssa was the only one paying attention. With just five minutes left in the class, Diego had already checked out, his gaze trained on the door, waiting for his father to retrieve him.

But little Alyssa had a fire in her eyes as she worked on a Rube Goldberg sequence. In just a few minutes, she'd managed to program her robot to walk forward fifteen steps, land on a lever, and open the compartment where we had stashed their coats. She completed her experiment just as the clock struck five, and the bells above the door in the lobby announced the arrival of someone's parent.

I busied myself putting away extra Lego pieces while the kids headed to the lobby to get ready to go.

"Marina," Mr. Chu said, popping his head into the room after seeing the kids off, "you're not biking, are you?"

I listened for a moment to the hard drops of rain tickling the roof and realized that my plan to bike home after the weather cleared wasn't working out. "I'll text my dad."

"Okay," Mr. Chu said, checking his watch.

"If you have to go, it's fine," I assured him.

"It's just with this weather, it'll take half an hour to get to my son's day care."

"It's fine." I smiled. "I've got homework to do. I'll wait in the lobby."

"You'll lock up when you leave?"

I smiled and nodded, appreciating that Mr. Chu always seemed to genuinely care what happened to me. His wife, Holly, and my stepmother, Laura, had become friends over the summer, often chatting over coffee during my Saturday class.

Mr. Chu turned to leave, but then the bells jangled over the front door again. "Shoot." He eyed his watch. "Someone must've forgotten something."

I grabbed my backpack and headed to the lobby with him but froze when the man who had entered moved a dripping umbrella out of the way, exposing his face.

It was Mr. Martel, a fact that took me a moment to process. It would have been weird to see any teacher from school out of context, but especially this one. He hovered in the doorway a moment as he shook the rain off his feet.

"I'm afraid we're closing up for the day," Mr. Chu informed him.

"Oh," said Mr. Martel, smiling as effortlessly as he had when I'd first seen him at the whiteboard. "I was hoping to sign up for a class."

"Adult classes are on Saturdays," Mr. Chu said as he grabbed his briefcase from behind the front desk and threw on his coat. "Ten a.m."

Mr. Martel turned to me. "Hello, Marina. I heard you worked here. Looks like the rumors were true."

In his distracted state, Mr. Chu didn't seem to think much of this interaction, but he looked at me for some sort of confirmation.

I cleared my throat. Mr. Martel and I had left things rather awkward, not getting a chance to discuss what had fallen out of his pocket.

Of course, maybe I was overreacting. Maybe the flattened penny in Mr. Martel's pocket wasn't from the train. Hell, they have machines at the zoo that flatten pennies, engraving them with little panda bears or sea otters. Maybe it was one of those, and I had just jumped to conclusions.

But then why did he follow me to work?

Should I ask Mr. Chu to stay, making him late to get his son?

He would demand an explanation. What would I say? I decided to give Mr. Martel a little rope and see what he did with it.

"Mr. Chu," I began, "um, this is my history teacher, Mr. Martel."

Mr. Chu turned to him with an outstretched hand.

"Adam," Mr. Martel corrected. "It's just Adam."

"Nice to meet you, Adam." Mr. Chu turned back to me, one foot practically out the door. "You'll be okay, Marina?"

I debated for a split second what to do, but then I realized I was going to have to talk to Mr. Martel at some point. Now was as good a time as any. I smiled at Mr. Chu, reassuring him.

"I'm a big girl," I said. "Everything's fine."

I waited several seconds after Mr. Chu left, until I could hear his car starting in the small parking lot, before turning to Mr. Martel. I decided to let him make the first move, just in case this was all in my mind.

"So, yeah, the adult classes are on Saturday. Maybe you should come back then."

"I think you and I need to talk, Marina."

The alarm bell that had started when he walked through the door was blaring louder in my head now, not so much because of what he had just said but because of how he'd said it: his voice low and cool, his eyes unwavering.

"About what?" I asked, feigning naivete while I furiously ran through the options in my head.

"I think you know," he said, stepping closer.

I curled my lips into the slow breathing I had been practicing. My heart was pounding, but I couldn't let him see that. I didn't know if this guy posed a threat or not. Maybe he really did just want to talk.

But then something occurred to me: in his classroom, when I had seen the flattened penny, the look on his face—he was pet-rified. He knew immediately that I recognized the penny, that I didn't think it was from the zoo the way most people would have. He seemed terrified of being exposed, terrified of . . . of me.

"Who are you?" I asked.

"I'm just who I say I am—"

"No, you're not."

He eyed me a moment, measuring what to say or, perhaps, what he didn't need to say.

"Okay, let's talk," I offered. "The second that penny fell out of your pocket, you knew you couldn't let me see it. You knew that I would know what it was. How did you know that about me?"

He smiled slightly, unsurprised by the question. His shoulders drooped, as though he was giving up some sort of ruse. "Because," he said, shrugging, "you're Rain's daughter."

And with that, the alarm bells exploded inside me. This man knew my mother's nickname from high school. I wasn't safe here. *Run, Marina. Run!*

I tried bolting past him, but his body was blocking mine from the front door. He reached out to grab me, and I could feel his giant hand clasp around my sweater for a moment. I was able to rip my arm away from him and yank it free. But just as I made it to the exit, he caught up with me and slapped his hand against the closed door, barring me from opening it.

"Let me out!" I screamed.

"Let me talk first."

"No!"

Instinctively, I thrust my elbow into his side. The jab was supposed to land in his kidney, but Mr. Martel spun at the last moment, and I got his ribs instead, which sent a jolting pain through my arm.

Still, it seemed to work. He doubled over with a grunt, allowing me to get my hand on the doorknob and get it open.

But once I had run out into the bombardment of ice-cold rain,

I realized I had nowhere to go. My bike and coat were still in the lobby. I hadn't called my father. Could I outrun him? An absurd thought popped into my head: Angela Peirnot slobbering over Mr. Martel's fit frame in class. He looked like he worked out every day. The answer was no.

I turned to face him, and he was already standing out in the rain, hunched slightly, eyeing me like he was scanning for weaknesses.

"I'm not gonna hurt you," he said, rain plastering his button-down shirt against his well-formed chest.

I pushed the hair out of my face, shivering as my finally dried sweater was soaked through again. Thunder clapped above me like a steel drum, reverberating through my skin. "What do you want?"

"Like I said, just to talk."

"I don't trust you."

"You should," he immediately retorted. "I'm the only one who can help you. Please, Marina, come back inside."

I looked around for an escape, but I was trapped. Taking deep breaths, I let the rain wash over me for a moment longer, as though it could carry me away somehow, take me somewhere magical, a place where Kieren or Robbie or even my dad would be waiting for me.

Somewhere I'd be safe.

But there was no magic here. There hadn't been magic here in a long time.

Reluctantly, I walked towards the building again, around Mr. Martel, who knew better than to try to touch me, and into the lobby, where I shook myself off.

And a second later, the bells above the door told me he had followed me inside.

CHAPTER FIVE

"I did know your mother, it's true," Mr. Martel offered as soon he could see that he had my attention, that I wasn't going to try to run again. "I met her when she was in high school."

The wording of this took me a moment to process. My mother was in high school in the late 1990s. Unless . . . "How old are you?"

"I'm twenty-three, like I said."

"So, then, you were what? Just visiting?" He must have meant he went through a portal to the past. But why?

"Something like that."

Mr. Martel's eyes scanned the stark, well-lit lobby and fell upon a coffee machine in the corner that Mr. Chu kept for parents. "Look, it's cold, right? Do you want a coffee?"

I didn't usually drink coffee, but I had to admit that something hot would be very welcome right about now, if only to warm my still shaking hands. I nodded a bit and watched him go find a clean mug on a small rack and plop a pod into the machine. When the whirring subsided, he came up and offered me the drink, the handle side facing me so I wouldn't have to touch him in order to take it.

It was like he was trying to make up for the way he'd been a minute ago, to signal to me that he was safe. I still wasn't sure I was buying it, however. "Tell me more," I insisted, blowing on the hot liquid and feeling its warmth tickle my upper lip.

"I was a curious kid, I guess . . . like you."

I nodded, watching him make his own drink while he kept talking. His voice was different than it had been in class. Younger. Like he wasn't pretending anymore, wasn't playing a part. I could see the kid he had been not that long ago dying to break out.

"Have you told anyone else this?"

"No."

"Why are you telling me?"

"Let me finish?" he asked deferentially. Like he needed me, somehow, to give him permission to continue. What was he hoping to get from me?

I sat down on one of the beanbag chairs in the lobby and motioned to him to do the same, a task that he pulled off with surprising agility for such a muscular guy. It struck me that maybe he'd been a gymnast or something at one point.

"I didn't mean to stay in Yesterday as long as I did. Honestly, I just wanted to see how it worked. Once I figured out how to open the doors, I wanted . . . I wanted to see everything."

"That's a dangerous game."

"I know that now."

"You met my mother, you said?"

"Yes."

"Did you—is she why you stayed so long?" Images of my

mother in high school zipped through my mind, mostly from the photo album that was still somewhere in the back of her closet. The album that showed her with her old high-school friends— Sage, George, Jenny, Dave . . . and John, her boyfriend at the time and her husband in this reality. John, who was obsessed with DW, who made it into a cult almost. A cult that none of them knew how to leave.

"No, it wasn't like that." Adam answered my question in a softer tone.

Relief flooded over me. It was hard enough to imagine my mom with John, but to think of her with this guy—

"It was for her friend, Jenny. Jenny and I . . ." He let the sentence trail off.

Jenny. That made sense. Jenny, who wore the tiny polka dot bikini in those old photos by the beach. Jenny, who was dating Dave. And a memory from long ago came back in a flash—my mother's voice: *They won't come out.*

In the old reality, before I had gone back into Yesterday and stopped the lake portal from being built, Jenny and Dave had been the first ones to go through it. They'd dived into the lake right after the portal was formed, and, in that timeline at least, they had never been heard from again.

But we were in a different timeline now—one in which they'd never had a chance to go under the lake. Jenny probably went on to live a normal life somewhere.

"I went back again and again," Adam continued. "Each time, I told myself it was the last. And each time, I couldn't stay away. I realize now that what I had with Jenny wasn't healthy. She had a boyfriend, and we . . . well, all she ever wanted to do was go through the portals with me. It was like a drug for her . . . and for me."

"You went through a portal while you were already in a portal? Are you crazy?" I wanted to be mad at him for risking the balance between the dimensions like that, but I couldn't. Hadn't I done the same and even worse? Hadn't I used the doors behind the boiler room like my own personal do-over machine? Who was I to judge?

He shrugged. "I thought I could conquer it."

"Okay," I sighed, "so what do you want from me? Why are you telling me this?"

"Because," he said, steadying himself, "the last time I saw Jenny, she was nineteen. We had plans to meet up a few months later. She was going to leave Dave. We were . . . talking about getting married. I was going to stay in the past to be with her."

"Jesus," I sighed. "You would have thrown off the balance of everything. And for what? Some girl who was cheating on her boyfriend and would probably cheat on you?"

"Well, I didn't get a chance, did I? Because she never showed. I looked for her everywhere. Every portal. Every existence I could imagine her living in. I never found her."

I swallowed hard, an ill feeling stirring in my gut.

If Jenny had never gone into the underlake world, she should have been up here somewhere in our reality. So where was she? She was sort of obsessed with DW, I remembered Sage telling me. Thought of it as a game. Did she go in another way? And if so, where had she been living all this time?

"I need to find her again, Marina. I need to know she's safe."

I struggled to think of what to tell him. I knew how he was feeling, of course, and I hated to sound selfish, but the truth was it just wasn't my problem. Maybe Jenny just got sick of him and ditched him somewhere. For all I knew, she'd settled down in another state or another country—living a life that had nothing to do with him.

"I don't know how to help you," I finally said, trying to excuse myself from the conversation.

"You have to. Your mother was the only one Jenny would listen to, the only one who could have found her. I begged Rain to give me a token, something that would lead me to Jenny, but she wouldn't. Said she would never mess with the portals again. Even though . . ."

"Even though what?"

"Even though if she didn't help me, it meant losing Jenny. Forever."

The words hit me like a punch. He wasn't acting like a guy who just missed some girl he'd fallen for. He sounded more desperate than that.

I couldn't pretend not to know what he was going through, and I really did sympathize. Obviously I did. But if I had to live without the people I loved the most in the world, the people I would give anything to be with again, then he could live without some girl he'd had a fling with.

He looked up at me with eyes rimmed with exhaustion and grief. I could swear he was almost begging. Maybe he really did love Jenny after all.

"Will you help me find her?" he pleaded.

All of a sudden, something that had been dangling just inches from my consciousness sprang into clear relief. Something Brady had told me once, on the bus heading to Oregon to see the Mystics. *There was another guy named Adam who went a few years ago to ask them about all this . . . he never came back.*

"Oh my God," I breathed. "You're Adam."

He screwed his eyebrows together, questioning.

"Brady told me about you."

"Brady?" he repeated. "Brady Picelli? That little freshman who was always following me around when I was a senior? You know him?"

"We're friends," I asserted, silently trying to picture Brady as a "little freshman." He had always been the tall, confident older boy I'd fallen hard for when I first got to school.

"Will you help me, Marina?" Adam asked again, bringing me back into the moment.

"Why should I?"

"Because I can give you what you want."

"And what is that?" I asked, honestly not sure what he might think the answer was.

But he only offered a coy smile, toying with me. He stood and took a couple steps towards me, standing just inches away. I gulped down some spit, feeling awkward being alone with him, still sitting while he hovered above me. "Don't you know by now?"

I stood to meet him. Before he turned away, he grabbed my hand from where it dangled by my side and pressed something into it. "Let me know tomorrow," he said casually before grabbing his umbrella and heading out the door. The bells jangled as the door slammed shut, a sound that continued to reverberate for a couple of seconds after he left.

I looked down at my hand and stared helplessly at the flattened penny Adam had just pressed there.

CHAPTER SIX

I stood in the shadows of our garage, watching my father at his workstation in the corner. He was doing his favorite thing in the world: fixing up an old computer, bobbing his head to a song on his headphones. The computer was splayed out before him in a million little pieces, waiting to be put back together by his callused hands.

After a moment, he looked up and noticed me there. A smile popped onto his face, and he pressed a button on his phone so the music switched from his headphones to a small speaker. Then he hung the headphones on a little wall hook—Dad's way of inviting me to join him.

It was one of his favorite old albums by Buffalo Springfield. Neither of us said anything for a moment as I approached the desk, surveying his progress so far, and the lyrics to the old song echoed off the concrete walls. Something about standing on the edge of a feather, saying goodbye to a loved one. Knowing that they'd gone. Knowing that it was too late to do anything about it.

Dad broke the spell by turning the volume down, his head still buried in his work.

"Hand me that DVI cable, will you, honey?"

"Sure, Dad."

After a moment of tinkering with the cable, he spoke again. "I Skyped your brother today."

My heart still caught in my throat whenever Robbie was mentioned. It was hard to believe, even to this day, that Robbie and I had barely any relationship. He'd been raised so far away from me in this reality, and in such a different environment, helping our mom run that little hotel outside of Portland.

"He said the classes are much harder this year at U of Oregon."

I nodded, always afraid of saying too much, giving anything away. "That makes sense," I finally added. "He's a sophomore now."

Somehow, the word *sophomore* struck me with a painful throb. A sophomore like I had been when I'd started a new high school without him, in the old reality where he had "died" at fourteen. A sophomore, meaning I had missed his whole first year of college, just like I had missed the nineteen years before that.

If I closed my eyes, I could still feel the cold night air whipping our faces as we ran from the pyramid house all those years ago, when Kieren had dared us to spend the night there. And now there was no one left to remember that night with me. My whole life, everything that had mattered, everything I had felt, ripped away day after day.

My brother and I were like two divergent rivers in this plane, twisting away from each other, never intertwining, wending through the earth towards two opposing oceans. I missed him so much sometimes that my bones ached with the pain of it.

A sob escaped my mouth, and once it had started, a tidal wave of sobs followed behind. My father dropped his tools and just held me, rocking me slightly against his chest.

"Oh, Marina," he whispered. "My sweet girl."

"I'm sorry, Dad," I whispered through my tears, not wanting to break away from his protective arms.

"I just don't know what to do for you, honey. You seem so sad lately, and I don't know why."

I nodded, knowing there was nothing I could say.

"Is it school? Is it a boy?"

I couldn't help but laugh at that, wishing it could be that simple. Of course, to a certain extent it was. I missed two boys. Kieren and Robbie. And to be honest, I missed Brady too. Brady was never supposed to go through the portal to Yesterday with us all those months ago. The plan had always been for him to remain above and to forget all about our experience together.

I suppose that had been my gift to him. Letting him forget the reality where Piper left him for Robbie, letting him live in a blissfully ignorant plane where she had never stopped loving Brady back.

But that meant erasing his memories of me too.

"Answer me, honey," my dad implored. "Do you need help? Do you need to, I don't know, talk to someone?"

I cleared my throat, wiping my face and taking my deep, calming breaths. Within a few seconds, I had managed to stop the tears but not the worried look on my dad's face.

"No, Dad, I'm fine," I insisted, hoping he would buy it. "I'm just, um . . ." *Think, Marina. Think of something logical. That's what you do best.* "I'm worried about school. Because I have a paper to write."

"Oh?" he asked, not quite believing the sudden shift in tone.

"On Genghis Khan. I have to go study now, in fact." I backed away, but my dad's eyes followed me. I offered him my best smile. "I'm fine, Dad, I promise."

Before I could get to the door to the house, my dad called my name one more time. I turned to look at him.

He seemed at a loss for what to say. "I just want you to be happy, Marina. That's all I've ever wanted."

I offered him the best smile I could muster. "I know, Dad. Good night."

"Good night," he said as I closed the door.

o o o

I fell asleep before even opening a book, buried deeply in my cocoon of covers, shutting out the world. I was so immersed in sleep, in fact, dreaming that I was swimming in the middle of the ocean, that the sound of pebbles clinking against glass registered only as a distant drumming. But as the clinking grew louder, the ocean water receded until I was back in my sheets, overheated and sweating.

The next pebble struck with a bit more force, and I was fully awake. A quick glance at my bedside clock informed me that it was after midnight. I tripped my way out of bed and stumbled to the window. When I looked out into the wet, moonlit street, I rubbed my eyes in disbelief.

Kieren was about to throw another stone when he saw me. He flushed, embarrassed, looking awkwardly over his shoulder to see if he had attracted anyone else's attention. But the street was deserted. A thin stream of visible breath escaped his lips under the blue light.

I couldn't help but smile at the sight of him there, waking me up in the night just like he had in the old dimension. I had no idea how he knew which room was mine. Maybe some weird sense memory. Or maybe the rather girly pink curtains my dad had hung when I was a baby and that I'd never gotten around to taking down. He held my ID tag in one hand and another pebble in the other. Behind him sat a tan Toyota Corolla, the door left open slightly.

His brow furrowed when he saw me—an expression somewhere between relief and annoyance. I held up my index finger to ask him to wait, then turned and threw on a hoodie and some gym shoes. I tiptoed down the stairs, even though I knew Dad and Laura could sleep through a hurricane.

I felt giddy, my stomach gurgling. I couldn't remember the last time I had been this excited about something.

Thinking quickly, I decided to leave the house by the kitchen door, knowing the front door would make too much noise. My feet tingled with anticipation as I all but ran around the house to get to him.

He lingered stock-still in the street, waiting for me.

"You found me," I breathed as I reached him, unable to fight the urge to smile when I saw his lopsided grimace and his unruly hair.

"I'm sorry it's so late."

"That's okay."

He stared at me for a moment.

"What is it, Kieren?"

A subtle twitch struck his handsome features. "Stop saying my name like that. You don't know me."

The smile was instantly erased from my lips, and I took a step back, chastened by his words. But he seemed to quickly regret his anger, or maybe to just forget about it. His shoulders hunched in the brisk night air. He rubbed his arms with his hands for warmth.

I knew I should feel cold too, but the adrenaline was keeping my blood flowing. I couldn't feel anything, really, except relief to be so close to him again. "What did you come for?" I asked.

"I was wondering," he said, clearing his throat, "why were you so upset that night? In my rec room, when we were . . . you know."

"Oh." I nodded, realizing instantly that I couldn't tell him the truth about the night he kissed me on his couch. I was upset that night because my mother had gone missing, and I was desperately afraid that she had followed my brother to the train tracks, that maybe she had even allowed herself to be struck and killed by a train just to follow my brother into death.

My world was shattering that night. Kieren was the only thing holding it together.

"It's hard to explain," was all I could say.

"Was that . . ." he began, shy suddenly. Was he blushing? "Was that our first kiss, or whatever?"

"Um . . ." Now I was blushing too. "Kind of."

I suddenly chuckled, a random thought occurring to me.

"What's funny?"

"Well, it's just . . . we'd kind of kissed once before." I started laughing even harder at the memory, and Kieren stepped closer, searching my face for clues.

"Tell me."

"Well, we had this dog when we were little—when I was little, I mean. He was a little dachshund, you know, the little hot dog ones. You used to call him 'Denny's' when you'd come over, and Robbie and I would get so mad at you."

Kieren nodded, seeming amused although he had no idea where I was going with this.

"Because his name was Denny, but you'd always joke that you were going to eat him. And one day, he was really old. He was like fourteen and blind and diabetic, and one day he went out into the street and just . . ." I took a breath, laughing for reasons that probably made no sense to him.

"And just what?"

"Died." I laughed again, my nervousness betraying me. "He just laid down and died. And you came over that night, and you were trying to comfort me."

Kieren shivered a bit, but his eyes never left me.

"You were trying to be all warm and nice, and you said . . ." Here I had to take a break to laugh again, my cheeks flushing with the memory. "You said, 'Don't worry. You can always get another dog!'"

Kieren snorted out a huge laugh, and I couldn't help but laugh with him. I hadn't realized at the time what a ridiculous thing it was for him to say, but now it struck me as preposterous.

"I did not say that?" he asked.

"You did! It was awful."

We both broke into a fresh round of snorting, and I looked around the empty street, suddenly conscious of the neighbors.

"Did I think that would make it better?" He laughed at himself.

"I don't know what you were thinking."

I slowed down my breathing, which only made me laugh once more. "And then you leaned down—you were, like, nine I think—and you were trying so hard to be all manly and strong, and I thought it was so cute even though I was so sad. And I had tears on my cheeks. And you leaned down, and you kissed me on my wet cheek."

I touched my right cheek at the memory of Kieren's soft, young lips grazing against it.

We were just inches apart now, both coming down from the high of laughing and letting the deadly quiet seep in to take its place.

Suddenly a buzz emanated out of Kieren's back pocket. He took out his phone and stared at it for a moment, his face falling. I knew immediately who it must be.

"Is she wondering where you are?" I asked, instantly regretting it.

He put his phone away, suddenly wary of me again. "Yes."

I nodded.

"How did you know I had a girlfriend?"

Shit. I was caught, wasn't I? *Talk yourself out of this one, Marina.* "I just assumed—"

"Are you stalking me?"

"No."

But he didn't believe me. He stepped back, his face growing hard and unreadable again. "I have to go," he muttered, heading for his car.

"Kieren, wait—"

"I won't be going through the doors again. Nothing good comes of it," he spat over his shoulder in my direction.

I stood frozen as I watched him walk away, feeling the heat that had been radiating off him seep away from me.

"Do me a favor," he said, looking at the wet street as he started to put one foot into his car.

"Anything," I promised.

He hesitated only a moment. "Pretend you don't know me."

He slammed the door shut behind him, started the engine, and revved the gas to speed away down my street, leaving me like an ice sculpture, moored in the black sea of concrete.

I always do, Kieren. I always do.

CHAPTER SEVEN

Just do it before you lose your nerve.

I faced the door to Today, twirling Mr. Martel's—Adam's—coin in my hand and letting the sharp edges of it press against my skin almost to the point of puncturing. It was seven in the morning. I could just leave, I told myself, pretend I hadn't even considered it.

Give him back his penny after seventh period and tell him never to speak to me again. Tell him I wouldn't play his games.

Or you could just do it.

The Today door wasn't like Yesterday, I assured myself for the millionth time. When you went into Yesterday, even the smallest changes could ripple away, affecting everything and everybody. Yesterday was dangerous. Today was something else entirely. The Today door was just another version of your life.

I had come to think of Down World like the hairs on a human head. They look the same, they may even fall the same, they're probably about the same length, and when seen from a distance, they look like one body. But really, they are individual strands, twisting around each other, free-falling. And if you pluck one, the others remain.

Today was just another strand of hair. Look at it, touch it, smell it. But the other strands won't be affected either way.

You're overthinking this, Marina. Do it or don't.

Damn you, Adam. You knew I wouldn't be able to resist.

Before I could hesitate another moment, I slipped the coin into the slot of Today and held my breath. A jolting crash, like something heavy falling in another room, exploded for only a moment. And then, under the cracks of the door, the yellow light began to glow.

I took a deep breath, cleared my throat, and reached into my pocket. There I had stowed away a tattered train ticket stub, found in the crevices of my father's old briefcase, from when he used to take the commuter train to work.

I clenched it in my fingers now and opened the door.

As always, it started small. Yellow light, fading into colors. Technicolor reds, deep-sea blues. A breeze struck my face—no, not a breeze, a whoosh of air. From the train.

I was on the platform of the train station, and the train was pulling in, chugging and churning, coming to a stop.

About half a dozen people were around me, suitcases in hand. This was the long-distance train. Westbound. The one I had taken with Brady two summers before. A suitcase brushed against my leg, metallic silver. Not my usual style. Had I borrowed it from someone?

"I'm so excited." Kieren spoke in my ear, leaning down from where he had been standing just behind me.

I gasped and tried to pass it off as a cough.

57

"Do you think Robbie will be surprised?"

I looked up at him, unsure, not wanting to give myself away. "Hmm?"

"When we show up at his birthday party? You think he'll be surprised?"

I caught up as quickly as I could and nodded in response. "Yeah," was all I could think of to say.

"And he doesn't know we're coming, right?"

I shook my head, taking in the glint of excitement reflecting in Kieren's warm eyes. His eyelashes looked blond in the sunlight. He squinted to look down at me.

"Sorry," he laughed. "I'm nervous, I guess. It'll be the first time I've seen him since he said he forgave me. And I just . . . well . . ."

"It'll be great," I assured him. "It'll be perfect."

"You think so?" he asked, breathing through tight lips. He chuckled again, jittery and awkward. Beautiful and warm.

An old, familiar sting behind my eyes crept up on me.

"What is it?" He smiled down at me.

"I'm just . . ." His crooked smile. His furrowed brow. "I'm just happy."

He put his arms around my waist and pulled me closer, tilting my chin up to meet him. "I'm happy too," he breathed.

I kissed him softly at first, shy suddenly. I hadn't actually kissed him that many times before . . . before I lost him. But he kissed me back with certainty, his lips firm, his strong nose nestling into the space beside mine.

"Okay, folks," said a middle-aged man in an official-looking railroad cap. "The overhead bins are full. If you've got luggage, hand it over, and I'll stow it for you."

Kieren broke away, laughing a bit. He reached down and grabbed my suitcase. "I'll give him our bag. Meet you on the train, okay?"

"Okay," I whispered, watching him approach the porter. I wanted to drink in every moment of this, to see how he walked, how his shoulders had grown broader, how his face had filled out. I watched him like a fleeting scene in a beautiful film, a perfectly composed image, there one second, gone the next.

I glanced up at the train, forgetting myself for a moment, ready to walk onto it and never come back.

At first, the image in the window seemed normal—just an old ticket taker walking past the rows of passengers. But when he was fully in view of the window, I could see more clearly that he wasn't just a ticket taker, and he wasn't just a man.

The ancient conductor turned his head slowly, as though churning through molasses, in my direction. His skeletal face had not changed since I'd last seen it, barreling through space and time with Robbie and Piper on the DW train. The day that I had handed him Kieren's flattened penny; the day that I had learned the power the coins possessed.

The conductor's hollow eyes bored through me now, his lipless smile twisting into a wicked grimace. He cocked his head slightly to the side, holding me in his vicious gaze. Then he raised his index finger and shook it from side to side like a pendulum: *tsk, tsk, tsk.* His wiry mouth mimicked the sound.

The message was clear: *You don't belong here.*

Panicking, terrified, I backed away. Farther and farther away. Until the colors began to melt.

I pushed away the reds and yellows and greens, the colors blending into formless mush, and the mush further melding into red brick.

I was back in the waiting room under the science lab, staring helplessly at the door to Today. My fists balled themselves into angry bombs and smashed away at the cold, cruel bricks over and over again, until my bloody hands couldn't take the sting of it anymore.

o o o

"My paper is on Joseph Stalin," intoned Angela Peirnot in her nasal voice. "So he was, like, the leader of Russia during World War II, right?"

We were sitting in another study group, just me, Angela, and Adrian Washington, while Adam circled the room like a hungry wolf, eavesdropping on everyone's conversations. I realized that I could only think of him as Adam now, not Mr. Martel, ever since I'd found out he was the guy Brady had known when he was a freshman, the guy who had disappeared after going to see the Mystics.

"And he was supposed to be, like, a Communist, so he was supposed to be all, like, 'equality for everyone' and stuff, but really he was just a dictator?"

Angela had one of those voices that shot up at the end of the last word in every sentence, so it came out as a question instead. I found myself resisting the urge to nod in agreement.

My knuckles ached from being scraped red on the brick hours before, and my stomach felt sour from missing the beautiful version of life that had taunted me briefly in Today. How did DW do this to me every time? How did it suck me in when I knew better? Closing my eyes, I could still smell the sweet odor of brewing coffee emanating from a nearby cart at the train station. I could feel the warm cotton of Kieren's sweatshirt rubbing against my cheek.

"And so, like, they really hated the Germans, because the Germans, like . . . wait, I can't remember this part."

Adrian Washington, who had been grinning like a circus clown the whole time Angela talked, didn't seem to mind the interruption. He took the opportunity to tickle her kneecaps under the shared desk, which made her lose her place again in her stack of notes.

"Stop it," she giggled softly.

I buried my face in my hands, exhausted with this exercise and not really giving a crap if Angela Peirnot ever figured out who exactly Joseph Stalin was. It was ancient history now anyway.

"Mr. Martel?" she called out, probably not realizing how flirty her voice was when she said his name. Adrian Washington, however, definitely noticed. "Can you help me with this part? I'm super confused."

Adam walked over, and I kept my eyes glued to the desk. I could almost feel the weight of him straining to *not* look at me. "Yes?"

"So, like, I thought Russia was our enemy, right? Like, there was a whole Cold War?"

"That's right."

"But, like, in this book I found a picture of Stalin and Roosevelt and the British guy—"

"Churchill."

"Yeah, him. Like, they were all hanging out?"

Unable to resist the urge any longer, I hazarded a glance up at Adam, only to find that he was staring right at me. He flinched immediately, regaining his composure and clearing his throat.

"And he was, like, this ruthless dictator. . ." Angela droned on. I took a deep breath, her voice getting under my skin. "I mean . . ." She flipped through some pages to find the right note. "Like, he starved his own people? And he sent all these people to Siberia?"

"What part don't you get?" Adam asked through tight lips, apparently as frustrated with Angela's obtuseness as I was.

"Why would we be, like, working with someone we hated?"

"Germany invaded Russia. They hated Hitler as much as we did."

"Okay?" Angela asked, still not getting it.

Adam cleared his throat again, his eyes darting momentarily to the other students before returning to our table. "Have you ever heard the old Sanskrit saying, Miss Peirnot?"

Her perfectly defined eyebrows furrowed up at him, and her mouth turned into a pouty smile meant to make her lips look fuller. "What's that?"

Now Adam looked directly at me, the heat of his gaze forcing me to look up and meet his eyes. "'The enemy of my enemy is my friend.'"

Refusing to break the staring contest first, I kept my head perfectly still until he broke away. Adam went to help another table, and Angela sighed.

"Whatever," she whispered to Adrian, who shook his head, charmed by her despite everything. He then began to tell us about his research into the Ugandan mass murderer Idi Amin.

When it was my turn to speak, I hurried through the choppy notes I had made on Genghis Khan, skipping many details as I knew my study partners weren't really listening anyway and the period was almost over.

The bell finally rang, and I tried to leave before Adam could stop me, but he was waiting by the door. One look from him told me he needed me to stay behind, and I knew that if I left, he would only find me later. I stood frozen in the room while the clamoring students filed out around me, feeling like a child left behind at the circus.

When the room was empty, he closed the door.

"What do you want, Adam?"

"Have you decided?"

I let out a deep exhale. And though I wanted to scream at him,

"No" or "I won't do it" or "It's not worth it" or any of the other denials that had been careening through my brain all day, all year for that matter, my mouth betrayed me by saying the only thing that I really wanted to believe, the decision that I had made the moment I saw Kieren's happy face smiling down at me at the train station.

I couldn't even look Adam in the eye to let him see my defeat.

"I'll do it."

CHAPTER EIGHT

I was already doubting my decision by the time I reached the school at midnight on Friday, my fingers numb despite their gloves and my hair windblown from the fifteen-minute bike ride. I shook my hands out and exhaled warm air onto them before reaching for the handle of the emergency door to the gym, which Adam had left unlocked for me.

I had learned the secrets of the school well in my three years there—where the security cameras were hidden, which ones actually worked, which hallways were chained shut after the school closed for the night, and which ones were still accessible.

It took me only a few minutes to weave through the halls to the boiler room, illuminating my way with the flashlight app on my phone. It didn't scare me to be alone in the school anymore, but there was another feeling creeping into my bones that night that I hadn't experienced in a long time.

Anticipation.

I was hooked on the fact that I finally had something to look forward to, something that excited me and got my blood pumping. Something that made me feel powerful. Now all of those emotions were gurgling to the surface, and I had to admit that I liked them. I liked them a lot.

I had been a good girl all my life, partially the result of the quasi-Catholic upbringing that had generally skipped the church part and settled instead for the part about constant guilt. I'd felt guilty all my life, I now realized. Guilty when Robbie and I had snuck out that night to take that photo in the pyramid house; guilty when I'd lied to my father about going to summer camp so I could visit the Mystics in Oregon; and even guilty when Robbie had been killed, because somehow I'd felt like it should have been me.

I spent so many years afraid, so many years ashamed. And for what? What did it get me? Loneliness. Anger. In the past fifteen months, I'd been floating through life like a shadow, the refrain constantly reprimanding me in my head: *Don't speak. Don't tell anyone how you feel. Don't tell them what you want. Don't let them see that you're absolutely breaking inside.*

I wouldn't break anymore. I was no longer made of glass.

I reached the science lab and steadied my breath as I twisted down that spiral staircase and my eyes adjusted to the dim light enough to make out Adam standing by the door to Yesterday, waiting for me.

"Did you bring it?" he asked.

"Yes."

I took off my backpack and grabbed the object Adam had told me to bring: my mother's old photo album, the one with pictures of her and her friends Jenny, Dave, John, Sage, and George by the beach behind the Portland hotel. The pictures were from about twelve years prior, the day I had returned to in order to prevent the dark portal under the lake from being built.

Adam grabbed the album from my hands and frantically flipped through it until his hand came to rest on a particular photo. It was of Jenny, the beautiful young woman he had apparently fallen in love with in DW. She was about twenty-six in the photo, very petite with flouncy blond hair and wearing that polka dot bikini, which I'm sure she knew she looked great in.

His eyes got a little misty. He sniffed slightly, and his fingers grazed her picture softly, as though he could somehow touch her if he were only gentle enough.

"This is a little older than she looked the last time I saw her. I've been . . ." He cleared his throat and removed his fingers.

"What?"

"I've been trying to find the exact moment she went in so I could follow her. I guess it must've been sometime after this day on this beach with your mother."

It wasn't until that moment that I realized why Adam had needed my help. He'd had no idea that there had been a lake portal. How could he have? In this reality, it hadn't existed. But in the old reality . . .

I was tempted to tell Adam what I knew: a couple of hours after this photo of Jenny was taken, she had gone into the lake portal and had never come out. And now it seemed that, in this new reality, she had disappeared around the same time.

Jenny had been giddy that day on the beach, I remembered, flouncing around in her little bikini. She was excited because she knew my mother was bringing the solution to make a new portal—a drug she had apparently missed very much. Was it possible that, after I had taken her drug away, she had simply found another?

Was I sitting on a secret Adam had spent four years trying to unravel?

The guilt gnawed at me. Yet another secret destroying yet another life. "Adam, I have to tell you something . . . about Jenny."

His eyes grew wide, and he took a step closer. "I knew you knew something. Rain told you, didn't she? You know where Jenny is?"

"No, Rain didn't tell me. I . . ." I thought for a moment. As cruel as it sounded, I didn't think it was a good idea to talk about that lake portal. Not yet anyway.

History repeats itself, I remembered. The fewer people who knew, the better.

"I'll tell you," I stalled. "I promise. After my turn."

He stepped back, examining me. "If you're messing with me, I swear—"

"I'm not," I insisted. "I'll tell you everything I know. But you have to help me first."

His chest rose and fell erratically, like it was taking all his effort not to pounce. "I told you I'd help you, and I meant it," he finally said. "But then you'll owe me. You understand that, right?"

"I know."

I looked around, uneasy. Even with the precaution of avoiding the security cameras, it still wasn't a good idea to dawdle.

"So, Marina," Adam began, the coy smile reappearing on his lips. His eyes regained the charming twinkle that had probably gotten him out of trouble his whole life, and he tilted his head down towards me. "What do you want to change?"

I took a deep breath. The secret had been lodged in my throat for so long, I wasn't sure I could force it out even if I tried. But it was now or never. "There was a moment," I began, "in this very room, a little over a year ago, when I went through the door to Yesterday."

Flipping through my mother's photo album, which I had to wrench back out of Adam's hands, I found a photo of my mother on the Portland beach. I took it out and placed it in my pocket, then returned the album to my backpack, which I leaned against the wall.

"My friends were supposed to come with me. They weren't supposed to do anything on the other side, just hide in the woods while I . . . took care of something." *Not yet, Adam. I can't tell you that part yet.* "And that way—"

"That way, they would remember everything when you came back out." Adam nodded. "I've played this level before, you know."

I cleared my throat. "My mother—Rain—beat us to the room by a few minutes, and she stopped my friends from entering. I ended up going in alone."

Adam closed his eyes and took a deep breath. "I knew it."

"You knew what?"

"When I saw you that first day, with your face that looks just like Rain's, I knew that you would understand what it's like."

I shook my head, not wanting to admit that I felt a deep connection to Adam, that somehow I could see in him the mirror image of a constant and echoing pain, the pain that kept me up at night. "What what's like?"

"Being this alone." He looked at me now with great compassion, but I still somehow sensed I shouldn't let Adam into my secret thoughts too completely. He hadn't earned my trust yet.

"You'll need something that takes you to a place a couple of hours before the event," he instructed. "I'll need that time to get to the school and create a diversion to keep Rain from beating you here."

"Okay." My mind was racing. Where had I been two hours before coming to the school? Well, we'd been at Kieren's house for a while. The boys had run out to make more flattened pennies for our plan. Then I had realized that I would need to go home and get the photo of my mother with her blue earrings in order to go back to the right day.

Kieren had offered to go with me, but I'd refused. I'd raced home, found the photo album, and then—

Brady. Brady had pulled up to the house in his Pontiac.

"There was a song playing."

"That'll work," Adam prodded.

"It was a sad song. I don't know—"

"How did it go?"

"It was like . . . a man who kept saying 'please' over and over again. Let him get what he wanted this time."

Adam laughed, and there seemed to be something condescending in the way he nodded his head. Like a melancholy song was somehow beneath him—but pining after a girl who'd ditched him years before wasn't, apparently. "Here," he said, taking out his phone and finding the song for me. "It's The Smiths."

The song echoed through the tiny little chamber, the deep, yearning voice pervading both our ears. Adam took a flattened penny out of his pocket and inserted it into the Yesterday door, which emitted the telltale yellow light.

"When we get there," Adam said, "you'll be wherever you were when you heard this song. I'm not sure where I'll be, but I'll meet you at the school."

I gulped, my heart suddenly beating too quickly.

"Now listen—this is important."

"Okay."

"When it's all over, when you and your friends return to this room, it'll still be the past. And unless you want to relive your junior year, you'll have to break away from them and sneak back down here. Go through Today again, holding this—" He handed me another flattened penny.

"What's this for?"

"It'll bring you back to tonight. When you go into Yesterday, the door to Today always brings you home, so long as you have a coin. Don't wait for me. I'll meet you here."

Suddenly, his eyes darted down to my hand. He surprised me by reaching down and grabbing my pinkie, sliding the ruby ring off my finger, and putting it in his pocket.

"My ring—"

"Collateral. You still owe me one after this."

I was scared suddenly, desperately sliding my fingers over my bare pinkie, feeling the indent from where the ring was supposed to be. But Adam put his hands on my shoulders, and I was calmed by his gentle tone and his knowing smirk. "Trust me."

Did I have a choice?

"Now take my hand so we end up in the same plane."

Steadying my breath, I did as Adam instructed, placing my small, trembling hand into his warm, stable one. Then we both stepped forward and let ourselves be swallowed up by Yesterday.

CHAPTER NINE

"I should have kissed you back when we were in the lake."

I blinked my eyes several times, clearing away the residual yellow light that always lingered a moment too long after entering Down World. I took a deep breath and got my bearings.

I was in Brady's Pontiac, sitting in my driveway. My mother's photo album was resting in my lap. My fingers traced the scalloped edges of the thick paper that overflowed from the book, and I dared myself to do what I was dying to: look into Brady's eyes.

He still looked tired, of course, just like he had at the gas station. But this was a different tired altogether. The eighteen-year-old boy in front of me was tired from a long night and from frustration—he had just seen Piper holding Robbie's hand. But that kind of tired would pass.

The man he would become, the one I had seen in the gas station days before, just looked bored and defeated, like life had been wearing him down so much he no longer even tried to get back up.

As I looked at Brady now, all the memories came rushing back.

Brady, who'd given me half a jelly doughnut the first time I met him, powdered sugar still rimming his upper lip like a milk moustache.

Brady, who'd held my hand the first time he had led me down into the boiler room.

Brady, whose idea of how to break into a building was to simply grab a rock and smash in the window.

And Brady, who'd gently kissed the top of my head when I was passing out in his lap after having an allergic reaction to the vaccine pellet in the underlake world.

He was real and beautiful and in front of me again, staring deeply into my eyes and telling me that he should have kissed me back in the lake all those months ago, when he had kept his distance because he'd still believed that Piper was out there in the world somewhere, loving him back.

I remembered this scene from the first time I had lived it. I had been embarrassed and stuttering, feeling guilty because Kieren was waiting for me at the house. That day, I had told Brady to drive to Colorado, knowing that if my plan worked, the world would mold itself to a new reality while he drove—that by the time he reached Boulder, Piper would have forgotten all about her fling with my brother, and she would be back in his arms.

I had wanted to give him that as my last present to him, my farewell gift.

But what had it gotten him?

The Brady that I'd met at the gas station was miserable and alone, his heart broken by Piper. But in that reality, he didn't even know why. Would he have been happier if he'd known the truth?

I knew that I would have been if I'd been him.

The first time I'd lived through this conversation in the car with Brady, I'd been too wrapped up in my own problems to think much about what the consequences of my actions might be for him. I was a kid, after all. Sixteen years old. My heart was breaking that day, the precarious plan to save my brother and close the portal to the underlake world hanging in the balance.

But now I wasn't a kid anymore.

It was time to admit something to myself: I didn't have to come back to this moment with Brady. Adam had just said a moment a couple hours before the event. I could have gone back to a moment at Kieren's house. I could have gone back to seeing the Mystics at the old grounds, where we had been just prior. But no, I had picked this moment.

And now I knew the reason. I wanted to fix the mistake that I had made with Brady—the mistake of not bringing him with us into the new reality, where at least he would have known the truth. After all that Brady had done for me with the Mystics, it was the least that I owed him.

And so, this time around, I did what I should have done that first day. "Brady," I whispered, covering his hand with my own, "come with me."

o o o

I felt like an archaeologist for the next couple hours, painstakingly re-creating every detail of that day as I had lived it two years before. Other than having Brady with me, which I figured should have had no effect on the outcome of my actions at the Portland hotel, I wanted to keep the day as consistent as possible.

Yet my emotions were threatening to overcome me as Brady and

I drove toward Kieren's house, anticipating heading for the high school. What if Piper caused a scene when Brady showed up, now that she was with Robbie? What if Kieren didn't like that Brady was with me, suspecting that perhaps we were more than friends? We weren't, of course, but would Kieren think we were?

And the most pressing concern of all: What if Adam didn't live up to his part of the bargain and wasn't able to distract my mother from beating us to the science lab that held the passageway to the three doors?

He had told me to trust him when we'd made this plan, but was I a fool to do so? After all, he had known my mother when she was in high school, had clearly spent a lot of time there if he was in love with Jenny. What if he was in cahoots with her? What if this was all some grand plan she had cooked up, exacting her revenge for the fact that I had slipped through her fingers the first time?

I wouldn't put it past my mother—or the evil version of my mother anyway—to go to any length to stop me from destroying the lake portal to the dark reality where she and John were powerful and rich.

But any concerns I had about what could go wrong with the plan were shelved when Brady and I reached Kieren's house. Because I was about to see Kieren and Robbie again, and for a blissful moment, nothing else mattered.

I tripped twice on the way from Brady's car to the door into Kieren's rec room, my unsure feet wobbling beneath me. And it wasn't until I had the sliding glass door shoved aside and saw Robbie standing in the corner with Piper that I realized I had stopped breathing with excitement.

Although I was dying to hug Kieren as well, I knew that my brother had to come first. I practically ran through the room and threw myself into Robbie's arms, almost knocking him over.

He laughed with surprise, and it took him a moment to hug me back. "You all right?" he whispered down at me.

"I'm fine," I choked out, but my voice broke in the middle of the word.

Robbie didn't ask any more questions but just held me for a second while Piper looked on lovingly. I grasped on to Robbie's middle, and I wasn't sure I would ever find the courage to let go again.

"I missed you too," he said into my hair, and I wiped my wet face on his T-shirt, remembering a time when I'd skinned my knee falling off my bike as a kid and he had let me do the same thing.

I finally pulled away, embarrassed by the show I was putting on, which must have seemed oddly dramatic to the people in the room.

"Sorry." I smiled.

"It's okay," Piper said, "you're making up for lost hugs."

Kieren was standing by the door, watching me with a light in his eyes that I had missed so profoundly I almost started crying again.

The moment was broken a second later, though, when Brady entered the room from the sliding door. His body had shrunken in on itself slightly, an awkwardness about his demeanor that told me he wasn't sure if he'd made the right choice in following me.

I realized it was my job to make this all seem normal. "Everyone knows Brady, right?"

Kieren, Robbie, and their friend Scott nodded in his direction, not terribly fazed by his presence. But then we all turned to Piper, almost in slow motion, to see how she would react.

She was flustered, something that I hadn't seen much from her since I'd discovered her living on the train with Robbie. She quickly shuffled away from my brother like a child caught cribbing notes from the textbook under her desk. Gone was her confident smile, her easy charm. She bowed her head and looked up at Brady with huge eyes—eyes that expanded with a trembling emotion that I couldn't quite decipher. Was she excited to see him? Scared? Ashamed? Her lips curled in on themselves, and she softly whispered his name.

She ran across the room to meet him, but he sidestepped her, and I saw his body turn in to a wall, not permitting even the slightest warmth to emanate in her direction.

The room had grown deadly silent. As we watched Brady and Piper's love for each other shrivel up and wilt before our eyes, the celebratory air of the room took on the unmistakable pallor of death and decay.

She was going to break his heart eventually, I reminded myself. *But this time, you were here to see it.*

"We need to go," Kieren said, breaking through the icy chill in the air. "It's time."

CHAPTER TEN

I sat on the bleachers with Robbie, just as I had done that first time, pretending to watch the basketball game while Piper took up her station in the nearby bathroom and Kieren and Scott stood guard in the hallway. The only difference was that this time, Brady was sitting with us. And, hopefully, Adam was already somewhere in the building. I was relieved that nothing else had gone awry from the original plan.

Brady followed our lead as Robbie and I discreetly left the stands before halftime, walking confidently past the guards who were not-so-secretly stationed by the doors, under the guise that we were headed for the bathrooms.

Once out of the gym, I retrieved Piper from her hiding spot in the bathroom, and we met up with the boys, trailing Scott, who had procured the large ring of keys he would use to lead us to the secret entrance of the science lab.

I was keeping my nerves in check so far. Despite the frosty air between Brady and Piper, the day had been progressing just as before.

After our rendezvous with our friends, after Scott's fumbling with the key ring that I had always suspected was a bit *too* clumsy—I never did learn if Scott had been working for my mother all along—and after we had made it into the secret alternate passageway to the abandoned network of halls that led to the science lab, that's when my nerves really began to kick in.

Piper and Brady were both acting as though the other didn't exist, with Brady staying noticeably close to me, as though I could somehow shield him from the avalanche of feelings he was going to have to deal with eventually.

We had reached the hallway where I distinctly remembered that Piper had told Robbie she loved him, and he had said it back. But this time, as if gagged by an invisible handkerchief, Piper remained silent.

Had I made a mistake bringing Brady? Was it stupid to add another factor to the plan—even one that theoretically shouldn't affect the outcome?

And would all of this be a moot point if we made it to the science lab and found that Adam hadn't fulfilled his promise to distract my mother?

I frantically looked for any trace of him as my friends and I began the perilous last stage of our journey—twisting through the once-deserted hallway that remained from when the high school had been a military complex in the 1940s. Our path dimly illuminated by windows placed at the tops of the walls, my friends and I progressed en masse towards the science room at the end of the corridor.

But there was no sign of Adam.

As before, the bricked-up doorways that had always lined this path were now mostly open, the droning hum of office workers filtering out of some of the rooms. But that only added to the surreal feeling that we were floating somehow, ghostlike, towards our destination.

Yet I wasn't a ghost. The telltale pounding of my heart against my rib cage told me that I was real, flesh and blood, and that I had only a short amount of time to relive this chapter of my life.

If a person spent too long in DW, especially in Yesterday where changes had huge consequences, it would eventually become too late to come back. That was something Sage had taught me when I had asked if my mother—my real mother, Ana—would be coming back home to me. I could still hear Sage's words in my head:

Your mother is gone. She's been in too long. That other woman, the one you saw under the lake—she's all that's left now.

I didn't know exactly how much time I had, but I did know this: if I stayed too long, I'd be stuck forever. And if the evil version of my mother succeeded this time in stopping not just my friends but myself as well from returning to that day when I had closed up the lake portal, the world I'd be stuck in was the hell that lurked beneath the lake.

Again, the thought came back to torment me: *Is that what Adam secretly wants?*

But my question was answered a second later when a loud crash came echoing out of one of the doors that lined the hallway. My friends and I all froze, frantically looking around for the source.

When a second thudding crash followed the first, Brady pointed to a door just a few feet up—one we would have to walk right past to make it to the science lab.

"What is it?" Kieren frantically whispered.

"It's our mother," I responded, nodding to Robbie. Of course, that wasn't exactly true, but I didn't have time to elaborate.

"How do you know that?"

"I—"

But I didn't get to finish the sentence, which was just as well.

Robbie moved his body to shield Piper from whatever might be lurking behind that door, and Brady, in disgust, started marching away from them in the direction of the crash.

But when I heard my mother's irate voice resonate from that same room, I reached out to grab Brady's arm and stop him.

"You'll never find her this way, Adam," I heard that evil version of my mother spit in her tersest voice. Mom was born in America, right after her mother had immigrated here from Mexico, and so she didn't normally have any trace of an accent. But when she was angry, I always thought I could hear remnants of my *abuelita*'s voice reprimanding us in Spanish to clean up our rooms or help her in the kitchen.

Adam's voice in response was calm but slightly higher than normal: "Then you won't either."

A deathly silence followed. Signaling to my brother to wait behind me, I began sneaking towards the open doorway. But Kieren tensed up before I made it more than a step.

"Marina, no, no," he whispered, stopping me with the forcefulness of his voice.

"I need to see," I responded.

But Brady wasn't having that either. "I'll go," he interjected, all but pushing me aside in order to approach the door. Stooping down low, he bent his head around the cracked-open door, but immediately whipped it back, cringing with an expression that told me he had been spotted. "Shit," he whispered.

"What was that?" my mother asked, her voice echoing out of the small room.

A slight Russian accent replied, a man saying, "It was that kid. Dark hair."

"They're here," my mother hissed.

"I mean it, Rain, stand back," Adam shouted, no longer sounding so cool.

"Do you understand that you're killing her, Adam? You're killing Jenny right now."

Brady stood up by the doorway, and I ran to meet him, no longer caring about Kieren's objections. What was my mother talking about? But Brady held me back before I could look in the room.

"No, Marina. There's a man with a gun. We have to go."

A gun? Did Adam have a gun on my mother?

But there was no time to find out. A struggle could be heard inside the room—feet shuffling, grunting. Suddenly, a gunshot rang out, followed by plaster raining down from the ceiling. My heart leaped into my throat.

"Mom!" I screamed, my voice boomeranging out before I could stop it. The next several seconds were an avalanche of chaos as panicking workers in the other offices shouted, slammed doors, and, in a couple of cases, bolted into the hallway, not pausing to consider what a bunch of teenagers were doing there before running for cover.

I realized I was on the ground, Kieren's body covering mine. But there were no more gunshots.

Over the receding din, I could make out Adam's voice: "Run, Marina!"

That was all the encouragement Kieren needed. He pulled me back up to my feet and grabbed hold of Piper's hand. He shouted to the others, "Now! Just run!"

As we passed the office, I peeked in just long enough to see that my mother had not been shot but that she and her Russian boyfriend—Alexei, that had been his name—were wrestling with

Adam over control of the gun. A small black hole in the ceiling revealed the final resting place of the bullet we had heard.

"Adam," I called out, not sure what to do to help him.

My voice was enough to distract Alexei briefly, and Adam regained control of the gun, pointing it at his attacker's head.

"I'm fine," Adam called to me, his eyes still trained on Alexei and my mother, standing side by side. "They won't hurt me. Just go."

Right before I could start running, however, I saw Alexei charge Adam, wresting control of the gun once again from Adam's fingers. The two strong men began what seemed to be a battle of gladiators, the gun perilously dangling between them as they faced off.

I didn't get a chance to see who would be the victor, however. I felt a hand grab my wrist and yank, and it wasn't until we were almost in the science lab that held the tent to the three doors that I looked down and realized it was Kieren's.

"Scott," Kieren yelled to his friend, "you got the key?"

"Got it!" Scott yelled, apparently as relieved as everyone else to have escaped my mother. Maybe I could trust him after all. He quickly found the correct key in his ring and pried open the door to the lab.

We were almost all inside the door when I heard footsteps barreling down the hall in our direction. A quick glance behind me revealed Alexei running at full speed towards us. He reached Piper first, who had been lingering in the door as she'd waited for Robbie to enter.

Grabbing a fistful of Piper's hair, he practically lifted her into the air and pulled her away from the door. Robbie threw his full body onto Alexei, trying desperately to free Piper from his clutches. But after his years on the train, Robbie's strength was still diminished. Alexei threw him off like he was shaking off a raindrop.

Kieren, Brady, and Scott had already entered the room, but they came back towards the doorway when they noticed me freezing behind them.

I was ready to abandon the plan altogether rather than risk leaving Robbie or Piper behind with this vicious man, but at the last moment, my sacrifice ended up not being necessary.

Before I knew it, a knife was in Alexei's face. The large Russian froze when he saw it, slowly raising his hands and letting go of Piper, whom he had still been grabbing by the hair.

Brady stepped even closer to Alexei, letting him know that he knew very well how to use the pocketknife that he had pulled out and that he would do so if needed. The Russian backed away, and Brady grabbed Piper's arm, pulling her behind him into the science lab.

Robbie followed suit, and once we were all inside, Brady slammed the door closed and twisted the bolt behind us to lock it.

"Let's go," Brady ordered the group.

Piper was still shaken, trembling and holding her hair. She started to cry, and Robbie, dazed by the whole experience, took her in his arms.

Brady folded up his knife and put it away in his back pocket, turning away from the couple. "I said let's go," he repeated, and we all followed him down the spiral staircase into the chamber with the three doors.

From my pocket, I took out the photo of my mother at the Oregon beach and focused on it for a moment. I then inserted the coin into Yesterday and watched as the door turned into a glowing yellow portal.

Taking Kieren's hand in my right one and Brady's in my left, I whispered to the others to join hands as well. And then, walking hand in hand, my friends and I entered the portal to Yesterday.

Something my mother had said the first time I'd tried this suddenly echoed in my ears.

Things end up the way they're meant to . . . nature finds a way.

CHAPTER ELEVEN

My whole body was sore.

That was the first thing I became aware of when I woke up in my own bed, while the harsh midmorning light illuminated my opaque pink curtains. The remainder of our trip into Yesterday hadn't actually been any more physically exhausting than the first time I'd done it, but the tension I had held in my body was now showing its effects in my tight muscles and aching forehead.

But relief also flooded over me as I remembered that the rest of our excursion had gone as planned: once we'd made it to the beach behind the Portland hotel, my friends had gone to hide in the woods while George and I buried the beaker that would have created the underlake portal.

There had been a brief moment of panic when it was time to return home and Brady could not be found anywhere. But he had reappeared a moment later, having wandered off to get away from Piper and Robbie.

And then we'd all returned through the door that George opened for us, which led us back to that night almost a year and a half ago. I had to wait until I'd reassured Kieren a dozen times that I didn't need him to walk me home and Piper and Robbie had headed back to her place to sleep before I was able to break away and return to the school.

I was so exhausted at that point, I couldn't even think to be scared. I simply used Adam's coin to return to the present day, retrieved my frozen bike from where I'd left it outside the school, and pedaled home as fast as I could, my teeth chattering.

Once in my warm house, I couldn't help but sneak a peek into Dad's room. In the faint moonlight that drifted through their white curtains, Dad and Laura were sleeping peacefully. Their gentle snores filled the room, flooding me with gratitude.

I was home. Everything was just as it should be.

o o o

My only regret was that I hadn't gotten a chance to talk to Kieren or Robbie more that night while we were all in the same time and place.

Now that it was morning, my fingers itched to reach for my phone to call and check in with them, to make sure it hadn't all been a dream. But I had to slow down. For me, it had only been about eight hours since we'd returned, but for them it had been almost a year and half. I was going to have to play catch-up on that time, figure out what exactly I had missed.

Of course, I'd been down this road the first time I'd come back from Yesterday, when I'd been plunged into a world where Robbie had been raised thousands of miles away and Kieren had no memory of me. It had taken me weeks to put the pieces of my life together then, sitting silently at the dinner table while Laura and my father acted out a strange new reality in front of me.

No one had caught on that time. I had played my part well. Would I be able to do so again?

I grabbed my phone out of its charging station and started to open Instagram so I could see what everyone had been up to, but I didn't even get a chance to start scrolling.

"Marina?" Laura called gently from the stairwell.

"Yes?"

"Aren't you going to work today, sweetheart? Those tweens aren't going to teach themselves how to make fart bubbles." Laura laughed at her own joke.

I looked at the clock on my bedside table. *Shit.* It was ten thirty on Saturday. I was supposed to teach the junior-high class at eleven. But, hey, at least this part of my life hadn't changed. I still worked at the Kids' Science Lab.

"Be right down," I called, throwing my phone on the bed and heading for the bathroom to brush my teeth. My image in the mirror was less than impressive, with blue half-moon shadows under my eyes and matted hair plastered to my cheeks.

I brushed with one hand and combed with the other while using my foot to open the top drawer where I kept my concealer. I didn't even know what today's lesson plan was. Not that it mattered much to the thirteen-year-olds. We could convert the Lego robots into a drum kit and just bang away at it for half an hour, and they would be perfectly happy.

"Shall I make you a Pop-Tart?" Laura asked sweetly from outside the door.

"Yeshh pleash," I called back through a mouthful of toothpaste.

Finishing up in the bathroom, I darted to my room to dig through the clean-clothes pile for a bra.

"Oh, your ride's here!" came Laura's voice, this time muffled from somewhere in the kitchen.

My ride?

I usually biked on Saturdays as my dad had the car with him at work. And then a realization shot through me like an electric charge: *What if it's Kieren?*

I whipped my backpack over my shoulders and tripped down the stairs, all while squeezing my feet into my Keds. I could feel my sweaty palms slip-sliding over the banister. A tall silhouette awaited me on the other side of the wavy yellow glass in the front door.

Laura appeared from the kitchen, a brown paper bag in her hand with a Pop-Tart–sized rectangle wedged inside.

"Thank you," I breathlessly whispered while my shaking hand opened the door, bright sunlight flooding into my eyes and making me feel, for a moment, as though I were entering another portal.

But this was no portal. This was real life—my real life now, as I must have wanted it to be. Because in front of me stood Brady, a smile as wide as Texas on his lips.

"Hey, beautiful," he said.

"Hi," I stuttered, my brain frantically trying to make sense of why he was here. Were we friends? Did he give me a ride to work on his way to the gas station?

But my questions were answered when he leaned down and kissed me. There was no trace of cigarette smell on his breath, only mint gum. A waft of the lemon-scented detergent his cousin used to use on all his clothes filled my nostrils with a warm, nostalgic sensation. And though my brain had not yet caught up with my body, I found myself kissing him back.

Things end up the way they're meant to.

Is this what I really wanted all along?

"You ready to go?" he asked, reaching out for my hand.

And having no idea what else I could possibly do, I took Brady's hand and headed for his car.

o o o

Brady scrolled through radio stations as he drove, not satisfied with anything. He lingered for a moment on a pop song before changing it again. Meanwhile, I stared out the window, trying to process what was going on, Laura's breakfast lying unopened by my feet.

Is this what I wanted?

Yes, there had been a time when being with Brady, feeling his soft lips on mine as they had been just moments before and knowing that he truly wanted me back, was all I could think about.

But that was before Kieren had brought me home from Portland and then spent the night holding me in my bed. Before he kissed me, and I realized that all I wanted to do was kiss him back. Before I forgave him for my brother's accident. In some ways, that was the night my real life had begun. And I hadn't really thought about Brady the same way since.

The next thought made me squirm a bit in my seat, flustered and grappling with my memories. Because the morning after Kieren and I had spent the night together in my bed, he'd tried to hurl himself in front of the oncoming train. And, pushing him out of the way, I had gone into the train portal instead of him.

I never blamed him for that morning. How could I? It led me to my brother. But is that why we weren't together now? Was I some-how still resentful of Kieren? Did I still not trust him?

Brady turned the radio off, his hand resting for a moment on my knee before returning to the steering wheel so he could make a left turn.

"You're being quiet."

"Am I?" I adjusted myself in my seat, trying to seem more open to him. Whatever had happened between me and Kieren wasn't Brady's fault. And though I was dying to scan my phone messages to try to piece together the past year and a half, I also didn't want to miss this moment to indulge in my current reality: sitting next to Brady, watching the sunlight dapple his brown T-shirt through the windshield.

"I'm just thinking about work," I improvised. "I'm not sure what I'm teaching the kids today." Brady laughed. "What?"

"It's just you usually have it planned out to the second. Isn't that what the bullet journal was for?" he asked, nodding towards my backpack.

I opened my bag and pulled out a large spiral bullet journal, a picture of Marie Curie glued to the cover. Opening it up, my eyes fell on the inside front cover: "For the smartest girl I know. I love you. Congrats on finishing junior year! Brady."

Hot blood rushed to my cheeks, both of embarrassment and something else—something like anger. Not at Brady but at myself. *I had been with Brady since at least June?*

What the hell had I done to myself? Brady and I had apparently already said "I love you." What else had we done? I didn't even know. Jesus, had we had sex? I had always thought that that was something I wouldn't do until college. But then again, I had apparently made a whole bunch of choices lately that I hadn't been expecting.

What other experiences had I robbed myself of?

I tried to calm myself down, suppressing an urge to scream. There was probably a logical explanation for this. I just needed time to figure out what had gone wrong. Still, every question just created a million more questions, and no one would be able to fill me in on what I had missed. No one except . . . maybe Adam.

If he even made it back alive.

I could feel my breath straining, my fingers clenching. Would I always be on a slightly different path than everyone else? Would nothing ever just feel right?

"What's that?" Brady asked, his eyes falling on my lap.

"Hmm?" I asked, trying to sound as normal as possible. I realized that, while grabbing the journal, I had also snatched up something else—a stack of papers, now jutting out from beneath Brady's thoughtful gift. Moving the journal out of the way, I could see words in thick black ink: *MIT Admissions. Part One. Biographical Information.*

Sorting through the stack, I saw that I had already filled out the whole first section. There was even a checklist with items such as Transcript, Standardized Test Scores (with "retake?" written beside it), and Letters of Recommendation. Next to the last one, I had scrawled giant red check marks beside the names Mr. Chu and Miss Yawani, my chemistry teacher.

So distracted was I with the forms, I didn't even notice at first that Brady had pulled the car over. I looked up, expecting to see the small storefront of Kids' Science Lab, but found instead that we were on the shoulder of the main road, still several minutes from work.

Brady removed his hands from the steering wheel and glared down at the forms on my lap. "I thought you said you weren't applying there." His voice sounded tight.

"I—I haven't. I mean, I haven't submitted it yet, obviously."

But his eyes fell on the words written in black Sharpie at the top: *Due Jan 12.* "That's due next week. How long have you been working on this?"

"I don't know."

"You don't know?" he asked incredulously. "Well, it's obviously been a while. You already got letters of rec and everything. Were you doing this over Christmas? During your birthday last weekend?"

"I don't know, Brady. Why are you yelling at me?"

"Jesus."

Brady sat back and ran his fingers through his hair. I still thought he was one of the most handsome boys I'd ever seen, with his caramel-colored eyes and broad shoulders. Although I guess *boy* wasn't really the right word for him now. He was twenty years old. Did he still live with his cousin? Work at the gas station? Was he happier now than he'd been before?

"I'm not yelling, I'm just asking. Because you've obviously been working on this awhile, and you didn't tell me." He inhaled deeply, and when he let it out, his whole body seemed smaller. "I mean, you said you were going to stay . . ." he said in a very soft voice, looking at his lap. "With me."

"I—" What could I say? The look of pain on Brady's face was killing me. First Piper had left him, and now me. Why would I have filled out this application if I'd told him I was staying? "I mean, you knew I'd go to college."

"Yeah, but you said state school. Or somewhere local."

"I can't study robotics at community college, Brady. I mean, not like I could at MIT."

"State school then."

"It's just an application!" I shouted, not sure why I was suddenly so upset. Did I even want to go that far away? I hadn't been sure before. What had changed my mind?

Brady sat silently, watching the cars go by.

I realized in that moment that what I'd said about MIT was true. If I really wanted to study robotics, engineering—if I wanted it to be my career—then I couldn't limit myself to staying here. I had been so afraid for so long to leave my father, to leave the only family I had left. But now that I looked around this town, I couldn't help but think about the fact that it had brought me nothing but misery.

We were less than a mile from the train that had killed Robbie the first time, a few hundred feet from the ice cream parlor where I'd run into Kieren last year and he'd walked right by me. And now? Now I had a boyfriend who I couldn't even remember my first real kiss with. The more I thought about it, the more I knew that I wanted to get the hell away from this place. Get on one of those dream-chasing trains to the coast and never look back.

"Why did it have to be Boston?" Brady asked.

"Because that's where the school is."

"No." Brady laughed, shaking his head. "That's not it. You're going to live with them, aren't you?"

"Them?"

"You know what I mean," he shouted, looking right into my eyes now. "You're going to live with your brother . . . and Piper."

I stared at him, my voice choking in my throat. Robbie and Piper? They lived together in Boston?

It was just as she had always wanted, just like she had talked about that night when she'd asked me if I would live with them by the sea. It looked like maybe Piper had gotten her color-coded boxes all in a row after all.

"I would live with my aunt Amalia," I protested, but it came out a beat too late to be convincing.

Brady put the car back in gear. "You'll be late for work." He didn't say another word while he drove the rest of the distance. And neither did I.

CHAPTER TWELVE

I stared breathlessly at the parade of images before me, cowering deeper under the tent of covers that I had propped up to protect myself. Somehow I had known that I would need a barrier from the world, that whatever my computer was about to show me would feel like arrows attacking me from all sides. As it turned out, my comforter was not enough to shield me.

The first image of Kieren on Instagram was one that his girl-friend, Stephanie, had tagged him in. So he was still with Stephanie, but this time, the pictures only went back about six months. In the most recent photo, dated just two weeks ago, she was standing next to him in a field, and he was wearing a camouflage army uni-form in desert beige. "So proud of my BF! Finished basic training today!" she had captioned it.

More pictures of them followed—date night at the movies; her BFF's birthday party at a bowling alley; just Kieren, taken from her perspective sitting opposite him, paddling a canoe up a beautiful, sunlit river.

And then, working backwards in time, on his page: "First day of basic," with the hashtag #GoROTC. In another of his photos, he was sitting at a large library table with books on chemical engineering splayed out in front of him. The caption: "They said college would be easy!"

I wasn't surprised, to be honest. His dad was a real jarhead, having served in the Marines after high school. He had never lost the close-cropped military haircut or stern demeanor that had always terrified me when I was a kid. I had expected Kieren to follow in his dad's footsteps, football and pride in service being the two religions in the Protsky household.

The pieces of the puzzle began to come into place: the Reserves were paying for Kieren to go to the state college, about half an hour away. Before that, though, he had helped out for a few months at his dad's store, and that's where he had met Stephanie.

The only part I couldn't figure—the part that I was most afraid to find out—was why I wasn't in the picture.

I scrolled desperately through my text messages, looking for clues. Right after the night we came back to this new reality, there had been a spattering of messages: *Meet me at my place* and *Did you say 7:00 or 7:30?* After that, very few texts passed between us for about five months, either because we weren't speaking or because we were together and therefore didn't need to text.

Then, almost a year ago, the messages started up again: *Miss you tonight,* I had written. And two days later, from Kieren: *Miss you too.* Then a few days later, from me: *Why aren't you answering?* And Kieren's reply: *Studying. Call u later.*

A week of nothing followed.

Then a message from me, sent at one thirty in the morning: *Is this really what you want?* No reply came.

The last exchange was from eight months ago. Kieren had written, *Got your message. Don't know what to say.* I had written back, *I'll always love you. No matter what.*

That was the last message.

I closed the computer, shut down the phone, and pushed both devices out of my cocoon of covers. A pervading blackness took the place of all the artificial light they had been providing. And in that darkness, I balled myself up like a seashell and cried myself to sleep.

o o o

"Marina?"

I was still enveloped in my sheets, and the voice floated to me in muffled waves. A moment of panic gripped me as I suddenly came to consciousness and couldn't remember what day it was, or even what reality.

"Marina?" my father gently called again.

I flung off the comforter and found him sitting on the edge of my bed, a mug of coffee in his hands that read, "Engineers unscrew things." It had been my Christmas present to him two years ago.

"What time is it?" I asked with a jolt.

"Nine o'clock."

"School," I muttered, wiping my eyes.

"Honey, it's Sunday."

"Mmm." My brain finally began coming to. I sucked in my dry lips to wet them and sat up more fully. "Is something wrong?"

"No." My father smiled. "I'm sorry, I couldn't wait for you to wake up. These were posted last night."

He held up his phone, but my eyes weren't awake enough yet to focus on the screen. Numbers, columns, something important-looking. I reached for my dad's mug and took a sip, blanching at the bitter taste of unsweetened coffee. "Dad, sugar. Seriously."

"It's your new SAT scores." He smiled wider, a barely contained enthusiasm seeping into his voice.

SATs? I remembered that I had written the word *retake* next to that item on my checklist. Guess I hadn't been happy with my first results. In my old reality, I had taken the test once in October, and my score had seemed good enough to me.

But now, there was apparently more at stake.

My stomach suddenly balled up, and a burp got lodged somewhere in my esophagus. The coffee mug turned slippery in my palms, and I put it down on my bedside table, swallowing repeatedly. "I can't read, just tell me."

"Fifteen-forty," my dad said, beaming, turning his phone back towards him and toggling to another screen.

"What does MIT require?" I asked, thinking ahead.

"Fourteen-ninety minimum, see?" Dad turned the phone to me again, having already anticipated the question and brought up the correct screen. "You're in, kiddo. You did it."

"Dad, you don't know that. Test scores are just one element."

"You're gonna get in, I can feel it. I texted your brother. He was so excited."

"You told Robbie? Dad, you gotta give me a minute here."

"I'm sorry, I'm too excited."

I hadn't seen my dad like this in years. He was giddy, like a kid just about to pull into the Disneyland parking lot. Despite my apprehension, I couldn't help but get excited too. Maybe it was just his energy rubbing off on me. I was proud of my accomplishment, but I hadn't even had a moment to process any of this.

It was like, overnight, my life had been decided for me. I would go to Boston and live with Robbie. With Robbie *and Piper*, I corrected myself. In my old reality, I hadn't been sure what I had wanted. Hell, in my old reality, I had just wanted to feel alive again.

Is this what feeling alive was like? Having life come barreling at me like, well, like a train rushing towards a station? But I hadn't even gotten a chance to choose where the train was going. Was I ready to leave my old life behind? Leave Kieren to the course he had set for himself, one that clearly didn't include me in any way?

And leave Brady? *Just like Piper did.*

"Were you studying last night?" Dad asked, eyeing my computer on the floor.

"Kind of."

"Oh, hey, how's that Genghis Khan paper going?"

I swallowed hard at the reminder, my hand instinctively grasping the pinkie where my sweet little ring was missing. I still didn't know if Adam had even made it back from the portal two nights ago. And if he had, well, then there would be a reckoning with him that I would have to deal with.

"It's due soon," I said through my dry throat.

Just then, my phone vibrated on the floor, and I looked down to see *Video call incoming* on the screen with Robbie's photo behind it.

Dad smiled. "I'll leave you two to talk." Standing up to go, he couldn't help but rub my head like he had done when I was a kid. "Proud of you, baby!" he cheered, pumping one fist as he left and chanting softly into his cupped hand to imitate a crowded stadium, "MIT, MIT, MIT . . ."

I couldn't help but laugh as I reached for my phone. No matter what I decided, knowing that I had made my dad proud was at least something.

"Hey, sis." Robbie smiled as soon as I swiped the phone. He looked like he was in a Starbucks, a chocolate croissant in the hand not holding the phone up.

"Hey," I said back, my heart leaping at the sight of him. Robbie looked great, tan and healthy. And there was something in his eyes that had been missing when I had first rescued him from the DW train. A liveliness, maybe. A spark. For a while there, I had been terrified that some intrinsic part of him had died on that train. It was the main reason I had been so hesitant to go back into Yesterday and redo the past—Robbie was happy with his childhood in Portland, happy not remembering his other self.

Seeing that glow in his eyes over the phone, I thrilled to the idea that maybe he was even happier now that he had gotten the best of both worlds—the safe childhood with Mom in Oregon, but also the memory that he had had a childhood with a dad and a sister who loved him. Now he truly had a life of his own choosing. A life with Piper.

"Dad told me the good news," he said, chomping off a bite of the croissant. "It's amazing. I'm not surprised, though."

"I haven't had time," I stuttered, "to process it all."

"There will be time when you get here," he said, smiling. "Then everything will be perfect."

"Robbie—"

"Congratulations, Marina!" a familiar voice shouted from else-where in the Starbucks, and Robbie turned the phone to show Piper's glowing face. "I knew you could do it, sis!"

"Piper, hi," I said, tripping over her name a bit. Where did she and I stand now, I wondered, since I was dating her ex-boyfriend?

But no matter how Piper felt about that, it didn't seem to be a problem. She blew me a kiss before curling her perfect lips to blow onto her hot drink. "Are you excited?" she asked.

"Totally." I cleared my throat, combing through my hair with my fingers. "Sorry, I'm still in bed."

"That's okay. Let's talk later?"

"Sure."

The phone swiveled back to Robbie as he and Piper walked out of the Starbucks and headed towards a car. I could hear the doors opening and a distant siren wailing.

"I'm really happy for you, M," Robbie said, standing by the car. A crystal-blue sky framed his face, and I wanted desperately to reach into the phone and hug him. Robbie had always made things make sense for me, even impossible things.

"Robbie, can I ask you something?" I realized I was whispering, although I was pretty sure Piper had already gotten in the car. I didn't want anyone to hear this but him.

"Yeah?"

"Did you . . ." I had to inhale some fresh air before finishing the question. "Did you ever forgive Kieren?"

Robbie's face froze for a split second, and I wondered if the call had dropped. But then he laughed. It was a strange laugh, coming from Robbie. Bitter and ironic. The kind of laugh I'd heard from him when he was trapped between dimensions. "For which thing?" he finally asked. "Daring me to get hit by a train or cheating on you?"

Now it was my turn to freeze. I could feel my facial muscles tense and harden with the words, petrifying like ancient wood. My face must've revealed everything that was happening inside my brain.

"Oh, God," Robbie said, realizing his mistake. "You didn't know. I'm sorry, Brady told me months ago, and I just assumed—"

"I have to go, Robbie."

"I'm sorry, M, I thought you knew—"

"It's okay. I'll call you later."

"M? Wait, Marina—"

But I had already hung up. I dropped the phone from my ear and let it plunk down onto the bed, then pushed and kicked it away from me like it was made of poison.

CHAPTER THIRTEEN

"My mother's gonna kill me," Christy muttered to herself, driving with both hands clutching the wheel and furiously scanning her rearview mirror. "I've never ditched school in my life."

"Well, there's a first time for everything," I offered, my eyes glued to the map on my phone to determine how many minutes remained before arriving at Kieren's school.

"I should have just loaned you the car. Then I could have gone to class."

"You really want me driving your car with no insurance? I'm the worst driver on the planet. Why do you think I bike everywhere?"

"'Cause you can't afford a car?"

"That too. Turn right here."

Christy drove for a few minutes in silence, twisting her mouth into anxious zigzags. "Okay, can I just ask you something?"

"If your mother finds out, I'll tell her it was my fault."

"Not that."

"It's another three miles, then turn left."

Christy turned the front defrost on, clearing up a fine layer of condensation that had formed on the windshield. She was waiting for me to respond, I knew, but I was afraid of what her question would be.

"What is it?" I finally asked.

She hesitated briefly before opening her mouth. "I just . . . I don't understand why we're doing this. You haven't talked about this guy in almost a year. And you seem really happy with Brady. He's actually warm with you, he has a sense of humor. He treats you well."

"Kieren treated me well."

"Really? When? When he went to college and didn't call you for a month? Or when you stopped by his dad's phone store and found him in the back room whispering with that girl?"

"When was that?" I asked stupidly, realizing immediately that it would seem like an odd thing to have forgotten.

"Seriously, you know when, Marina. It was like two weeks before last Christmas. Remember? Because you had gone in to ask him what he wanted."

"They were just whispering," I said, more for my own benefit than hers. "It could have been about work or something."

"Marina, honey, you are fooling yourself. You told me you were over this guy. What is this about? Did something new happen? Did he drunk-dial you or something?"

"No, it's not that. I just . . . I can't explain it, Christy, but I need to talk to him."

Christy made the right turn in to the campus gate, and we waited our turn for the car in front of us to finish checking in with the security guard.

"I just don't want to see you get hurt," she said as she pulled into a parking garage before softly adding, "Again."

○ ○ ○

I could only assume that the address I had for Kieren in my phone was still his dorm, although it occurred to me that it might have been old information. What if he'd moved this year, now that he was a sophomore? What if he wasn't even living on campus anymore? Was I standing outside this dorm, freezing my butt off while Christy went to find a coffee place to do homework, for absolutely no reason?

I was about to give up when a tall blond man that I didn't even recognize at first came out of the front door with two other young men. He zipped up his winter coat as he walked and laughed at something his friend was saying. Jesus, could that really be Kieren? How had he aged so much in less than a year and a half?

I knew from his pictures online, of course, that he had filled out some. Maybe the Reserves had him lifting weights or something, but he looked like a totally different person. Like a grown man who had swallowed up the kid I used to know.

It took him a moment to recognize me too, or maybe it was just the disconnect of seeing me standing there, but he almost walked right by me. When his gray eyes finally did latch on to mine, I swear he almost fell over.

"Guys, I'll meet you in class," he finally said to his two friends, one of whom sported an actual full beard. They sauntered off while Kieren walked up to me, and I realized I was shivering all the way down to my spine. It was freezing out, but that wasn't the reason. I wrapped my scarf more tightly around my neck.

"Hi," I said, wanting to run to him and throw myself into his arms. But that's not where we were, was it?

"Hi." There was a sadness in his voice, even in such a short word. A defeat.

"Can we talk?"

Instead of answering, he just drew in a huge breath and slowly let it slide out of his tight lips. I was clearly opening up an old wound here, but I didn't care. I needed answers.

"I thought you didn't want to," he said.

"Well, now I do."

"Jesus, you're freezing. Let's go in the lobby or something."

"Right here," I insisted.

"M, there's nothing left to say," he began to protest, but then a thought seemed to occur to him. "Are you in trouble?"

"Trouble?" I shook my head in confusion. What kind—Jesus, did he think I was pregnant or something? Is that what he thought of me, that I would come to tell him something like that when . . . when it wouldn't even have been his? "No."

"Then what?" He seemed tightly wound, anxious, like he just wanted to get to class and I had screwed up all his plans.

"What happened to us, Kieren?"

"M, we've been over this a million times, I can't do it again." His voice cracked with exhaustion, and I swear I saw a tear start to form in his eye. Or was that just the cold?

"One more time."

"It's like I told you on the phone that night—things were just different when I got to school. I was alone, I was confused. You were still in high school half an hour away—"

"Stephanie?" I asked, barely able to spit out her name.

He sighed deeply, clenching back an emotion that was either anger or frustration, I couldn't tell which. "I asked you to give me some time to think," he said with hard, measured words. "You said you would."

"And I told you I would always love you," I insisted.

"Yeah, you did. And how about that?" He took a step closer to me, the seed of anger I had sensed a moment before coming to the surface. "Did you know I called you a couple nights later to talk about that?"

I shook my head. Obviously I didn't know what the hell he was talking about.

"And Brady answered your phone."

I swallowed hard, trying to make sense of it. Had I really moved on with Brady just days after telling Kieren I loved him? Was that something I would do?

"Why are you acting like you don't remember this?" he asked, throwing up his hands. "Like we haven't been over it to death?"

I could only stand there dumbly, shaking my head and fighting back a new wave of tears. "I didn't . . ." I began, not sure what to say. "I didn't remember."

Suddenly, a new light came into Kieren's eyes—this time, one of fear. "M, what did you do?"

"I can't tell you," I said meekly, starting to walk away, but he didn't let me get far before grabbing my arm.

"Have you . . ." He looked around quickly before continuing. "Have you been in DW?"

I didn't want to admit it, but my silence seemed to answer his question.

"What the hell have you done, M?"

"I had to."

"You had to what?" he demanded.

"I had to go in and fix something."

But he wasn't accepting that answer. He clenched my arm even tighter and stepped even closer, so that he was right above me now, and I had to tilt my head up into the harsh, freezing air to look at him. "We promised," he whispered.

"The night we went through Yesterday, Kieren, the night we went to Portland . . ."

"What about it?"

"The first time we did it . . ."

"First time?" he asked, his face a wall of apprehension.

"The first time . . . you didn't make it."

The words hit him like a tsunami. He stepped away from me, shaking his head.

"I went back for you." I answered the unspoken question in his eyes. "For us."

Kieren buried his face in his hands, wavering on his tall legs. I thought he might fall over, and it took him several seconds to steady himself.

"Because I didn't think anything could hurt worse than living without you," I continued. I knew I was digging the knife in deeper, but I didn't care. I wanted him to feel this pain twisting inside me. I wanted it to be fresh for him, like it was for me. Maybe just so that, for one minute, we could finally be in the same place at the same time.

"M."

"But I was wrong," I finished, finally finding the courage to walk away from him. I had to get as far away as possible, find Christy in that coffee shop and beg her to take me home. I never wanted to come here again, never wanted to look into his cold, hard eyes and see something I never thought he was capable of: indifference.

I ran as quickly as possible down the street, and I only looked back once to see if he was following me.

He wasn't.

CHAPTER FOURTEEN

I sat at the dinner table, staring at the uneaten bowl of Cheerios I had made myself for dinner. The little oat rings had been floating in the milk for so long they had started to bloat and fall apart, like defective lifesavers.

"Marina?" Laura asked gently from the kitchen door. "Can I make you something else?"

I cleared my throat, pushing away the bowl. "No, I'm just not hungry. Thank you, though, Laura."

"Okay. Your dad and I are going to head up to bed."

I glanced at the clock above her head. It was 10:00 p.m. God, I'd been sitting here for an hour. "Good night," I said, forcing a smile.

"'Night, sweetheart."

I waited a full minute after she left before getting up and dumping the soggy remains of my dinner in the sink. I was scrubbing the bowl out when my phone buzzed on the counter next to me. A text from Brady.

I'm sorry.

I put the bowl in the drying rack, wiping my hands on my jeans. *I'm sorry too*, I wrote back.

No, it's my fault.

I sighed, not knowing what to write back. It wasn't his fault that he didn't want me to go to Boston. It was totally understandable. His ex-girlfriend and the guy who stole her from him were both there. He wanted nothing to do with the place, and I couldn't blame him.

But a gnawing worry came back to taunt me as I stared at his text. Brady had told me once that he didn't have a family—or rather, that he had a family of his own making. His cousin. His friends. And Piper.

Now that Piper was gone, was I just some sort of replacement— some way of filling that Piper-sized hole she'd left behind? And if it weren't for me, would he have filled that blank space with some other girl?

He had told me twice now that I reminded him of Piper. Is that why he was with me? And if so, why was I with him? Did I love him? I had always been wildly attracted to Brady, and for a while, when we were in Oregon together, I had really started falling for him hard. He was funny. He was protective of me, shielding my body with his whenever he sensed danger.

I'd always thought Kieren was the one looking out for me. But maybe it had been Brady all the time.

I'm outside, came a new text. *Can I come in?*

I walked to the front door and opened it, seeing his car in the driveway. "Brady?" I called out.

"Over here."

He was over by the kitchen entrance, but he walked around to meet me.

"Hey," I said, smiling at the sight of him. After my day from hell, seeing his open, friendly face was like taking strong medicine.

"Hey." He smiled back. He was hesitant for a moment, but then came up and opened his arms. I threw myself into them and let him hold me in the doorway for a minute. He kissed the top of my head, and I squeezed him even tighter.

"Come inside," I offered.

We walked to the kitchen, and he grabbed himself a soda from the fridge before sitting down. I couldn't help but smile to see him so at home here. Brady had never had much of a real home. His cousin was nice to him, but he wasn't exactly loving. And even if he had been, nothing could have taken the place of the mother who had left the family and then died when Brady was just a kid. Maybe he'd found a home here, I realized. With Laura making sure he got a warm dinner, and my dad shaking his hand when he came over. And with me.

"I really am sorry I acted that way."

I shook my head, not sure what he meant.

"That school means a lot to you. You should go."

"I haven't even been accepted, Brady."

"You will be."

I hesitated a moment, not sure if this was ground we had already covered. But I needed to say it. "You could come with me."

He took a sip of his soda, and I could hear the little bubbles popping against his upper lip. "Yeah," he said, nodding. "There are lots of gas stations in Boston I could work at."

"Hey," I said, waiting for him to look up at me. When he didn't, I went to him and sat on his lap. He opened up his body to bring me even closer to him and gently pushed some hair behind my ear while I looked up into his impossibly beautiful brown eyes. "Don't talk about my boyfriend that way."

He laughed and kissed me, then looked in the general direction of the stairs. "Are they asleep?" he whispered.

I nodded.

"Come on. Let's go to your room."

My throat suddenly turned dry. Here it was, the moment I had been both afraid of and anxious for. I had dreamed of going to my bedroom with Brady since the day I'd met him. Was it really happening now?

Once we tiptoed upstairs and closed the door, I plopped my phone into its speaker cradle and put on some soft music, just in case Laura and my dad could hear anything.

He kicked off his shoes and lay down in my bed like he had done it a hundred times.

"I'm just gonna brush my teeth," I said, trying to sound casual.

"Mmm," he mumbled, his eyes closing and his body spreading out on my soft pink comforter. His head almost touched the headboard, and his feet hung off the end. Yet he looked so comfortable, I wondered if he would fall asleep before I got back.

I calmed myself down a bit in the bathroom, going through my nighttime ritual of washing my face and gargling mouthwash. Is this what it would be like if we went to Boston together? Familiar and sweet like this, Brady snoring lightly in the bed while I did a night mask to unclog my pores or folded laundry or made popcorn? Peanut butter and jelly sandwiches for breakfast. Baseball on the TV. Brady touching my feet gently while I studied.

A bead curtain in the kitchen doorframe.

Could it really be that perfect?

When I got back to the room, he looked up at me through groggy eyes and smiled. I climbed into his waiting arms and snuggled in close, kissing his neck and then his cheek, breathing in the lemon scent of his clothes and the warm, musky air on his skin.

He kissed me deeply, his hand traveling absently under my shirt. I fought back an instinct to flinch, letting his hands work their way up my back to my bra clasp. Could he tell that I was nervous? Maybe. Before going any further, he pulled his hand away.

"Why'd you stop?"

He shrugged with a smile, as though I already knew the answer to that question. Then he rolled away a bit.

"Don't—" I began. "Don't stop. Come on."

He laughed slightly and touched my cheek with the back of his fingers. "I know you wanted to wait till you were eighteen, but that doesn't mean we have to do it right away. It's not a finish line we have to cross."

"Oh," I said, swallowing hard. I guessed some things hadn't changed. But did I really even care about some childish idea I had formed about sex years ago, when I was nowhere near ready to have it? Did it really matter to me now—now that I was with someone who I trusted so completely? "We don't . . ." I began, searching for the words. "We don't have to wait."

He smiled softly. "When you're really ready, I'll take you somewhere special, okay? Not this tiny little bed."

I laughed in embarrassment and buried my face in my palm. "Right."

"It's okay," Brady said, pulling me closer to him again, and bringing my head to rest on his chest. "I don't mind waiting for you."

It felt so good to lie there, so comfortable and easy.

"We've got all the time in the world."

And as I drifted off into a deep sleep, his words continued to echo through my mind, over and over again.

All the time in the world.

CHAPTER FIFTEEN

The whispers of Mr. Martel's black eye reached me before I'd even made it to my locker Tuesday morning. By third period, the black eye had morphed into ten stitches in his forehead; by lunchtime, the gossip was that he'd broken both arms; and by sixth, Mr. Martel had been mugged and almost killed on his way home Friday night.

It was a bit of a letdown, to be honest, when I made it to seventh period and found that Adam was not in a wheelchair, nor was he in a cast. He did, however, have quite a shiner on his left eye, apparently the handiwork of a large, irate Russian man.

I couldn't help but notice the flicker of relief that passed through Adam's darkened eyes when he saw me walk in, and I felt a moment of guilt. It hadn't even occurred to me yesterday when I'd ditched school to go visit Kieren that the last time Adam saw me, I had been in a fair amount of peril. He must've panicked when I didn't show up Monday morning.

I offered him a weak smile as I headed to my seat, raising my shoulders in a sort of "I'm sorry" shrug. But my apology was not accepted, apparently, as his hollow eyes narrowed in on me and his lips curled towards his teeth. He shrugged it off, however, and headed back to his desk.

"Your essays are due Friday," he began in a forceful voice, causing the rest of the room to quiet down. "We're going to spend the day reviewing your work, making sure you've completed all necessary elements. If you have any last-minute questions," he hammered on, his voice a smidge too loud, "now is the time to ask them."

"What happened to your eye?" Angela Peirnot asked, but Adam ignored her.

"You may begin," he said to the rest of the class.

A general hum of commotion broke out all around me as people started digging through their bags for their work. The essay was supposed to be in five parts, and while I had completed all five now, I had to admit that at least two of them were, well, thin. As in, one-page thin.

Whatever. MIT was really only going to be interested in my science and math grades, which hadn't suffered despite the fact that I'd been a bit distracted lately. As long as I got a B in this class, which would count as an A since the class was AP, it wouldn't affect my GPA.

God, I couldn't wait to get to college, I suddenly realized. I didn't want to ever think about any of these obnoxious initials again: AP, GPA, SAT. In college, it would be about the work, not the initials. Images of the campus that I had looked up last night on my phone flitted through my brain. The place was a perfect microcosm of the students who went there: half green lawns and stately buildings with Doric columns, half fun-house buildings designed by architecture geeks that looked like toppling-over Legos or glass eggs.

Slow down, Marina. You haven't even been accepted yet.

"Where were you?" Adam whispered between clenched teeth as he stooped down to inspect my feeble offerings on Genghis Khan.

"I'm sorry," I mumbled. "It's a long story."

"Is this all you've written?" he asked a little more forcefully as he flipped through my limp pages.

"Yes."

"Stay after class."

He stood up and moved on, leaving me to stare in shame at the work he had so summarily dismissed.

The minutes ticked by with an audible click, like soldiers' feet marching towards an inevitable war. I scrolled through my tablet, ostensibly looking for more dirt on Genghis Khan to fatten up the underwhelming parts of my essay. But my browser had landed on an article titled, "MIT Uses $350-Million Gift to Bolster Computer Sciences." What would it be like to be in a place like that, where every resource would be at my disposal?

When the bell rang, I didn't even hear it, but I snapped to attention when the other kids started packing up their bags. I stayed in my seat while the room emptied, feeling like I was in a doctor's office awaiting inevitably bleak results.

Adam closed the door when we were the only two left and then leaned against his desk, keeping his distance from me.

"We need to talk about my turn."

"I know."

I looked down at my lap. I knew that I owed Adam something, but I wished more than ever that I could never have anything to do with DW again. Kieren had been right: *Nothing good comes of it.*

Although, remembering the feel of Brady's warm chest under

my head last night as I fell asleep, I realized that maybe it had been my mother who was right about DW: *Nature finds a way.* Maybe everything really did happen for a reason. But if so, would it have worked out that way even if we didn't try to conquer the very nature in question?

"Where were you yesterday?" Adam asked again, but he didn't sound angry anymore. In fact, his tone had softened to something that sounded almost like concern.

"I had to . . . take care of something."

He chuckled, shaking his head.

"That's funny to you?"

"Let me guess." He pushed himself away from his desk and walked a bit closer. "You didn't get everything you wanted."

"It was . . ." I shook my head, clearing away images of Kieren standing like a rock behind me as I walked away from him, not making any effort to stop me. ". . . not what I expected."

"I'm sorry to hear that," Adam retorted, his voice dripping with sarcasm. "But it's still my turn."

"I said I know that." My voice came out sounding harsh and angry, which of course I was. How had I let this guy rope me into this—into being beholden to him?

"You have to bring me something. That picture of her from the beach."

A movement in the little window of the door revealed that several students were milling about, waiting for their class to start.

"We can't do this here," I whispered fiercely, although no one else could hear me. I stuffed papers in my backpack to try to make it seem normal that I was lingering behind, the only student left from the previous class. People in this school loved to gossip. I didn't want anyone getting any ideas about me and Adam.

"Where?" he asked. Did he sound desperate?

I thought for a moment, my mind racing through possibilities and immediately rejecting them as too obvious, too public. "You know the pyramid house, on the other side of town?"

"Yes."

I took a deep breath, my eyes avoiding his at all costs. "Midnight."

I grabbed my things and stormed out of the room, not waiting to hear his reply.

o   o   o

I couldn't help but feel an old, familiar thrill as I pedaled my way across town to the pyramid house, despite the bitter frost eating away at my fingers through my useless woolen gloves. My leg muscles finally warmed up enough to stop stinging about halfway there. By the time I pulled up to the great, towering structure, I had ceased to care about my chapped lips or wind-dried eyes.

How long had it been?

The night I'd biked here with Robbie and Piper after rescuing them from the train came into sharp relief as I ditched my bike and peeped into the deserted window. But the memory of that night was a bittersweet one, because that was when I had seen my mother's evil doppelgänger and her own version of Robbie inside the house, throwing some grand party.

I hated to think of it—of their horror-show faces, malicious twins of my real family, or of the fact that I had been waiting for Kieren to come pick us up, and Scott came instead.

I shook away the cruel memories and replaced them with one I had imagined hundreds of times before. The night Robbie and I came here as kids, dared by Kieren, and Robbie took the photo of me on the floor of the living room.

What I wouldn't give to have Robbie with me now, I thought as

I climbed in through the all-too-familiar window and heard my hollow footsteps echoing through the dilapidated old house. Why hadn't they torn this place down yet? No one would ever live in it again. Too many ghosts, both for those of us whose loved ones would never walk these floors again and for the town itself, which had been a booming utopia a century ago when it was built.

"I thought you weren't coming," Adam said from his perch in the corner, scaring the ever-loving shit out of me.

"Jesus, Adam."

"You're late."

I checked my fitness watch—a Christmas gift from Laura—and sighed. "Just ten minutes," I panted, catching my breath from the difficult ride.

He stood up to meet me, in his anxiousness standing a bit too close. "Water?" he asked, handing me a bottle from his bag.

"Thanks."

"Had a feeling you'd need it. Do you bike everywhere?"

"Don't have a car," I said.

I backed away instinctively while I screwed off the lid and took a big gulp, realizing that I had been dying of thirst from the dry night air. I looked for a place with more light. "Sit by the window," I instructed, and he followed me there. Once cross-legged on the floor, I took off my backpack and pulled out the old photo album once again.

"I can't give you the picture from the beach," I began.

"Why not?"

"Because that day is—there was too much going on that day. It's too delicate."

His lips pursed, and I could see his fists start to ball up, anticipating that I was rescinding my offer somehow.

"But I'll give you something else. Something even better."

He looked at me with a wary expression, but his fists relaxed a little.

"My mother didn't leave much behind when she . . . when she left," I began, opening up the book to the back page. "But there is one thing."

There was only one photo in the back of the album, and it was of my mother and Jenny in high school. They both had that layered haircut called the Rachel, after the TV show *Friends*. My mother was a huge fan. I used to come downstairs and find her in the den watching reruns early in the morning when she couldn't sleep. Her laughter would wake me up sometimes, and I'd come down and watch with her.

Or, at least, in my old reality I had. It was one of the few positive things that my mother and I had left after Robbie was gone. One of the few things I missed about her now.

In the photograph, Mom and Jenny were hugging, smiling wide as the sea. Mom was wearing a bracelet with *FRIENDS* spelled out in white beads, in the same font as the TV show logo. Jenny had given it to her, she'd told me once. And the bracelet itself was affixed with yellowing Scotch tape to the album page, overlapping the picture.

I ripped the bracelet off now, although it wouldn't budge at first. When it finally came free, the brittle tape sucked off some of the white paper of the album with it. I peeled the remaining tape off, and it cracked and disintegrated in my fingers.

Adam shook his head, his eyes narrowing on me like he thought I was just jerking him around. "You know I could just take that picture from you now," he threatened.

I swallowed hard, hoping that as someone who knew Down World as well as I did, he would understand what I was about to tell him.

"I'll tell you why you can't," I explained, "if you'll listen."

He sat back a bit, giving me the slightest nod that I should go on.

I understood his frustration, of course. It was the not knowing that was the torture of losing someone. The endless questions. If I could offer Adam anything, maybe it was just an answer or two. If nothing else, maybe that would help him to let her go.

He steeled himself, his broad chest growing stiff with anticipation.

"There used to be a portal under the lake," I confessed all in one breath before I lost my nerve. "The lake behind the hotel outside Portland, the one in the pictures."

He nodded, not wanting to stop me as I clearly had more to say.

"Jenny and Dave originally went in there, twelve years go. Right after the photos I showed you were taken."

Adam let this sink in for a moment before muttering something to himself that sounded like "Portland," although it might have been "portal." Then he turned back to me. "What do you mean, 'under the lake'?"

"It was in the bottom of the lake, in the sand bed."

"How do I get in?"

"You don't," I told him. "It doesn't exist anymore. I destroyed it when I went into Yesterday. It's *why* I went into Yesterday."

"Why would you do that?"

"It was . . ." How much to reveal? Could I really trust Adam at all? "It was a bad portal . . . to a bad place."

His eyes squinted as he looked at me, as though he was waiting for me to reveal more. But I never wanted to talk about that place again. It didn't exist now anyway.

"I don't understand," he said, and I could see tiny beads of sweat starting to form at his temples. "How do you destroy a portal?"

"I mean I destroyed the thing that would have built it."

"What thing, Marina?"

"I don't know what it was. Some pink solution in a beaker that my mother brought. I buried it in the woods before Jenny ever got a chance to see it."

Adam's face froze momentarily, and then his eyes flicked back down to the photo album, as though he was looking for the evidence of what I was saying. But of course, there were no pictures of that beaker, which my mother had been careful to hide in a secure suitcase.

"Okay, fine," he said, steadying his voice. He paused for a minute, collecting his thoughts. "So where is Jenny, then?"

"I don't know, Adam. I really don't. She—she had been waiting that day for my mother to build the portal. I guess she was really looking forward to it. When I destroyed it, maybe—maybe she went in a different way."

"Then I'll go back to the beach and follow her," he decided, leaning over me to reach for the album. But I grabbed his shoulders and used all my might to push him back. I knew he was only humoring me by letting me do so. He could have taken it if he'd really wanted.

"You can't. It doesn't matter where she went in, only where she came out. Please, Adam." I handed Adam the bracelet. "This is what you need. I promise you. You don't need to go to that beach." He hesitated, his eyes untrusting, and I all but forced the bracelet into his hands. "Please."

"What am I supposed to do with this?"

"It was important to her," I explained, and then indicated the picture of Jenny with my mom. "To both of them. It will lead you to her."

Adam nodded slightly, encircling the delicate beads with his strong fingers. "I guess it's a start," he said, beginning to stand.

Before he could break away from me, though, I reached out and grabbed his arm again. "Adam."

He raised his eyebrows at me, still questioning what I was telling him, I supposed . . . and what I wasn't.

"What will you do if you find her?"

He smiled through closed lips, his focus drifting to a faraway place—a place with Jenny in it. "Bring her home."

I stayed on the floor while he headed for the window. "Do you, um, need me to give you a ride or something?" he asked, almost as an afterthought.

"I'll get myself home. Don't worry about me."

He nodded, turning to me once more before climbing back out. "Thank you, Marina. For telling me the truth."

I didn't have time to ask him what he meant by that before he was gone. I knew I should get up and go. It was late, and I was shaking with exhaustion—suddenly dead tired. God, when had I last slept? I knew I should have been terrified alone in the abandoned house, but somehow a warm, glowing feeling came over me instead. A euphoria that was either from memory or sheer fatigue, I couldn't tell which.

This was the room Robbie and I had snuck away to that night; the room where Kieren later told me that Robbie wasn't dead, giving me hope again for the first time in years. This was the place where I had conquered fear, where I had become the warrior I was always meant to be.

And it was these thoughts—Robbie, Kieren, loss, hope, and strength—that lulled me to sleep on that cold wood floor, my backpack doubling as a pillow, my mother's photo album just inches from my face, opened to the last page, robbed now of its most precious possession.

○ ○ ○

The sun was in my face.

Shit. I had slept through the night in the house, and now dawn was finding me alone and stiff, miles from home. I swallowed down a bitter taste and rubbed my tongue over my chalky front teeth. As I sat up, the crick in my neck felt like a noose, and I knew I had to shake out my sore back and get myself home before my dad woke up.

Rubbing sleep out of my eyes, I was surprised to feel metal scrape against my cheek. I pulled my hand away and saw what I had forgotten to ask about: my ruby ring.

It was back on my finger. For a second, I tried to remember if Adam had given it to me. But no, he hadn't. That meant he must have come back in the night and put it on my hand while I slept.

Why would he do that? Maybe he'd just remembered it on his way home and didn't want to wake me when he saw me sleeping here? Still, it seemed suspicious.

I didn't want to linger on my doubts for too long, though. I had to get home before Dad and Laura woke up and found me gone.

I reached for Mom's photo album and was about to snap it closed and throw it in my backpack when my eye caught on something that didn't seem right: the page it was open to was empty. I blinked twice, turning it back another page.

This one wasn't empty at all. And that's when I knew something was very, very wrong.

My heartbeat screeched to a halt, then sped up like a bullet train. I forgot to breathe, my suddenly shaky fingers struggling to turn the pages.

It was the pictures. These were the wrong pictures.

They weren't of my mother. They were of me. Picture after picture of me. Me in a diner, a coffee cup on the table. Me on a street with half-built houses. Me with Brady. No shoes on our feet. Wet hair. Me in a school that wasn't a school. Me in a long line to see a nurse in a 1950s outfit. Me with Sage. And Caryn. And Milo. In the basement of Sage's diner.

Me in the fancy hotel with the evil version of my mother—the one who had no idea who I was.

They were surveillance photos, in black and white. Taken under the lake. One after another after another, filling the place where my mother's photos had been.

And the pictures that had been there before—they were all missing. Adam had taken every last one of them while I'd slept.

I looked around frantically for the thief, but I knew he'd be long gone. I had been asleep for hours. Dead asleep. Drugged? The water bottle from the night before sat by the window, clear as light, half empty.

I shook out my head, trying to make sense of this. There was only one conclusion to draw.

Adam knew.

He knew about the world under the lake the whole time. Was he even looking for Jenny at all, or was that just a ruse to get me to help him? He knew there'd been a portal leading to a world where my mother and John were very powerful, a world where maybe he could be too.

The only thing he didn't know—he couldn't have known—was how to get back in now that the portal was gone.

Until I told him. *Pink solution in a beaker.*

Oh my God. What had I done?

CHAPTER SIXTEEN

I reached the school in record time, my sides stitching up with the effort, and my head pounding from the residual effects of whatever Adam had put into that water bottle. It was probably 6:30 in the morning when I arrived, and I prayed that the custodian had already unlocked the service entrance behind the gym.

When I got there, hopping off my bike and not even bothering to lock it up, I saw that the entrance wasn't just unlocked, it was open. Someone had already been through it—someone too excited to remember to close it.

I worked my way cautiously through the school to the boiler room, just in case Adam was still lurking in the hallways for some reason. Just in case he had his gun.

Please don't let me be too late, I repeated frantically inside my head.

By the time I'd made it through the boiler room and past the door leading to the twisting and turning abandoned hallways, I was on the verge of exploding with nerves. But my feet moved of their own volition, faster and faster, knowing time was seeping by—time in which he might be escaping.

Reaching the science lab at last, I cautiously turned the knob, anticipating that Adam might be waiting on the other side. I didn't have any kind of weapon, nothing to fight him off with. My mind flitted briefly to the time I had managed to elbow him in the ribs, temporarily deterring him. But he had recovered quickly. He was far too strong for me to beat.

Still, I had to try.

But when I entered the room, Adam was nowhere to be found. Someone had definitely been there, however. A rack of six empty glass vials that usually sat on the back countertop had been carelessly knocked over; one of the vials was conspicuously missing.

What did he need a vial for?

On the blackboard, a familiar symbol caught my eye. A circle, like a large white sun, being bombarded on all sides by glowing red arrows. The first time I had seen this symbol, I hadn't had the slightest idea what it was. But I did now.

It was a uranium core, being compressed on all sides to create a nuclear chain reaction. This was what Sage had warned me about, that the first experiments with splitting atoms actually happened in our town, in this very lab. This was the nuclear fission that had made the portals appear in the first place.

And this was the lab where my mother had found the beaker with that mysterious pink solution. All Adam would need was a small sample of it, and he could create any portal he wanted anywhere in the world. And thanks to me, he now knew when in history to find it.

That would explain the missing vial: if he used the photos from Mom's album to go back to the beach on the night I buried Mom's beaker, all he would need to do was hide somewhere and wait.

Eventually, he would spy George and me burying the pink solution. Then, after we left, he could dig it up and help himself to a vial of his own.

He must have gone through Yesterday.

My head whipped to the green tent that held the spiral staircase. Was I already too late? I flung myself down the stairs, my body whipping around the central post like a ballerina.

I landed with a thud as my eyes widened in horror. The door to Yesterday was closed, but the edges were still emitting a slight yellow radiation, confirming my initial fear: someone had been through it tonight. But that wasn't what shocked me.

No, what was really shocking was the door to Today, which was wide open, glowing with a translucent blue that washed the entire chamber in undulating ripples. This was clearly the door he had just gone through.

My mind raced to catch up with the logic behind Adam's actions. He'd gone into Yesterday, nabbed a vial of solution, made the portal somewhere—maybe in the woods this time—and then . . . he'd come home and gone back to the underlake world through Today?

Why would he do that?

Unless . . . unless he didn't want to go to the past. He wanted to go to the modern-day version of the world under the lake. Why?

There was a small pile of something on the floor by the portal, barely visible in the dim light. I leaned down and picked up a handful of it and was surprised to find that it was very fine gravel. Was this the token he had used to bring him back to the world under the lake?

But as I struggled to understand, I was yanked back into the present moment because now the waves of aquamarine were fading. Before my eyes, the color was seeping away from me, turning duller and duller until the outline of red bricks began to emerge from the remnants. *No*, my mind screamed, *no, don't let him get away!*

Before I could even decide what to do, I hurled my entire body into the dimming blue glow, letting it swallow me up and suck me in. And then I was fully surrounded by churning bubbles, which faded to yellow and finally to murky brown.

It was like being plunged into an arctic sea. I was in the freezing water, being tossed around like a jellyfish, completely immersed in an ocean of blue so dark it was almost black. No, not an ocean. A lake.

Oh, God. He'd built the portal in the lake, just like last time.

The icy water seized my entire body. My muscles clenched, and my clothes felt like a straitjacket pinning me into place. I used all my might to swim for the surface, but the light was playing tricks on me. Just as I was about to break through to the air, my head smashed against the lake floor. I had been here before, I remembered. *Down was up.* I followed the direction of my air bubbles, only to find that they were going towards my feet.

Panic overtook me as I started to follow them up, my fingers already numb.

But that's when I saw Adam, just inches from me. His eyes were blasted open in panic. He was drowning, lost and flailing.

I reached out and grabbed his shirt. He resisted at first, but then all strength seemed to seep out of his body. With the last of my power, I pushed the water away with my free hand, grabbing on to Adam for dear life with the other.

A second later, just before all my breath was gone, we burst through the top of the lake water. The frigid air seared my lungs. Adam bobbed to the surface beside me, stiff as a board. And looking around, I knew immediately that I was a million miles from home.

PART TWO

CHAPTER SEVENTEEN

"George!" I screamed, still trying to tread water in the middle of the lake without letting Adam's rigid body slide off my chest where I was holding him up. "George, help!"

I scanned the shoreline desperately for George's little cabin— the structure he had converted from a small boathouse that had resided on the shore on the other side of reality. But the cabin seemed abandoned. The telltale plume of smoke from the chimney that indicated he was home and cooking in his small kitchen was absent.

I struggled to catch my breath; Adam's body was growing too heavy for me to hold up as my arms started to give way and my icy lips chattered just above the waterline. But then George appeared in his doorway, confused at first, looking around for the source of the sound.

"George, here!" I shouted with what little breath I could spare.

"Help," I whispered, no longer having the lung capacity to shout.

I saw him run for the water and dive in. I turned my attention back to Adam's stiff face, using one hand to try to slap him back to consciousness while I dog-paddled with the other. Finally, George reached us and took over the duty of towing in Adam so I could focus on getting myself to shore.

Halfway there, I flipped over to a backstroke, both because it was easier to float that way and so I could confirm that George was successfully towing Adam in.

It seemed to take forever to get there, but finally, I was able to crawl from the water and hurl my body onto dry sand. I was panting and scraping at the beach, trying to bring feeling back into my ice-cold fingers, as George dragged Adam onto the strip of ground next to me.

George tried to shake Adam, but nothing came of it.

"I don't—I don't know how—" George began.

"I do," I said, wracking my brain to try to remember the details of the CPR lessons we had been forced to take in gym last year. I laid Adam's arms out by his sides so he was flat on his back and tilted his head up a bit to open his airway.

Taking a deep breath, I began compressions on his chest. *One, two, three, four.* I couldn't remember how many, so twenty would have to do. My hands warmed slightly with the contact, and I pinched his nose and tried breathing into his mouth.

Nothing happened.

I tried again, but he was cold as ice, his lips almost blue.

I steadied my anxious mind, pressing my left hand over my right and thumping away at Adam's chest again. *One, two, three, four.* "Breathe, Adam," I whispered through my tight throat. "Please breathe." I looked up at George, who sat hopelessly staring down at the dying man before him.

And then Adam's whole body exploded. He flipped over onto his side and threw up what seemed to be a gallon of water. He was breathing.

Oh, thank God. He's breathing.

Although George must have had no idea what was going on, he bent over in relief, letting out a sound that was half chuckle, half moan.

"George," I began, catching my breath again while Adam recovered. Relief was quickly replaced with something more necessary: reality. "Go get your shotgun."

o o o

George ran towards the cabin while I watched Adam pant and catch his breath. My shirt had turned into an icicle, and I struggled to wring it out. I stood up to my full height—all five foot four of me—and did little jumping jacks to try to heat up my core.

Adam started to prop himself up onto all fours, then stretched back onto his bent legs. I could hear his teeth chattering, which I took as a sign that he was warming up. But as his strength came back to him, I knew I had to keep the upper hand before he recovered completely.

Hurry up, George.

"Just stay down, Adam." I pushed the icy strands of hair out of my face, keeping my eyes trained on him.

"Why the hell . . ." he wheezed in a scratchy voice. Coughing a couple times, he was able to speak again. "Why did you follow me?"

"Why did you build a portal?"

"You lied to me."

"You roofied me!"

"It was just a sleeping pill! It's over-the-counter."

He started to stand, and George wasn't back yet. Panicking, I gave in to an instinct to keep Adam down, and I threw myself onto his back before he could rise. But I instantly realized I'd made a huge mistake. In one fell swoop, Adam flipped his entire body over onto his back, pinning me beneath him. I smashed against the sand with a grunt.

A split second later, Adam had flipped over again, pinning my arms up over my head, his legs on either side of me.

"You really wanna wrestle me?" he said, his forceful voice almost teasing me. "I was all-state for three years."

"Get off me!" I screamed, my knee rising on its own to smash him in the groin. I must have hit the mark because his eyes crossed slightly, and he fell off me onto his side. I started to crawl away, but before I'd made it more than a couple of inches, he grabbed hold of my ankle.

"Ahem!" George's voice shouted loud and clear above our heads. We both stopped what must have seemed like a comical mismatch of flailing to look up at him, standing calmly with the shotgun in his hand, pointed at the sky. "Who was the shotgun for, Marina?"

"Him," I screamed, at the exact same time as Adam shouted, "Her!"

"Don't trust her, George," Adam continued, pulling me closer before I could stand and holding me in a half nelson with one arm twisted behind my back. It hurt like crazy, and I couldn't help but turn in to the twisting arm to relieve the pressure, making me face Adam again. "She's working with her mother."

"You lying sack of—"

"Keep the gun on her, George."

I blanched for a second, trying to figure out how Adam even

knew George's name. But then I remembered—he'd met all of them in high school, when he was with Jenny.

What kind of nonsense had he filled their heads with?

"He's lying to you, George," I explained, trying to keep my cool, although I was still forced to face Adam. I tried whipping my body left and right to free myself, but it was useless.

"I have the pictures to prove it, George."

"Those pictures show me helping Sage!"

Before this charade could go on any further, we were both stopped in our tracks by a shotgun blast. Adam, seeming to be acting on instinct, pulled me into him and covered my head with his hand. But a moment later, we both realized we were fine, and I pushed myself away from him, childishly slapping at his chest.

George had fired the gun into the sky.

"I wouldn't do that if I were you, Adam," George said in his calm voice. "She just saved your life."

Adam and I sat next to each other, both panting from exertion, while he took this in. I glared at him out of the corner of my eye and saw that the news was having an effect on him. He looked chastened.

"Is that true?" he asked George.

George only nodded, and I could feel Adam's body shrink a bit by my side.

"Let's get inside," George said, scanning the trees that surrounded the lake. "They'll be coming now."

CHAPTER EIGHTEEN

I toweled off my hair by George's small stove while Adam went in the bedroom to scavenge for a dry shirt that might fit him. The cabin was littered with a million small reminders that this was indeed the world under the lake and not the one above: a mug with Russian writing on it; a photo of a pinup girl wearing one of those furry Russian hats. Even George's shotgun had a hammer and sickle engraved on it. It just didn't make any sense to me. This world was never supposed to exist.

George stared out the window, shotgun in hand, in case any Russian soldiers came to investigate the source of the gunfire.

"I don't get it, George," I said through significantly warmer lips. "Why is any of this still here if there was never a portal?"

George seemed confused by my question for a moment, but then he nodded slowly to himself. "I'm sorry, Marina, I thought you understood how this works."

I shook my head in frustration. Did he mean that I had some

basic principle wrong? "What are you talking about? The portal was never built, so the world beneath the lake should have been erased."

"No, that's not how it works," he said, his voice turning gentle as though I needed to be coddled. "All you did was remove a door. But the world on the other side continued to exist."

My mind caught up with what George was saying. If that was true, then this world had been here this whole time while I was living above, obliviously thinking I had fixed everything. And that raised another question.

"This dimension was already here even before my mother brought the beaker? She wasn't creating a new dimension, she was just opening a door to one they wanted to go to?"

"I don't know," George admitted. "It's possible that it was just a fresh slate, but something changed in it, something in the past, and the effects of whatever that was rippled out to today."

"Okay," I said, trying to remain calm. "But you're the George from above, aren't you? You recognize me and—" I had to bite down anger at his name "—and Adam."

"Yes." George sighed heavily. He'd gained a few pounds since I'd last seen him, and some gray hairs had sprung up around his ears. He looked tired and, frankly, kind of sad. Finally, he turned to face me. "I have to admit something to you," he began. "The day after you and I buried the beaker, I made a choice. I knew someone would have to guard this world. Before the solution could dissolve, I used it to come down here. And I've been here ever since."

"George, that was almost twelve years ago," I said, my tongue tripping over the words. "The balance between dimensions, it—"

"It's okay," George said calmly. "You know how, when someone stays in another plane too long, the other versions of them disappear from every plane?"

"Yes," I said, though the word *disappear* hit me hard. That was exactly what had happened to my mother in the old timeline—only the dark underlake version of her remained. That is, until I created a new timeline in which my real mom, the one I remembered, stayed up above with John and Robbie.

"Well, there was something I had always suspected about that, and it turned out to be true," George continued. "When that happens, you're no longer borrowing energy from one dimension and displacing it in another. The consequences become smaller, so you can stay longer. Maybe even forever. So long as you lie low, don't interact so you don't cause a butterfly effect . . ."

His words trailed off. I looked around his tiny little cabin, isolated out here in the woods. "You've been alone this whole time?"

He nodded sternly. "I keep an eye on this world. There's not much I can do to keep it from getting worse, and it has gotten much worse. But at least by being down here, I can try to protect . . . what's left."

And by "what's left," I knew he meant Sage. Had he always been in love with her? Even in high school?

I looked up and realized that Adam was in the doorway, wearing a shirt that was comically too tight for his broad chest. He had been listening with a sober expression on his face.

Suddenly, a rustling outside made George raise his hand, indicating that we should be quiet. "It's probably nothing," he said softly. "I'll go check it out. Stay here." He stood to leave, turning just before he made it to the door. "And, um, try to get along, all right?"

With the door closed behind him, Adam came fully into the room and sat down at the small dining table in front of George's half-eaten breakfast. He leaned over and squeezed a little more water out of his pant legs.

An awkward silence filled the air between us as we both continued trying to get as dry as possible.

After a moment, Adam came over and sat down near me in front of the stove, munching on a slice of bread. He must have noticed me swallowing down some spit when I saw it, and he silently handed it to me and went to get himself another.

We sat stiffly next to each other while we ate.

"Did you really save my life?" he finally asked.

I turned my head to him slowly. The yellowish remains of a fist-sized bruise still formed a halo around his left eye socket. I had to admit that he had been quite brave when facing off against Alexei—that he had upheld his part of the promise.

"Yes," I said, and he nodded silently, eating the last bite of bread. Then he laughed bitterly at himself. "Winter," he muttered.

"What's that?"

"Winter," he repeated, this time for my sake. "I didn't think how cold the water would be. That I'd run out of breath so quickly. Stupid mistake." He cleared his throat. "I owe you one, I guess."

"You don't. We're even," I insisted. "But I need you to tell me something." A ball of nerves formed in my stomach at the question I had to ask. "You used my mom's photos to come back to this beach on that night twelve years ago."

"Yes."

"Did anyone see you?"

"No," he answered, not having any way of knowing why I seemed so nervous but clearly seeing that I was. "No, you told me you buried the beaker in the woods. I waited until late at night, when you and George were done, and I dug it up. I poured out a vial, just enough to make the portal in the lake but not so much as to tip anyone off to my presence if they went looking for it—which apparently George did the next day, so I'm glad I thought of it. And then I remade the portal in the lake before I headed home."

"My mom didn't see you? She didn't . . . know about the portal?" I asked, and I could hear the thin whisper of desperation in my voice.

"No one saw me, Marina. I promise."

My body collapsed with relief. Everyone was okay. As long as Mom didn't know there was a portal, then nothing would have changed for her. She would still have raised Robbie in Oregon, which meant that Robbie was fine. I could breathe again.

"You can never go back to that night, Adam," I said with as much force as I could muster. "Ever. It's too fragile. You could ruin everything."

"Why? 'Cause if it gets screwed up again, your boyfriend won't remember you?"

"No, you idiot, it's my brother." My hands were shaking, but not just with cold. I could feel the prickling of tears behind my eyes.

Adam froze, watching me like I was a figure in a dark alley he couldn't make out.

I steadied my breath, feeling the emotions threatening to overtake me. "I saved my brother that night. In the old timeline, he died at fourteen. In this one, he's alive. He lives in Boston. I'm—" The tears were forming in my eyes, but I shook my head, knowing I had to convince Adam to trust me, or he could ruin everything. "I'm supposed to go live with him in the fall. Please, Adam." I fell to my knees before him, not caring how desperate it must have looked. I was begging. "Promise me. You said you owe me your life."

"Stand up," he said softly, his hands now under my elbows as he guided me to my feet.

"Do you promise me?"

"I do," he answered, a softness seeping into his voice and his eyes. "I promise. I won't go back to that night."

I nodded, calming myself again. It was okay. He wasn't going to hurt Robbie. That was all that had ever mattered to me.

Finally, perhaps sensing that he had me in a vulnerable moment, he leaned in closer, his eyes moving from the warm stove to me. "I thought, when I saw the surveillance photos—I thought they proved you were a spy for your mother."

"You mean the woman down here? The one who's, like, Secretary of Death or whatever?" That made him chuckle, but then he turned serious again.

"Well, *are* you?"

I shook my head. "That's not my mom. That's just some twisted version of her who never even had me. My real mom is on the other side of the lake," I said with a subtle nod to the water that had almost killed us both a few minutes ago. "She has nothing to do with this place."

"You're sure they're not the same person?"

"They're not," I insisted. "Don't get me wrong, the real one is a piece of work too, but she's not evil. Those photos you stuck in the album while I was asleep—creepy, by the way—show me and Brady when we got trapped down here. And now, to be honest, I'd really appreciate it if you'd explain how in the hell you got them."

"Milo gave them to me. About a year and a half ago, after the two of you came down here. He's hacked into every camera in this place. Told me to check you out, that he didn't trust you. I was going to ask Sage about you, but I didn't get a chance."

Milo. Of course, that jerk from Sage's diner. He'd never trusted me or Brady. Figures he would turn on me the first chance he got. But everything Adam had just said raised a million more questions. I shook my head, not getting it.

Finally, Adam stood, warming his hands by the fire. He rolled out a crick in his neck, turned to me, and said, "Okay, Marina. Let me tell you the truth."

o o o

"I met Jenny when we were both seventeen," Adam began. "Whenever I'd get a chance, I'd go down and visit her and her friends—John, Sage . . . and your mom. I mean, the nice version of her anyway. Not the one from down here. After a while, I started to feel like they were my only real friends. They seemed more real to me somehow than the kids from our time. Maybe it was just that their noses weren't constantly buried in cell phones. Of course, who needs cell phones when you've got portals? I swear, Jenny was obsessed with them. She wanted to do it all the time, said it got her . . . excited."

Adam's eyes twinkled when he talked about Jenny, and I had to look away, feeling very awkward suddenly.

"I know what you're thinking," he said, still lost in his story. "I was throwing off the balance. But I never stayed more than three days, and I never had any problem returning after that. If the world got screwed up around me, I didn't notice. Jenny would cry whenever I left. She said she didn't love Dave, that she wanted to be with me instead. But it was impossible. I even started thinking about finding her in my own time, even though she'd be a lot older. But when I looked her up, I couldn't find any trace of her. In fact, it was weird—none of the gang was still living in town by the time I was a teenager. There were no forwarding addresses, nothing. It was like they had all vanished.

"And then one day, I hear this rumor floating around. Something about Mystics living out in Oregon. And somebody says they found a journal entry, and it was written by someone with the initial S. And I just knew—it was Sage.

"I told my folks I was going to a friend's for the weekend, and then I drained the college savings they'd put aside for me and flew out to Oregon. When I got here—or, I guess, the 'here' on the other side of the lake—I asked where Jenny was. They wouldn't tell me at first. And then finally George let it spill. Jenny and Dave had gone into a new portal in the lake years before, and they'd never come out. I screamed at him. I went crazy. 'You just let her go? You never looked for her? What if she's not okay?' They started to say something, but I wasn't even listening. I just dove in, went through the portal, and discovered, well, this place.

"There was no sign of Jenny anywhere. I figured maybe she'd hopped over to another parallel dimension, so I went home and revisited every plane we'd ever been to. We would keep souvenirs so we could always go back. She wasn't in any of them. That was six years ago. I've been looking for Jenny ever since—the Jenny that I knew. She'd be thirty-eight by now."

He stopped talking, and only the crackle of the fire broke the silence between us. "Why?" I finally asked. "Why not just keep visiting the young version of her back in the Yesterday door?"

"I did for a while. When I couldn't find any adult versions of her, I went back into Yesterday and met up with her when she was about eighteen. We kept things going for a couple years. I tried to warn her to stay away from the lake portal, but she would never let me tell her anything about the future. Butterfly effect and all that." His eyes took on a glassy appearance for a moment, and the whisper of a smile crossed his face.

"The last time I saw her, we were both nineteen. She told me she was going back to Dave. And by that point . . . things had changed for me. I'd spent a lot of time down here, just hanging out with George, exploring this warped, messed-up version of our world, and I'd done a lot of thinking. Something clicked in my mind. Because the more I discovered how much the world down here had diverged from ours, the more I suspected something.

"This world is like this because of Jenny. She did something, I don't know what. But she was always taking risks in the portals, always. I think she altered something in this timeline, and the result is the hellscape you're looking at. And I knew there was only one way to fix it, to put it back the way it should be, and that was to find that adult version of Jenny who went through that lake portal all those years ago and bring her home."

"Why didn't you just grab her before she went through? I mean, she was here that night, wasn't she?"

"I thought about it," he admitted. "But there was no way to get her away from the others. And if they'd seen me, it would have upset too many things. Don't forget, I have my own history with these people."

I waited for him to elaborate, but he just shook his head, a dark shadow hovering over his eyes. "Besides," he finally said. "You don't know Jenny. She would have just tried again. History has a way of repeating itself. I should know."

I cleared my throat, shivering a bit from the cold.

"No, the only way to fix this dimension was to come down here and get to the bottom of whatever Jenny did in the past to create it. It's not about her anymore, not for me. It hasn't been for a long time. Honestly, I don't want anything to do with her now. That's over.

"I am only here to try to save my friends," he said, looking out the window at the bare branches of the nearby woods. "I owe that to George. And to Sage—the one who works at the diner down the street, I mean."

"You know the Sage in the diner?"

Adam looked at me for several seconds, his mind landing on a decision. Finally, he rolled up his left sleeve and turned his hand over to show me something I hadn't seen in a long time— something I never thought I'd see again.

It was three dime-length scars, running in parallel lines next to the protruding tendons of his wrist.

"I'm part of it," he confessed.

The air forced its way into my lungs. How did I not know that? Sage had never mentioned him.

"When I saw you didn't have your scars," he continued, "I just assumed—"

"That I wasn't part of it?" I finished his thought, using the same phrase that he and Caryn and the other members of Sage's little gang had coined to show they were working against my mother's corrupt government.

He nodded. "I need to find Jenny, Marina. It's the only way to find out for sure what happened down here. Assuming she's . . . still alive. Sage and the others at the diner were helping me look for her. But then last summer, I tried to come down here to search again. I dove into the lake, but I couldn't find the portal. I figured I was in the wrong place. I tried again."

"But you were locked out." I nodded, his words stinging with something that felt awfully close to guilt. "You shouldn't have even remembered the portal existed. We live in a timeline where it wasn't built."

"When you're between dimensions," he reminded me, "you remember everything from the ones you've left. And I've spent the last several years almost constantly between dimensions."

Right. Of course. I walked away from Adam, needing to pace and think. But the room was so small, there was nowhere to go.

I thought about what George had said—if there's only one of you, the others evaporate. And then something dawned on me. "There's no other adult Jenny," I said softly. "That's why you couldn't find her anywhere. The only version of her that remains is the one from the old timeline—the one who went through the lake portal." I looked to Adam, and his face confirmed that he'd already figured that out. I swallowed down a sudden onslaught of fear and sadness. "I'm sorry, Adam."

"You kept me away from my friends all year," Adam said with a bit of venom in his voice. "I could have found her by now. I could have . . . I could have fixed it."

He was right. This was my fault. All the time lost, all the people down here suffering. It was because of what I'd done that night twelve years ago. Because I'd selfishly wanted everything to work out for me and for my brother, and I didn't even think about how it might affect anyone else.

A horrible silence lingered between us, and the weight of shame threatened to crush me.

George came back into the cabin then and leaned his shotgun against the wall. I turned away to collect myself while Adam returned his attention to his shoes.

"Haven't you two killed each other yet?" George asked.

"Not yet," Adam replied, his voice betraying no hint of anything we'd just said. He seemed focused on trying to pry his damp shoes back onto his feet, but they wouldn't fit, as the leather had shrunk.

George's eyes fell on the half-devoured loaf of bread he had left on the table, then on me. With a weariness in his body that had gotten worse over the years, George plopped himself down at that table in front of his depleted breakfast.

"What do you want to do, Adam?" he asked.

He wasn't talking to me, but I knew what my answer was.

"We need to go to Sage," I said.

Adam seemed shocked, his eyebrows furrowing together in my direction. "Why?"

I smiled at him, an effort at reconciliation. Of redemption, perhaps. This dark world may have gotten worse over the last year because of me, but that didn't mean I was powerless to help them now. "So I can get my scars."

Without waiting for a response, I leaned down by Adam and grabbed my own wet shoes. All the poor people here were always barefoot anyway. He and I should both fit right in.

CHAPTER NINETEEN

"Ow!" I screamed as Milo sliced into my raw skin with the edge of a razor blade after having soaked it for several seconds in rubbing alcohol.

Milo laughed at me. Apparently he hadn't become any less of an asshole since the last time I had seen him. He wiped my blood off on a towel and brought the razor back to my wrist for the second slice.

We were in the basement of Sage's diner. George had escorted us here through a twisting path in the woods that hadn't existed last time I'd been here—a path that allowed us to completely circum-navigate the hotel and its insidious residents.

Caryn, the sweet waitress who'd had a bit of a crush on Brady the last time we were here, sat nearby, concealing a chuckle as she watched me grimace. She looked thinner than she had when I'd last seen her, and her light brown hair hung limply by her ears.

But it was her pale blue eyes that showed the effects of the passing time the most—there was something dull and tired about them that made me look away in pity.

Sage hadn't said anything to me when we got here, ignoring my awkward attempt at a hug. Instead, she just let us into the diner, and Milo and Caryn took us downstairs while Sage stayed above to deal with any potential customers.

"It hurts like hell, doesn't it?" Caryn asked.

"It really does."

"You ready for the second cut?" Milo asked, relishing my pain a bit too much.

I felt woozy from the sting of the first slice, but I didn't want to admit that to Milo, who would have gotten too much pleasure out of my pain. He was a big-boned guy with dark skin and glinting brown eyes who might have been handsome if his belligerent personality wasn't always getting in the way. Trying not to give him the satisfaction of seeing me squirm, I simply turned my head away, squeezed my eyes shut, and groaned something that sounded affirmative.

For some reason, this cut hurt twice as much. Maybe it was hitting a nerve.

"Shit!" I screamed, embarrassed immediately as I heard Caryn and Milo laughing again. But Adam, who had been sitting in the corner waiting, didn't seem to think it was funny. He walked up to me now, inspecting the damage.

"You're cutting too deep," he told Milo.

"It's the same as I was cut."

"Let me do it."

Milo gave him a look that said he wasn't interested in handing over the razor, but Adam didn't seem to care. He grabbed it from Milo's hand and then pushed him aside.

"I don't do well with pain," I admitted to Adam, looking around the basement of Sage's diner. The door the bathroom was open, and my eyes landed on the picture of President Koenig they kept over the toilet—the one with the bull's-eye on it.

"No kidding," Adam sarcastically responded, taking Milo's seat. He then grabbed an extra towel, rolled it up, and handed it to me. "Bite down on this."

I did as he instructed, and closed my eyes while the searing pain of the third cut ripped into the delicate skin of my arm. Before I knew it, he was done.

I looked down at the three identical bleeding slashes on my wrist while Adam went to get some iodine and cellophane. When he got back, he poured the liquid into the wound, causing me to grab on to his arm in agony.

He held still a moment, letting the wave of pain pass over me. Then he wrapped the new scars up in the plastic, very tight, so no air would hit them.

I looked up at him as he did it, relieved that it was over. "Do you believe that I'm part of it now?" I asked.

He only smiled and nodded in response.

Milo, having been displaced to Sage's empty bed while he waited, seemed restless. "Where's your boyfriend?" he asked me, looking to stir something up, apparently.

"He didn't make it this time," I answered, still looking at my arm as Adam finished wrapping it.

"Too bad," Milo replied. "I was hoping to see him cry again."

"Shut up, Milo," Caryn and I both responded in unison. I couldn't help but chuckle at that.

"And his other girlfriend," Milo continued, really enjoying himself now. "How is she?"

Adam seemed annoyed at the interruption, which was causing me to stir angrily as he worked.

"Don't talk about Brady like that," I told him. "You don't know anything about him."

Adam glanced up at the mention of Brady's name, then snapped off the plastic wrap and threw the remainder of the roll onto a table.

Just then, the entire building began to rumble slightly, and the fluorescent lights overhead flashed on and off a couple times. The rumbling grew louder and louder. I panicked, looking around to the others for some indication of what it might be. An earthquake, maybe? Adam was the only other one who seemed concerned, however.

"What is it?" I asked Caryn.

She shrugged. "Tanks. They pass by sometimes to try to scare us. Clear the streets."

"Yeah, can't you see I'm terrified?" Milo asked with his usual amount of sarcasm.

Despite the nonchalance our friends seemed to be feeling, Adam and I remained frozen in place. The shaking did not subside for several minutes, and it made the table I was sitting on wobble beneath me.

Just then, the door to the basement slammed open, and even Caryn jumped to her feet. I stood by Adam, who placed an arm between me and the door the way a mother might do to shield a child from hitting the windshield at an unexpected traffic stop.

I had to physically push his arm out of my way to see who was coming down the stairs.

Relief flooded over me when George's feet began to descend. But he had someone else with him, and it took me a moment to process the face that appeared before me.

"Kieren," I said, not able to hide the excitement in my voice. He made it down the stairs to ground level, and, without even remembering that we were in a fight, I threw myself across the room and into his arms. His shirt and hair were wet, and I knew he must've come through the lake portal too.

He held me for a second, closing me up completely in his long arms as his tense body relaxed. "Thank God," he whispered.

"What are you doing here?" I asked, pulling away just enough to see his face. "How did you even find me?"

Instead of answering, he opened his palm and showed me a handful of the small gravel stones that had been piled up by the door to Today. "You left these by the portal. I assumed they were the token you used to get . . . wherever the hell we are. George explained when I came out of the lake that you were here."

I sighed, relieved but also panicking a bit at how easy it had been for Kieren to track me down. What if someone else tried to do the same thing?

"And why'd you follow me?" I asked softly. Even I could hear how childish the words sounded.

"Why do you think? I came to get you. I knew you were up to something, M, but if I had known what—"

"I'm so happy to see you," I couldn't help but gush. I didn't care anymore what had happened between us when I realized that he had come for me. Could this mean he was changing his mind about us?

"What is this?" Kieren asked, pulling my arm away and examining the plastic wrap.

"It's—"

"Did you cut her?" Kieren demanded suddenly, his gaze whipping up to Adam. He pushed me away and marched towards the table, where Adam was wiping off the bloody razor blade in the even bloodier towel. Adam put the blade down as Kieren got closer, taking a defensive stance.

"No, Kieren, it's not like that—" I started to protest, but he wasn't listening to me.

"What the fuck?" he asked now, the back of his neck turning red with anger. Before I could stop him, he had made it to Adam, and he pushed him back with all his might.

Adam, of course, immediately recovered and took up a wrestler's position. "Try me," he said lightly. And that was all the encouragement Kieren needed to lunge at him again.

Milo actually cracked his knuckles with glee at the show he was about to watch, and Caryn plastered herself against a wall to get out of the way.

"Stop it," I shouted, running to try to break them up.

Adam had already managed to catch Kieren's punch midair and twist the offending arm into the same half nelson he had pulled on me earlier. Kieren was in the process of turning into the maneuver to regain the upper hand when I managed to get my fingers on Adam's arm.

"Damn it, Adam, I said stop it."

It took both the men a second to stop when they noticed that any punch they might throw at that point would probably hit me instead. I placed my hands on Adam's chest to push him back, forcing him to look me in the eyes and see that I was serious. "Back off," I insisted.

Adam held up both hands, as if to say, "I didn't start it." But I kept pushing until he was several inches away. Then I turned back to see that Kieren was still glaring at him and was apparently disgusted with me as well for getting in the way.

"Kieren, let's go upstairs and talk," I said.

He finally looked down at me, although his forehead was still rumpled with rage, and I was afraid he might make another leap for Adam. I came up and gently touched his upper arm to lead him away, and I was relieved when he let me.

"Come on," I said again, softer this time, and he followed me up to the diner.

CHAPTER TWENTY

As soon as we made it upstairs, I saw the last tank inching past—a mountain of slowly creeping metal capable of obliterating everything in its path. The diner booths were mostly empty, but a few stragglers remained, anxiously clutching their coffee cups as they stared warily out the window. A little girl with a red ribbon in her hair had her face plastered against the glass, her eyes turned in the direction the other tanks had gone. Her mother, a hollow-looking woman with deeply sunken eyes, pulled the girl back by the ponytail and held her close until the last of the rumbling had stopped.

I realized I had been standing painfully still, watching the scene transpire before me. A glance over at the counter revealed Sage, looking a decade older than I'd last seen her just eighteen months earlier. She poured a cup of coffee for the lone customer before her—a skinny old man in a bowler hat.

When she glanced up at me, a flash of something passed through her eyes. Was it anger? Or embarrassment? She flinched and turned away, plopping the coffeepot back in its holder and hovering over the pie table, hiding her face from me.

George had been telling the truth then. Things here had gotten worse, a thousand times worse. This underlake version of Sage had already started to look defeated when I had last been here, too tired to fight back anymore. But now . . . now she couldn't even look at me, didn't want me to see what had become of her. I clenched my fist. It looked like that dark, evil version of my mother had truly won.

An impulse to go and talk to Sage came over me, but Kieren's hand on my back led me in another direction.

We sat down in the corner booth—the same one I had once sat in with Brady—and wordlessly we both scooched in all the way to the middle. I didn't think I could get close enough to him. Just feeling his warmth next to me made me feel like, despite everything happening around us, I was safe.

I had forgotten how much Kieren used to make me feel that way. After our last confrontation, I didn't know if I'd ever have that with him again.

"George said we have to wait a few minutes," Kieren began, speaking almost in a whisper. His face was inches from mine, and he was being very careful that our conversation had no audience. "Until the last of the tanks is long gone. Then he'll bring us back through the woods."

I took a deep breath, the sting of the cuts in my arm still throbbing slightly. "I can't do that, Kieren."

"I don't want to hear your excuses, M."

"I'm not leaving yet."

"You are."

"You're not listening to me," I whispered a bit too loudly. Kieren touched my upper arm as a gentle warning to keep the volume down while his eagle eyes scanned the restaurant, looking for eavesdroppers. "I made a commitment."

"To do what? Get yourself killed for these people?"

"*These people* are my friends," I explained, glancing momentarily at Sage only to find that she still had her back turned to me. "They helped me when I needed it. And it's my fault things are this bad here."

"No, M," Kieren pressed on, almost begging me to understand. "It is not your job to fix this." He nervously peered out the window again. I followed his line of sight and saw that the last tank was no longer visible. Slowly, very slowly, a few people had started to reappear in the street, walking with bowed heads and shuffling feet towards wherever they had been heading before.

"I won't get hurt, Kieren. I promise you."

"You can't promise that. You know what happens if you stay too long."

I nodded. The fact was, nobody really knew how long a person could stay in another dimension before the other versions of them disappeared. But Adam said that he had stayed for up to three days before. So as long as I was back in three days, I should be fine.

I had to risk it. I couldn't betray my friends again. Not when it was my fault their lives were like this. "I won't stay too long."

"M—"

"A few days, Kieren. Just to see this through."

"And what about your dad?" he asked, his facial muscles tensing. "What do I tell him?"

I had to admit to myself that I hadn't even thought about that. I was in the Today portal, which meant every minute that passed down here was passing up there as well. "Tell him the truth," I finally said. "I'm helping friends, and I'll be back in a few days. Tell him . . . tell him that he would be proud of me."

He hesitated a moment before asking the next question through clenched teeth. "And Brady?"

I shook my head, the weight of realizing how many people cared about me suddenly feeling a little suffocating. "Tell him the same thing."

"That's not what I meant."

Kieren's eyes turned towards the door to the basement, resting on it with a bitter resentment. I followed his line of sight until it occurred to me that the reason he was looking at the basement was because Adam was in it.

"Oh my God, he's my teacher," I all but spat at him. I couldn't believe he would even think that about me. "It's not like that. And I wouldn't do that to Brady. I wouldn't cheat on him."

The words hit Kieren like a punch. He winced painfully and let out a slight grunt.

"I didn't mean it like that," I added.

But he just shook his head. We sat in silence for what felt like an eternity. Finally, I cleared my throat, knowing that it was up to me to ask the most difficult question.

"Do you love her?"

He closed his eyes, wrestling with some internal thought. He couldn't even look at me when he answered. "Yes."

Now it was my turn to feel punched. Tears raced down my cheeks, and my throat clenched shut. How did this happen? Kieren was mine. We had finally found each other again, after so many years. How had I let him slip away?

"I love you too, M, but it's just different."

"How?"

He exhaled slowly, still not able to meet my eyes. "When I

looked at you, all I could see were the years of pain. Years of regret and hating myself. It just hurt too much."

"And it didn't hurt with her?"

"She was . . ." He hesitated, but I think he knew he had to say it. "She was a new beginning. A fresh start."

A new wave of tears followed the first, and I didn't even bother to try to stop them. Instead, they fell like tiny bombs onto my pants, exploding on impact and splattering on the bench all around me.

"Please don't cry, M."

I felt like I was suddenly imprisoned in a shell of sadness. I could feel Kieren's arms around me, but it was like they weren't real. They weren't even touching me. Nothing could touch me. This was it. We were really over.

I hadn't actually accepted it until that moment. Even when I was with Brady when he was holding me the other night, a part of my brain had still been trying to make sense of it all. That part would have to be at rest now. Because I had the answer, whether I liked it or not.

A shadow fell over me, and it took me a second to realize that it wasn't just from how I was feeling. Adam was standing next to the table, waiting for me to look up.

I wiped my eyes frantically with my palms, not wanting him to see me like this.

Kieren pulled away and stood beside the table, carefully keeping his distance from Adam. "You need to decide, M," he said coolly. "What are you going to do?"

I caught my breath and wiped away the last of the tears on a napkin, then crumpled it up and threw it on the table. By the time my face was dry, I had made my decision.

I stood up and took a step towards Adam, standing with my arm almost touching his. My head was still bowed, but I dared to look up at Kieren, seeing a reluctant acceptance in his eyes. He nodded and pushed his hair back with his fingers.

"If you're not back in three days, I'm coming to get you."

"I know that."

He straightened his shoulders. Looking up, I saw that George had also come back upstairs and was talking with Sage over by the front door. He noticed me looking and turned towards us, his arms slightly raised as if to say, "Who's coming with me?"

Kieren began walking towards George alone, but he stopped briefly as he passed us, leaning in towards Adam. "If anything happens to her, I swear . . ." His eyes bored into Adam's momentarily, and though Kieren was a couple of inches taller, Adam's imposing physique puffed up to let Kieren know he wasn't intimidated.

And I stood like that, my heart beating a thousand times a minute, my arm barely grazing Adam's, as I watched George and Kieren head out the front door and disappear from view.

"Any more of your boyfriends coming, or can we get to work?" Adam asked.

I only glared at him in response, heading back downstairs to get started.

CHAPTER TWENTY-ONE

"You all right?" Caryn asked me gently when I got back down-stairs. I guess my puffy eyes and Kieren's absence tipped her off to the fact that our conversation hadn't gone very well.

"Fine," I grunted, my throat still sore from crying. But I didn't want to be rude to Caryn. She had always been so nice to me—to us—the last time I was here with Brady. "Thank you."

Milo pulled up a couple of chairs when he saw Sage heading down with Adam to meet us. I followed Caryn's lead and grabbed another chair for myself, forming a semicircle with the others.

"Caryn, man the floor," Sage said in voice that reminded me of a dry riverbed.

"But I want to be part of the meeting."

"And I want to not get arrested when the MPs show up and we're all clearly down here conspiring. Do it, please."

Sage dismissed Caryn with a forceful plop into the nicest of the chairs Milo had procured, and Caryn had no choice but to do as she was told.

That left just the four of us in this secret meeting, whatever it was, once Adam had claimed the seat next to mine.

"I want you to know," Adam began before Sage could say anything, "that I never meant to be gone so long."

"It's not important now—" Sage began.

"It is important," he countered. "I did everything I could to get back here."

I bowed my head, feeling ashamed once again that I had inadvertently cut these people off from someone who was trying to help them. When I glanced at Adam, I realized he was looking to me for reinforcement. "He's telling the truth," I offered.

But Sage just sighed in response.

"It's my fault, Sage," I continued. "I didn't do it on purpose but . . . but it's my fault."

"Nothing's your fault," Sage said to me, although no warmth radiated in my direction. "It was inevitable."

Milo had remained uncharacteristically silent through this exchange, maybe because he just wasn't interested in blame or true confessions. Milo wasn't the type, I understood, to spend too much time thinking about stuff that made no practical difference in the end. And while I still didn't like him very much, I had to admit that his philosophy made a lot of sense to me.

What difference did it make whose fault this was? It was real. What were we going to do about it?

"Now that I'm back," Adam said, addressing Sage directly, "we can begin again. We'll just pick up where we left off." He glanced momentarily at me as he continued, as though the following was being said for my benefit. "We had kids at the high school scouring history books, looking for any mention of Jenny. And then there were the assets in Koenig's palace. Have they had any luck?"

Adam was getting so excited as he listened to himself talk that he didn't seem to notice—maybe didn't want to notice—that Sage's and Milo's body language was shutting down everything he said.

"If not, no worries. We can use Marina for that." He barely glanced in my direction when he said this before hammering on. "Rain will take her under her wing when she learns who she is. It might take a while to gain her confidence—"

"Adam," I gently prodded, dipping my head in his direction to try to meet his eyes.

"What?"

He finally looked up long enough to realize that Sage and Milo were still staring bleakly into the distance, letting his speech slide off them like water over ice.

Sage finally opened her mouth to speak, and even Adam seemed to realize that he shouldn't interrupt her. "It was a good idea, Adam," she began. "And everyone appreciated that you . . . that you wanted to help us."

The fact that Sage was using the past tense pretty much told me all I needed to know. And yet my throat clenched shut with anticipation as I waited for her to confirm it. Adam's body shrunk next to mine as the same realization seemed to dawn on him.

We sat in silence for a moment, and when Adam spoke again, his voice was an octave lower.

"The kids at the school?" he asked.

"The disease got half of them," Sage said, any emotion she might have felt about this buried deeply beneath a steely resolve. "Some disappeared . . ."

I took a deep breath, trying to keep the room from spinning around me.

"And some . . ." She finally looked up at me, her glassy eyes unreadable. "Some work for your mother now. True converts. Kids who used to come in here for a hot cocoa, a cookie. Kids I watched grow up. Kids I loved. They'd arrest you now in a heartbeat if you crossed the street without your papers."

I shook my head, not wanting to accept it.

Sage turned back to Adam. "We have no assets in the palace. They were discovered, tried, and hanged in the middle of town. The MPs sold tickets. They handed out cotton candy as the bodies swung from the gallows."

Milo shot up from his seat now, pushing back so forcefully that the chair beneath him skidded halfway across the floor before toppling over onto its back. He headed into the bathroom and slammed the door.

Sage seemed unaffected by the outburst. "You should go home," she said to Adam, but she meant both of us. "After dark tonight. Take her back."

I felt her words like a slap. *Her* was me. She couldn't even look at me. Couldn't say my name.

"Back where she's safe," Sage concluded. Then she stood up and straightened her dress. "Excuse me. I have to get back upstairs."

Before Adam could react, Sage left us, her heavy footsteps thudding as they ascended the staircase. She closed the door at the top with a fateful click.

Adam hadn't moved an inch.

"Adam?" I asked, trying to gauge how was reacting.

"Don't talk to me," he said under his breath. He pushed his chair back and looked around for somewhere to escape to. But we knew we couldn't leave. Trapped in this room like a mouse in a maze, he simply sat on the edge of Sage's bed and buried his head in his hands.

I stayed in my chair a long time, having no idea where to go.

CHAPTER TWENTY-TWO

Eventually Milo came charging out of the bathroom, his face impassive once again, as though nothing had happened. He scanned the room to find me sitting stiffly in my chair and Adam passed out on Sage's bed. I raised my index finger to my lips to let him know he should be quiet and let him sleep. After all, Adam had been up all night waiting for his chance to steal the portal solution.

Milo raised his middle finger to me in response. Then he marched up the stairs and slammed the door closed behind him.

Adam stirred slightly but didn't wake.

I got up to explore the cold, barren room. It really was depressing to think that Sage had been living down here. The walls were just gray plaster, no pictures or decorations of any kind. A metal bookshelf against one wall was half empty.

I couldn't help but think of the other Sage's apartment, the airy, chic top floor of the hotel she lived in with John. The one with the fire-engine-red bathroom and the flowing curtains over the majestically tall windows. The one that had haunted my memories as a child, knowing it was a place I needed to get to someday but not remembering where I had seen it.

That was the real Sage. A bright, lively woman in a flowing white dress, beads on her wrists, a musky perfume, a ready smile.

How could the same human being live two such disparate lives? How could life—even a sad and oppressive life like this—kill the spark in someone who had been so very alive?

And this led me to another thought, one that made me hold my breath: Were we all just one fateful moment away from losing everything that defined us?

My eyes fell on Sage's half-empty bookshelf, a very familiar-looking spine suddenly catching my eye. I did a bit of a double take, trying to make sense of why my mother's photo album was on Sage's shelf. It wasn't until I picked it up and looked at the well-worn cover, with unfamiliar markings and stickers all over it, that I realized it wasn't the exact same one; Sage and my mom must've gotten identical albums together.

They were good friends in high school, so that wasn't really surprising. I wondered if the albums had been bought to commemorate their graduation or just on a whim one day, maybe down at Groussman's Pharmacy after school. I liked to think of them like that, young and innocent.

For the second time in a day, I flipped through an old photo album, expecting to see familiar and comforting images.

And for the second time in a day, what I saw instead made me shiver down to my bones. A sensation oddly like brain freeze grasped hold of my frontal lobe for a second: a kind of cognitive dissonance. Because there was something very disturbing about this album too.

But this time, it wasn't because the pictures were of the wrong people.

They were the right people: Mom, Sage, and John; their friends Jenny and Dave kissing; a photo taken in what looked like a friend's basement, Mom and John smiling together on the couch, George sitting several inches away with a forced look of happiness creaking across his face. In fact, some of these pictures seemed to have been taken on the very same days as the ones in Mom's album. Various outfits, a bright yellow hair scrunchie, and even a glimpse of a red plaid backpack all harkened back to similar photos I'd seen before.

It was the backgrounds that were wrong.

They weren't taken at East Township, as they had been in Mom's album. Instead, they were at a sterile-looking school with all-gray walls. Flipping madly through the pages, I found one of Jenny and Dave smiling in front of the school's entrance, a sign above the portico welcoming new students to Good Citizen Academy. The words were repeated underneath in Russian.

I went back and frantically reviewed each and every picture. They were all like that. A movie theater with the film titles written in both languages. A guard in a red military uniform could be seen behind John in that one. A picture of Mom—or this world's version of her anyway—sunlight streaming through her hair as she sat in a windowsill, reading a book with a Russian title.

I was so rapt looking at the photographs, I didn't immediately notice that Adam had woken up and was standing behind me, looking at the book over my shoulder. I was about to turn a page when his hand shot out, slapping down on a photo of Jenny in a plain gray school uniform.

The slapping sound make me jump with shock, and I turned to look at Adam over my shoulder. His eyes were glued to the photo, however. And then he looked at me.

"Do you still have the photos from my mother's album?" I asked.

He blinked a couple of times while his ears caught up with his brain. "Y-yes," he stuttered, producing a waterlogged stack of pictures from his back pocket. They were a bit stuck together from being wet, but he managed to slowly peel them apart, one by one, holding them awkwardly in his trembling hands.

"Over here," I said, indicating the table where I had gotten my scars. I laid the album I was holding at the top of the table, and Adam began spreading the photos from his pocket out in rows beneath it.

We both took a moment to scan the evidence before us, comparing and contrasting the two similar but eerily different realities that were coming into focus before our eyes.

"There," I said, pointing with my finger to the one photo I'd remembered—the one where Jenny had been wearing that bright yellow scrunchie in a makeshift bun at the top of her head. I traced my finger up to the same exact photo from Sage's album, this time with Jenny standing in front of the Good Citizen Academy.

Adam had to back away, swallowing hard as he thought the pictures through.

"You said you suspected Jenny went back in time, did something to create this dimension?"

"Yes."

"These pictures are from when they were seniors. That's the year 2001. And the Jenny in these pictures, she's the one from *this* timeline, not the one you knew. Not the one who went through the lake portal when she and my mom were twenty-six."

"So?"

"So, Adam, don't you see? Whatever your Jenny did—whenever she did it—it was way before this. All we have to do is find the moment that this reality and ours diverged."

Adam nodded as his eyes flitted back and forth between the two sets of images, finally landing where my finger was pointing, on that picture of Jenny in the gray school uniform.

"We'll take the Yesterday door back from this dimension," I continued, keeping my eyes on Sage's book, "and we'll just keep going until we find the place where the worlds were the same."

"We?"

"Yes, we."

But Adam bowed his head. "Marina, I can't let you—"

"I'm not going home yet, Adam. You heard what I said upstairs."

He shook his head, wrestling with some quiet struggle. But I had already made up my mind. The truth was, I wasn't just staying because I felt guilty. I had seen firsthand what happened when the evils of Down World were swept under the rug. I had already watched once as this dark and ugly reality found a way to slip through the cracks between dimensions and permeate my own.

Darkness finds a way. If I had learned nothing else about the portals, it was that. Darkness never lies idle for long. Ignore it at your own risk.

No, this whole world needed to be destroyed, for good this time. It's what I thought I had accomplished the first time I went through Yesterday, when I buried that beaker in the sand. But now I knew better: this world wasn't created when the lake portal was built; it was created by Jenny, who must have altered something far in the past.

Just then, the door to the basement shot open, and I almost jumped out of my skin. Adam pushed me back, turning to face our visitors, only to find that it was just Sage, wearily clomping down the cold, tiled stairwell.

"Sage," I asked as she made it to the ground, stepping out from behind Adam, "can you tell us something?"

Sage's disapproving eyes fell with a sad resolve onto her photo album on the table. Meanwhile, Adam, perhaps realizing that the damper set of pictures would be more than she could handle, started frantically gathering them up and shoving them back in his pocket.

"What do you want to know?" she asked in a smoky, tired voice, heading for her little cot to sit down.

"How long have the Russians been here? I mean, when did they first come?"

Sage looked at me like I had asked her why the sky was blue. She didn't seem interested in humoring me, and for a moment I wondered if she would even answer. But then she sighed and laughed to herself. "How nice it must be," she muttered, "to be an Otherlander."

My pride was a bit hurt at that, but Adam stepped forward to take up the baton.

"Can you just tell us, please?" he asked.

"The Russians came in the midforties, after World War II was over. At first, it was just to help us out, bring some industry. Everyone was glad to have them. After all, they were the most powerful country in the world, and we were one of the weakest. It made sense to let them in. Or so the history books tell us."

"And then?" I asked, my voice wavering with fear.

"And then they weren't so helpful anymore."

Next to me, Adam's body betrayed no obvious reaction to what Sage was saying. But as he was standing so close, I could hear his unstable breath seeping out of his throat.

"If you think about it," Sage said, nodding to herself and shrugging in a resigned kind of way, "America was really over the minute those Russians dropped that atom bomb on Hiroshima."

Adam's hand instinctively thrust out to grab mine, but I was so numb with shock I couldn't even feel how tightly he was squeezing until, looking down, I watched in horror as my compressed fingers turned a blazing shade of red.

CHAPTER TWENTY-THREE

"This isn't my best work," Milo said from between his teeth as he peered into an ancient relic of a microscope at my fake identification papers. With tweezers, he began to painstakingly affix a very thin sheet of translucent paper with a hand-drawn pattern on it. "The real papers have watermarks on them," he explained, "which is pretty much impossible to duplicate. This will do, though. As long as you don't let them look too closely."

Adam's ID had been finished first, and it was hanging to dry on a clothespin over the tub in Sage's bathroom.

From her perch on the edge of her little cot, Sage watched Milo work with an impassive face, betraying only the slightest flicker of worry in her eyes. "When will you leave?" she asked.

"As soon as they're dry," Adam answered for me. "The longer we stay, the longer people might start talking about us being here. We'll take the overnight train."

Sage nodded, and I wanted desperately to hear her confirm that she didn't think our plan was insane. For a minute, it seemed like her silence was closest thing to an answer I was going to get. But then she shot up out of her seat and headed to a corner of the room, where she inched an old filing cabinet out of the way.

From behind it, she opened what appeared to be a hidden door in the wall and brought out a small locked box, which she now placed on the table next to Milo's work.

"Once you get back to the forties, you'll need some money. Obviously, everything I have will be dated wrong, so . . ." She pulled out an old jewelry box and revealed a delicate diamond ring with a simple silver band. It was clearly quite old, given as an engagement gift by someone who had probably spent half a year's salary on it.

"That's beautiful."

"It was my grandmother Golda's. You can pawn it when you get there." She tried giving it to me, but I held up my hands, refusing to take it.

"Absolutely not; we'll find something else."

"I want you to, Marina."

"I'll pawn my own ring," I suggested, holding up my pinkie, which once again was encircled by the small ruby ring my parents had given me.

"That won't be enough," she said. "No offense. And besides, you didn't know my grandma. She would have loved that it's being used to help the freedom fighters. I would go with you, but the MPs are onto me. If I disappear, they'll be on us like flies."

Once again, Sage tried handing me the ring, but I just couldn't bring myself to take it from her, until Adam settled the argument by yanking it out of her hands. "Thanks," he muttered, practically dumping it in my palm.

It felt sacrilegious to put it on my left hand, so instead I slipped it onto my right ring finger for safekeeping. "We'll try to get it back to you if we can," I offered, but she merely shrugged, already dismissing the possibility.

o o o

The walk to the train station had the ominous feel of approaching a gurgling volcano. The sky had turned to pink and purple as evening settled around us, casting everything in shadow. Every corner seemed fraught with peril; every set of eyes seemed to bore into mine, as if knowing what I was up to. As if they could see that Adam and I did not belong. The town had built up considerably in the time since I'd been there, now having the feel of a midsize European city. There was something timeless about the attractive but sterile new structures and the well-ordered streets that divided them into neat, orderly blocks.

I tried to keep my eyes straight ahead, my face neutral, but my wobbly knees betrayed me by making me miss several steps. Frustrated with my pace, Adam finally grabbed my elbow and guided me along like a misbehaving dog on a leash. I tried yanking my arm away, but he simply grabbed it again. "Just be cool," he whispered to me, and I forced myself to begin my deep exhaling trick that was designed for exactly that purpose. It didn't work.

As we were approaching the square in the center of town, about halfway to the train station, a booming voice suddenly echoed down from above, making us both freeze in our tracks. In an instant, the side of every building turned into an enormous screen, projecting in stereo the crystal-clear voice of the woman whose face appeared on those surfaces.

Since we were surrounded by buildings, that meant that over a dozen iterations of my mother now surrounded me. I hadn't seen her—or this version of her anyway—since the night I'd gone through Yesterday with my friends. But of course, I'd had only a glimpse of her that night.

Here she was now, a couple of years older, although it was impossible to tell under the heavily caked-on makeup, the plastered-on smile, and the glassy eyes that made her look more like an android than a woman.

"Citizens." Her voice boomed down all around us, so loud I could feel the ground rumbling beneath my feet. "I have wonderful news. President Koenig, in his benevolence, has decided to create an opportunity to visit him in the palace."

Now images of the man they called President Koenig filled the screen, smiling broadly under his own thick layer of foundation and obviously dyed jet-black hair. An array of images of a beautiful palace, bedecked with golden furniture and an impressive collection of world art, played under the next words of my mother's evil twin: "Young people will have five days to submit to the palace a letter, in your own words, extolling the virtues of our president. Do not hold back. The authors of the most impressive letters will be treated to a fine meal and a relaxing afternoon in the palace grounds."

Looking around through my horrified eyes, I saw all the thin-cheeked children of the town clinging to their mothers' coats, gazing up in wonder at the parade of fantastical images before them. A sumptuous meal, fresh fruit overflowing from a Grecian urn, a roast leg of lamb, and golden goblets filled to the brim with clear water.

The parents watched the screen too, all with the same hardened and desperately sad look in their eyes.

"One lucky winner," the woman with my mother's face continued as the screens cut back to her, "will even have a chance to ride a real pony through the garden."

Now the children could hardly contain themselves with excitement. Their sunken-in eyes glowed with a new promise as they turned up to their parents and tugged on their coat sleeves.

"Five children will be chosen," the woman said, beaming. "Will you be one of the lucky few? Only if your letter to President Koenig is impressive enough. Again, hold nothing back. List all his accomplishments, and don't forget to be grateful and gracious. Good day, citizens."

And with that, the Down World version of my mother evaporated as quickly as she had appeared, and the building wall screens went back to projecting almost real-looking bricks.

As the commotion around us died down, Adam resumed walking, but I couldn't bring myself to move. He glanced over his shoulder and whispered fiercely, "Walk, Marina," but even he seemed to soften a bit when he saw the tears brimming in my eyes.

He circled back slowly, his eyes darting around to make sure I wasn't attracting too much attention. When he reached me, he simply dipped his head down towards mine, his emerald-green eyes conveying as much warmth as he could muster. "We'll talk about it on the train, but now you need to walk. Do you understand me?"

I nodded dumbly, and a solitary tear wound its way down my cheek. Adam wiped it away with his sleeve, took my hand, and continued walking at the same abrupt pace.

We stormed along that way for several minutes, and we were almost at the train station when a guard stepped before us, her arm outstretched and her hand flat in our faces, telling us to stop.

"Papers," she demanded.

CHAPTER TWENTY-FOUR

Adam and I dutifully took out our new IDs, and I said a silent prayer that the glue holding them together was fully dry. The guard, a very young woman—seriously, was she even older than me?—held my photo a bit too close to her nose for Adam's comfort.

"We're late for a train," he ventured, but she was unimpressed.

Staring at the teenage girl, I couldn't help but remember what Sage had called kids like her: *true converts*. Did this girl really believe in what that twisted version of my mother was doing, or did she simply have no choice? In another reality, would she have been in school with me? Would we have been friends?

"You're not from here," she stated, still peering at my paperwork.

I felt a globule of spit get stuck in my throat, and I strained to swallow it down. But the guard didn't seem particularly disturbed by what she had just discovered as she switched her focus to Adam's ID.

"When did you two arrive from Seattle?"

Adam stepped forward, a subtle hand on my upper arm informing me that I should let him do the talking. "Recently."

"Why did you transfer here?"

I looked to Adam, hoping he had another answer ready to go, but I could see his mind was racing just like mine.

"We were hoping to find work," I blundered, still looking to Adam for confirmation.

"I'm a carpenter," he added without missing a beat.

Her eyes finally flitted up from the paperwork in her hands to Adam and me, scanning us from head to foot like an X-ray machine. "You're newlyweds?"

I almost choked on that bit of spit, once again lodged in my throat. But Adam caught on quicker than I did, grabbing my right hand—the one with the diamond ring on it. *Of course*, I realized, and I forced a smile of what I could only imagine might appear to be wedded bliss.

"So where are you going on the train, then?"

I swallowed hard. That was a very good question. An impulse took over me suddenly—from where, I had no idea. "He got a gig." I beamed, rubbing my hand over his in a way that I hoped looked loving and not creepy. "Building houses."

Adam smiled awkwardly back at me, and we held the pose as long as we could.

"Congratulations," she stated flatly, handing us back our documents. "You should hurry for that train."

"Yes, ma'am," Adam agreed, all but yanking my arm out of its socket as he pulled me the rest of the way to the station.

It turned out that the diamond-ring trick was good for more than just getting out of police interrogations. Once we were on the eastbound overnight train, Adam slipped a porter a small amount of the money Sage had given us in order to score an upgrade to a sleeping berth. "We're newlyweds," I overheard him whispering to the frail old woman, and I swear I even saw him wink.

I had to admit, however, that any weirdness I might have been feeling was allayed when I realized we wouldn't have to spend the night sleeping upright in rigid little seats.

The berth was a tiny compartment with a set of bunk beds along one wall and a luggage rack against the other. As soon as we were inside, Adam hurled his body onto the lower bunk, muttering something about waking him when we got there.

"You want a sandwich first?" I asked as I climbed up to the top bed, fishing a bag with Sage's takeout meals out of the backpack she'd loaned me. But he was already breathing deeply into the pillow.

Unable to sleep, I watched the night sky pass outside the window for a bit, lying on my stomach and nibbling on a turkey and cheese sandwich. The world didn't look too different once it started to move. I had noticed a similar phenomenon on the interdimensional train with Robbie and Piper—no matter where we were or which plane we were visiting, once in motion it was all a blur of green and brown. The earth didn't change; only the people in it.

Different clothes, different hair, but mostly different eyes. Happy and bright in certain worlds, empty and longing in others. The world was only what we made of it. And in the underlake world, what people had made of it was a travesty.

I unwrapped the plastic from my arm to let the air heal it. The blood had dried into three identical scabs, and I laughed silently at the fact that I looked like the world's most inefficient suicide attempter.

I fell asleep remembering the warm feeling of Brady's arms around me, his heartbeat pulsating gently against my ear. Would I ever get to feel those arms again?

Would he still love me if he knew how much of our lives together I couldn't even remember?

I slept long enough to dream that I was looking for my brother, Robbie, in a dark cave, frightened by the echoing thrum of silence. Then the silence became the constant churning ache of the train passing over the rails. And the ache became a grunt. The grunting grew louder and louder until I felt the cave slipping just out of my reach.

Inhaling through shocked nostrils, it took me a moment to remember where I was, and I almost rolled off the top bunk, catching myself at the last moment.

My eyes peeked open enough to find that the grunting was Adam, doing pull-ups against the metal bars of the luggage rack, his back to me. My inner clock told me it was probably the middle of the night.

"Jesus, do you have to do that?"

"Couldn't sleep."

"Read a book."

"Can't get soft," he grunted again as his chin made it to the level of the bar and then just a couple inches above it.

I tried to cover my head with the pillow, but it was no good. The grunting seemed to seep through the cotton. I just lay there, my face turned towards him inside a taco shell of bed and pillow, watching him go up and down for a second.

"Were you really a wrestler?" I asked.

"What do you think?"

He plopped down on the floor now, squeezing his body into crunches and exhaling sharply at the top of each one.

"Did you like it?"

"Wrestling?"

"High school."

"Loved high school," he grunted, corkscrewing his elbows to touch the opposite knees. "Best time of my life. I had a cute girl-friend, shelf full of trophies. Good grades. Plus, my dad liked that I was a wrestler 'cause he'd been one."

"Then why'd you do it?" I wondered out loud, so softly I wasn't sure if he'd heard me.

"Do what?"

"Leave."

He fell flat onto his back now, catching his breath. A thought seemed to be on the tip of his tongue, but he shook it off, piked his legs up above him, and began twisting his way up to touch his toes. But he only made it to the count of five before collapsing to the floor again and staring up at the ceiling, breathing in short bursts through his mouth.

"If I could take it back, I would," he said. "If I could just . . . start over."

"You know you could, right?" I asked, taking the pillow off my head. It was a touchy subject—the door to Yesterday. The impulse to undo all our mistakes.

"I was fourteen the first time I went down. I couldn't go back to fourteen even if I wanted to, and I don't want to. What's done is done."

I let this information wash over me for a moment. When given the same choice, I had tried to redo the past. But it turned out that some things can't be fixed.

"You didn't go to college?"

"The world was my college."

"The world doesn't give out teaching credentials."

He smiled sardonically at me as he flipped over to do push-ups. "I got my degree online. Almost every dimension has the Internet." He paused briefly, exhaling at the top of a push-up, then lowering again. "I would just come home to take the tests so they would count."

He did about twenty more, then flipped over again and sat down, letting his upper body collapse a bit over his legs. I thought maybe he was done talking to me, and I started to drift back off to sleep. "It's not enough anyway," he said, making my eyes pop back open.

"What's not?"

"I really should have a master's. The school only hired me because they were desperate. It's only a year-long gig."

"And then?" I asked, my eyes settling into a half-open state. "When this is over? Will you just—I don't know, take over some happy version of yourself somewhere on a tropical island and live out your days?"

He finally turned to look at me, his breath returning to a normal pace. "I've been down for six years. There *are* no other versions of me. I'm all that's left."

"You said you never stayed more than three days."

"When I was younger, I didn't. But over the years, I got a little reckless. I don't know which trip did it or how long I'd stayed. But after a while, I began to realize that in every new dimension I visited, there was no record of me."

I picked my head up to look at him. How could I have not realized that? It seemed so obvious now that he was saying it. Six years, in and out of every dimension he could find. There's a price to pay for that.

"So, what's in Boston?" he asked, finally done moving around. "Besides your brother?"

"I'm applying to MIT for the fall."

His lips pulled down into an impressed face, and I laughed at how shocked he seemed.

"Yeah, I'm smart."

"Oh, I know you're smart, Marina," he laughed, shaking his head. He hauled himself up off the floor, airing out his sweaty shirt. "I have to change my shirt. Turn around."

I laughed a bit at the fact that he was suddenly shy, but I rolled over as instructed while he rifled through a bag of extra clothes Milo had given him. "M," I said after a bit.

"What's that?"

"My friends call me M."

When no response came, I glanced back over my shoulder to find one of Milo's T-shirts halfway over his sculpted abs. I whipped my head back towards the wall before he caught me.

"Let's get some sleep," he said, climbing back onto the lower bunk. "M."

"I was trying to," I joked.

"And don't snore."

"I don't snore!"

He was silent for several seconds as I tried to will myself back to sleep. "You snore a little," he joked, and I couldn't help but laugh.

CHAPTER TWENTY-FIVE

I had seen this version of our town before, of course, but it still broke my heart to lay eyes on it again. The minute we stepped off the train, I could see the influence of the invading Russians: the guards in stiff uniforms roaming the train platform, the signs in dual languages. But the biggest anomaly was the division between the people: rich and poor.

On the rich side, the same 1950s fashions that had been trending in Portland seemed to be in vogue—lots of red lipstick, bouffant hair, and what appeared to be fox-fur coats. Near as I could figure, the '50s had been some sort of heyday for the Russians and the Americans who had been glad to have them. Money was pouring in, they were all living the high life. There was still a cultural fascination with that time period that had never really died out. At least, not for the rich.

But on the poor side, kids younger than me shuffled aimlessly around the tracks with no shoes on their freezing feet, begging passersby for change.

As Adam and I threw our backpacks over our shoulders and started walking away from the station, I wondered how we must look to the people all around us. Which group did we seem to fit into? Or was it obvious that we didn't fit in at all?

My instinct was to head to my house, but I dreaded to discover what it might look like in this reality. Would my dad even still live there? Would he be married to Laura, or would he be on a completely different track just like that demented version of my mother was? I reminded myself that it didn't matter, that if we were successful in finding Jenny and figuring out what had gone wrong down here, this version of events would cease to exist. But for now, it mattered very much, both to me and to everyone else around me.

"What's the plan?" I asked Adam once we were across the street in front of Groussman's Pharmacy and safely out of earshot of the Russian guards.

"We need to get a more specific idea of where in history Jenny went—exactly when the paths of our world and this one first separated."

"Okay. So should we go to the library or—"

"Oh, you mean the library where you did your Genghis Khan research?" he teased. I could only blush in response. "Word to the wise," he continued, "don't crib off Wikipedia. We have software to detect that."

"It wasn't *all* from Wikipedia," I protested, but I had to admit he had caught me.

"It's not important right now. We can't go to the library."

"Why not?"

"Because history is written by the victors, M. We'd only get the official Russian version of events. We need to talk to real people."

"What real people?"

He pulled out a couple of the pictures he'd borrowed from Sage's album, flipping through them until he found one of Sage herself, sitting awkwardly in front of a statue of Stalin. "Sage's mom. She was very smart and always nice to me. She's not alive anymore, but we could use this picture to go back to this date and talk to her there."

"Yeah, but Adam, this is a different timeline than when you met her. She won't remember you." I hesitated a moment before saying anything else, but then I couldn't stop myself. "And neither will Jenny."

"I know that."

"Do you? Because if this is just some excuse to go see your ex-girlfriend, I really don't have time for it."

"Do you have a better idea?"

"The adult Jenny left our timeline, came down to this one, and then went back to the forties. That's when the timeline diverged based on what Sage said. She's the one we're looking for—the adult from our timeline—not a seventeen-year-old, which will be a different version of her anyway. We shouldn't waste our time—"

"Where in the forties, M? What year, what day?"

"Well, when was the bomb dropped?"

He sighed, reining in what appeared to be frustration with either my tone or the fact that I knew so little about history that I had to ask that question. "August 6, 1945."

"Okay, so sometime before then."

"Oh, great, that narrows it down. Do you know how long I've looked for her? This is the first real lead I've got. Why are you giving me a hard time?"

"Why are you mad at me?" I asked, realizing that we were

drawing attention from too many people. I took a step closer, trying to keep the volume down.

He shook his head, looking down at his feet, crammed as they were into a pair of Milo's stained old gym shoes. "I'm sorry, I'm really hungry."

"Well, I offered you a sandwich."

I opened up the backpack and dug out what was left of the food. The turkey and mayo had been sitting out all night, and I made an executive decision that he shouldn't eat it. "Stale French fries or a Danish?"

"Danish, please."

I handed it to him, and I could see the tension physically deflate from his body as he chewed and his blood sugar came back to a normal level.

"Thank you."

"You're welcome." I waited another moment, looking around at the tired masses of people roaming around us like zombies and nibbling on a few of the stale French fries. "Do you really think Sage's mom can help?"

"Unless you've got a better idea?" he responded, his tone significantly softer than a moment ago.

"I don't."

He held up the picture of Sage again, and I could only nod in agreement.

o o o

I spent the walk to the high school mentally preparing myself for what it would look like, remembering the nurse who had been dispensing vaccine shots after I had rescued Robbie and Piper from the train fifteen months ago. And yet no matter how much I tried to be ready, the actual sight of it still felt like a punch in the gut.

The words *Good Citizen Academy* now adorned the front portico, just as they had in Sage's pictures, with the Russian translation beneath it. But the building looked even more cold and imposing than it had in those twenty-year-old images. There had been some trees then, at least, at the corners of the building. Now they'd been removed, two stone guard towers having taken their place.

There was no nurses' station set up in front. I guess by this point, everyone in town had either received their vaccine or the disease had already taken them.

But there were lines of people anyway. One line for bread. One for socks. And another line—the longest one—winding its way through the parking lot held people queuing up for an empty table. Whatever was supposed to be there had apparently run out. But the people waited anyway.

There weren't any children in the lines, however. It was after 8:00 a.m., and they were probably inside already, being force-fed whatever information that horrible version of my mother and President Koenig had decided they should know.

The study of mathematics makes women infertile. I still remembered that particular little nugget from last time.

Or maybe they were just working on their letters to President Koenig, expounding on how perfect and amazing he was so they could win the chance to ride a pony. The more I thought about it, the angrier I got. Adam and I were standing frozen at the edge of the parking lot, watching the sad progression of desperate people lined up before us, and I could feel my breath growing heavy with impending rage.

"You okay?" Adam whispered to me.

But I only shook my head.

"Marina," he continued.

I tried regulating my breathing, but it only made my cheeks grow hotter. How had these people let it get this bad? Why hadn't they revolted when it first started? Or had it started too quickly? Was it the threat of the disease that kept them pacified? Or were they just so enthralled with their godlike president they didn't see him for what he was?

Don't forget to be grateful and gracious.

"M?"

"What?"

Adam was still looking down at me, waiting for me to snap to attention.

"We have to get into the school."

He was right, of course. There was no time for my feelings right now. We had too much to do. I nodded in response, shaking off my anger so I could pay attention.

"Follow my lead?" he asked, and I nodded again.

He took my arm and led me with a forceful push towards the school entrance, where another guard in that same overstarched uniform was surveying the people before him, a smirk of disgust on his sallow face.

"Caught this one ditching," Adam explained as we reached the guard.

The man swore to himself in Russian. "What were you thinking?" he said to me in English, rubbing a hand through his thinning black hair.

"I needed to—"

"Don't talk," Adam reprimanded, smacking me on the back of my head. I knew he was doing it for the guard's benefit, and yet it still made me want to throttle him. The heat of anger returned to my cheeks, but I swallowed down the urge to say anything more. "Can you believe these kids?" Adam added to the guard.

"They're bad seeds," the guard agreed, but his eyes fell to my chest when he said it, a fact that Adam didn't seem to miss as his hand tightened around my upper arm. "I'll take her in for you," the guard offered, stepping up to meet me.

"No, I'll do it myself," Adam insisted. "I want to have a word with the headmaster."

"I insist," the guard replied, a sleazy smile now oozing over his thin, chapped lips. "Get back to work, citizen." Before I knew it, the guard had yanked me away from Adam and was leading me through the hallway, his hand on my lower back and working its way even farther down.

I risked a look over my shoulder towards Adam, only to find him stranded by the door.

Shit. What do I do?

I could wait until we got to the principal's office—if there was even a principal in this godforsaken place—and then try to ditch this guy. Maybe Adam would meet me at the boiler room? But for now, I was too distracted by the fact that the guard's hand had reached its goal: cupping my ass as we walked. I tried to pull away, but he only forced me closer. We were about to turn a corner, and then I'd be alone with him. Was I strong enough to fight him off?

Before I could think of an answer to that question, the guard was suddenly hurled away from me. I turned in time to see Adam punching him in the face. I heard a pop and then a tinkling sound a few feet away. It took me a second to understand that the red object that had gone flying was one of the guard's teeth.

"Run!" Adam shouted before the guard had time to recover.

I didn't need to be told twice. I ran with all my might after Adam, my body in pure adrenaline mode and every muscle in my thighs tensing as we wound our way through hallways that were utterly foreign in appearance and yet completely familiar in layout.

Before I knew it, we'd reached the door to the boiler room, only to find it locked. Adam quickly fumbled through his backpack, pulling out his school keys.

"They won't be the same," I warned.

"It's a master key. It might work," he muttered, the shaky fingers of his now bloody right hand almost dropping the whole ring as he tried to insert the biggest of the keys. A moment of breathless anticipation followed, and a second later, I felt a flood of relief as the door opened.

We hurried inside and slammed the door shut behind us, locking it from within. We'd made it into the boiler room. Now we could only pray that the science lab was still there, that the Russians hadn't sealed it off.

Rushing down the stairs, I was relieved to find that at least the wooden key that opened the second door to the winding hallway was still lodged above the doorframe. It wasn't until we were through it and working our way down that mysteriously curved hall, thankfully now devoid of office workers, that I realized Adam was holding his shaking hand.

"You okay? Did you hurt yourself?"

"I'm fine," he panted.

"Let me see it," I insisted, turning his hand over to inspect what would surely soon be very bruised knuckles.

"I haven't punched someone out in years."

"Yeah?" I asked, letting go of his hand as there was nothing I could do for him until we could get hold of some ice. "What's it like?"

"Honestly? It's fucking great." He smiled, and I couldn't help but smile back, wishing more than anything that I could have been the one to knock that jerk's tooth out after he'd grabbed my ass.

"Thank you, Adam."

He simply touched the top of my head with his still trembling hand in a sort of kind, protective gesture and then nodded towards the science lab. "Let's go."

"Yeah."

We ran the rest of the way, not pausing to consider some new computations that had been scrawled over the whiteboard before racing down the spiral staircase towards the portals. Once we were in the room with the three doors, Adam pulled out the picture of Sage, grabbed my hand, and inserted a penny into the door to Yesterday.

CHAPTER TWENTY-SIX

The statue of Stalin was coated in bronze. Sitting on a rearing horse with a flowing mane that just grazed the muscular leg of its rider, the figure towered over the stone base designed to hold it. In the dull light of this cloudy day, it reflected a distorted golden version of Adam's and my faces back at us, our expressions unreadable in the dark metal.

"A fearless leader, boldly guiding the people into the future," I read the plaque out loud.

Adam said nothing in response but simply turned away. "Sage's house is over by the old grounds."

"Okay."

We started walking in silence, taking in the streets and the people of our town as we went. It was 2001, and the twenty years we had shaved off history showed in subtle ways.

Gone were some of the fashions I had been expecting to see based on Mom's photo album and reruns of old TV shows: black chokers, slips worn as dresses, and overplucked eyebrows. Fashion was as malleable as politics, I guessed, and the cultural influences that had inspired those looks were apparently absent in this version of history.

We had come back to a month in the dead of winter, and the thick coats and fur hats many people sported seemed instead to be inspired by Russian styles. The barefoot children were mostly absent as well, and in fact, the whole town seemed somehow less bleak than it had in the present day we had just left.

Maybe it was the thin layer of snow dusting the sidewalks or the dove singing on the bare branch of a newly planted tree that produced the effect. There was a promise in the air of this place that was nowhere to be found on the other side of those twenty years.

I shivered a bit with no protection from the chill. "If we have any of Sage's money left, we should buy some coats."

"Agreed. We'll find a store in town."

I inhaled a sharp gust of cold air, and my teeth began to chatter.

"Almost there," Adam assured me, putting his arm around me and rubbing my shoulder.

"Okay."

It was awkward walking like that, and after a moment, he pulled his arm away again, and we both put our hands in our pockets and continued on a few inches apart.

I realized that I needed to be careful. Down World can make people feel close to each other, like coconspirators in a crime. It had happened with Brady too.

But Adam wasn't Brady.

After a while, we reached the old grounds, which existed now not as the shiny amusement park they would become after the Russians renovated them nor as the gas station and fast-food restaurants they had been in my reality. Instead, they were somewhere in between: rusted and abandoned structures, vaguely meant to emulate a Nordic village but sadly neglected by time and covered in a blanket of dirty snow.

Adam nodded to the neighborhood across the street, and we walked one more block to a small, simple house painted a dull white with two spiny, bare bushes plopped haphazardly on either side of the front door. Only a wind chime of little moons and stars jangling into a shooting comet indicated that, somewhere inside this house, a woman of great spirit lived.

We stomped our feet on the cement stoop, leaving boot-shaped clumps of caked-on snow behind. Adam cleared his throat, and I offered him an encouraging smile.

"Lose the Fitbit."

"Right," I stammered, loosening the band and shoving it in my pocket.

Adam knocked on the door, but his hand froze in midmovement. "Oh," he said, remembering, "and hide the ring."

I looked down at Sage's ring on my frozen finger and pried it off just as the door was opening, wedging it into the tight inner pocket of my jeans. I looked up when I heard Adam gasp.

A teenage Jenny was standing in front of us, a smile on her welcoming face, arms crossed over her ample chest to protect herself from the chill. "Can I help you?" she asked.

And although she clearly didn't know who Adam was, his face still exploded with happiness at the sight of her.

o   o   o

We sat around the small living room balancing little cups of hot cocoa in our laps—Adam, me, and Sage's mom, who introduced herself as "Cherie pronounced Sherry."

"Now," she said in a warm-honey voice, "what did you say you were looking for again?"

"I'm doing research for a paper," I improvised, glancing quickly over at Adam to see if he wanted to add anything, but he was distracted by the chatter from the other room. Sage and Jenny were in the den, watching TV and laughing over something I couldn't hear. "It's an essay on the history of the town."

"I see."

"I heard you were the one to talk to."

Cherie turned to Adam. "Now, you're a little old to be writing a paper?"

Adam came back to the conversation, flustered as he hadn't been listening.

"This is my history teacher," I said, covering for him. "Mr. Martel."

Cherie put her cup and saucer down. "That's nice. None of my teachers ever came with me to do research."

Adam cleared his throat, turning on the charm that always made his eyes glint and that could make certain women not ask too many questions. "Your mother worked at the facility?" Adam stated more than asked. "At the base?"

"And how did you know that?"

"Public records," he said, smiling. "I'd love to hear more about it."

I couldn't tell from the slight smile on Cherie's face if she was believing all of this or not, but she certainly didn't seem to mind the attention. There was no evidence of a man in the house—only women's coats on the rack; only Cherie and Sage in the pictures on the mantel. I had noticed Cherie quickly removing a bandana from her head and combing her hair with her fingers when we walked in. It's strange what women will say when a handsome man is asking the questions.

"My family were Russian Jews. They came here in the twenties, speaking only Yiddish, desperate to escape the ghettos they'd been living in. They were given a new name, one that was supposed to sound American: Wexler. My mother, Golda, was the first person in my family to learn to read and write. She was eighteen when she started working at the facility, and she had no idea what it was she was working on. They had her monitoring these little knobs and gauges, trying to keep them within a certain range. She didn't learn until years later what they were for."

"What were they for?" I asked, swallowing hard as I anticipated the answer.

"Monitoring the enrichment of uranium. We were working on our own atom bomb. They had brought in hundreds of young women who were working day and night, with no idea what they were working on—no idea that when those little gauges started spinning, it was because the uranium was reaching high levels. In fact, my mother was there in November of 1943 when the uranium went critical for the first time—meaning a sustained nuclear reaction. Of course, she didn't know that then. The men in lab coats started running around the facility, cheering and crying, and the women had no idea why. She wouldn't learn the real reason until much later."

I nodded, imagining the room as she described it and remembering from an old physics class how the uranium had probably been shot through a racetrack-shaped series of tubes, magnetized to separate the useless isotopes of the element from the rarer ones that could power a sustained nuclear reaction.

"By early summer of 1945, we were close to finishing the bomb, really close," Cherie continued. "But then . . ." She looked around, into the high-up corners of her living room, then down at the lamps. It was as though she suddenly remembered that someone might be listening, and she corrected her posture and placed her hands on her lap. "Thankfully," she continued, "the Russians beat us to it. The day they announced they had the bomb, the government shut down the facility and sent all the women home."

"When was that?"

"July 16, 1945. Although I'm sure you know that part. 'The date of our great salvation' and all that."

I remembered what Adam had told me on the street: the bomb had been dropped on Hiroshima in August of that year, so the Russians had had the bomb for at least a month by that point.

Whatever Jenny did, she did it before July of 1945.

Adam was momentarily distracted by a fresh wave of laughter from the den, but then he turned back to Cherie. "What happened to your mother after that?"

"She did what all the girls did, I guess. Married the first soldier that stepped off the bus after the Russians dropped the bomb. My sister was born a year later, then three boys—two who lived—and finally me. I always joked that my family came all this way to get away from the Russians, and then they followed them here."

I smiled along with her. Adam had been right—this woman was very nice, but maybe a little too trusting.

"Mom," came a familiar voice from the archway connecting the two rooms. "We're gonna go out," Sage said, nodding over her head to Jenny, who was waving her fingers by her head in an effort to dry what appeared to be fresh red nail polish.

"That's fine, Sage."

"Can I have the car?"

"I need it for work." Cherie smiled at us, embarrassed by the interruption.

"Why do you need to work? They're not even in town."

"Because they'll be back in a few days, and the colonel wants his house dusted."

"Maybe we could do it," offered Jenny between breaths on her nails. "We don't mind cleaning."

I couldn't help but notice Adam turn away and smile at that. Was it some private joke between him and the other Jenny—the one he had known?

"Yeah, you work too hard, Mom," Sage seconded, seeming to get excited about the idea.

Cherie seemed to be considering it, but she obviously knew better than to think this was some altruistic offer. "Not after last time."

"I swear, we'll just clean this time," Sage insisted.

"If one beer bottle is missing from that house, Sage—"

"It won't be, I promise."

Adam seemed to sense an opportunity here, and he stood up, doing his best impression of the responsible adult. "Maybe I could help?" he offered. "What exactly are we doing?"

"We're gonna go clean a house," Jenny said, smiling a bit too enthusiastically. "You guys could come out with us after," she offered, looking at me but clearly meaning Adam.

"Yeah," Sage agreed, smiling maliciously at her friend, "you could meet Jenny's boyfriend, Dave, after."

"Shut up," Jenny whispered, but Sage just laughed.

"We'd be happy to help," Adam agreed, gesturing to me that it was time to go.

"Thank you," I said to Cherie, placing my hot cocoa on the table. Once she had walked over to the girls, I leaned in to Adam. "What are you doing?" I whispered.

"We need more info," he whispered back. "Something specific. Maybe the girls know more."

I gave him a warning look, not wanting to push it since everything we'd told them so far was a lie. But he wasn't interested in my hesitation, pulling me up by the arm and leading me to the door.

We started to walk out with the girls, who grabbed their boots and coats, pulling each other's hair out of the way of their scarves almost like sisters. I had never realized that Sage and Jenny were so close. I'd always thought my mom was the glue that had held all their friendships together. But maybe things were different in this plane.

It was the small things that tended to change from one reality to another.

"Hey, are you Mexican?" Sage asked me, a warm energy radiating off her.

"Half. Why?"

"Mmm. You look like a friend of ours."

"She does, doesn't she?" Jenny whispered to her.

Adam stiffened by my side, eager to change the subject. "Where is the house?" he asked, following Jenny out the door a bit too eagerly.

"Oh, it's wicked, you'll love it," Jenny said, smiling at Adam a beat longer than necessary. "It's got like a million rooms."

"And the best part?" Sage added. "It's shaped just like a pyramid."

CHAPTER TWENTY-SEVEN

"Jesus," Adam whispered through almost closed lips once we were inside the pyramid house. It was the first time I had ever walked through the front door, and I was surprised to find we were in an enormous two-story atrium, complete with twenty-foot-tall trees and ivy dripping from the balconies.

"I told you." Jenny smiled.

"It's fucking *klass*," Sage agreed. "You should check out the upstairs."

But Adam didn't need the invitation. He was already roaming through the entryway and poking his head into one of the rooms. We were on the opposite side of the house from the window we usually crawled through, and I was dying to see the transformation.

"Come on," Jenny offered, while Sage headed for what I could only assume was a laundry room, emerging a second later with a tray of cleaning supplies.

"I'll give you the grand tour," Jenny continued, tugging at my sleeve in a welcoming way.

We headed down the hall to the only room I'd ever seen before, the one Kieren and Brady used to have meetings in. I didn't recognize it at first, as it had been wallpapered to look like an eighteenth-century sitting room. Every surface was covered with something lush and soft, from the tapestries on the wall to the silken bobbles placed delicately on the antique tables. It was tastefully done, despite being so ornate I found myself looking around for Marie Antoinette.

"Who lives here?"

"Some colonel," Jenny answered, and I turned to realize she wasn't looking at the room but at me. "Where do you go to school?"

"Um, it's called St. Joe's. It's private."

"Yeah, I know it."

I smiled, peeking my head into a small door I had always assumed was a closet but that I now saw was a powder room complete with a gold-handled sink. "That's not real gold, is it?"

"I don't know, maybe."

Jenny was still staring at me, thoughts that may have been doubts apparently whirling through her head. It occurred to me that they were awfully trusting to let us come with them to this house. Unless, of course, they had something in mind that I hadn't discovered yet.

"Is that guy really your teacher?"

"Yeah. Mm-hmm."

"You're lucky. My teachers all look like trolls."

Now she picked up a little box from one of the tables and opened it, spinning a little key at the bottom. It was a music box with a mermaid diving in and out of a white-capped wave. A tinny little version of a song from *The Nutcracker* came echoing out of it, until Jenny snapped it shut a moment later.

"And you just wanted to talk to Sage's mom?"

"Yeah. For a paper I'm writing."

There was something suspicious in her tone, and I busied myself flipping open the top cover of a coffee table book on wild horses.

"Cherie's like a second mom to me," Jenny offered. "But she'd believe the sky was purple if a friendly face was the one saying it."

I only smiled in response. "What's upstairs?"

Jenny's face shifted, a smile replacing the questioning look that had been there a moment before. "Come on."

Not surprisingly, the house got narrower as it went up, but the staircase had been strategically placed right in the middle, so it climbed all the way to the attic. The second story was all bedrooms, one more magnificent than the other, with two exquisitely appointed children's rooms on one side.

"Do they have two kids?"

"No, only one. But I guess they figured the other room looked empty without a fancy imported German crib in it."

I smiled and nodded, sensing the resentment beneath Jenny's words. Everything in this house cost more than someone like Cherie would make in a dozen years. So much for the Russian idea of equality for all.

The other side of the hallway had only one bedroom, the master suite, which was roughly half the size of my house. A sea of silk met my eyes, drooping from the bed and the tabletops in gray and pink. I poked my head into the bathroom and found a clawfoot tub surrounded by an endless assortment of pink and golden perfume bottles.

"It's his mistress's room," Jenny offered from the doorway. "His wife stayed behind in Russia." Jenny entered the bathroom and picked up a bottle of perfume almost the size of a toaster, spritzing herself generously. "Her name's Anastasia. She's our age," she whispered to me, a little secret for the two of us to share.

"Holy shit," I heard Adam mutter from upstairs, and I went out into the hallway and looked up the giant stairwell to the landing above, calling out to him.

"What is it?"

"The view!"

I rushed up the extra flight and followed Adam's voice into a room that occupied most of the considerably narrower third floor, with the stairwell passing right through the middle of it. It was clearly the colonel's office, decorated on all four walls with bookcases jammed full of thousands of books, an enormous sepia-toned globe balancing in a golden arch that allowed it to spin all the way around.

The view, as Adam had promised, was spectacular. Our entire town was spread out before me, all the way to a distant lake that I knew was over fifty miles away. The land was quite flat around here, and I had never seen it from an angle like this before. Everything looked to be in miniature, all the little rows of war-era houses and the park where Kieren and Robbie and I used to play when were children, all covered in pristine white snow.

Standing by Adam's side, we stared at it like little kids seeing Santa for the first time. It was just another town from here, another lovely place to grow up. The distance and the snow hid all evidence to the contrary.

"It's wild, isn't it?" Adam said softly.

"Looks so innocent from here," I whispered back.

But then Adam nodded to his right, tugging gently on my sleeve, and my eyes followed his lead until I saw what he was looking at.

Even from this distance, the Good Citizen Academy was an ugly blot on the land. Occupying the greatest chunk of terrain, it marred the otherwise lovely view like an oil slick, surrounded by razor-wired chain-link fences and those few trees that I now knew would soon be replaced by guard towers.

It was clear that parts of the building that were no longer used in our reality—the ones that had been part of the abandoned military fort—were very much in use in this one. Ominous spirals of dark smoke rose from the chimneys, invading the otherwise opaque air above the building.

"You all right?" he whispered to me.

"Yeah, I'm thinking about what Cherie said, about the reactor going critical. When did she say that was? November of '43?"

"Mmm. Why?"

I shook my head, trying to piece it all together. "I'm just thinking, that's all." After a minute, another question occurred to me. "What's the farthest you've gone back?"

"What do you mean?" he asked, sneaking a look over his shoulder to make sure we were alone. "Like, in time?"

"Yeah."

He laughed. "Tried to go to Woodstock once. It was wet and miserable. I left after fifteen minutes."

"And you call yourself a rebel," I joked, pleased to see that I'd made the tops of his ears turn red.

"Why do you ask?"

"Because I'm just wondering how far back a person *can* go. Sage told me once that the nuclear reaction was what made the portals possible. I wonder if it started that first time the reactor went critical. November of '43. All those scientists in lab coats running around and cheering about the plutonium they'd made, and they had no idea what they'd really done."

We stood in silence for a moment, watching the tendrils of smoke escape the building in the distance like steam from a cauldron.

Adam put a hand on my shoulder and said something very softly about how it would all be all right.

Jenny cleared her throat behind us, and we both turned to look at her. "What are you two whispering about?"

I stepped away from Adam, scratching my head. My empty stomach growled suddenly, and Adam chuckled under his breath. "Hey, um, do you think there's any food here?"

Jenny smiled, her body twisting a bit as she thought about it. She really was very pretty, and I was starting to see why Adam had fallen so hard for her when he'd first met her. "Hey, Sage," she called down the stairwell.

"Yeah?" came the echoing response.

"We're going to raid the fridge!"

The kitchen, once we got down to it, put all the other rooms to shame. It took up half of the back of the house, with enormous panes of glass taking the place of the entire back wall, angled and cut perfectly to fit into the pyramid shape. The room flooded with golden streams of sunlight that filtered through the giant elms outside, their long branches tickling the tips of neatly arrayed rosebushes.

Every surface was glistening, and I could imagine the long hours Cherie must have spent meticulously polishing the stainless-steel refrigerator and dishwasher, scrubbing the grout between the floor tiles until it matched the unblemished virgin white of the tiles themselves. A shelf over the oven overflowed with loaves of fresh bread and bottles of herbs.

While Adam and I stood and gaped at it all, Jenny opened the double-wide fridge to reveal a bounty of every color imaginable: red apples and green lettuce, jars of pickles and olives, a platter of cold cuts with freshly shaved prosciutto and salami, a jar of bloodred beets, and, on the top shelf, an entire chocolate cake decorated with little yellow flowers and pink buds.

"Are they having a party?" I asked.

"No," Sage laughed, coming fully into the room with a bottle of window cleaner still in her hand, "this is just the way they keep it, in case they decide to come home early. If they don't, Mom and I get to take it all."

I held back, hesitant to touch anything in case we were discovered and remembering what Cherie had said about the missing beer from last time.

But Sage didn't seem to share my concern. "Honestly, help yourselves. They called this morning and said they won't be back for several days. I was gonna take it home anyway."

I looked at Adam for encouragement, and I could see him practically salivating. We'd had nothing to eat but that Danish and stale French fries since yesterday.

Before we could second-guess ourselves, Adam and I rushed the fridge and started grabbing everything we could reach with an insatiable hunger. He piled what must have been twelve pieces of salami onto a huge chunk of the fresh bread while I pried one of the jars open and started popping blue-cheese-stuffed olives into my mouth. It tasted so good I started laughing. I don't think I'd ever been so hungry.

I rolled up thick slices of cheddar and Munster from the cheese platter and gobbled them up in two bites. When I was done, I grabbed a nearby butcher knife and brought the cake to the counter, where I hacked off a huge slice.

Jenny and Sage were sitting at the kitchen table, giggling as they watched us eat and helping themselves to a canister of cookies with a Russian label on it.

I wolfed down a huge bite of the cake, its gooey goodness landing on my tongue with the perfect amount of sweetness. Meanwhile, Adam finished his sandwich and started making himself another.

"This is the best cake I've ever had," I said through chocolatey bites.

"I could eat eight of these sandwiches," he returned.

"I'm sticking with the cake."

"All right," he said, smiling and putting his sandwich down, "let me try."

I hacked off another slice, and he came up and grabbed it from the platter with his bare hands. "Oh my God," he laughed, stuffing his face with it.

"I told you."

"I'm gonna eat that whole thing."

"Careful, Adam, there are calories in that."

"I don't care!" he joked, chocolate landing on his cheek as he took another bite. I pointed it out to him, but he missed it when he tried to wipe it off with his hand, so I had to get it for him with the back of my sleeve.

We looked up from our feast just long enough to realize that Sage and Jenny were no longer talking but instead staring at us with knowing looks on their faces. I cleared my throat and started to put the cake away, silently chastising myself for letting my guard down.

This house was messing with me—everything was so nice and clean and pretty. An Eden on Earth, paid for by the work of those children at the train station who had no shoes. I had to remind myself where all this luxury was heading, what kind of waste this self-indulgence would eventually beget.

And I had to be careful to stop calling Adam by his name in front of others.

"Thank you for the food," Adam said over his shoulder as he wrapped up the bread and put the rest of it back on the shelf.

"No problem," Sage said, her warm voice sounding almost eerily like her adult self, despite the youth of this version. It was hard to reconcile what she looked like now—young and happy, maybe thirty pounds lighter—with the Portland version she would eventually become.

The two different adult Sages I had met floated before my eyes like constellations—one happy, one miserable. In this timeline, the one standing in the kitchen with me would become the latter. If I warned her now, would she even believe me?

But before I could take that line of thought much further, a thumping sound outside and the front door opening and closing told me someone else was joining our party.

Adam and I froze with fear, but the girls both stood, excited suddenly.

"They're here," Jenny said, and she and Sage ran for the front door. Adam put a protective hand on my back. I wasn't sure why, as I had no idea who "they" were. But maybe Adam had intuited it.

Because when we stepped into the atrium, we were confronted with a whole gang of visitors, all fresh-faced and seventeen years old: John, Dave, and George entered first, followed by my mother, looking for all the world like my clone.

We stared at each other through the warped mirror of time, and an ominous silence fell over the crowd.

"It's wild, isn't it?" Jenny asked. "You two could be sisters."

CHAPTER TWENTY-EIGHT

"*Bozhe moy*," my mom said after a beat. "You look exactly like my abuela."

"Really?" I couldn't help but ask, imagining the great-grandmother in Mexico I had never gotten a chance to meet. I was torn between wanting to stare at my mother and not being able to look at her. It was too surreal, and even the part of my brain that had become used to such things simply couldn't handle this level of absurdity.

The strangest part of it all was that I was mad at the girl standing in front of me. Or maybe I was just mad at the woman she would become. This version of my mom would never marry my dad. She would never have me. Instead, she would stay with John, who stood nearby giving off a distinctly menacing aura. She would become something ugly and cruel. And here she was, standing not two feet away, looking at me like I was a stranger. It seemed like, on some level, she should sense her connection to me, like she should embrace me. And yet no warmth seemed to radiate from those deep brown eyes.

After all this time, after the year and a half I'd spent in purgatory without my friends, seeing this teenage version of her, completely indifferent to me, was the moment that hurt worst of all.

It was John who broke up the awkward moment by entering the room more fully. At seventeen, he already exuded some of the alpha male swagger that had made all the girls follow him. It was some sort of pheromone he was giving off. Adam had the same thing, I now realized, and I wondered if they had gotten along when Adam first went down and met Jenny. After all, a pack can only have one alpha.

"Who are *they*?" John asked Sage, eyeing Adam.

"They're nice," Jenny said before Sage could speak, taking a step closer to me. "They came to Cherie's house, and they're spending the day with us."

"Why?" John asked.

"Why do you think?"

"Hey, Jugs, you don't make the decisions here."

"Don't call her Jugs," Dave insisted. It was the first time I'd ever heard him speak. He pushed John aside and walked up to put his arm around Jenny.

"You can be such an asshole," Jenny said, her eyes not wavering from John.

"Enough," my mother said, and I was impressed with the way everyone, even John, seemed to obey her by shutting up. Sage had told me once that my mother was the real brains behind this operation; she had been the one to put the signs on the portal doors, the one who had figured out where to get the pink goop that had created the portals in the first place.

She walked up to me now. "What's your name?"

"Mara." I repeated the lie I had told Cherie back at the house, having decided when we first got here not to use my real name. I wasn't sure why; maybe it was just because I didn't want to give too much of myself away. My real name was the only thing I could still say I owned.

"And who's he?" my mother continued, nodding slightly towards Adam but still looking at me.

"He's her history teacher," Jenny answered for me, but there was something in her tone that told me she was messing with me somehow, that Adam and I hadn't fooled her for a second.

"John," my mother finally said, turning to her boyfriend, "what do you think?"

"I think," John began, seeming bored with this whole conversation and ready to leave the atrium where we all still stood like tin soldiers, "that we should see if there's any beer in the fridge."

"Hell, yeah," Dave agreed, following John towards the kitchen.

Adam eyed me with a cautious expression before falling in with the crowd. But before I could do the same, Jenny pulled me aside. "Just so you know," she whispered, "St. Joe's closed down eight years ago. You should come up with another story."

I swallowed hard before I could reply. "If you knew," I whispered back, "why are you trusting us?"

"Because your boyfriend's really hot."

"He's not my—"

"Shh." She stopped me with a finger to my lips. "This is the fun part."

o o o

The sun had begun to set behind those towering elm trees, casting the kitchen in abnormally long shadows and making the people who had been partaking in the beer seem even drunker than they were. That group involved everyone but Adam, who had refused politely with a sly smile on his face when offered a beer by an underage kid, and me, because I hated the taste of beer.

With the impending night, everyone seemed to be getting a second wind.

"It'll be dark soon," my mother said to John, and something in her tone informed me that they had been waiting for this part of the day; the beer and the hanging out at the pyramid house were just time-killers. But until what?

"Mmm," John replied, polishing off the last of his drink and dropping the bottle onto the table next to the two he'd already finished.

"You're going to have to pay for those beers, John," Jenny teased him.

But John just smiled a huge joker smile back. "I'll steal you some more, Jugs."

Jenny glared at him in response, but this time, Dave was too drunk to come to her defense.

"Why do you keep calling her that?" Adam asked. I knew him well enough by now to understand when he was about to pop. He'd been careful to keep his distance from Jenny all day, especially after Dave showed up. But one more inappropriate comment from John and this was going to end the way Adam solved most of his problems: with a fight.

"'Cause she looks like a pinup girl," John said, laughing.

"Stop it," Jenny whispered, her cheeks reddening with embarrassment.

"It's a good thing," John insisted.

"We should go," my mother interjected, once again stopping

213

the conversation dead. She had other things on her mind than retreading already tired ground. "Before it's too late."

"Agreed," said Dave, finally roused by something after being completely checked out while his girlfriend was being insulted.

Sage finished up her beer and dropped it down next to John's, letting out an enormous belch that temporarily distracted everyone into a gale of laughter.

It was George who stood up first. He'd been drinking too, but he didn't seem drunk. And he hadn't said a word all day, although I had noticed him watching Sage the same way I kept catching Adam looking at Jenny. "She's right. It's getting late."

The others moaned various forms of agreement, and slowly the party began rising from the kitchen chairs and cushions and making their way towards the powder room and the front atrium, eventually blobbing back together by the front door.

"Well, come on, you two," Jenny said before leaving the kitchen after noticing that Adam and I hadn't moved, not sure if we were invited.

"Not them," John insisted, lingering with a suspicious gaze towards Adam in the doorway.

"Come on, it'll be more fun that way," Jenny insisted.

Dave settled the matter by popping up next to John, his coat now in hand. "Jenny, let's go."

Adam motioned to me that we should follow, and, not knowing what else to do, I stood and headed for the atrium.

"Here, you two can wear these," Jenny said once we got there, pulling two coats—fur for me and leather for Adam—from the front closet.

"Is this real?" I asked Jenny, weighing my disgust at wearing a dead animal against my desire to not freeze to death.

"It's already dead, honey," Jenny said, smiling, "you might as well wear it."

We piled into a couple of different cars once we were outside. Adam and I shoved into the back of Cherie's Honda next to George, with Jenny and Sage in the front, and the others all hopped in John's truck.

I took advantage of the blaring radio and the fact that George seemed lost in his own thoughts, staring out the window, to whisper in Adam's ear.

"Adam, they're onto us. We should lose them."

"Not yet. She likes you," he whispered back, nodding towards Jenny in the front. "Talk to her more, try to get her to open up."

"She doesn't like me, she likes you. That's why she's being nice. I know you miss her, but we don't have time for this."

"Miss her?" he said a bit louder, pulling away to look me in the eye. As he glanced at Jenny, who was talking about some homework assignment with Sage, his face hardened and his jaw muscles clenched. "I told you. I don't want anything to do with her now. I'm here for George and Sage. That's it."

I sat silently beside him for a moment, feeling the weight of his words like an anchor around my neck. The pain he was hiding was palpable, and I wanted desperately to tell him that I understood. But of course, he already knew that I did.

Giving in to an impulse that I didn't want to give too much thought to, I took hold of Adam's hand, and I was relieved when he squeezed mine back.

A moment later, we both let go as the cars pulled up to their destination.

This was it, what Sage had told me about once. Their preportal ritual, the one that made their escapades into the other worlds feel more like a rite of passage instead of what they really were: a trespass.

There was nothing to do but get out of the car. We were at the old grounds.

CHAPTER TWENTY-NINE

"Well, come on then," John called to me when he saw me hanging back in the car. "This is what you came for, right?"

Adam had already gotten out, walking towards the center of the abandoned structures next to Sage and Jenny. I struggled to make out the outline of what the place had looked like when I'd been here last. The fun house where Sage and John had been drinking their coffee was now just a shack with a bunch of cracked mirrors nailed to the surface, reflecting pops of color as we all gathered in front of it.

Nothing else was recognizable at all. Half the small buildings were missing parts of their roofs; inside a nearby shack, I could make out the corner of a soiled mattress. Graffiti on the wall was full of sloppily written expletives naming some of the activities that had happened there.

My stomach turned as I looked at it, a feeling overwhelming me that, just by being here, I was somehow complicit in something sleazy and immoral.

The group of friends had gathered in a circle right in the middle of the clearing that formed the center of these ramshackle buildings. They all took hands, and I looked to Adam for some clue as to how I was supposed to behave.

"If you're here, then be here," my mother suddenly demanded. "You came all this way—"

"Rain," Sage admonished her.

"What? Let's be honest, shall we?" She turned to me, her cold eyes bearing only the slightest resemblance to the ones I had once loved more than anything. When had I last seen love in those eyes?

You are my warrior.

"You came here to see what it's like, right?" she teased, her gaze unrelenting. "Everybody wants to know what it's like. So come have a taste."

"I told you," I protested weakly, "I'm just writing a paper."

John laughed to himself, and the girls all followed suit. Even George sighed, tired of all the pretense. "You think you're the first ones to try this?" John demanded. "Kids show up here all the time. They come in on the train, or they hitchhike. They heard a rumor somewhere. Someone in their school had a story. Although I will say," he laughed, looking at Adam, "this is the first time I've ever heard the 'he's my teacher' line. You like 'em young, huh, dude?"

Adam clenched his jaw, and I could see the fire burning in his eyes. If John said one more thing, this whole experiment could explode before we learned anything useful.

"You're right," I blurted out, trying to defuse the tension. "You caught us. Sorry. Didn't mean to lie. We were just curious. Weren't we, Adam?"

His mouth twitched with a burst of anger, but then he looked at me, and I smiled, trying to get his eyes to soften. After a moment, they did, and he nodded to me with a kind of apologetic shrug.

"We shouldn't have lied," Adam said. "She's not writing a paper. We came to learn what you know. We won't tell anyone."

"Damn right you won't," John countered.

"Can we get started?" Jenny asked no one in particular. "It's cold, and I want to get there."

Sage cleared her throat, and everybody took hands. She waited a moment for Adam and me to catch up. I entered the circle and held George's hand on my left and Jenny's on my right.

"We bless our journey," Sage began, her head lowered and her voice solemn, "that we may be safe on the other side, that we may become enlightened in our travels . . . and that we don't get caught."

"So say us all," everyone said in unison, except Adam and me.

"All right." My mother broke away from the group. "The clothes are in the truck. I'll get them."

"Whose turn is it?" Jenny asked.

"Mine," she called back as she walked to the car, "and John's."

"It was your turn last time!"

"We didn't get to finish," John answered for my mother as she crawled into the back of John's truck, retrieving something.

"How is that fair?" Jenny asked. "Dave, say something."

"What do you want me to say?" Dave asked.

"I don't know, maybe grow a pair and stand up for us!"

A chorus of "Ooohs" escaped the others' throats as my mother came back with what appeared to be two Russian guard uniforms dangling from hangers, complete with crisp little caps.

"Don't worry, Jugs, I'll take you down next time," John teased, grabbing the jacket that my mother tossed him and swapping it for his winter coat.

Jenny looked to Dave for support, but he had tuned her out

again, rubbing his chilled hands and talking with George.

"Why do you need the uniforms?" I asked my mother, feeling braver now that they had already shown us so much.

She was stepping into the guard's pants over her leggings, and she looked up to smile at me. "Aren't you the curious one?"

"How do you think we get in?" John asked. "It's a military fort."

"Through the high school?" I asked, feeling that somehow they were all just laughing at me, that this was part of the fun for them—stringing us along as some sort of twisted game. Like any drug, you can get numb to the portals after a while, so the stakes must always be raised.

"Come on," my mother offered, "we'll show you."

We piled back into the cars and drove to a place just a few minutes from the school, then pulled over to the side of the road. When we all got out, my mother and John had completed their transformation into young Russian guards. With her hair pulled tightly back under the cap and the jacket buttoned to her neck, she looked eerily like the adult version of herself who ruled over this world twenty years in the future.

The drawing wasn't completed, but the outline was there.

"We go in two at a time," my mother informed me as I stood, cold and obviously confused, at the lip of the woods near the Good Citizen Academy. "The school part is guarded at night, but the fort has deliveries at all hours. Most of the soldiers are about our age anyway. You just need the right paperwork."

"Why keep the fort connected to the school at all?" I wondered out loud. "You'd think they'd just build a new school somewhere."

"Are you kidding?" my mother asked, condescension dripping from her voice. "This is the perfect arrangement for them. The Russians ship their new curriculums directly to the fort. With the buildings connected, it's a one-stop shop to filter their propaganda into the school. We're sitting ducks in there, waiting to be spoon-fed whatever they're serving."

John came up and took my mother's hand, tugging her along. "Rain, let's do it."

"Now, that's all you're gonna see tonight." My mother smiled, tipping her cap in my direction. "Hope you had enough of a thrill."

"I still say it's our turn," Jenny protested.

But John just laughed at her, and for some reason—maybe because he knew he could get the reaction he craved there—he turned to Adam. "It's hot when they're so anxious, isn't it?"

I had to grab Adam's arm to keep him from lunging at John. But that just made John laugh even more as he and my mother walked towards the imposing lights of the fort. He made it a few steps before turning back to face Adam, dying to get one more jab in. "You're a slave up here, my friend. They own you up here. But down there," he said, nodding over his shoulder to the buildings and the portals they contained, "down there, we take what we want. Down there, I'm a king."

Adam's muscles clenched even tighter under my hand, and it was all I could do to restrain him.

"Get yourself home now," John teased before turning and taking my mother's hand. I stood by Adam's side, watching them walk away until they turned the bend.

Adam jerked his arm away from me with a ferocity that made my bones rattle. He paced away a bit, collecting his breath.

Sage turned to me, a softness in her expression. "Sorry about John."

I could only shake my head, not sure what to say.

Jenny was still irate as well, turning on Dave. "You never defend me!" she shouted. "He says whatever he wants to me, and you never do anything about it!"

"Well, what do you want me to say, Jenny?"

"He's basically calling me a whore!"

But Dave just shrugged in response. "Is he wrong?"

"Screw you!" she screamed, hitting his arm.

"No, screw you. I'm outta here." And with that, Dave stormed off, leaving Jenny fuming behind him, breathing heavily and pulling at her hair.

Sage actually yawned at this point, and it was pretty obvious that this was not an atypical way for one of these evenings to end. Then Sage turned to me.

"Listen," she whispered, "do you have a place to stay tonight?"

I looked into her generous face, an urge to lie coming over me. But to what end? "No," I admitted.

She sighed, shaking her head to herself. "Okay," she mumbled, taking out her mother's keys to the pyramid house. "Don't make me regret this."

Adam came back up now, having cooled himself down.

"Just leave it exactly the way you found it, okay? And you have to be out by morning."

"Of course, I promise."

"George?" She turned to her friend. "Will you give them a ride and then bring my car back? Jenny and I are going to walk home."

"Yeah, you got it," he said, nodding. It occurred to me that he and Sage probably had the purest friendship in the whole group, and I was glad that, at the very least, they remained close well into adulthood. That was why George had let himself be trapped under the lake, after all. To keep an eye on Sage. I had to wonder if I would do the same if a friend needed me.

"Actually," Adam interjected, "you can just take her, George." He nodded towards me, not even saying my name. "I'm gonna walk the girls home."

222

The look I gave Adam must have revealed how I felt about this arrangement. After all that, he was going to leave me so he could take Jenny home? What happened to "I don't want anything to do with her"?

George looked to Jenny to make sure it was okay with her, but she was already eyeing Adam with a coquettish grin. Before I could protest, Adam had already walked off with Jenny and Sage, his hand on Jenny's back.

I looked at George, who offered me the most pathetic of shrugs.

CHAPTER THIRTY

Once in the house, I busied myself with something I'd been dying to do for two days: namely, wash everything. I headed up to Anastasia's bathroom, peeled off the clothes that had become like a filthy second skin, and slipped into the luxuriously soft kimono-style robe she had hanging on the door. I found a better hiding place for Sage's ring in a deep pocket of the backpack, then ran all my clothes down to the all-in-one washer/dryer in the laundry room.

Adam wasn't back yet, but I told myself I didn't care.

Back upstairs, I ran the water in that huge bathtub until it reached the proper temperature of burn-my-skin-off hot and searched Anastasia's chest of drawers for something to change into after.

Everything she owned was preposterously girlie—lots of silk nighties and imported lingerie with European labels, not a T-shirt or a pair of sweatpants to be found. I laid out the only pajamas I could find that at least had pants instead of bootie shorts, then headed back into the bathroom and let the steam from the water finally warm me up as I sat on the edge of the tub waiting for it to fill.

I felt like I'd been lost a snowdrift for days, constantly chilled to the bone and without any real sense of direction. The only thing that had been keeping me anchored was knowing that Adam was with me, that if nothing else, I had an accomplice in all this mess.

Now my eyes wandered to the delicate gold clock on the wall above the tub. It was almost midnight. I was ashamed to admit to myself that I was scared here without him. What if he didn't come back? Was I strong enough to finish this mission on my own? If I went home now, gave up on finding the adult Jenny, could I really live with myself?

I slipped into that cauldron-like tub, trying to clear my mind of everything but how good it felt to be immersed in heat, to let my muscles finally relax. My half-opened eyes fell on a bronze bottle of Anastasia's perfume. What must it be like to be her, I wondered. Surrounded by every luxury, a seventeen-year-old mistress in a fantasy house.

Twisting off the cork-style top of the bottle, I was struck by how delicate the rosy scent of the perfume was, how it transported me somehow to a place I couldn't identify at first. But once I had poured a few drops onto my wrists, the memory came charging back at me.

My mother. She used to wear this perfume when I was very little. Maybe it was something that had been in vogue in the early 2000s. Maybe all the girls wore it.

Maybe she had stolen it in DW, from a house very much like this one.

I poured a generous amount into the hot water, letting the sweet smell of it drown me completely. Then I closed my eyes and tried to imagine that the hot water was Brady's hands, that in front of me his beautiful brown eyes were floating, full of that warm connection I had been so desperate to feel for so long.

But then I opened my eyes, ashamed at the vision that had usurped my thoughts. Because the eyes I was imagining weren't brown.

They were green.

o   o   o

It was the crashing sound that woke me up, followed by annoyed cursing. I rolled over in the silken sheets, almost slip-sliding out of the bed as Anastasia's camisole top was made of the same material. The clock on the bedside table informed me it was 1:00 a.m.

Groggy and a bit disoriented, I headed downstairs. My clothes were still in the dryer, and my arms instinctively crossed over my chest as I got closer to the source of the sound.

Even in the dim light of the elaborately decorated sitting room, I could immediately make out that the liquor cabinet was open. A slumped figure that I recognized as Adam sat on one of those upholstered love seats that cost more than a car, a bottle of what I assumed was vodka clenched in his fist.

"What are you doing?" I asked, turning on a light, which made him flinch and glare at me.

"Drinking."

"Why?"

"To get drunk."

I watched him for a moment, knowing that if I had half a brain

I would just let him be. But I couldn't leave. He had knocked over some of the trinkets on a nearby table, and, not knowing what else to do with my hands, I walked up and started straightening them.

"Can you not do that?" he asked in a small voice through clenched teeth.

"She said to leave it the way we found it."

I tried to remember where everything had been sitting before, re-creating it as best I could. I balanced the mermaid box in my hands, not sure where to place it, and I looked up to see Adam staring at me through angry and distant eyes. "Why do you smell like a whorehouse?"

A deep flush of embarrassment came over me. I swallowed down the painful effect of his words, trying to calm myself. "It's that girl's perfume. I put it in the bath."

"Don't use her stuff, Marina."

"Don't worry, she won't know it's missing."

"That's not what I mean. I don't like the smell."

"Well, don't smell me then!" I turned to go, but I was stopped by a crashing sound. Adam had knocked over a lamp, whether intentionally or not I wasn't sure. It clattered to the floor. I heard him groan to himself, picking it back up, and once he had it teetering upright on the table, his body tensed up again, and he took another drink.

"Are you going to tell me what happened?" I asked, trying to soften my tone enough for him to trust me.

"Nothing happened."

"Well, did Jenny tell you anything?"

"No." He wasn't looking at me but down at the bottle in his hands.

"Did you . . ." I couldn't finish the question, both because the answer was none of my business and because I didn't want to know.

"Did I what?"

"Did you two . . ." I let the words hang there, swallowing down anything else that I was thinking.

Adam stared at me now, a sly smirk on his face and something that I could only read as resentment in his eyes. "Dave came groveling back, she let him in, I walked back here. Happy?"

"Oh." I didn't know where to go, and I was suddenly aware of how ridiculous I must look, wearing Anastasia's silk pajamas, planted like a lighthouse in the middle of this obnoxiously expensive room.

"I honestly don't care," he insisted. "She's just some stupid fucking kid who thinks everything is a game."

I couldn't help but feel that he was no longer talking about Jenny, and I flinched with wounded pride. "Wow, you're even meaner drunk than you are sober, you know that?"

"Go home then."

"I wish I could," I insisted. "You didn't see what happened last time this world leaked into ours because you were too busy chasing after your precious Jenny. I won't let that happen again."

"Are you really accusing me? After everything you've done to me? I was right about you the first time, Marina. You're as selfish as your mother."

Before I could control my rage, I hurled the music box at his head, but even in his drunken state his reflexes were good enough to dodge it. It smashed against a wall and let out a few strained notes of tinny music, the mermaid suspended in middive, before it came to a stop.

"I am doing everything I can think of to help you!" I screamed once it stopped. "Why do you think I'm here?"

"I don't know!" he yelled back, the vodka swishing around in the bottle as he raised his arm in anger. "But I'm starting to wish to God I'd never let you come."

"You didn't *let* me do anything, Adam. I've never asked you for anything, least of all permission!"

"You asked me not to go back to the Portland beach."

"How dare you hold that over me? I told you why!"

"And so I haven't."

"Just admit that the only reason you want to is to see your own perfect little Jenny again. You said you were done with her."

"I am!" He turned and kicked the table I had just straightened up, knocking everything to the floor.

I could feel myself getting angrier and angrier. I knew he was drunk, but it was no excuse. "You think you're the only one who's had to look into the eyes of someone you loved more than anything and see a blank stare coming back at you?"

"Try doing it for six more years and see how it feels then," he returned, a bitter sarcasm working its way into his already hostile tone. "Do you know how many Jennys I've met? Do you know?"

"No, I don't. You never told me that—"

"Hundreds," he spat at me, raising the bottle to his lips but exploding with another thought before it could get there. "Hundreds of times I've looked into those eyes and seen a stranger." He started pacing a bit but then, realizing that he had nowhere to go, returned to where he'd just been. "She was all I had."

"I know that."

"I don't care what you know!" His voice came out anguished and pinched. "I'm alone!"

Despite my anger, the voice in my head couldn't help acknowledging that he was really crying out for help. I was furious at him for taking it out on me, but I couldn't pretend not to understand. How many times in the last year and a half had I wanted to throw a television set through the window? How many times had I cried myself to sleep? I measured my voice carefully, keeping it as calm as possible. "I'm alone too."

He laughed now, shaking his head, the bottle dangling precariously from his fingers. "What about all your boyfriends?"

"Which one?" I asked, laughing myself at how ridiculous it all was. "Kieren, who dumped me because it hurt too much to look at me? Or Brady, who I can't remember dating?"

He took a drink, closing his eyes and letting the alcohol seep down his throat.

"I am completely out of sync with my whole life," I reminded him, "and there's no way to fix it."

But he wasn't done feeling sorry for himself, waving away my words with a dismissive hand. "At least you have a life."

"What do you want, Adam?"

"I want . . ." He hesitated, looking around restlessly. "I want someone to look at me and actually know who the hell I am."

"Well, congratulations, you found her."

He looked up at me now, his shoulders slumping and a desperate emotion coming into his eyes. It hurt to even look at the rawness in his expression. There was no wall between us now, maybe for the first time.

I had spent so many months wanting to be in the same exact place as another person, an honest and exposed place where I didn't have to remember which of my myriad lies I was supposed to recite.

Now that I was here, I trembled to the bone, more afraid than I'd been since the day I'd heard that my brother had died. It was all too real now. There was no escaping what was passing between us. We really were the only two people on the planet who could understand what we were going through, what we were fighting for. The weight of it was suddenly oppressive.

I couldn't help but break away, turning my attention to the bottle in his hand. "This isn't helping things," I insisted, walking up to him and snatching the bottle away before he could protest.

"Give that back, M."

"No. You've had enough."

"I said give it back."

"And I said no," I said over my shoulder as I went to put it back in its cabinet.

Before I knew it, he had rushed up behind me and was reaching around my side to grab the bottle back out of my hand. I held it up as high as I could, a ridiculous and futile gesture as Adam was probably six inches taller than me. His fingers worked their way up my arm, but I stubbornly refused to lower it.

It took a moment for it to sink in that he wasn't really reaching for the bottle anymore, which he could easily have retrieved at that point. He was just holding me from behind, his body curled around mine like a mollusk's shell.

His other arm came around my waist, and I held still for fear of losing his touch, just feeling his strong stomach pressed against my back and his warm breath blanketing my neck. He let out a choking sob, his embrace turning more desperate with each passing second, the desperation morphing into something more primal.

When his fingers grazed my hips, I knew I was done for. I forgot to be angry or scared or anything at all. My body grew weak in his arms, the vodka bottle slipping out of my grasp and crashing to the ground, its contents gurgling out and soaking my feet.

Finally, I couldn't take it anymore, and I turned around to face him.

I don't know if I leaned in first or if he did, but his mouth was on mine, and every inch of my body was screaming to be even closer to him. Our stomachs seemed to plaster together, our mouths like opposing magnets, inextricably pulled towards each other. I couldn't believe how well we fit.

"We have to stop," he breathed into my cheek, but instantly his mouth was back, his strong lips devouring mine with an untamed hunger.

"I know," I whimpered between kisses.

"I mean it, we have to stop," he repeated, his fingers pressing weakly against my cheek.

"Stop then," I offered, though I made no effort to follow through.

He shoved himself away from me, his strength too much for what little power I still held in my weak knees. I wobbled before him, utterly defeated, my wet lips open in a desperate invitation, pleading with him silently to come back. To give me back the warmth he had ripped away.

He stood a few inches from me, holding his position for seconds longer than I thought I could stand, leaving my whole body alive and stinging, a raw nerve exposed to fresh oxygen. Finally, deliriously, he came flying back into my waiting arms.

Suddenly I was in the air, weightless, as he lifted me up, and my legs wrapped around his firm torso.

"Do you want this?"

"Yes."

"Are you sure?" he whispered, already carrying me towards the staircase that led up to Anastasia's bedroom.

"Yes," I promised, "I'm sure."

Sage had warned me once, back in Portland, that this is what could happen inside the portals. When there are no consequences, you do unspeakable things.

At sixteen, I hadn't really understood what she meant. But I understood it now.

Adam's mouth on mine, my hands in his hair, my legs wrapped

tightly around him as he carried me up the stairs, and the sweet, dense musk of another girl's perfume radiating off my overheated skin.

I knew the shame would come crashing down in the morning. I knew I should be thinking of Brady, but all I could think about was this moment and how good it felt to be carried like that, to have Adam's strong arms under my legs, holding me up.

Down here, we take what we want.

Down World makes monsters of us all.

PART THREE

CHAPTER THIRTY-ONE

The snow fell lightly outside of Anastasia's bedroom window, illuminated in the stark winter air by the soft light of a full moon. Unable to sleep, I simply lay in the bed and watched it trickle down from above, dancing silently past on its way to the ground, burying the world in white.

Adam spooned behind me, encasing me like a suit of armor, his left arm nuzzled under my pillow, his wrist lying on the purple-tinged sheets beside mine, our scars stacked side by side like dominoes. Ready to fall.

"What are you thinking about?" he whispered.

"That if we succeed in erasing this timeline," I answered, my voice coming out soft and distant, "we'll be the only two people left in the world with these scars."

His right hand came over my body, grazing my waist and working its way slowly down my arm. His fingers passed over his own weathered scars and landed gently on mine, freshly healing now, the scabs bright red in the soft light. He kissed my temple as his hand traveled on, landing in my own. Our fingers intertwined, our bodies warm in their perfectly formed half-moon.

"I should go," he said in my ear, starting to pull away from me.

But I pulled him back, clutching his hand even tighter. "Not yet," I insisted. "Just give me tonight. We can hate ourselves in the morning."

He hesitated only a moment, then clung on to me even tighter. So tight I couldn't tell where his body ended and mine began. So tight that, for a moment, we were one.

o o o

"Rise and shine!" Jenny laughed, and I was jolted awake as she tugged the blankets down from around us, plunging our bodies into a shock of cold air. I opened my eyes to see her standing at the foot of the bed in the flat morning light, next to Sage, who looked embarrassed to be there. "I told you so," Jenny whispered to her friend.

Adam, coming to consciousness in a heartbeat, yanked the sheets back and covered me with them. "Get out of here," he said in a forceful tone that sent chills down my back.

"Oh, we're just teasing," Jenny continued, not seeming to understand that Adam was only going to get angrier the longer she stayed.

"I swear to God—"

"It's okay," Sage said, "we'll meet you downstairs. Sorry we burst in."

A rush of humiliation overcame me as I fully woke up and took stock of the situation. There was no undoing this. We'd been caught. What the hell were we going to do now? I buried my face under the covers, the harsh daylight too cruel to face.

"We're taking you to breakfast," Jenny said as they headed out the door, in a voice that was a little too happy with itself. "Why don't you two get cleaned up first?"

"Jenny, give it a rest," Sage scolded under her breath as the two of them finally left the room.

Adam ripped his body away from me and started putting on the jeans he'd left by the bed, stepping into them while still sitting. Coming back up for air, I reached to place a hand on his back, but he flinched violently at my touch. A small noise escaped my throat, one of surprise and more than a little fear.

But then I saw Adam's broad back deflate with a forced exhale.

"I'm sorry, Adam," I whispered, my hand resting on the bed in a sort of purgatory, halfway to his body.

With what seemed to be great effort, he reached back and took my hand, giving it a peremptory squeeze. "It's not your fault," he said through tight lips. "I'm gonna go find a shower. I'll meet you downstairs."

He zipped out of the room in a flash, leaving a chill like frostbite in his wake.

Wrapped in a sheet, I headed for Anastasia's bathroom and took a long look in the mirror—at my bleary eyes half-shut with sleep and my hair falling in messy waves over my bare shoulders. I didn't even smell right, the faint whiff of last night's perfume intermingling with Adam's skin and my own sweat.

A million emotions flooded over me at the sight of my reflection. I had to admit that the first one was exhilaration. Despite everything, it had been the most beautiful night of my life. And I did feel different, as I'd always known I would, now that it was over.

But then the shame settled in, and I knew in my heart that it would be a constant presence, returning in unrelenting waves for a very long time.

I wasn't ashamed of what Adam and I had done, although I knew most people would feel that I should be. I was ashamed because I had betrayed Brady, who'd done nothing to deserve it. Yes, it was true that I couldn't remember the last few months when we'd begun dating. But that was no excuse.

I remembered Brady. His kindness. His humor. The way he'd looked out for me when we went under the lake together. The way he'd held me as I'd fallen asleep, just a few short days ago. God, was that even possible?

And it was all my fault because I hadn't let him go to Boulder like he'd planned. I'd brought him with me into my new timeline, telling myself that it was to spare him the pain of having Piper leave him.

I was worse than Piper.

You're as selfish as your mother.

Adam really knew where to dig the knife in with that little zinger.

There was a time when all I'd wanted in the world was for Brady to love me. And now that he did, what had I let myself do to him? Even if Adam and I succeeded in this impossible task, even if we found out where the adult Jenny had gone and managed to stop this evil, twisted timeline from ever occurring, it would never erase the knowledge in my head of what I'd done to someone who truly loved me.

There was no fixing this. Not a portal in the world to hide behind.

This one I would have to live with.

I stepped into the shower and washed the last of Anastasia's perfume off my skin.

CHAPTER THIRTY-TWO

We sat in a booth at a restaurant with a 1950s aesthetic, a jukebox in the corner churning out a constant stream of Elvis songs. The air was thick between the four of us, nobody speaking as Jenny and Sage looked over their huge laminated menus. Adam's eyes stared distantly into an abyss of thoughts, the menu untouched before him. He hadn't looked at me once on the way over.

"You two are being really weird," Jenny said out of the blue.

Adam closed his eyes a moment, then opened them onto nothing again.

"Well, I'm having pancakes. Sage?"

"Me too."

I cleared my throat, unable to focus on any of the food options in front of me. I didn't have the stomach to eat anything in any event. Adam's silence stung me across the table like a constant, blaring punishment, telling me over and over again that I was the reason he looked so devastated.

Choking back a weak inhale, I tried to calm my hands from twitching on my lap. Was this the way it was going to be now?

"Jeez." Jenny laughed after another moment of intense silence. "You guys are a barrel of laughs. Was that your first time or something?"

A slight grunt escaped Adam's mouth as he shot up from the table and headed for the bathroom.

Sage sent me a worried look, but Jenny seemed bored with the fact that her little game was falling so flat. She had clearly thought that taking us to breakfast would be a fun way to rub it in our faces that she knew our secret. Turns out, it wasn't so fun after all.

Meanwhile, I tried to think about anything but how I was feeling inside, and yet the tears were forming hot and heavy in my eyes, and it was all I could do to hide them behind a napkin.

"Whatever," Jenny said, dropping her menu. "I'm going to call Dave."

"I should call my mom first," Sage said.

"Well, there's only one phone. You can go after me."

Jenny stood and walked over to a payphone by the front door. I watched her for a minute as she dug some coins out of her pocket, and it occurred to me that this was probably the longest I'd ever gone without looking at my cell phone. It was like I had left one of my limbs behind, but I had been too distracted to notice.

Getting lost in these thoughts helped my breath regulate, and the tears stopped on their own. Still, Sage scooched over and put a comforting hand on my upper arm.

"You all right?"

"Yeah."

I pretended to look back at the menu, just to bury my face for a minute.

"Was it?" she asked gingerly. "Your first time?"

A flood of embarrassment came over me again. I was never comfortable talking about things like that. But I supposed that my face answered the question for me. I nodded slightly.

"Oh," she said warmly. "Are you being careful, sweetie?"

"Yeah," I answered quickly, feeling awkward again. "That girl Anastasia had condoms next to her bed."

Sage smiled. "Well, that's good. But that's not what I meant." She looked up at the bathrooms where Adam had disappeared. "You're a sweet girl. You need to protect yourself . . . in here." She touched her heart lightly.

Her words brought on a fresh onslaught of guilt and shame. "I'm not sweet. I have a boyfriend."

She nodded and looked around for a beat, her eyes landing on Jenny at the payphone. "We all make mistakes."

"Not like this. He won't forgive me."

"How do you know that?"

"Because I wouldn't."

Jenny glanced over at us, lazily swinging the metal cord of the payphone back and forth like a jump rope.

"What should I do, Sage?"

She sighed, a look of regret passing over her face as she watched Jenny. It wasn't until that moment that I remembered what the Sage above the lake had told me once: she'd had an affair with Dave when they were in DW and later confessed it to Jenny. It was the beginning of the end for them, of the innocence they had once had.

From the guilt-ridden look on the face of the girl before me, it was probably safe to assume that the same had happened down here.

"Tell him the truth," she finally suggested. "Everything else just hurts more . . . in the end."

Jenny came galloping back to the table then, seemingly with-out a care in the world, and Sage got up to take her turn at the payphone. Sage hadn't told her about Dave yet, apparently. She was just sitting on the secret, letting it infect everything they did together. Is that why she was counseling me to do the opposite?

I looked at the bathroom door, but Adam wasn't coming out.

"I don't know why everyone's being so dramatic this morning," Jenny said as she plopped into her seat, gulping down a huge swig of orange juice. "Even Dave's being weird. I swear it's the portals. They make people crazy."

"You don't seem crazy," I said, looking at her porcelain-white hand on the glass.

"I just hide it well," she said, laughing. "The River Styx gets to everyone eventually. Messes with your mind, you know. You guys should get out while you can, honestly. You saw how John was last night. He didn't use to be that way. He was nice once. I actually—" She looked around, making sure no one was listening.

"You what?"

"I almost dated him instead of Dave. When we were younger. I'm glad I didn't now. Look how he's become."

I nodded, guarding my own secret thoughts about John and the even more ruthless and cruel man he would eventually devolve into in this timeline.

"I swear, sometimes I wish I could go back to the exact moment the portals were created, you know? And just stop it from happening."

My throat clenched shut when she said that. I could feel the shock seizing my face as her words sunk in. *The moment they were created?*

"Oh, well," she sighed, "I don't think I'd ever actually have the courage. But it's a nice thought. Hey, where's our waitress?"

"Excuse me," I muttered, stumbling away from the table and bee-lining for the front door. I needed some air. I needed to think.

All this time, we'd been trying to figure out when exactly Jenny had gone to—which country, which year. Wasn't it obvious? How could I have missed it? And with that thought, another one fol-lowed—a feeling of wrongness that had been sitting inside of me since we'd arrived here yesterday.

Something was off. Of course, something was always off in DW, that's just the way it was. The bright colors and the still air. But this was different. There was an image in my head that my brain was struggling to catch up with. What was it?

I started walking away from the restaurant, my feet moving on their own towards . . . towards the train station. I'd gone about thirty feet when I made out my name being carried to me on the breeze.

I turned to see Adam running to catch up with me, a relieved look on his face. "Where are you going?" he asked as he reached me.

"What do you care, Adam?"

"Don't do that. Answer me."

"I'm walking."

I turned to keep going, but he ran in front of me, stopping my path with his wide shoulders. He was finally looking at me, which I supposed was some progress.

"You know," I began, "when I said we could hate ourselves in the morning, I didn't mean starting at dawn."

"I know that, I'm sorry."

"Then why are you treating me this way? Do you know how you're making me feel?"

"I'm sorry, Marina, I'm—"

"What?"

"I'm mad at myself, okay?" He ran his fingers through his hair and paced a bit, his face contorting in agony. "I'm furious with myself. I've done some horrible things in the portals, I've done a lot of things I'm not proud of, but . . ."

"But *I'm* the worst?" I nodded, seeing where he was going with this. It only made the pain double to hear him confirm it.

"No." He shook his head, looking even more tortured. "No, sweetheart, it's not your fault. I didn't mean that."

"We both knew what we were doing, Adam. I made my own choice. I don't regret it," I insisted, finding my voice now. "Do you?"

His head fell in utter defeat, and his eyes clenched tightly for a moment before he responded. "Only because you're too young."

"I'm eighteen."

"That's not the point, and you know it."

I watched him grapple with his thoughts, overwhelmed by the feeling that I was destroying lives left and right. First Brady and now, apparently, Adam. "You came in wearing that—whatever that was."

"They were the only pajamas I could find."

"And that perfume."

"What is your obsession with that perfume?" I demanded, growing irritated again.

"Jenny used to wear it."

This new revelation hit me harder than any of the others. So that's why my mother had had it when I was young. She'd gotten it from Jenny. Or maybe it was the other way around. And the smell of it brought him back to—

"So, what?" I asked, swallowing down my hurt. "Were you thinking of her the whole time?"

I had been worried that Brady was using me to replace Piper.

Now it seemed I had walked into the same trap twice.

"No," he insisted. "No, the opposite. The whole time I was walking her home, I was thinking of you."

I sighed in relief, finally feeling like I had him back with me—like he was looking at me and not through me. "I was thinking of you too."

A thin smile cracked his lips, and he relaxed his shoulders enough to open his arms and let me into them. I wrapped myself up in him like a blanket on a cold morning, letting his comforting warmth seep into my skin.

"What do we do now?" I asked.

"We just can't let it happen again."

I closed my eyes, knowing that he was right, of course, but not quite ready to accept it.

"I'm sorry I was so angry," he whispered into the top of my head. "That guy John really got under my skin. He's such an asshole."

"He's my stepfather," I reminded him.

"Oh. Well, then you know."

Still nestled into Adam's arms, I felt relaxed enough to finish the thoughts that had begun when I left the restaurant. Images swirled before me—everything we'd seen here, from the moment we got off the train twenty years in the future. Something wasn't quite right. What was it?

"Adam, did John used to call Jenny 'Jugs' when you knew him before?"

"No, that's new. He's really taking this power trip to a new level here."

I pulled away from Adam, searching his eyes as I tried to put the pieces together. What had John said? *She looks like a pinup girl.*

"Oh my God," I mumbled, walking away from Adam and crossing the street to the dead-end road with the train station on one side of it. He followed behind, unsure of where I was going but obviously realizing I had good reason to be going there.

When we reached the end of the road, however, he saw that I wasn't heading for the train station but across the street. To Groussman's Pharmacy. To the very place we had been standing when we ate that stale Danish and French fries.

My trembling finger pointed at the cause of my discomfort—the image that wouldn't quite settle in my mind. Because there, under the faded letters spelling out DANCE HALL GIRLS, left over from the town's World War II boom, lurked the ever-so-faint relic of a picture: a beautiful blond with bouncing curls. But not the one who had been immortalized there when I was a child.

The girl in the picture was Jenny.

CHAPTER THIRTY-THREE

"When Rain comes home and sees that these are missing," Sage said as she climbed out of my mother's bedroom window, two Russian uniforms draped over her arm, "she'll go ballistic."

"We'll have them back before she gets home," I lied, taking Sage's hand to help her climb out while Adam reached for the uniforms.

After discovering Jenny's portrait on the pharmacy wall, Adam and I had realized that the picture itself could be the token to take us to her. He had carefully chipped off a bit of the painted brick and handed it to me. Now we just needed a way down to the portals. And that meant getting past the guards at the school.

"There's another problem anyway," Sage added now that she was back on her feet, straightening her crumpled pants. She held up the two military IDs she had taken from my mother's drawer. My mother's photograph looked enough like me that I could pass for her. I wasn't the problem.

The problem was Adam.

I held up John's fake ID next to Adam's face, and it was immediately obvious that they weren't the same person. Everything from their coloring to their jawline was different. Adam looked at the picture and frowned.

"We could cut the photo out of the ID Milo made," I suggested.

"It won't look the same."

"Close enough, though?"

Adam shrugged, digging out the paperwork Milo had prepared from his pocket and comparing it to the Russian ID. "It'll have to be."

While Adam got to work peeling back the plastic cover of his ID to remove the photograph, Sage pulled me aside. Her mouth had turned down, and she seemed to be balancing too many thoughts in her head.

"What is it?" I asked softly.

"Are you sure about this? Once you go down . . ."

I stiffened as a military car drove by slowly on the road in front of my mother's house—very slowly. The two men inside were looking around the neighborhood, their jaws stiff under their caps, like they were looking for someone they could mess with. They slowed to a crawl when they saw the three of us standing on the lawn by the side of the house.

Sage waved to them with a sarcastic smile on her face.

One of the men clenched his already stoic face, and then the two of them drove on.

"If you look right at them, they figure you have nothing to hide," she advised.

"Good to know."

Sage looked aimlessly around the street, her body slumping with a weariness that I knew would eventually overtake her in this world. Even at seventeen, life was taking its toll on her. Some people, I figured, never really get a chance to be young.

"Once you go down, you were saying?"

"Yeah." She nodded, looking back at me with a resigned smile. "Once you get a taste, you just want more and more. The best thing to do is never start."

"I understand. But we don't have a choice."

"Everybody has a choice," she countered. "But it seems like you've already made yours."

I glanced over at Adam, who nodded to me that the photograph was fitting in well enough. Then I turned back to Sage, giving her a warm hug. "Thank you, Sage. For everything."

o   o   o

I rubbed my thumb somewhat neurotically over the rough nugget of brick that Adam and I had chipped off Jenny's painting—a bit with a swirl of golden hair—which I now kept in my uniform pants pocket.

We were standing at the edge of the woods by the school, exactly where we had been the night before, and Adam was finishing shoveling the dirt back over the hole in the ground where we had buried our backpacks. I twirled Sage's grandmother's ring, which was back on my right ring finger now, and took a deep, steadying breath. Adam laughed when he noticed me.

"What?"

"This cap is too big on you," he said, trying to straighten it, but it kept sliding back down. "Hold your head up."

I did, which left me staring right up into his eyes. He cleared his throat, taking his hands away.

"How's mine?" he asked, jutting out his chin a bit under his own cap.

"You look perfect." I smiled, admiring how Adam's broad shoulders stretched the thin fabric of the uniform a bit too taut. He seemed to enjoy the compliment.

"Hey, we got this, right?" he said, a shade of worry overtaking his face.

"Yeah, of course. Just look like you know what you're doing and you're in a huge hurry and you're really important. That's what Sage said."

"So, be myself?" he joked.

"Exactly."

With stiffened backs and heads held high, we marched past the high school entrance, around the side of the building, and into the fort.

Following Adam's lead, I confidently flashed my ID badge at the guards who stood sentinel at every turn and entryway. They were mostly kids, as my mother had said they would be, somewhere between my age and Adam's. Their eyes ranged from bored to vacant, with the occasional peppering of cruel. Being handed a gun in a holster and the instructions to stand still for hours on end tends to bring out one of those two dispositions in people.

Frankly, I was more afraid of the bored ones than the cruel ones. Idle hands and all that.

We had never gone to the portals this way, of course, but my intrinsic knowledge of the layout of the building, of the placement of those portals and the curve of the decades-old hallways, gave me a sense of where to go. Adam seemed to have it too, because every time we reached a fork in the road, we both seemed to turn, acting completely on instinct, in the same direction.

Finally, we reached a hallway that, despite the erasure of two decades, looked almost the same as it had the night—or the two nights, rather—that I had walked down it with my brother and my friends, heading for Yesterday.

"This is right," I whispered to Adam, and the slight "Mmm" he gave in response made it all feel real suddenly.

I had taken a lot of risks in the portals before. I'd gone into other dimensions and other times. I'd survived the interdimensional train that showed me glimpses of a thousand other lives led by a million other people, all blissfully ignorant of one another's existences.

But this would be the farthest I'd ever gone.

The moment the portals were built.

What would it look like? This was the very facility where the first fission reactor went critical—the splitting nucleus of one atom smashing into the neighboring atoms and splitting them in turn, creating a chain reaction. Somewhere else on these grounds, the enriched uranium itself had been produced. That was where Cherie's mother had worked, monitoring the gauges. Would I be able to get back onto the grounds, see that lab? Watch those scientists at work?

The greatest physics lesson in history was on the other side of the door I was about to cross. The most significant scientific breakthrough of all time. The most brilliant minds. I had never been so excited. I rubbed my sweating palms on my pants.

Adam and I flashed our IDs one more time to the guards at the end of the hallway that led to the science lab, and one of them—a young man with acne on his chin—actually yawned as he looked at them.

No wonder it had been so easy for John and my mother to sneak in the other night. Nobody was really paying attention. People only balk at the unusual. That was one thing I'd learned in my travels. As long as things seemed normal, *felt* right, you could get away with murder. And everything can be normalized in the end.

We made it to the science lab, locking the door behind us. I couldn't help but laugh. It looked exactly the same.

"Has this place ever changed?" I asked.

But that's when I noticed that Adam looked a bit green.

"Are you all right?"

He coughed into his palm, and when he looked at me again, his face had turned deadly serious. "We're going a long way back, Marina. I've never gone this far."

"Me neither."

"It's a risk. The physical portals won't even be there yet. We'll have to wait for them to be built before we can come back."

Footsteps in the hallway were followed by an older man's booming voice, asking a series of questions. A squeaky voice, which I could only assume belonged to the kid with the chin acne, answered back, uncertain in tone. And then the man's footsteps grew closer.

"We don't have time for this, Adam. What are you saying?"

His eyes searched mine for a moment, affection tinged with sadness. He reached into his pocket and held out a flattened penny, offering it to me. "I want you to go into Today."

"No."

"Your father will be worried about you."

"He won't. We'll go back home together . . . when we're done."

"*I'm* worried about you. It's too risky."

"You need me, Adam. I need to get into this lab and see how exactly these portals were built—what it is that Jenny did that gave all the power to the Russians."

"I can get into the lab myself."

"What do you know about physics?" I teased, but he only looked angry in response.

The rattling of the doorknob told us that our new friend was close. The man outside could be heard muttering to himself as his keys began to jangle.

Adam grabbed my hand, and we ran together down the spiral staircase. We had only moments to decide. He pressed the penny into my palm, his eyes imploring. We were standing in front of Today.

But with my other hand, I brought out the piece of brick with Jenny's yellow hair on it, and I pulled him with me towards the Yesterday door.

"You told me to trust you once," I reminded him. "Trust me now. We'll go home when we've finished this."

Footsteps passed overhead, heavy and stiff. It was now or never, but Adam's face had not relaxed.

I reached to put the flattened coin into the slot of Yesterday, but Adam stopped my hand in midair before it could get there. He took a step closer then and slid my cap off my head, peering down at me, our faces almost close enough to touch. My heart was racing as I got lost in the bottomless well of his green eyes.

Was he right? Could he continue without me?

Am I just not ready to leave him yet?

All these thoughts would have to find some other refuge, because the heavy soles of officious feet were clomping down the spiral stairs, and, holding tight to Adam's hand, I inserted the penny into the slot and all but pulled him with me into the past.

CHAPTER THIRTY-FOUR

It was a bright and sunny summer day in front of Groussman's Pharmacy as a painter in a white jacket and pants put the finishing touches on a golden curl of hair, advertising a dance hall just opening down the road.

We had landed in an alley on the side of the building, and as we stepped out into the stark daylight, I couldn't help but feel like we were entering a Technicolor film, bursting with a shock of blue sky and white puffs of cloud. Bacon was frying somewhere, and the unmistakable stench of diesel fuel wafted towards our noses, competing with the bacon for our attention. A radio somewhere was blaring a tune with lots of brass horns and piano.

Spinning slowly in circles, Adam and I must have looked like we'd blown in on a strange wind, wearing our incongruous Russian uniforms and gaping open-mouthed at the enormous automobiles buzzing by, their fenders shining in the afternoon sun.

The town was alive, with many of those huge cars pulling into the parking lot of the train station across the street to catch a shiny silver passenger train brimming with commuters. Women wearing elaborate updos and bright red lipstick gave us strange looks as they passed by, some pushing white-lace-covered baby strollers or balancing packages from a day of shopping.

But there were other women too, wearing men's trousers with their hair tied up in bandanas and smudges of dirt on their faces, carrying paper sacks stained with grease in the direction of Fort Pryman Shard—racing back to work.

I turned in awe towards Adam, but he didn't seem to be noticing any of it anymore. His eyes were glued on just one thing: Jenny's portrait, being constructed in front of our eyes like Frankenstein's monster rising from the dead.

Her crystal-blue eyes had an innocence in this picture that they lacked in real life, clearly an intentional effort on the part of the painter to entice men with a certain kind of fetish into visiting the dance hall.

I felt like an intruder standing there, watching him have this private moment with a girl who now seemed as close as that fresh wet paint.

A nearby newspaper dispenser was full to bursting, and I leaned over to look at the date: July 7, 1944. It was a full year before the bomb would be dropped on Hiroshima, but after the date Cherie said the nuclear reactor went critical. And Jenny was already having her likeness painted on a wall. I had no idea how long she'd been here, but she'd apparently made quite an impression.

"Adam, take off the hat and the jacket," I whispered as more people began to stare at us. He finally seemed to come back into the moment, and once he had removed the two articles of clothing, he actually looked a lot like all the other men passing by. Except all of them were in a different kind of uniform: American World War II fatigues.

I took off my own jacket and draped it over my arm, trying to look like the girls heading back to the fort. It wasn't quite right, however. I needed something in my hair.

"We should walk," I suggested, and he nodded. As we did so, I tried to rip the sleeve off the coat, but I wasn't strong enough. Adam chuckled when he realized what I was doing and grabbed it out of my hands, finishing the job for me. I took the sleeve and tied it up in my hair like a bandana.

"Perfect," he said, smiling.

As we passed the corner, we threw everything else into a trash bin.

The ad for the dance hall said it was in a building that had already been a dozen other things by the time I was born. In my world, it had been a Sears at one point—a fact that I was aware of only because they didn't take the signage down for about a decade after the last Sears had come and gone—and then it was temporarily a community center that no one in the community ever actually used.

For a while, when I was maybe ten years old, a sign had advertised church services in the abandoned building. But one day, about a year after that, I was driving by with my dad and roughly a dozen police cars were surrounding the place, leading people away in handcuffs. I had asked my father what was going on, and he had mumbled something about bad men.

It took me years to discover that it had never been a church but only a front for drug dealers.

The last time I had noticed the building, maybe a year ago, it had become a *quinceañera* emporium, selling everything from flowing, flouncy evening gowns to piñatas. I never went inside it, though.

After my mother left, anything Mexican had only reminded my father of her. I'd never had a quinceañera.

None of that mattered now anyway, eighty years in the past, because here it was something else entirely.

Squatting alone on an otherwise not-yet-developed street, it was a fat, white two-story building with a large sign over the front door that simply said GENTLEMEN'S CLUB. As we approached, a gruff-looking man with a shaggy beard opened the front door and set up a stool to block it from closing again, plopping his oversized behind on it and sipping at a tin mug of coffee.

"We don't open till six," he informed Adam when he noticed him standing there.

"We're just looking for an old friend," Adam answered, angling his body a bit to shield me from seeing anything inside the door.

The man on the stool noticed me then, peering around the large chest blocking his view to try to check me out. "You lookin' for work, sweetheart?"

"She's not," Adam answered for me. "Like I said, just looking for a friend."

"Well, that's just as well," the man returned in his sandpaper voice, his eyes working their way down my legs, "owner likes 'em whiter than that."

Adam must've heard me inhale in shock because he all but pushed me behind him at that point.

"No offense meant," the man laughed. "I think you're beautiful, honey. If it were up to me."

"Her name is Jenny," Adam interrupted, his fists clenching by his sides. "I believe she works here. We just want to have a word."

The man's face changed then, falling under a bit of a dark cloud. "You Jenny's man?" he asked, his tone sounding suddenly disappointed.

"I am."

"Thought you were overseas."

"I'm back."

The man burst out with an enormous chainsaw laugh, so loud that I actually flinched away from the sound. "Yeah," he said between raspy breaths, "I'm back too!" And with that, he pulled up his pant leg to show us the wooden stump in place of his foot.

Adam's muscles softened at the sight of the false appendage, and his voice came out softer than a moment ago. "I'm sorry."

"I'm not," the man joked. "Rather have no leg than still be in that hell swamp in the South Pacific!"

Adam nodded in response. "I hear you."

"Eh, go on in. But have that girl out by six, you hear me? This is a gentlemen's establishment."

"Yes, sir," Adam replied as he led me under cover of his arm into the building.

The place was still being set up for the night, with a frail old man taking chairs off small, round tables and a couple of girls on stage stretching out their legs. "Stay close," Adam whispered at the sight of the girls.

"Where am I gonna go?" I whispered back.

My eyes were still adjusting to the darkened lights inside, distracted temporarily by the clanking of glass as a middle-aged woman lined up bottles on the shelves behind the bar, when I heard a gasp several feet away.

I turned my head, and there she was. Jenny still looked the same age she had on the beach that day twelve years ago, which made me realize that she probably hadn't been down here that long. And it was also immediately clear that John had been right about her: she had the exact right kind of look for the 1940s. Her hair was pin-curled and her makeup done to perfection. She was wearing some sort of spangly showgirl outfit that managed to be even more revealing than the bikini I'd last seen her in.

And she was staring right at Adam, who was staring back.

"Adam," she breathed, and tears sprang to her sapphire eyes.

She dropped everything she was holding—various shiny costume pieces and fringed belts—and her hands flew to cover her mouth. A moan of happiness escaped her lips as she practically flew across the room and landed in his arms.

I watched in silence as his strong arms wrapped around her hourglass waist, holding her with all his might.

"I knew it," she cried. "I knew you'd come. I just knew it."

She looked up into his eyes, the tears glinting in the reflection from the gold-hued stage lights, and his thumb passed over her cheek, wiping away all her grief.

My body shrank into itself, crumpling like a deflated balloon, as she pressed her lips to his, and I watched him kiss her back.

"Jenny gets all the luck," a showgirl whispered to me as she passed by, taking in the scene. "Of course her man comes back early. I haven't heard from mine in weeks."

I turned to look at the girl, mostly just as an excuse to not have to look at Adam and Jenny anymore. Underneath the pancake makeup and the false eyelashes, she was probably only a little older than me. Not knowing what to say, I offered a sympathetic look.

"Don't know if he's alive or dead. We aren't married yet, so I wouldn't even get a telegram."

"I'm sure you'll hear something soon."

She smiled at me, all her anxiety seeming to disappear under the three pounds of foundation. "Your man overseas?"

"No," I stammered, my eyes drifting against my will towards Adam, who was holding Jenny at arm's length, examining her body as though checking a used car for dents.

"Oh!" the girl exclaimed, her attention falling to my hand and the diamond ring that was hanging a bit too limply on my right ring finger. She smiled to herself as her gaze moved from the ring to Adam and back. "Well, that serves Jenny right," she mumbled to herself as she walked on.

I shuffled backwards a step or two, not sure what to do with myself. When I looked up again, I realized that Jenny was staring at me. And she had noticed the ring too. I awkwardly tried to cover it with my other hand, but it was too late.

"Who's that?" Jenny asked Adam, though she was still looking at me.

Adam seemed to remember suddenly that I was there, and yet it took him a second to pry his attention from Jenny.

"I'm Marina," I answered for him. "I'm just a friend. I'm here to help you."

Her eyebrows rose at the word *friend* and she turned back to Adam, whose eyes hadn't wavered from taking in her showgirl costume with a look of repulsion on his face.

"Come on, Jenny," he all but ordered. "Let's get out of here. We need to talk."

"I can't go right now, Adam. I have to work."

"You're not working here anymore," he commanded in a tone that was lower and more forceful than I had heard from him in a while.

"Adam, don't be possessive. You know I don't like that."

His hand was on her upper arm, and I could see the tendons of his wrist clenching. "I've come all this way for you," he whispered fiercely.

"Yes, I realize that, Adam." Her eyes flitted to me for a moment before returning to him. "But you always do this. You show up out of the blue after how long?"

"I couldn't find you."

"I've been here almost a year already, and I'll be here tomorrow too, and I'll need my job. Where will *you* be tomorrow?"

Adam stiffened, not having an immediate response.

"That's what I thought. For years, I dropped everything every time you decided to show up. And what did it get me?"

I aimed my head at the floor, feeling like I was invading something private but unable to stop listening. Adam let go of her arm, chastened by her tone, and Jenny turned the full force of her vicious glare on me again.

"You should probably go," she stated flatly. And while she continued to look at me, the next thing she said was for Adam's benefit. "The owner doesn't like children in here."

She marched off, and I found my feet shuffling of their own volition towards the door.

"M, wait a second," Adam blurted out in frustration, looking at me sideways.

"I should probably . . . wait outside."

My body couldn't move itself fast enough to get the hell out of there. I was out on the sidewalk again in a moment, sidestepping the man on the stool, who chuckled when he saw my face, assuming that I was somehow traumatized by what I had seen inside. He wasn't exactly wrong.

Adam followed me out a second later. "Wait up, M. Where are you going?"

"It's okay, Adam," I insisted. "Really."

He was clenching his jaw again, trying to calm himself down.

"Listen," I whispered, stepping a bit closer. "She'll be more willing to talk to you if I'm not here. Trust me."

He looked at me, worry shadowing his handsome features.

"I'll go take care of some things, get us set up somewhere. Try again with her. She was just surprised to see you."

"I can't let you walk around by yourself."

But this just made me laugh. "I've been walking around by myself for a long time now, Adam."

He nodded, looking torn.

A large blue car came buzzing by, its radio blaring a bebop song, the teenagers inside laughing and shouting. Someone spit a piece of gum out the window, and it landed with a thud on the sidewalk by my feet, making me step back a bit.

"The hell?" Adam asked, but then the car sped off, the music fading with it, and soon it was silent again.

I looked down the length of the street towards the corner where other businesses had already sprung up, their paint so fresh it almost looked like it was still drying.

"There's a restaurant on the corner," I observed. "I'll meet you there after."

"When is after?"

"After." I shrugged, already walking away and leaving him behind me on the sidewalk in front of Jenny's club.

CHAPTER THIRTY-FIVE

The large sign at the entrance to the compound was written in clear, bold letters: WHAT YOU DO HERE, WHAT YOU SEE HERE, WHAT YOU HEAR HERE, PLEASE LET IT STAY HERE.

Sneaking past the guards onto the grounds of Fort Pryman Shard wasn't the hard part. In fact, it was deceptively easy. All I had to do was wait beside the gate for a group of those women in the bandanas with their lunch sacks to make their way past the guard, smiling and flirting, asking him about his mother in a way that made him blush, and insinuate myself into the group. Within minutes of arriving at the front gate, I was in.

But now I stood rootless in the middle of the roundabout by the front entrance, trying to get my bearings. The entire edifice had been transformed once again, now containing no high school, as I'd known it wouldn't. My father had explained to me when I was young that the place was originally built to be the fort. The school was an afterthought.

In the place of the sign that had read either East Township High School or Good Citizen Academy, depending on which reality you happened to be in, there was instead just an American flag. It hung in bold colors, fresh creases from its nightly folding still visible throughout its surface, flapping occasionally in the whiffs of warm summer air.

Near the main building was a series of other buildings, mostly sitting in the area that would eventually become the track field behind the high school or the wooded patch of land that wasn't used for anything anymore by the time I was growing up, except a convenient place for ditching students to make out.

Now an entire complex of buildings occupied that space, and as I walked with purpose from one end to the other, trying to avoid the suspicious gazes of the roaming guards, I saw that each building was marked with only the smallest sign, designating it with a series of letters and numbers—Y12, X10—instead of a name.

Hundreds of people milled about, making it easier for me to avoid detection, and they made their way with swift steps through the muddy clearing in the middle of all these interconnected buildings, all with one thing in common: ID tags. Lots of them. In several colors, all seeming to identify which buildings they were—and were not—allowed to enter.

There seemed to be three types of people entering the buildings: white men in even whiter lab coats; workwomen, some as young as me, all wearing either simple shift dresses or blue men's work pants and blouses, their hair tied up in yellow scarves; and the Latina women who entered all the buildings with their cleaning carts in tow, mumbling almost inaudibly to each other in Spanish and making eye contact with no one.

I must have paced back and forth for over twenty minutes, a determined look on my face to indicate I was in a huge hurry, while I scanned the faces for any variance.

White men in lab coats.

White women in overalls.

Latina women in drab gray dresses, a broom seemingly glued into their hands.

Finally, I realized that I would either have to make a move or leave. The world wasn't going to change around me while I sat there. I tentatively approached the front door of the building labeled Y12, wiping my hands on my trousers even though they weren't actually dirty. I took a deep breath. Could I just sneak in?

What would they think of me if I walked through time into that building?

"*¿Estás perdida?*" a voice asked me.

I turned to see one of the cleaning ladies facing me, a wrinkle of confusion on her tired forehead and a rag in one hand.

Shoot. Spanish. Not my strong suit.

"Um . . . no, *no estoy perdida. Gracias.*"

I was fairly certain I just told her I wasn't lost, although that wasn't exactly true. I smiled awkwardly and excused myself, walking with purpose across the grassy knoll and back past the guard in his little booth. He looked at me with a million questions almost on his lips, but I was long gone before he ever got a chance to voice them.

o o o

The window of Groussman's Pharmacy—which was apparently one of the oldest businesses in town—contained a random assortment of personal items, including a couple of wedding bands displayed within well-worn clamshell cases. Scanning the rest of the offered goods—an old watch, a scuffed-up guitar with only three strings, a small radio—my eyes finally fell on what I'd been hoping to see: a handwritten sign that read, LAYAWAY/PAWN, SEE OWNER.

I had already checked out the rest of the street, and this was the only business that seemed promising. If they couldn't help me, I didn't know how I'd get any cash.

I retied the sleeve around my hair, trying to emulate the look I'd seen on some of the girls at the base, and walked inside.

The little bells jangled overhead, announcing my presence.

A young woman, maybe twenty-five years old, was standing behind the glass display counter, which had even more wares arranged within it. Her hands were busily moving in steady loops, sewing a hem on a dress.

"Excuse me?"

She looked up, a helpful face with a ready smile sitting under a generous pile of curly brown hair. "Yes, dear?"

"I was wondering if, um . . ." I twisted the ring nervously on my finger, then slid it off and placed it on the counter. "If you'd be interested in buying this. Pawning it, I mean."

Her face fell when she saw what I had offered, and she put down her sewing, giving me a pitying smile. "Wait right here." She got up and stuck her head into the doorway of a little office behind the counter. "Dad," I heard her say, "there's another one."

I cleared my throat, my fingers resting nervously on the ring. The casing around the diamond scratched lightly against the glass.

Another one?

I thought about grabbing the ring and running. Did she know it wasn't mine? But before I could make a decision, an older man with a potbelly and two identical tufts of white hair springing out over his ears emerged from the little office. Peering at me over wire-rimmed glasses, he looked like a kind little elf. The thought made me smile to myself, which in turn made me trust him.

His daughter took her sewing to a bench over in the corner. The message was clear: I had been passed off. I would be dealing with the father now. He leaned over the ring, grabbed a loop from a chain around his neck, and inspected it closely.

After a moment, he sighed heavily, placing the ring with the utmost gentleness back in front of me.

"Did your man not come home, dear?"

I inhaled sharply at the question, specks of dust from the ancient goods and musty old clothes filling my nostrils in the process. "Oh, no," I said, tripping over my own mouth. "No, it's not that. He's fine. We just—we need some money."

This made his eyebrows knit together in worry. He looked down at my belly and then back up to my face. "Now listen, dear, if this is for something . . . untoward, I can't—"

I wasn't immediately sure what "untoward" referred to, but I could venture a guess. I was just making things worse. "No, it's not that, I—" *Pull it together, Marina. Speak clearly.* "We're new in town. We're looking for work. He's back from the war, and we need some money to get settled. That's all."

He nodded slowly, his mouth forming a small O as if he was finally getting it.

"You two hoping to work at the base?"

"Yes."

"Well, that clearance will take a long time. But you might be able to secure housing while you wait."

I nodded. "That would be great."

"Don't you have any savings, dear? Any family you can call?"

I shook my head slowly, trying to say as little as possible. "No."

He dropped his eyes back down to the ring with a determined sigh. "Well, I'll tell you what I'm gonna do . . ." Scooping up the ring, he gently placed it in a cigar box sitting up on a tall shelf behind him, letting the lid fall over it. "I'm gonna keep that ring right in there, you hear me?"

"Yes, sir."

"I'm not going to sell it. When your man gets his first check—or when you do—you come on in here and you give me three dollars a week to buy it back. In the meantime . . ."

He disappeared into the back office, and I could hear him clattering around in there. I looked over to his daughter and saw that she was smiling pleasantly in my direction. After a moment, her father came back out and handed me one hundred dollars in ten-dollar bills. "That ought to get you through the month."

I opened my mouth to protest, pretty sure that even in the 1940s, that ring was worth more than a hundred bucks. But what leverage did I have to negotiate? Was I going to go to the other pawnshop in town? There wasn't one, and we both knew it.

"Now, you stay here while I make a phone call," the old man instructed, shuffling back into the office. "I'm going to try to get you into one of the new married units they're putting up out in the fields."

"We don't need a married unit—" I began.

"Oh, you'll need it." The man smiled warmly. "Now that your man's back, you'll be glad of the second bedroom soon enough." His glance wafted down to my stomach again as he turned to enter the office.

I knew I should be happy since this transaction had worked out pretty well, but I couldn't help but feel grossed out instead. The complete freedom with which men were talking about me and my body was beyond surreal. I knew it was a different time and all, but I didn't realize it would be this bad.

I turned while I waited for him to come back and examined a

rack of dresses nearby. They were all made in the same style, but from a range of different fabrics. I picked up a nice green one, rubbing the material between my fingers.

"You like that one?" the daughter asked, coming around the counter to check on me now that her father was gone.

"Did you make it?"

"I did. I make them all," she said proudly. "Truth be told, they're from a pattern, but I always like to add a little extra flair."

"It's really lovely."

"Try it on," she urged, a gentle hand on my back guiding me in the direction of a curtained changing area.

"Um . . ."

"Oh, it's all right, I'll give you a deal for it. I know you're saving your money. I couldn't help but overhear."

I hesitated, the dress clutched in my hands, and her eyes fell down to my feet. A soft look came into her brown eyes as she took in my black boots—part of the Russian outfit. "Do you only have the men's shoes, dear?"

I nodded awkwardly, trying to hand her back the dress.

But she seemed undeterred, taking me aside and whispering in a conspiratorial kind of way, "When the war first started, I had to sell my very last pair of stockings. Oh, it broke my heart. I wore my brother's pants for a week to hide my bare legs."

I smiled, grateful that she was taking the pressure off me to explain my clothes. Her hand reached up and lightly touched the sleeve I was using to wrap up my hair, and she nodded affection-ately. "The sacrifices we make for the war effort, eh?"

Then she pulled back the dressing room curtain. "I'm going to make you my pet. You go right in and try on that dress, and I'll fetch you some stockings. They're rayon, I'm afraid, but no one will know the difference."

Once I had on the dress, stockings—which I eventually figured out how to secure into the garter belt she passed me—and some shiny new pumps, my new friend led me over to the counter again.

She was pinning up my hair, rouging my cheeks, and painting my lips red by the time I got around to asking her what her name was.

"Call me Mimi. Everyone does."

"Thank you for being so nice to me, Mimi."

"Oh, I'm happy to do it. You know, dear, you really must wear a hat when you work in the sun. You could be a great beauty, but you're much too tan."

Despite the voice in my head telling me to let it lie, I just couldn't. "I'm not tan, I'm Mexican."

To Mimi's credit, her hand only hesitated for a quarter of a second before she leaned back in to finish up my lips. "Well, I won't tell anyone," she whispered, offering me another friendly smile.

I glanced over to the small office, where I could hear Mimi's father finishing up his phone call with the sign-off, "And a pleasant day to you and yours." Before he came back out, Mimi leaned in one more time.

"You know, I've got a little bottle of lilac cream in the back." She smiled. "You just massage it in every night for a month," she continued, demonstrating on herself how to rub the cream into her cheeks, "and it'll lighten you right up. It's what Rita Hayworth uses."

Mimi's dad came out of the office then. "Good news," he said, beaming, "I've secured you one of the new units. You can move in tonight." Father and daughter both clapped their hands in delight, and I could only offer them what I hoped looked like a genuine smile in return.

CHAPTER THIRTY-SIX

The owner of the restaurant was giving me the stink eye as I sat alone at a large table, one of every dish on the menu spread out before me. Maybe he thought I was going to dine and dash. Maybe he didn't like my skin color. He stood with arms folded over his stout little body, twitching his moustache in my direction and tapping his fat foot.

I didn't care. I was starving and annoyed, and I ripped off a huge chunk of bread and dipped it into a bowl of tomato soup, then started twirling my fork into a towering plate of spaghetti.

"What the hell did you order?" I heard Adam ask, and I looked up to see him standing with an expression of dismay over the table.

"Everything," I answered, hovering the fork over the plate en route to my mouth. "You can get an entire steak here for only eighty-five cents."

"These people are on rations," Adam whispered, embarrassed, as he sat down opposite me. "You just ordered enough food for ten people."

I hesitated before bringing the fork to my mouth. I hadn't thought of that. Okay, so maybe the owner had good reason to be gaping at me. Whatever. Nothing to do now but eat it all.

Whatever judgment Adam had about the food dissipated as he sat down and started shoveling bites of steak into his mouth, all dripping in a thick, brown gravy.

"You sold the ring?" he noticed.

"Pawned it. The man said he'd hold it for us . . . for me. Until I could pay him back."

Adam watched me eat for a moment, devouring forkfuls of food like they owed me a favor. "I have no idea where you put all this food."

"It's feeding my rage."

He laughed, adding a large portion of chicken parmesan to his plate. "Did you learn anything today?"

"Oh, I learned lots of things today," I answered between bites. "I learned that the career options for a Mexican woman in 1944 range from cleaning lady to maid. Can't be a stripper, unfortunately. Not white enough. But if I bleach my skin with the lilac tonic stuff that Rita Hay-something uses, I can pass for white, and then I can watch needles spin around a gauge at the base, so long as I don't ask what they're for."

Adam chuckled into a bite of steak, washing it down with a gulp of water. But he was also looking over his shoulder, making sure no one was listening.

"And basically," I continued, "the only way I'm ever getting into that lab now is if I wake up tomorrow morning looking like you."

At this, Adam's fork froze in midair for a moment, his eyes questioning.

"What?" I mumbled through a mouthful of spaghetti.

"It's not a bad idea."

"What isn't?"

"Go in as a cleaning lady, and you can sneak in and steal me a badge."

I dropped my fork, which made a louder clanking sound than I had intended, catching the attention of the already suspicious owner. I offered him an apologetic wave, and he eventually went back to staring indignantly at the other diners.

"I can't do that, Adam."

"Why not?"

"Because I can't pass as a cleaning lady."

He simply held out his hands as if to ask, "Why not?" The anger that had been brewing inside me all day was starting to work its way up into my throat again, and I swallowed it down with a cold sip of water before continuing.

"There are no mixed people here, Adam. I'm too white to be Mexican. I'm too Mexican to be white. The other ladies would know. Also . . . my Spanish sucks."

"You don't speak Spanish?"

"I speak some Spanish. I'm not fluent."

But Adam didn't seem to understand that either. Had he never heard of assimilation?

"My abuela tried to teach me, and my mother wouldn't let her. There's a stigma. You wouldn't understand, Adam."

"Can we skip the white privilege lecture, Marina? I'm just trying to get us in the building."

"So am I."

"Then what are we fighting about?"

"I'm angry, and you're here." Even I had to laugh at that, realizing as I said it that it wasn't the best argument. But I was just so frustrated. "I belong in the lab."

"I know you do, sweetheart, but we can't change history."

I could only laugh at the irony of that statement, and Adam laughed too.

"We can't change *all* of history," he clarified.

But it was the word *sweetheart* that had caught me. I stared at the pile of food in front of me. "Is that what you're gonna call me now?"

He put down his water glass and placed his hand over mine. "Hey."

"Stop," I said softly, pulling my hand away. I sliced up little bits of the rest of the chicken. "What did Jenny say?"

Her name sat between us for a moment like I had placed a gun on the table. "Nothing much after you left. She had to work." He flinched at the final word. "And afterwards, she was meeting someone. I told her to blow it off, but she said, 'He'd be mad.'"

"*He*? Who do you think it is?"

"I don't know. She said she'd meet me in the morning to explain."

I let that information lie for a moment. "So, you just . . . sat there and watched her dance all afternoon?" *What are you doing, Marina? Don't torture yourself.*

"No. I didn't want to watch that, so I've just been walking in circles for hours . . . looking for you."

I couldn't help but smile as I took one last spoonful of soup. I was finally feeling full, and I was a little embarrassed that I had ordered so much. But even the owner seemed to have gotten over it at that point and had returned to his post by the front door.

"I got us a place to crash," I said, grabbing the paper sack with all my belongings from under the table. "Let me pay for this, and we can catch the shuttle."

Adam looked nervous suddenly, his eyes darting around.

"Don't worry," I assured him. "It has two bedrooms."

o o o

About two minutes outside of town, the packed shuttle fell off a cliff. Well, maybe not an actual cliff, but that's certainly what it felt like. Suddenly, the paved road underneath the tires fell away, and the large bus wobbled and lurched its way forward on the pockmarked dirt path that shot out like a broken arrow into the untamed sea of fields beyond the town.

All civilization—every street and business, every tree and park that I had known by heart from the time I was conscious of my surroundings—evaporated into the warm summer air. It was like someone up above had taken a great eraser and simply wiped it all away. Nothing remained but wide open fields, billowing with summer growth of wheat and corn under the soft light from the crescent moon.

The bus shot farther out into the dark, occasionally bobbling left and then right, causing Adam and me to bump into each other on our bench for another ten minutes until it reached its destination. I clung to the paper sack on my lap, holding it like a baby. The driver suddenly pulled over—although it wasn't immediately clear why, as we hadn't reached any landmark that I could see—and announced that we were there.

All the people aboard the bus—mostly young women in work clothes or simple dresses, and the few men who were apparently husbands judging from the way the women clung close to them—flowed off two by two into the night.

Adam and I stood, waiting our turn, and I tried to peer out the windows into the darkness to see where exactly we were being dumped.

It wasn't until I'd made it off the final step of the bus, landing in a soft, wet patch of dirt that soiled my brand-new shoes, that I saw something that looked like a street sign. It was made of wood, jammed into the ground at a slight angle, and it held the name of a street that I actually recognized.

"Where are we?" Adam muttered as he came up behind me. The bus pulled away, its tires grinding temporarily in that wet mud before spinning themselves free and allowing the driver to leave us there, in the midst of the endless wheat.

The other couples had already started walking off towards what I could now see were a series of small cottages, each identical to the next with only a number painted on the front to tell them apart. They were lined up as far as the eye could see for the length of the dirt road.

"We're in my neighborhood," I answered, still not quite able to process it. These little cottages would one day occupy a paved street lined with elm trees that shaded the sidewalk where my dad taught me to ride a bike when I was seven.

We were the only two left on the road, and I pulled out the little slip of paper from the sack with the information the old man at the shop had given me—the number eighty-seven written in his small, crisp handwriting.

"Marina, look up," Adam said.

Panicking for a moment, I looked at him, only to see his eyes trained on the sky above, a childlike look of wonder on his face. As I tilted my chin up into the night, my mouth fell open with a look that must have mirrored his. I had never seen so many stars in my life.

And not just stars, but whole galaxies. Swirling and bright, distant and alive. Billions of twinkling constellations and star clusters. Jupiter bright and blinding, painfully white under the moon. We walked slowly side by side, occasionally looking down to sidestep a puddle or a pothole in the raw earth, only to find our eyes pried upwards again into that inviting envelope of light.

We didn't speak; nothing I could have thought of to say seemed important suddenly. It felt like the world had hit pause for a moment, the silence as comforting as a lullaby.

By the time we reached number eighty-seven, it was all I could do to force myself to put the key in the door and walk inside.

Adam flipped the light switch, showing every detail of the tiny house I had agreed to rent for eighteen dollars a month—two bedrooms, a bath, and a kitchenette. We stood awkwardly together in that small entryway while I dug into my shopping bag again.

"I got you a toothbrush," I said, breaking the spell of silence that had overtaken us outside.

"Thanks."

He took it, and we continued to stand there for a moment, lost in our own thoughts.

"I don't love her anymore," he finally said. "But if she's in trouble, and she needs me, then I have to help her."

"I know that," I answered, realizing that I would do the exact same thing if Kieren needed me.

Or if Brady did.

Adam inhaled sharply, his mouth twisting around words that couldn't seem to find any way to escape his brain and make their way out of his mouth. Instead, he simply cleared his throat and nodded.

"Good night," he said quickly, heading for one of the bedrooms.

"Good night," I answered, but he was already closing the door.

I walked into the other bedroom and lay down on the bare cot by the window, looking up into that impossible night sky. How many galaxies did this universe contain? How many lives might exist in them? How many dimensions?

And if space and time were infinite, if it was all just a never-ending sea, the waves crashing ceaselessly into one another, smashing and combining, blending into one only to separate again, then where did all of this end?

Somewhere in this universe, there was a dimension where

Robbie was killed at fourteen. Somewhere, a dimension where Kieren and I were in love. Somewhere, another where I loved Brady and he loved me back.

And somewhere, in the multitudes of time and space, my mother and I, two planets orbiting the same sun, were what mothers and daughters were meant to be: faithful to our bond, proud to belong to each other, innocent and true.

But this was not that dimension.

I waited ten minutes before I went to his bed.

He was awake and waiting for me.

CHAPTER THIRTY-SEVEN

"How did you choose 2001 anyway?" I asked, my head resting on Adam's broad chest, his fingers stroking up and down my back like the strings of a violin. "The first time you went?"

"Oh, the Kubrick film," he answered. "*A Space Odyssey.* It's a really awesome movie."

Clouds had shrouded part of the night sky, leaving just enough of a glow to feel like God had turned on a night light. It was weirdly silent outside until a distant owl began to hoot, somewhere far off beyond the wheat fields.

"Are you serious?" I asked.

"No, I'm messing with you."

I laughed, picking up my head and slapping his arm just to have the pleasure of replacing my face on his warm skin after.

"No, I'd had this—this epically, and I mean really, colossally, bad wrestling match. I'd gotten my ass creamed . . ." He laughed at the memory, and I couldn't help but laugh too, trying to picture what teenager could ever beat Adam. "And there was this trophy in the display case at the front of the school. You know which one—"

"Yeah. I've got a trophy in there."

He looked down at me, impressed. "For what?"

"Robotics. I was on a team that went to regionals last year."

He chuckled to himself, shaking his head and twirling his index finger around a loop of my hair.

"What's so funny?"

"Nothing." He laughed. "I love how smart you are."

I couldn't tell if he was messing with me again, but I decided not to push it. "So, there was a wrestling trophy?"

"Yeah, the school had had a really good wrestler that year, and I decided, what the hell. I've been everywhere else I can think of. I'll go back to the year this kid won this trophy, and maybe I'll learn a couple things."

"Right."

"And I go back, and I sit myself down in the bleachers, and I look up across the gym. And there's this face of an angel staring back at me. And that was it. I just kept going back."

He must have felt me hold my breath for a moment because his fingers stopped twirling my hair.

"Yeah, she's really pretty," I offered, a beat too late and dripping with way too much hostility.

He laughed, holding my chin up to look me in the eyes.

"What?"

"Is that jealousy?"

"No, I want to hear more about how pretty your ex-girlfriend is. Seriously, don't skip any details." I started to pull away, but he pulled me back by my left arm and held it up to his own.

"Look at this," he said, and though I wanted to stay angry with him, I couldn't do it. I looked at our arms together, our two different skin tones, his almond-colored and mine caramel, pressed up against each other. "That's beautiful to me, Marina," he whispered, kissing my shoulder. I flipped my arm over to show my scars, and he did the same, pressing his to mine and letting our hands fall into each other.

I smiled at him, realizing something.

"What is it?" he asked.

"You've stopped calling me M."

He smiled back, shaking his head and holding my hand tighter. "That's someone else's name for you. Marina is mine."

I put my head back on his chest.

"Why robotics?" he asked.

"It's the future."

"Humans make the future."

"Hate to break it to you, but it's actually gonna be robots." I swirled my finger in slow circles on his chest while I talked, and his hand went back to stroking me idly and working its way into my hair. "Which is a good thing," I continued, "because, as you know, human history is just people destroying everything in sight over and over again."

"That's what you think history is?"

"It's white people killing brown people, Adam."

"If you don't study history, you're doomed to repeat it."

"We are repeating it. Literally."

A silence came over the room, and even the owl seemed to have drifted off to sleep. The light was changing outside the window, growing darker and more ominous with the late hour, telling us that time was passing.

"Imagine an airplane," I continued, letting my mind drift and the images become vivid and real, "flying through the sky, running on the power of its own wind resistance. No gas. No engine. It's basically a huge wind-powered drone, adjusting for height, temperature, turbulence. Landing perfectly on time. You go from point A to point B, and you don't destroy the world in the process."

"Something would go wrong. It always does."

"And we would fix it. With robots!"

I could feel his chest shake a bit, laughing at me, and I knew I should be falling asleep, but the moment was too perfect to let go.

"And this is why I teach history," he said, laughing.

"You're a great teacher."

"Don't say that when you've got your leg draped over my stomach."

"You are. This doesn't count."

"Everything counts."

He finished twirling my hair then, letting it slip out of his fingers like water.

"We're only five and a half years apart," I said, and somehow it came out sounding like a prayer.

"And in a couple years, that won't matter at all," he agreed. "But right now, it does."

"So go meet me in a couple years then."

A chill passed through the room, so real and cold that I swear I could almost hear it. I shivered despite Adam's heat, and I could feel his breath catch and then release beneath my ear. Because it was too real. With the portals, anything was possible. Any timeline could be altered. We could spend the rest of our lives this way, shaving off a year here, a minute there, trying to achieve a perfection that would never come.

I dropped everything every time you decided to show up. And what did it get me?

"Marina," he began, his voice tight, "we have to promise our-selves. No more portals after this."

"I know."

"We have to leave it all behind. All of it."

"We will," I said, holding him even closer, clutching him to me like he was my last breath. "This will be the last time."

Several minutes passed, the night air thick and hot, the silence deafening.

"Tell me about your brother," he whispered, already half-asleep.

"Robbie." I smiled, my voice far away. "Robbie was my best friend growing up. He was my whole world . . ." In a voice that grew softer and softer as I spoke, I told him about the pyramid house, the games of Monopoly. A deck of cards with the geography of the world on it. A packet of stolen M&Ms. And a train . . . the rumbling of a train.

CHAPTER THIRTY-EIGHT

The bus finished its chaotic thrusting as soon as it hit paved road again, and it was like we had suddenly entered another dimension, not just another street. The wheat fields and the dirt gave way to cement and brick, the town that I had known my whole life beginning to take form in front of me like the first strokes of a pencil drawing. It wasn't flesh and blood yet, not as I had always known it, but the bones were there.

"Are we meeting her at the club?" I asked.

"No, she gave me another address. She's, um . . ."

"What?"

He hesitated. "She's only expecting me."

"Well, she's about to be disappointed," I said, my eyes trained out the window as the bus pulled up to the same stop where we had gotten on it the night before. I knew it had been my idea to leave the two of them alone at the club, hoping it would loosen her lips, but now I had thought better of it. Maybe my presence would let her know that Adam wasn't kidding around, that we were here for something more serious than a reunion.

Adam shot me a smile out of the corner of his mouth but said nothing. "We stay on the bus. It's another mile or so, she said."

"Fine." I thought about our situation as the bus chugged on, a thick, noxious black smoke puffing out of the exhaust behind us. "You know, I was thinking. Maybe we don't have to get into the fort at all."

"How's that?"

"Well, when I went into the past before, I came back home through the place where I had entered. It was like the outline of the door stayed behind, and I just needed a coin to open it. If we could get her to the alley where we first showed up, maybe we could go back that way . . ."

But I stopped talking when I saw the disappointed look on Adam's face. "Sorry, Marina, I thought you knew," he finally said.

I swallowed hard, waiting for him to say something. *Knew what?*

"That door remains only for a few hours. If you miss that window, then the Today door is the only way to go home."

"Oh." I nodded, trying not to look freaked out. "I see."

"Is that why you agreed to come, Marina? Did you think it would be that easy?"

Yes.

"No. Of course not."

He smiled and patted my hand, letting his warm fingers rest over mine. "We'll get into the fort. Don't worry."

"We should do it soon, though, shouldn't we? I mean, before Jenny gets a chance to do . . . whatever it is that she did."

"I was thinking that too," he agreed. "Unless—"

I looked at him, but his eyebrows were knit together, and he was staring distractedly out the window. "Unless?"

"Unless she's already done it."

I followed his gaze out to the street as we wound our way past the newly erected buildings and into a wooded area, the bus jerking a bit as we left the town behind and continued on to a very different part of the landscape. It took me several minutes to realize these were my woods—the ones I'd ridden my bike through hundreds of times. In fact, maybe some of these trees were the exact same ones I had touched and run through and played beneath during my childhood.

Soon the bus pulled over to the side of the road, and Adam signaled to me that it was time to get off. Somehow, despite the fact that these trees should have been the most familiar sight we'd yet seen, I felt even farther from home than I had in the wheat fields.

Adam let me get off first, and feeling his warmth radiate behind me was the only thing keeping me from being afraid. After the bus pulled away, we were stranded at the side of the narrow road, with nothing but bark and green leaves in every direction.

"Are you sure about this?" I asked in a weak voice.

He scanned the woods behind us, the look of worry on his face replaced with a reluctant determination when he saw something that apparently looked encouraging. "There," he said.

He had spotted a freshly painted white mailbox, and I could now see that it stood sentry at the end of a long, narrow driveway. We began walking down it, plunging ourselves even deeper into the shaded canopy of tall trees, the singing of two mating birds above the only noise breaking up the silence. I wobbled a bit on the uneven ground, not quite used to the heels Mimi had sold me.

"It should be on the left, just a bit farther."

"What is she doing out here?"

"I have no idea." Here his voice turned tight again, the pinch of worry sitting on top of his words.

Around the next bend, we saw a beautiful ranch-style house in the shape of an L, with lots of sliding glass doors and windows reflecting the trees in every direction so that the house itself seemed to be made of forest. The timeless, natural setting stood in sharp contrast to the bustling town and the military fort just a mile down the road.

Adam approached the large wooden front door first, edging his body in front of mine in what was an attempt to either protect me or shield Jenny from having to see me when she opened the door. In any event, she did open it, wearing a bright yellow dress with polka dots that reminded me of the bikini I had first seen her in, and her face couldn't hide her disappointment when she saw me behind Adam's shoulder.

"Oh," was all she said. But then she caught herself, forcing a smile, and moved aside to let us in.

The house was even more beautiful inside, with skylights in the slanted roof flooding the large sunken living room in natural light. Jenny led us to a couch and then sat herself primly on the love seat facing us. There was something very formal about her posture suddenly, like she was playing the part of a housewife in a sitcom. Maybe it was just because I was there. Or maybe because Adam was.

"You look like Rain," Jenny said, breaking the ice. Her tone wasn't harsh so much as frank. She was trying to put together the puzzle of why Adam had finally showed back up in her life with another girl in tow.

"I'm her daughter." I smiled.

Jenny nodded, the pieces starting to come together. Her eyes flitted to Adam, who was awkwardly looking around the house, probably trying to determine who exactly lived here and what kind of trouble Jenny had gotten herself into.

But Jenny wasn't done with me, her face turning quizzical, bemused somehow by my appearance, dolled up as I was in Mimi's dress and stockings. "How old are you?"

"Eighteen," I sputtered, realizing that it probably sounded very young to her. Adam shuffled a bit by my side, not looking at either of us.

She nodded, smiling ironically to herself before turning to Adam. "Okay, so what can I do for you, Adam?"

"We're here to take you home, Jenny."

"That's bold."

"Today," he added. "Right now. Or as soon as we can. Once the portals—"

"Once the portals are built, yeah. Sounds like you've got it all worked out." She stood up then and poured herself a cup of coffee from the bar at the side of the room. "You still take it black?" she asked Adam, pointedly ignoring me.

"I don't want any," he answered.

She brought back her delicate cup and sat down, placing it gently on a saucer. "Well," she began again, twisting her soft mouth into another forced smile, "your timing isn't great, as usual, Adam. There's a lot going on today, and I really don't have time to be rescued just now—"

"Where's Dave?" I asked, realizing I was going to have to steer this conversation if it was ever going to get anywhere.

The words changed her face somehow, a flash of shock and sadness passing over her delicate features, ripping away the facade she was trying desperately to maintain and exposing the scared child underneath. Her lips grew tight, and she took a shaky sip of coffee before replacing the cup on the table. After a moment, she moved her hand to her neckline and pulled aside the collar of her dress, removing a chain with two dog tags on it.

"It was my fault," she said softly, not looking either of us in the eye. "I was always riding him. 'Be a man.' 'Grow a pair.' He didn't tell me he was going to do it. Because he knew I'd stop him." She laughed ruefully, her face falling again after a beat. "He had a friend tell me instead, when it was too late. He had already enlisted."

I could feel Adam stiffen beside me, his hands kneading his kneecaps as he sat uneasily on the sofa.

"Six months later, they sent me back these. He was in the Pacific theater somewhere. I don't know where exactly. They wouldn't tell me." And with that, she tucked the dog tags back into her dress and straightened up the neckline to hide the chain, giving the unmistakable impression that she was somehow burying Dave all over again, this time deep inside her own body.

"I'm so sorry, Jenny," I said. I looked to Adam, but he didn't seem capable of saying anything in that moment.

Jenny waved my words away, a chirpiness coming back over her face—but one that seemed even more forced than before. "My boyfriend takes care of me now. He'll be here in a minute. He took the car into town to get us eggs."

It was Adam who spoke next, and his voice came out rough and tinged with anger. Whether it was at Jenny, me, the mysterious boyfriend who was about to show up, or just at time and the over-whelming feeling that too many things were out of our control, I didn't know. But his voice scared me, and it seemed to scare Jenny a bit too. "How did you get here, Jenny?"

"What do you mean?" she asked, her fingers clutching at the hem of her dress.

Adam looked directly at her now, and I could see the tendons of her neck tighten. "You know what I mean. When there was no lake portal. How did you get here?"

Jenny sighed deeply, letting go of any pretext of superiority she had been trying to maintain. It was like her whole body shifted, shrank, and caved in before my eyes. The scared girl she was hiding inside was all that remained.

"It wasn't my idea, Adam," she blurted in a significantly smaller voice. She swallowed down her emotions and continued. "It was John. John made us do it." Her eyes darted to me on the word *us* and then nervously to the front door.

Adam followed her darting glance to the door and then leaned forward, casting a shadow over the table. "Explain. Now."

"Rain was supposed to build a portal under the lake. John had been planning it for years. He was going to send Dave and me back here. He had it all worked out; he had studied all the history. If the Russians had gotten the bomb first, they'd have all the power, and then whoever did business with them would have it too. But then the night Rain was supposed to do it . . ."

"Go on," I encouraged, although I already knew this part of the story.

"I don't know, someone . . . took it or something. Someone broke into the apartment and took the beaker that Rain had brought to make the portal. John was furious. He blamed Rain and Sage and even me for not guarding it. He said we had sabotaged it on purpose. That we didn't believe in him."

I thought about the pull that John had maintained over these women. My mother had loved him, and then Sage. Even Jenny had wanted to be with him at one point, when she was just a kid, maybe fourteen. He'd had them all wrapped around his finger. Why? What was so special about John? What made them follow him so blindly? And with that thought, I couldn't help but look over at Adam.

"He ordered Rain to go get more solution. She refused. She said it was for the best. But then . . ." And here, she looked at me again. "John grabbed little Robbie."

I gasped at my brother's name, and my hand flew over my mouth as though to protect him somehow.

"He said Robbie would stay with him until Rain got back with more solution." Jenny looked sympathetically at me. "She didn't have a choice."

My heart was beating too fast in my chest, and I tried to steady my breath. *She didn't have a choice.* Did that mean she would have come back to me otherwise?

"When she got back with it, he said we weren't taking any more chances. The lake was too accessible, so he bought that old estate outside of town—the botanical gardens. There was a huge house in the middle, almost a castle. I guess the man who built it was obsessed with medieval Europe or something, because it looked like that. John put the new portal in the cellar."

I inhaled sharply at the mention of the botanical gardens. Sage had told me about them the first time I'd visited the Mystics with Brady. At that time, two years ago, the John that I met was a small man painting little figurines in his apartment, consigned to a life where he'd never amounted to much. Maybe the loss of Jenny and Dave had scared him straight. After all, in that timeline, his friends had disappeared into the lake a decade before.

But it seemed that there had been another consequence to my creating a new timeline when I went back to that beach and buried Mom's beaker. It woke something in John—that lost opportunity of what the lake portal had represented to him.

Or maybe it was just that without losing Jenny and Dave that day, there had been nothing to scare him away. And so he'd tried again.

Yet another way I had failed that night when I'd buried the beaker. I bowed my head in guilt while Adam chimed in with another question.

"Where did he get the money?" he asked.

She laughed bitterly. "Every time John pulled a wad of cash out of his pocket, he would say the same thing: 'My grandma left it to me.' It was one thing when it was just the hotel. That seemed believable. But when he bought the gardens . . . well, was his grandmother a multimillionaire?"

Adam's eyes had drifted to the table between us, thinking, working out the solution. "He took it from the portals," he concluded.

"It's easy enough, isn't it? Just go back a couple days and pick some winning lottery numbers. I told myself it was a victimless crime. After all, someone was going to win the lottery no matter what, right?" Jenny said.

"About a year went by. John would disappear from time to time into his work at the castle. Your mom wanted nothing to do with it, though," she added, turning to me. "She wouldn't even go see it. I asked her once if she was curious, and she said all that mattered to her was keeping Robbie away from all that. I understood. I think John did too because he never pressured her. But one day, he asked me and Dave to come see what he'd been doing, and so we went and looked."

Jenny stopped talking for a second, her eyes soft with a memory.

"And?" Adam asked.

She cleared her throat. "The portal he built was a Today door, just like the one beneath the lake was supposed to be. He would use a flower from the garden above as a token to lead him where he wanted to go: the parallel botanical gardens on the other side. It's the dimension we're in right now. He had bought the gardens on both sides, and he would just take over his other self while he was down. And in that garden beneath the castle, he had built his dream life. He planted mazes and weeping willows and an entire field of wildflowers. He even bought some horses and put them in the stable."

Adam and I must have had the same realization, because we both gasped at once.

One lucky winner will even have a chance to ride a real pony through the garden.

"Jesus," Adam sighed, "it's President Koenig's palace."

Jenny's eyes grew wide, and she burst out into a choking laugh that belied the fact that her eyes looked scared. "Is that what he decided to call him?"

"Decided to call him?" I repeatedly dumbly, my mind not able to catch up with the words.

"He always said all you needed to convince people to follow you was a symbol—a figurehead that represented to people what they really wanted to believe about themselves. It doesn't even have to be a real person—just a bunch of images and an idea."

My mind was reeling. Was she saying that . . . that there was no President Koenig? That it had just been John the whole time? I realized my mouth was hanging open. Adam shot up out of his seat and walked to the bar, just to let his body slump over it a bit while he listened.

"President Koenig." Jenny laughed strangely again at the name. "It's almost too perfect."

"Why?" I asked, my throat dry around the word.

"Because *König* is German for *king*."

The air settled in the room while Adam and I took this in.

"John was living a double life," Jenny said now, her eyes on Adam's back. "And his plan to send me and Dave on this mission hadn't changed. The truth is, I think John was planning to come live full-time beneath the gardens. He was just waiting for us to finish setting everything up down here, and then he would become his other self permanently. I have no idea if he ever did it or not. I've been stuck here for almost a year."

I waited for Adam to speak, but he didn't turn around, so I answered her question myself. "He didn't do it, Jenny. He's still up there, living with my mom at the hotel."

She nodded, shaking her head in self-admonishment. "Of course," she said softly. "He abandoned me here. That bastard was just gonna let me rot."

Before Adam or I could ask any more questions, the rumble of a loud engine could be heard pulling up outside, followed by a car door opening and closing with great force.

Peeking out the front window, I could see a large red car had pulled into the detached garage facing the house.

Suddenly, Jenny leaned over towards Adam, her voice turning urgent in a way that made him acknowledge her. "Adam, I need you to know this. I wasn't going to do what John wanted. I just told him that so he'd let me go. My plan had been to stop the creation of the portals." Her eyes darted to the door now, to the man who was approaching. "Alex said he could help me do it, that he knew all about the physics behind them. That's why I trusted him when I met him at the club. That's why I stole him an ID to get into the building. I didn't find out until later that . . ."

Carefree whistling came out of the mouth of whoever was walk-ing towards the house now, his feet crumbling the soft stones with an audible crunch. He was getting closer.

"That what?" Adam asked, a painful sympathy in his eyes.

"He's a plant. He was working for John the whole time."

Before she could say another word, the front door opened, and a booming voice preceded its owner into the room.

"I'm back!" the man shouted, joyful and bright, his footsteps heavy as he came into the room, his arms full of grocery bags.

And I froze in shock and fear, my mind going blank of anything but what was before me. Because the man who had walked into the room was my mother's Russian boyfriend, Alexei.

"Alex." Jenny beamed. "We were just waiting for you!"

CHAPTER THIRTY-NINE

Alexei's face didn't change in any discernible way when he saw me sitting on the couch or when he looked over and noticed Adam at the bar. Instead, the smile only grew wider on his chiseled face with its icy blue eyes. Putting the groceries down on an entry table, he reached out a hand to Adam as he crossed the room to meet him, and my body shivered like an ice cube had dropped down my spine. But when they had finished shaking hands, I was relieved to see that Alexei still seemed oblivious as to who we were.

I breathed a quiet sigh of relief. This wasn't the Alexei responsible for Adam's black eye. That meant he must have been the one from the world above the lake, the Russian investor John had been so excited about a dozen years ago. I didn't know when he had crossed over to this dimension, but all that mattered now was that he didn't know us.

"So, you're the competition," Alexei joked in his crisp, clear voice that betrayed almost no hint of an accent. Every time I'd heard him speak, I'd been struck by the idea that he must have studied hundreds of hours of American television to emulate our speech patterns and ended up speaking a hybrid that was almost too perfect to be believable.

Now he stood back and appraised Adam from a foot away, that knowing smirk never leaving his face. Then he turned to Jenny on the couch. "Well, I think I could take him, honey. What do you think?"

Jenny only giggled in response, playing her part again. Meanwhile, Adam stood as still as a statue, only a glimmer in his eyes letting me know that his mind was working overtime to assess the risk and to make a plan to get us out of it.

And then Alexei turned to me, his eyes drinking me in from head to foot like I was new furniture. "And you didn't come alone," he continued, still addressing Adam. "What a lovely girl you are. What is your name?"

"Mara."

"Ah, like *el mar*, the sea." He smiled, proud of himself. "And you're as pretty as an ocean."

I shivered again despite myself, Alexei's eyes boring through me and making me feel suddenly naked. Was I wrong that he didn't know us? Why was he still staring at me? Unable to hold still anymore, I started to get up. I didn't really have a plan, except to stand near Adam. To feel safer by his presence.

"No, don't get up," Alexei said before I could fully stand.

"I'm just going to get a coffee."

"I'll get it for you," he offered, and his tone let me know that it wasn't an offer. "Sit back down."

I swallowed hard, my legs trembling in a way that I hoped wasn't noticeable as I sat on the couch again.

"Jenny, sit next to her."

Jenny looked up at him, surprised, from the other side of the coffee table. "Why?"

"I want to look at you both at once," Alexei said, heading behind the bar to get me the coffee that I hadn't really wanted.

And as Jenny slowly stood and made her way over to my side, I looked over to Adam, whose anxious eyes now landed on a decision.

"We actually have to go," he said, his voice straining to sound steady despite the nerves that I could clearly make out.

"Not yet." Alexei smiled again, pouring the coffee. "You came to see Jenny, right? From a long distance, she says. You must have had good reason."

"Just to visit," Adam continued, every muscle in his body clearly tensing.

"So visit," Alexei snapped, his voice turning harsh as he slammed the coffee down. "Look at her. That's what you came for, right? To see her again?"

Adam started to back away from the counter towards the couch, but he was stopped in his tracks by something I couldn't see behind the bar. He whispered something I couldn't make out, though it sounded like, "Please."

"Stay where you are," Alexei said, and when he walked around the bar again I could finally see what Adam was reacting to. He had a gun in his hand, pointed at Adam's chest.

"No," I begged, standing without thinking, "please, stop. We'll go."

"Sit down, Marina, please," Adam pleaded, his attention still on the gun as his hands went up by his sides.

"You should listen to him . . . *Marina*," Alexei added, not blinking for a second as he looked at Adam. "Did you think I wouldn't know you?" he continued, and I knew he meant me. "You look just like your mother."

"Alex, baby, please," Jenny begged by my side, "they didn't do anything. Let's just let them go."

Alexei just shook his head at this, apparently disappointed. He nodded to the corner of the room, indicating the direction he wanted Adam to walk. "Go sit in the corner and don't move, or I'll kill you."

Adam looked tortured as his eyes darted to Jenny and me on the couch, locking with mine for only a second; the look of anguish on his face made me want to cry out. But I knew I couldn't. No matter what, I had to keep my wits about me now. I had to think as clearly as possible. There was a way out of this. I had to find it.

Adam moved to the corner as he was told, and I sat back down by Jenny, not wanting to upset Alexei even more by ignoring his order.

Alexei continued to shake his head in frustration as he backed away from Adam, coming back over to where he could clearly see the two of us on the couch, sitting side by side, powerless before him. I knew from the smirk that returned to his face that he wouldn't just let us go. Men like him got too much pleasure out of making others suffer, especially women. Watching the two of us trembling before him was probably the greatest thrill he'd had in a long time.

"I'm just so disappointed, Jenny," he said, although his face still looked smugly satisfied. "I really thought we'd have more time. I didn't expect you to be faithful—" At the word, a sob squeaked out of Jenny's throat. Her body began to tremble forcefully by my side, and I instinctively took her hand. She grasped mine back.

"Please," she whispered, barely able to form the word.

"But I did think we'd have more time—"

He was standing about five feet in front of us now, moving

the gun back and forth between my stomach and Jenny's. Adam's body lurched forward, almost crawling towards us, but Alexei stopped him with a forceful glare before turning back to us.

My stomach muscles began to clench uncontrollably, bracing themselves for impact. The moment lasted so long, I felt like I was floating above the room. Like, somehow, I was already dead. My father's eyes appeared before me. Kieren was right. I should have never come.

I'll never get to say goodbye.

"—before I had to do this." Alexei finished his sentence. And then the gun fired with a bang so loud I screamed and covered my ears.

Blood was on me, like it had been painted there. Speckles of it covered my arms.

Shaking violently, my hands lowered from my ears and seemed to move through molasses as they worked their way to my stomach, searching desperately for the bullet hole.

But there wasn't one.

Instead, Jenny collapsed into me, her body heavy and hot, blood gushing out of her, soaking her yellow dress in red.

I looked up just in time to see Alexei running out the door, and before I knew it, Adam was on top of us, holding us both in his strong arms and choking back moans of abject fear as his eyes fell on the gushing blood.

"Who's bleeding?" he asked in a high, terrified voice. "Who's bleeding?"

"It's not me," I answered, my hands going to hold up Jenny's face as it began to wobble forward, her skin turning white and her pupils beginning to dilate.

"No, no, no," was all Adam said, over and over again, as we laid Jenny down before us. I looked around frantically until my eyes landed on a throw blanket on the couch. I grabbed it and pushed it into the entry wound.

"Adam, push here," I said, taking his unsteady hands and pressing them into the blanket. "Keep putting pressure. I'll call an ambulance."

"Hurry, Marina."

"I am."

Outside, the rumble of a car engine was followed by the squealing of spinning tires and the crunching of the driveway stones, and then silence. Alexei was racing off, and I knew where he was going. But I couldn't do anything about it until Jenny was safe.

I scanned the room, finally seeing a phone on an end table. I picked up the receiver and prayed that rotary phones really did work the way they seemed to in old movies, barely able to control my nerves as my finger made the long, circular journey around the dial to turn the 9.

"You've reached emergency services. What is the nature of your call?"

"Someone's been shot," I said, trying to keep my voice steady and clear, not wanting to waste time repeating myself as I scanned the table in front of me for a piece of mail to give the address.

On the floor, Adam was crying over Jenny, stroking her hair with a bloody hand and pressing down the blanket over her wound with the other.

"Keep talking to her, Adam," I coached while I waited for the operator to respond. "Keep her awake. Ask her questions."

"Right." He nodded, shaking off his emotions to focus on the job before him.

The operator bombarded me with questions of her own: where the gunshot entered, how many shots were fired, how many victims. It was all I could do to focus and answer her as accurately as possible while I desperately observed Jenny on the floor, looking for signs of a response.

I was encouraged by the fact that her eyes were still open, straining to focus on Adam as he cooed soft questions that I couldn't quite hear.

"The ambulance is on the way," the operator finally confirmed. "Five minutes."

That was all I needed to hear. I placed the receiver down on the table, facing up in case Adam needed to say anything further to the operator. And then I started for the door.

"Where are you going?" Adam demanded before I could make it out.

"I have to follow him, Adam."

"No, Marina, no."

"I have to try."

Adam's hands didn't leave their task of applying pressure to Jenny's wound and stroking her forehead, but his face turned up to me with a new desperation. "I'll do it. You come help Jenny."

"You won't be able to get into the building, Adam. You don't have a name tag."

"Neither do you!"

"I can get one, though."

"Marina, please," he begged, his face turning red with emotion, his eyes wet. "Please. I can't lose you both."

"You won't," I promised, backing even farther towards the door. "Just get her on the ambulance. Stay with her."

He only shook his head, paralyzed on the floor, Jenny's hand lying weakly on top of his as he continued to push the blanket into her stomach.

"You're doing it, Adam." I nodded, trying to offer him the only comfort I could in that moment. "You're saving her life."

Before I could see the effect the words had on him, I turned and ran out of the house. If I waited any longer, I would lose my nerve. And I couldn't let that happen. Not if there was any chance I could still stop Alexei.

At least one mystery was solved: why Jenny never came back from the past. Because the first time this had happened, Adam hadn't been there to save her. But now he was. I could only pray it was enough, that the gunshot wasn't fatal. If nothing else, we would have saved one life.

But was it too late to save all the others who would be lost if Alexei wasn't stopped?

I ran to the garage, just on the off chance that he had a second car. There wasn't one, which was just as well, considering my driving abilities.

But there was something even better waiting for me, something that gave me a shred of hope, as though it were a good omen: a bicycle.

I hopped on and started pedaling towards Fort Pryman Shard one last time. My feet were slipping a bit in Mimi's heels, and the was seat propped up too high, but I wasn't going to let any of that get in my way. I wasn't stopping for anything in the world, not even the blaring, careening ambulance that sped past me on its way to the house, leaving a gush of hot wind in its wake.

CHAPTER FORTY

I ditched the bike around the bend from the guard's station, hoping against hope that another group of women might be making their way back from lunch, providing me with a cover in which to disappear. But I had no such luck this time. It was too early in the day.

Alexei's car was nowhere to be seen from where I was standing near the entrance. In fact, there was nothing about the sunny, bright day to give any indication of the stakes that were riding on whether or not I could get on the grounds.

I cleared my throat, quickly checking my skin and dress for any signs of blood, which I rubbed off as discreetly as possible. Then I approached the guard.

"You're not gonna believe this," I began, and I was immediately relieved to see that the guard was a young man, handsome if a bit skinny, with the beginnings of what I'm sure he hoped would soon be a moustache tickling his upper lip.

"What's that, honey?"

"I left my ID at my station yesterday, and I'm just going to be in a heap of trouble if I don't get to work on time."

The young man shook his head, a discouraging sign, but I couldn't help but notice that a slight smile never left his face. I was admittedly very inexperienced at flirting, but if there was ever a time to figure it out, it was now.

"Oh, please," I begged, leaning forward onto the little shelf of the half door between us in a way that I hoped was sexy and not just klutzy, my eyes landing on his name tag. "Please, Edwin, I wouldn't even ask, but my supervisor's been riding me lately, and this would just be the last straw."

Young Edwin turned the shade of a pomegranate when I said his name, so I decided to double down. "I don't know if I've even met you yet, have I? How long have you been here?"

"Two weeks," he answered, still shaking his head, unable to make eye contact with me.

"And I didn't even notice." I smiled.

He chuckled then, his face ripening to an even darker shade of red, and he started looking through what seemed to be a directory before him. "What's your name?"

My mind went completely blank for a moment, when suddenly, by the grace of whoever it is that is supposed to be looking out for us up there, the name popped into my head clear as day: "Golda. Golda Wexler."

He found the name on his list somewhere, looked up at me, and blushed again. Then he nodded for me to go in, and I was so excited I actually leaned forward and kissed him on the cheek before I did so.

Once on the grounds, I didn't have a clear plan of what to do next, as there would be another guard stationed at any of the building entrances, and I couldn't expect to flirt my way past all of them. It wasn't until my eyes landed on a small building off to the side of the main road with two Latina women coming out of it with cleaning carts that I knew what I had to do.

I approached the building tentatively, steadying my breath and praying silently that this would work. Knocking gently on the open door, I stepped inside the small structure—almost a shack, really—and squinted to adjust to the darkened room.

"*¿Sí?*" asked a short, squarely built woman before me, and it took me a moment of focusing on her stern face and wrinkled forehead to realize she was the same woman I had met yesterday. "*¿Qué quieres esta vez?*"

What do you want this time? It was a good question, and one that I didn't quite know how to answer. But I knew this woman was my only hope.

"*Por favor,*" I began, my hands trembling suddenly and my breath uneven. "*Necesito ayuda.*"

Her eyes turned a bit softer when I asked for help, and her head tilted back so she could judge me with a bit more perspective. Finally, after what seemed like an eternity, she lowered her head and spoke. "*¿Qué tipo de ayuda?*"

I smiled at the question. She wouldn't want to know what kind of help I needed unless she was considering it. I took a step forward, gesturing to the extra pairs of work boots and overalls folded neatly on shelves against the wall. "*Un trabajo,*" I said, and she nodded with a certain kind of acceptance that let me know I wasn't the first girl to walk in here looking for a job, and I probably wouldn't be the last.

o o o

I adjusted the overalls that had been at least three sizes too big when I first put them on, tightening the straps so that the waist actually fell somewhere in the vicinity of the middle of my body, and then leaned over to roll up the pant legs one more time.

For the first time in my life, my terrible Spanish had probably been my biggest asset with Lorena, which I now knew to be the name of the woman who had helped me, because it was just the tipping point to convince her that no one as incompetent as me could ever pose a threat to the fort.

I pushed my cleaning cart up and down the main road that ran the length of all those weirdly named buildings two times before my eyes finally fell on what they'd been searching for: Alexei's red car. It was parked in front of Y12, a two-story building that was not attached to the main entrance, but I could see from its layout that one day it would be—it was the senior wing of East Township High, the one with all my science and math classes.

Next door was a building called X10, sitting on what would be a vacant lot in my day. But after tilting my head this way and that and closing my eyes a moment to imagine the walk from the boiler room through the twisting hallway into the science lab—

I opened my eyes. X10 was over the portals. It had to be.

The question was, if X10 would have the portals one day, then why was Alexei in Y12?

Pushing my cart with my head bowed down, I flashed my temporary work pass at the guard at Y12, who was thankfully distracted with the cigarette he was attempting to light in the soft breeze. He waved me in without any questions.

No one seemed to notice me as I pushed the cart down the unfamiliar hallway. Several people were marching with great purpose past the blandly painted walls, in and out of offices where the clacking of typewriters could be heard. I kept my head low, busying myself with some item in the cleaning cart whenever it seemed someone might be looking at me suspiciously.

I wasn't exactly sure what I was looking for, other than trying to ascertain where in the building Alexei might have gone off to. But my mind whirled endlessly as I walked, trying to piece together what I did know:

Jenny had stolen Alexei an ID, one that had let him come and go from this building whenever he pleased.

He'd had the ID for a while, probably months, or at least since Dave had died and Alexei had swooped in to take his place. That meant he'd had time to ingratiate himself to the workers here. They would trust him, think of him as one of their own.

And finally, Alexei was working for John, and whatever it was he was planning would ensure that the Russians got the bomb first. No, not the bomb—the fuel for the bomb. The enriched uranium. That must be what this building was for.

As I was turning these thoughts over in my mind, I became distracted by an incessant noise that started almost like a hum and continued to grow louder and louder the farther I got down the hallway. It was a clicking sound, like the gurgle of a car motor just before it runs out of gas.

Cherie had said that her mother monitored gauges and that they would click and spin whenever they detected high levels of enriched uranium. Maybe that clicking could point me to the source of the uranium itself.

I entered the compact room, full of what appeared to be telephone operators—young women in practical dresses and pinned-back hair, their fingers hovering over knobs with looks of great concentration on their faces. I took out a duster and began to lightly brush it over some of the unused equipment, grateful that nobody seemed to think this unusual.

"Esther?" a woman behind me asked an older woman who had been sitting nearby on a stool watching her own gauges.

"Yes?"

"There's something wrong with mine," the woman said, sounding apologetic that she was being a nuisance.

"Let me see, Golda," Esther said as she left her station and approached the other woman's. My eyes couldn't help but dart up curiously. Golda looked exactly as I would have imagined—very much like Sage and Cherie, with dark blond hair, a strong nose, and deep-set eyes. I was trying not to stare, but I couldn't help but steal another second to observe her, marveling at the odd sensation that a character from an almost mythological story was coming to life before my eyes.

Golda, and everyone else in this room for that matter, had no idea the significance of these little dials and knobs, nor did they have any way of knowing that a Russian traitor had been in their midst for months, sabotaging all their work.

But just as I was finishing this thought, mindlessly circling that duster over some machinery so as not to give myself away, something changed in the room.

At first, it was just that Golda's gauge wouldn't stop making the clicking sound. And it was growing louder, the needle itself starting to spin a bit more rapidly.

And then another woman's gauge started clicking too. "Esther?" she asked in a nervous, high-pitched voice that made her sound about twelve years old, though she was surely at least eighteen.

And another gauge. And then another.

Before Esther could do anything about it, all the dozen or so gauges in the room began to spin and click, whirring ever louder as they picked up speed. The clicking grew in volume until all of the young women were sitting back on their stools, looks of worry on their faces telling me that this was not an everyday occurrence.

"Is it happening again?" Golda asked.

"I don't know," Esther stammered. "I'll . . ." she stuttered, "I'll get a supervisor."

I dropped the duster as Esther ran out of the room. There was no more time for charades. Approaching Golda, I leaned over by her stool and made eye contact.

"You don't know me," I began, whispering loudly over the cacophony of the gauges, "but I need your help."

Golda looked confused, searching for Esther or someone to save her.

"It's okay," I continued.

"What do you need?" she asked, worry knitting her brows together, still clearly thinking about her hyperactive gauge and not about the strange cleaning lady suddenly bothering her.

"There's a room around here somewhere with a bunch of tubes in it. Pipes. Maybe shaped like an oval, a racetrack?"

She nodded, still not sure why I was asking about this. "And?"

"Where is it?"

She shook her head, looking around again for Esther or someone else to take over.

"Golda," I said, more forcefully this time, "please, just answer me. Where is the room?"

Golda only shrugged, her eyes darting to all the other girls who were staring in fear and disbelief at their clicking, clacking machinery, the din of it echoing off the metal panels that lined the little room. "It's in the basement," she finally answered, shaking her head in doubt.

And with the cleaning rag still gripped in my trembling hand, I turned and ran towards the stairwell.

CHAPTER FORTY-ONE

The sight that greeted me at the foot of the stairs actually made a small sound of surprise escape my lips. The entire basement was just one giant lab, with a small entryway partitioned off from the rest by a glass window.

What was on the other side of that window made me stop in my tracks. Pictures from a dozen history books on nuclear energy and particle physics suddenly came into blinding reality before my eyes. I wanted to cry at the awe-inspiring enormity of what I was looking at.

It really did look like a racetrack, the magnetized tubes that were processing raw uranium atoms and separating out the much-needed lower-neutron isotopes creating a Frankensteinian element nearly impossible in nature: plutonium. Men in white lab coats buzzed about the apparatus as the humming of the magnets grew louder and louder.

I approached that reinforced glass now like a kid at the zoo seeing an exotic animal for the first time, unable to hide the amazement in my eyes as I took in the scene and watched the handful of scientists assessing the quality of the machine's output.

The scientists looped around a central figure like electrons around a nucleus, and my heart stopped when I saw who was at the center of all that energy: Alexei.

And he was looking right at me.

Or, at least, that's how it seemed at first. Only after a moment of my heart leaping into my throat did I realize that his gaze was actually focused on a point behind my head. In the reflection of the glass wall between us, he couldn't make out my face.

Still, I spun around quickly before his eyes had a chance to adjust or he took a step that reduced the glare, exposing the fact that I'd followed him here.

With the rag in my hand, I busied myself cleaning the lamps in the small lobby, trying to think of what I could do to expose Alexei to the other men in the room. If I simply came forward and announced what I knew about him, who would believe me? Even if this time period weren't proving to be even more racist and sexist than the future, it would still be hard to believe a cleaning woman over a revered scientist.

But my indecision was settled for me when I looked up again.

A small canister, about the size of a coffee can, was now sitting under a protective glass case on a wheeled cart that Alexei was carefully pushing through a doorway at the back of the glassed-in room. Turning in unison, almost like they were one interconnected blob and not individual men, all the white-coated scientists in the room followed right behind him.

That canister—such a tiny, insignificant-looking thing—was the reason this whole place existed. It was hard to believe that something so small would be the death warrant for hundreds of thousands of people.

I waited a few seconds, making sure the coast was clear, before venturing into the lab and letting my eyes rest for just a moment on that incredible piece of machinery—still humming and radiating off a slight warmth from its efforts. Then I proceeded through the back doorway, following Alexei and that precious little canister.

The hallway that lurked behind the door had the feel of a secret tunnel—dark and narrow, lit only by a few overhead mining lights. It traveled on for maybe forty feet, turning a couple of times, before letting out through an identical door at the other end.

Once I reached that door, I took a deep breath, not sure what might greet me on the other side. What if Alexei was waiting for me there? What if a security guard was?

I shook off my nerves, took a deep breath, and opened the door.

It took me a moment to process that the room I had entered was the size of an entire building. As I tried to get my bearings, my eyes latched on to something that was oddly familiar— high-up windows that lined the edge of the room, like storm windows, revealing that we were just underground. And it wasn't until I stared at them for a moment that I was able to place them.

They were the windows that lined the twisting, turning hallway that led to the science lab, the one beyond the boiler room. I had always said that the hallway looked like it was built to avoid hitting the trees in an invisible forest. It weaved this way and that, seemingly with no rhyme or reason, and doors on either side of the corridor led alternately to bricked-up rooms or long-abandoned offices.

Now that I was finally seeing this subterranean maze in its original form, my brain superimposing the future version of the hallway over the one before my eyes, it was like a light of understanding had been turned on in my head.

The parts of the floor that were missing in the future were now occupied by enormous tubes, pipes, and machinery. Computers the size of a living room. Pipes so wide a person could walk through them without ducking. Things that would become obsolete over the years, hulking machinery that would eventually be replaced by nanotubes and memory sticks containing more gigabytes of data than this entire building.

In the future, when the hallway was being carved out of the remnants of this place, they would simply brick off the odd assortment of parts that were no longer needed.

My eyes zeroed in on the very back of the enormous room—a room that must have spanned almost the entire area of the basement of what I now realized was the building called X10, the one that would eventually contain the portals. And the men in the white coats had made it to the exact spot where those portals would be— or rather, they were hovering about fifteen feet over the exact spot.

I watched in stunned silence, keeping my distance and making the most rudimentary show of cleaning whatever happened to be nearby, as the canister was taken off the rolling cart and emptied carefully by a cadre of scientists into long, cylindrical tubes. The entire back wall of the place was an enormous board filled with dozens of circular holes, and a quick glance informed me that they were just the right size for the tubes to fit into.

It was a reactor. This was it—the ultimate experiment. They were going to try to make a sustained nuclear reaction with the plutonium in those tubes. I knew from what Cherie had told us that this wasn't the first time they'd pulled it off. That had been months before, in November. But judging from the scared faces of Golda and the other women upstairs, I was willing to bet that it hadn't happened often. Was I really lucky enough to be witnessing this pivotal moment in history?

317

But whatever it was the men were expecting to see from that reactor, it probably wasn't what happened next.

The frantic shouting of a man with a thick foreign accent made me drop all pretense of being a cleaning lady. Panic seized my stomach when I saw the other men's nervous faces.

There had been an accident. The smooth, interweaving dance of the men who'd been assisting Alexei had been replaced by chaotic bumping and careening bodies. Something was wrong. People were huddling into a small human mountain, covering those desperately important cylinders, their backs strained by tightening muscles.

I could only make out glimpses through the sea of chaotic bodies. The men surrounding Alexei encouraged him softly in worried voices. The words *Don't lose a drop* seeped out of one man's throat, muffled by the tension in his voice. For a moment, it seemed as though maybe they had controlled the problem.

But then another moment of panic seized the people in the room, causing every one of their bodies to tense and flail. "Oh, God!" someone shouted. "Oh no!"

And finally, one more voice, quiet and spooked: "What in God's name—"

Now other workers from the room behind me had joined me in gaping at the men, a fact that relieved me as it took away any focus I might have been attracting. We all stood powerless together, our mouths open, as we helplessly watched the show before us.

"Get it, get it!"

"I can't!" shouted another man. "It's too late."

Looking down, I finally made out something that took my breath away: a slow, oozing trickle of neon pink, seeping its way past the feet of all those men and wending through the ground beneath them towards the corner of the room.

"What is it?" a desperate-sounding man behind me asked.

"I have no idea," panted another.

The scientists in the room seemed equally fazed, backing away slowly with their hands on the sides of their heads as if trying to hold their disbelieving brains in place. It wasn't until the men had backed away that I could see one figure in the middle—a man who didn't seem shocked or frightened by the lava-like flow of pink goop that was now burning a hole into the ground as it traveled.

Alexei and I were the only people in the building who had any way of knowing what the hell we were looking at. But it still chilled me to the bone to see it again.

Suddenly, the trail of pink ooze began to separate, branching like a river hitting a bed of rocks into three separate streams, all skinnier and slower than the first. As if on cue, the three separate branches stopped in their tracks and slowly—painstakingly slowly—began to melt their way into the earth below, boring deep and irreversible holes into the floor. Holes that glowed and radiated out a menacing pink aura that filled the room with an eerie sense of doom.

The three portals had taken root. They could never be undone.

Enthralled as I was by the sight, and as much as the terrified clamor of those around me was making me uneasy, I had the presence of mind to look up at that moment, away from the newly formed portals towards the one person who wasn't watching this scene unfold.

Alexei had the container with the remaining plutonium in his hands. And under the cover of the confusion in the room, he was sneaking away towards the unguarded door.

CHAPTER FORTY-TWO

"Stop!" I shouted before I even realized that I had opened my mouth. An immediate rush of embarrassment, mingled with fear of exposure, made my cheeks burn hot and my throat suddenly go dry.

Everyone in the room, from the scientists who had been staring dumbly at the new portals to the workers who had been buzzing anxiously around me, stopped like they'd been freeze-framed and stared at me.

Not knowing how I could possibly explain my presence or get anyone to believe my story, I instead decided that the best course of action was simply to point out the obvious fact before me. My finger pointed up towards the door where Alexei had disappeared with the canister of plutonium wedged under his arm.

"Stop him!" I choked out, my voice thin and airy. "He's getting away."

All the men in the room, still shaking their heads and muttering as they tried to decipher what exactly had happened just moments before, now looked even more perplexed as their eyes followed the line of my finger.

"Where is he?" asked the man with the thick accent.

A clamor of confusion followed, all the men in their white lab coats seeming to arrive in unison at the same conclusion that I had: Alexei was no longer in the room.

The man with the accent locked eyes with me for a moment, seeing what must have been abject panic on my face. He then turned to the little rolling table where the canister had been and, seeing that it was just as absent as Alexei, his face contorted from confusion to terror. "Oh God," he muttered. "Where is Dr. Rostoff?" he asked the room, but no one responded.

And that was when I heard a sound that was so familiar to me I almost didn't think anything of it at first. It took my brain several seconds to latch on to the understanding that, yes, I really was hearing the thumping, chugging cacophony of a train approaching—the squeal of the brakes, the vibration of the floor as the massive behemoth approached, the swoosh of the releasing steam.

But how could a train be here? We were over a mile from the station.

I ran through the room then, hoping that people would be too distracted to have the presence of mind to stop me. I ran right past all those befuddled men in their lab coats, past the white-haired man with the thick accent, and through the door from which Alexei had escaped.

It led to the base of a small flight of concrete stairs, revealing that we were roughly fifteen feet below ground level. Blinded temporarily by the harsh daylight as I ran up two steps at a time, I froze in shock once my eyes landed on the sight before me.

The train track had been rerouted so that it ran directly behind the fort. One glance at the train spelled out the reason: it was only five cars long, and the middle three were all empty barrel-shaped hopper cars. Perfect for hauling in large quantities of raw uranium. Meanwhile, the last car, the one right in front of my face, was shaped like a silver bullet, encased in what appeared to be armored steel.

As I stood there gaping at the enormous train just feet from me, the man with the accent caught up with me.

I turned to him in desperation, my palms slick with fear. "I can't explain right now," I began, "but you need to believe me. The man who took the canister is a traitor. He's a Russian spy. We need to stop him."

To his credit, he didn't take too long to come around to this new information. I suppose it was a conclusion he had already begun to draw as soon as he saw his would-be colleague sneaking off with a canister of plutonium.

"He must be inside," he said, nodding his head towards the sleek bullet-shaped car before us. His thick Eastern European accent made the words sound crisp and urgent.

I watched uselessly as the man stepped onto the train car in front of me. I didn't dare follow once I saw the guard stationed at the door. There was no way he would let me on.

From where I was standing, though, I could see that the inside looked eerily like a stripped-down submarine. For a moment, my mind reeled with memories of the train between dimensions where my brother, Robbie, had been trapped for almost four years—a train that was devoid of any discernible humanity, floating endlessly into the black hole of time and space.

But this was not the same train. This one was quite real, as was the guard who stopped the scientist in front of me before he could fully step aboard.

"Sorry, Dr. Kleiner, but Dr. Rostoff has given strict orders. No one else is to board today."

"Daniel, you don't understand—" the man in the lab coat, Dr. Kleiner, began to protest.

"It's only for today," Daniel continued, his hands raised slightly in a definitive but gentle gesture. These two clearly had met before, apparently under less stressful circumstances.

My eyes darted left and right, my feet locked in place, as I half listened to their conversation. Dr. Kleiner continued to try to sway Daniel to let him on, but Daniel clearly had strict orders. Encouraged by the distraction the scientist was providing, I willed my feet a few inches to the left, down towards the front car of the train.

No one was watching me, I realized as I continued to shuffle down the length of the train cars. I was never going to be allowed onto the bullet car, but maybe there was another way.

That's when the chugging started up again.

A quick glance to my left towards the first car at the head of the train revealed a chimney. The train was steam-driven, meaning that first car was the engine. And the engineers in that room would need to breathe, so there would have to be windows.

I doubled my speed, heading towards that first car, but the train was starting to lurch away from me. Soon it would be going too fast to jump aboard. I let go of all thought and threw myself forward. I hadn't quite made it to the engine yet, so I had to settle for the first of the hopper cars. It had a slight shelf at the base, barely big enough for my feet to land on. My fingers grasped on to anything they could find—namely the molding that ran horizontally across the barrel of the car.

I was mere inches from the front of the car. If I could just slide the rest of the way, I'd be able to leap for the engine. But the shaking and rumbling of the train made that a very precarious proposition. At least we were pulling away from X10, and there didn't seem to be any prying eyes on my back.

Now the train was really starting to go. The wind whipped against my face, thrashing my hair loose of the bandana and into my eyes. Terrified of letting go of the quarter-inch of metal that was keeping me upright, I could only shake my head in fast circles to try to get the hair away.

The train reached full speed within minutes, and I knew it was too late to jump. We were pulling away from the complex of buildings that formed the fort now, heading through a patch of trees. In a few minutes, we would probably be in town.

Would the train stop at the station? If not, it might be miles before it did.

What the hell had I done this time?

My fingers began to sweat, but I took deep breaths and willed them not to cramp up—not to let me fall. Looking towards the front of the train, I flinched for a moment at a slight movement before me.

Then I saw it again. It was a human hand, sticking out of the front of the engine car and flicking ash off a cigarette. That was it, I realized with a gush of relief—the window. I was right about the engine. That was the way in.

Gathering all my courage, I slid my left fingers a quarter-inch to the side, willing my right fingers to follow suit.

You can do this, Marina, I chanted to myself softly. *You have to do this.*

Left fingers, then right. Then the feet. Just a quarter-inch more. Fingers. Feet. Breathe.

Fingers. Feet. Breathe.

And then a mighty leap of faith, my fingers grasping across the chasm between the hopper car and the engine, and I found a firm handhold to clutch. With all my might, I pulled myself the few inches between the two cars, and I was officially clinging to the outside of the engine, just inches from the window.

We were in the shadow of the trees still, and the flickering spasms of light that managed to hit the train were playing tricks on my eyes, messing with my depth perception. I reached a bit too far with the left hand and almost slipped, gripping the metal again so tightly I could feel three fingernails bend in on themselves.

But I knew I could breathe now. Because I had reached the window.

Grasping on to the window frame with a mighty effort, I yanked my whole body towards the comforting warm air inside. I didn't have time to register the shocked eyes of the man who turned in my direction.

"Holy—" he muttered.

"Help," I gasped, and before I knew it, he had grabbed my arm, high up by the shoulder, and was all but picking me up in his thick, hulking hands and lifting me into the car.

Once fully inside, my body collapsed to the floor with relief. *That was the craziest thing I've ever done*, I thought with a self-chastising grunt. My fingers were still shaking with tension, my knees clutched up to my chest.

The man who had saved me took one last drag of the cigarette before flinging it out the window. "You'd better have a good story, kid."

"I do," I stuttered, still collecting my breath.

"Well?"

I swallowed hard, looking up into two crinkled deep brown eyes. His skin and hair were so covered in soot from the coal that I couldn't tell if he was thirty or seventy, but he was a large man, both in height and girth. He looked like he could bench-press the train if he wanted to.

"There's a man on this train named Alexei Rostoff. He's a Russian spy, and he's stolen something very important from the fort. We need to find him and stop him before he gives it to the Russians."

Those two deeply cave-like eyes squinted down at me for a moment, then burst open with what I assume was amusement as a snort of disbelief escaped his bark-like lips.

"I'm serious."

"You're getting off at the next station."

"It's a canister of plutonium. Enough to build a bomb."

"Look, I don't know anything about all that—" the man protested, already shutting me down.

"It's not just a bomb, it's—it's the biggest bomb in the world. You have to believe me."

He took out another cigarette and covered his hand with his map-sized palm to light it. His eyes traveled out the window for a moment, one hand returning to an enormous metal clutch that I assumed was some sort of brake.

"There's a war on, sweetheart. Lots of bombs."

"Not like this one."

He considered my words for a moment, the cigarette dwarfed by the sheer size of his weathered face as it dangled from his mouth. "What do you mean?" he finally asked.

"This one could blow up a city the size of Chicago."

The cigarette dangled limply for a moment, then plummeted to the ground. Coming back to reality, the man looked down at the floor where the burning embers were touching the wooden plank by his feet.

Then he furiously stamped it out with a reverberating thump.

CHAPTER FORTY-THREE

My new friend's name was J.P., and he wheezed like an asthmatic child every time he took a step around the small, confined space between us. I had told him everything I could think of to sway him, and near as I could tell, he was still considering my words.

The fate of everything was now in his hands. I couldn't stop this train myself. I didn't even know how. But he could. And once it was stopped, we would just have to get to Alexei.

The train continued to rumble beneath my feet, swaying and lurching suddenly as it emerged from the cover of trees and plunged into the stark, unrelenting light of the bright summer day. My nostrils filled with J.P.'s sweat, mixed with coal dust, cigarette smoke, and what I assumed was the metallic odor of his hair tonic. Despite everything, though, I found the smells comforting. I was reminded of the late nights in my father's workshop, when he'd get so caught up in a project he'd forget to come in to eat or even shower until Laura or I would all but drag him back inside.

A sting of tears lashed at my eyes as my father's memory became more vivid in my mind. I knew I had committed to finishing this mission; I knew that the future of everyone in the underlake world was riding on it, that Adam was depending on me, that Jenny getting shot and maybe even dying would be all for nothing if I didn't pull this off. But all I could think about was getting back to that garage—back to that jumble of computer wires and hard drives that he called an office. Back to my father's arms. Back to the girl I'd been when I'd last seen him.

If it wasn't too late.

That's when J.P. pulled the huge metal lever, and the painful screeching of the train's brakes whipped me back into reality as the imposing behemoth beneath our feet ground its way to a determined halt.

We had stopped in the middle of sunlight, but I had no idea where.

Without so much as a word, J.P. yanked open the steel door of the engine car and descended with a thud to the ground below. Though he didn't even acknowledge me as he did so, I got the feeling I was supposed to follow him, and so I did.

I kept myself safely hidden behind his broad back as we walked in a terrifying dual beat towards the back car of the train. One of J.P.'s feet—the left one—was apparently smaller than the other, making him twist awkwardly at the end of each stride, and he sometimes had to stop and collect his breath before continuing.

I stayed a couple inches behind his back like it was a force field, my eyes popping out in intervals to scan the scene before me for any sign of Alexei.

Just a few feet down the track, there he was, facing me in a standoff that could only end with one victor.

He held the canister of plutonium in his hands. If he escaped with it, he would be able to follow through with his original plan: bringing it to Russia so that the Soviet Union would beat us to obtaining the atomic bomb.

The world beneath the lake had been built, or rather designed, based on the power that this twisted, evil man held before me. I had one chance to stop that from ever happening, and that chance was now.

I knew that if I hesitated, it would be too late. Sirens could be heard in the distance, growing louder. The scientist in the lab coat—Dr. Kleiner—and the guard, Daniel, now descended from the back silver bullet car, standing behind Alexei, who stood dead center. We had him surrounded, with J.P. and me before him and the other two men behind.

But Alexei had the real power in this situation, clasped between his steel-like hands, and everyone seemed to realize it at once.

Still, I had to try.

I began to approach him, my hands in the air. I knew he still had the gun on him, that he wouldn't hesitate to shoot me. But if he did that, the police would open fire when they arrived. He would surely be stopped from delivering the package to the Russians. I had to risk that he wouldn't take that chance.

I kept walking towards him.

"Wait, girl," J.P. called from behind me. "Is that it in his hands?"

"Yes, that's it," I answered over my shoulder, my eyes not wavering from Alexei, caught like a mouse before me.

"Wait for the authorities, girl."

"I am the authorities, J.P."

I kept walking, almost to him now, and Alexei's eyes began to dart around, looking for an escape route. He was getting twitchy, and finally he turned and began running away from me. Daniel and Dr. Kleiner moved to block his path, but he held the canister up.

"I swear I'll drop it. It's unstable. Move back."

The two men, realizing the gravity of the situation, did as they were told.

But was the canister unstable? There was nothing exerting any pressure on its contents. So long as that remained true, it should be safe. I kept walking.

"Wait, child," Dr. Kleiner said as I got near him.

I smiled at him, and his kind eyes locked with mine for a moment, but I knew I had to keep walking.

Finally, Alexei stopped, standing now in the middle of the track. He turned to face me.

My breath caught in my throat, but I didn't stop moving.

"You stupid bitch," Alexei muttered.

I kept walking.

"You'll ruin it all."

I kept walking.

As I reached him, he suddenly lurched forward and grabbed me, the canister clutched in the hand that smothered me to his chest. A gasp of shock escaped my lips. He had turned me now to face the men who stood frozen in fear before us. They all had their hands slightly raised, their eyes on the canister.

Something hard jabbed my ribs—the gun barrel. It was cold through the coarse fabric of the work overalls.

I'll never get the ring back.

What a ridiculous thing to think.

That's when I looked up from where we stood on the tracks and caught a glimpse of Groussman's Pharmacy across the street.

Wait a minute.

I suddenly knew exactly where we were—in town, maybe a

hundred feet from the station I had known my whole life—the one where my fate had been changed more times than I could count.

It was the station where Robbie and Kieren and I had waited for our fathers to arrive on the evening commuter train from work when we were kids.

It was the station where Piper McMahon had gotten on the westbound train in another reality—a reality where I was a scared sixteen-year-old kid following her hopeless crush on what would turn out to be the most fateful day of his life.

And it was the station where my brother, Robbie, and his best friend, Kieren, had been popping wheelies and playing chicken with the train when Robbie, only fourteen years old—Robbie who had been my hero, my best friend, sometimes my only friend—had followed Kieren down the track, within feet of where I now stood, and been struck by the oncoming train.

It was fitting, then, that this was where I would have to confront Alexei. Because if I was going to die today, I might as well do it in the same place my brother had.

I wasn't afraid of death anymore. I had seen it with my own eyes. I had conquered it with my own hands. And I was ready to do so again.

I turned my head back towards Alexei.

"Stop!" came a man's voice to my left. Our heads whipped in unison towards the sound, and somehow it was Adam standing just twenty feet away. His shirt was covered in blood, his eyes red. How had he found me? Why wasn't he with Jenny?

Was she already dead?

Adam began to creep closer, and so did the men by the train. They were encircling us. Even if he shot me, Alexei would have nowhere to run.

"Goddamn it," Alexei whispered behind me.

Before I knew it, the canister of plutonium had been shoved into my stomach, my hands grasping it by instinct alone.

I closed my eyes. For a moment, I felt myself floating above the scene, as I had when Alexei's gun had been aimed at me hours before. I tried to be brave, but I could feel myself shaking. There was liquid on my face, in my mouth. Bitter salt. My legs unsteady. The world spinning too slow.

And then arms around me.

Adam's arms.

A gunshot blasted into the sky. I opened my eyes and saw Alexei running away, the gun pointed towards the heavens. Another gunshot—a warning. *Don't follow me.*

And then he was gone, and I was still in Adam's arms.

"How did you find me?" I asked.

"Followed the sirens." He kissed the top of my head, and I squeezed him tighter, but then I was brought back to reality by the soft echo of a plopping sound by my feet.

I looked down, and a surreal feeling encircled me as I realized what I was looking at. In between my feet and Adam's, the slightest dollop of neon pink had dripped from the canister in my hands. It sizzled into the track, making us both step back from each other. It covered only a few inches of the rail, which glowed an ominous pink for a few seconds and then faded back to metal.

Adam and I continued to back away from the spot—the spot where the future coins would be made, the spot where Robbie would be killed but not killed.

It was the train portal.

I had backed off to one side of the tracks, Adam to the other. We stared at each other, the gulf of the tracks—of the most dangerous portal of all—now lying between us.

I didn't see where the man came from. He appeared as if on the wind. Was he real? Was he not? I couldn't tell. At first he looked like any man from the 1940s. Tan trousers and a button-up shirt. A hat to block his gaunt face from the sun. He walked onto the tracks and leaned down at the spot where the radioactive material had dripped onto the metal. He touched it with his long, skeletal finger. He touched it slowly, mournfully, as though placing his finger for the last time on the head of a sleeping child who would never wake up.

And then he looked up at me with piercing blue eyes, eyes that looked right through my soul.

He was alive. He was real. But he wouldn't always be.

The conductor stared at me, and with silent words his eyes condemned me.

Shame. Shame. Shame.

Dr. Kleiner was beside me now, his hands outstretched. I handed him the canister, and when I looked back at the tracks, they were empty. The conductor—or the man who would become him, rather—was gone. The sirens were almost upon us. Adam and I would have to explain ourselves somehow. We would have to get ourselves out of this.

But during the brief moment of reprieve before that happened, I crossed over to the other side of the tracks, stepping carefully over the place where the portal would forever exist, as though stepping over my own fate.

Then I fell into Adam's arms and pretended they were the only truth in the world.

CHAPTER FORTY-FOUR

Even pale and free of makeup, a cannula in her nose, her face gaunt from the loss of blood, and her lips chapped with dehydration, Jenny managed to look beautiful. She looked like one of those heroin-chic models from the '90s, all cheekbones and shoulder blades. She held out a long, trembling arm towards Adam when she saw us at the foot of her hospital bed, and Adam obliged by taking her hand in his.

I was surprised, however, when she then held out the other hand to me. I stared awkwardly at it for a moment, misinterpreting the gesture as weakly hostile. But then a strained smile across those whitened lips informed me that she meant for me to come to the other side of her bed and comfort her too.

I did so, and her hands were so cold and bony that it was hard to believe she was still alive.

The military guard who had escorted us here was kind enough to wait out in the hallway while we visited with Jenny. Adam had been quick on his feet while we were being questioned back at the train track. He seemed to pull every answer out of his head ready-formed, as though he'd been thinking ahead the whole time.

Jenny was a friend of mine from the base, he'd told the MP—a stout, middle-aged man with round glasses who would probably have been a bank manager or a vice principal had the war not come.

We had gone to Jenny's house for brunch, he'd explained, and her boyfriend had attacked her. Shot her in the stomach. No, sir, we didn't know he was a spy until Jenny told us. No, sir, we'd had no idea he'd had a gun. No, sir, we didn't know what was in the canister, just that it belonged to the base.

We were just being good citizens, Adam had explained.

Good Americans.

I had stood silently while they talked, grateful for once that the sexism of the time precluded me having to add much. My voice had been lost somewhere in the hot summer air that had enshrouded us in afternoon heat.

We had done everything we'd set out to do in this world. We'd stopped the Russians from obtaining the plutonium. They wouldn't get the bomb before we did now, and so this dimension would not diverge from our own. Sage and George, our friends in the diner— they would be safe now.

It should have been a moment of jubilation. But somehow all I could think about was that it felt like something deep inside of me was dying.

Turning my attention back to Jenny in the bed, I tried to offer her a sympathetic smile. I tried to think about her and stop thinking about myself.

"They gave me a transfusion," she whispered now through a dry throat. "Seven bags, the doctor said. He had never used so many before. He didn't think I was going to make it."

"You'll be fine," I insisted, although I had no idea if that was true.

"You're cold," Adam noticed. "I'll find you another blanket."

"Not wool," she called as he walked off.

"Not wool, I know."

She smiled, turning back to me. "Wool upsets my skin."

I nodded, secretly stung to realize how many little things like that Jenny and Adam must have known about each other. Their long history hovered over the room even after he had walked out of it, just as it had always seemed to hover just above the surface of every conversation he and I had ever had.

I shook the selfish thoughts away, trying to stay present for Jenny.

"What happened with Alexei?" she asked.

"I stopped him from taking the fuel for the bomb. He got away, but I don't think he'll be able to try it again. Everyone knows what he looks like now."

She nodded, but her face looked pained. "I'm so sorry. I should have never let it get to this point. I should have stopped him myself."

"He just would have shot you sooner."

Her eyes darted up at me, surprised by the frankness of my tone. I flinched, realizing how it had sounded. Bedside manner was never my best quality. I had a dangerous tendency to say things exactly as I thought them.

No medical career for you, Marina. Luckily, robots don't have feelings.

But Jenny smiled despite my mistake. "You're right. He would have."

Adam came back into the room with a small white blanket that appeared to be made of cotton. "From the pediatric ward," he explained as he tried to stretch the square of fabric over her delicate body. "It's the only nonwool one they have."

He sat on the edge of her bed now, his hand lying awkwardly near hers but maintaining a couple inches of distance. "Jenny, I have to make sure Marina gets back home. But then I'll come back and help you—"

"No," she said, her voice calm and certain. "You go back too."

"I'll wait until you're out of here."

"Adam . . ."

She didn't seem to know what else to say, so she simply took my hand, still linked with hers, and placed it into Adam's open palm. It took his warm fingers a second to adjust to the shock and to wrap around mine.

"I've been down nearly a year, Adam. Anyone who knew this version of me assumes I'm dead, if I can even go back."

"You're going to stay?" he asked.

She shrugged. "I like it here. It's simpler. Now that the war is ending, it'll be a good time to live."

"Jenny," I protested, ripping my hand from Adam's and leaning in towards her. "You can't just stay here."

"Don't worry, kid. I won't disturb anything. The truth of the matter is, I never really felt like a part of the modern world. I was always a square peg in a round hole. I just didn't fit."

Adam sat frozen on the bed, unable to look at her or say anything.

"Adam, kiss me goodbye."

But he only shook his head.

With a great effort, Jenny propped herself up onto her elbows. She reached a weak arm towards his downturned head and tilted his chin to her. Then she leaned over and gave him such a gentle kiss on the lips that I wasn't sure he'd even be able to feel it.

It felt strange and very intrusive to be watching this scene, but somehow I was afraid it would be even more distracting if I got up and left in the middle of it.

Jenny collapsed back into the bed, having exerted herself too much. She trembled with exhaustion, her eyes fluttering closed.

Adam couldn't take it anymore. He stood and kissed her one more time on the top of her head and then bolted out the door, leaving me there like a dinghy abandoned at sea.

Jenny smiled again, whispering to me, "Take him home, Marina. Promise me you'll take him home."

I nodded, but Jenny's eyes were already closed. "I promise," I whispered, patting her hand one more time before standing to leave the room.

I bypassed the guard who had been smoking a cigarette and reading a dirty magazine while he waited for us. He gave me a cursory glance, but I waved him off, finding Adam several feet farther down the hall.

His back was plastered against the stark, white wall, and his green eyes were a sea of pain. His usually stoic face crumbled before me into grief. I walked up to him and put my arms around his middle, letting him collapse into me, his body doubling over. My kisses peppered the top of his head as he laid it upon my shoulder.

I wished I could be a giant, so I could hold him in my hands and press him to my heart.

CHAPTER FORTY-FIVE

The first part of our problem was solved for us: the MP escorted us in a jeep back to Fort Pryman Shard for questioning by a senior official. "Just a formality," he insisted as the jeep jostled its way down the bumpy road between the hospital and the fort. "You should be cleared for leave after a few routine questions."

Adam nodded, and I offered a half-hearted smile. Only the slightest brush of Adam's hand against my thigh in the back of the jeep informed me that he was thinking the same thing I was: at least we'd be on the grounds.

Now we just had to get down to the new portals somehow.

The same guard who had flirted with me in the morning was still on duty, and I saw a quizzical look pass over his bright, freckled face when he noticed me in the back of the car while waving us in. Adam had yet to see the school in this condition, and the shock was evident in the way his mouth fell open slightly while looking out the window.

"We'll be in here," the guard called over his shoulder, pulling into a parking spot at the building called Y12. It was the exact entrance I had used earlier, which relieved me, if only because it meant I would be in a place that was somehow familiar. Yet once inside, the click-clacking of the typewriters filling the halls seemed somehow incongruous with the dramatic events of the past few hours. It was as though nothing here had changed at all.

Of course, for the secretaries behind the desks, nothing *had* changed. The world was exactly as it had been this morning for them: America on the brink of winning the worst war in world history; Germany on the brink of defeat. They were part of a winning team, these secretaries, and you could hear it in the decisiveness of their undulating fingers.

While I knew it was a good thing that the world under the lake had been prevented, I couldn't help but feel that the victory was bittersweet.

The bombs would still fall. The people would still die. What had we really accomplished?

The officer who had been escorting us opened the door to one of the offices—a clean, nondescript room painted in the same shade of greenish beige as the rest of the building. It could have been anyplace, and I guess that was the idea. It looked innocent and boring, not like what it really was: a factory. A factory that made only one thing.

"He'll be in in just a minute," the officer informed us, depositing us in our chairs like we were packages he had to deliver before he could get back to work. He left the room, and the knob clicked behind him as he locked us in.

We didn't speak for a moment, but a glance at Adam revealed a sea of thoughts overtaking his brain.

"Adam?"

"Yeah."

"How many people die in Japan?"

"Don't think about that."

"I have to."

He nodded, taking in a deep breath and slowly letting it out. "A lot."

"Thousands?"

"Over a hundred thousand. Two hundred with the radiation poisoning."

The words floated from his mouth and hung over my head. They expanded into the room like helium, filling every crevice.

My body began to shake beneath me, and before I knew it, I was sobbing. "We didn't stop it."

"We weren't supposed to stop it. They were going to die anyway, Marina."

"No, we should have stopped it," I insisted through my tears, my throat clutching around the words.

"Then the war wouldn't have ended at all. And millions more would have died."

"You don't know that. Maybe there was another way."

"Don't, Marina. Please."

I was still shaking, my head buried in my hands. I could feel Adam crouching in front of me, his palms on my knees. He waited patiently for me to finish. "We did the only thing we could do," he whispered. "We stopped the Russians from getting it. We saved Sage and Caryn and even that jerk Milo. Their world will be the same as ours now."

But I could only shake my head. I was happy our friends' lives would be better, happy that the dark world under the lake could never take over ours again. But what difference did any of that make to the people of Japan? What difference did it make if we didn't even save any lives?

We'd just moved pieces around the chessboard. The outcome of the game would always be the same.

I had handed that canister to Dr. Kleiner, glad to be rid of it, knowing that it was on its way to New Mexico. And all I had felt in that moment was relief because handing it off meant it wasn't my problem anymore.

Despite what Adam might have believed about my education, I did remember certain things from history classes over the years. I remembered what happened in New Mexico: the mushroom clouds. They showed as an old movie called *The Day After* in class once. Mannequins melting in their chairs.

And Dr. Oppenheimer, on seeing what he had done, thought of an ancient Sanskrit text. I couldn't remember how it went, but Adam had quoted Sanskrit to me once before, and I had a feeling he would know it.

"What did Dr. Oppenheimer say about seeing the bomb for the first time?"

Adam bowed his head low before me, his face falling in my lap. When he looked up at me again, his lip was quivering. "'Now I am become Death,'" he answered. "'Destroyer of worlds.'"

I gulped down an unsteady breath, trying to calm myself. But I couldn't find any rhythm to it. "Are we good people, Adam?"

He sighed, heavy and long, then leaned up and kissed me tenderly on the lips. He stood and started pacing without answering me. There was nothing more to say.

"I want to go home," I whispered. Hearing the words escape my lips solidified them in my brain. "I want to go home. I miss my dad. I miss my brother."

"We will."

"Now."

He rolled his head as he walked, shaking off his frustration. Then he padded over to the door and tried the handle, even though we both knew it was locked. Looking futilely around the room, he seemed to be seeking something—anything—that could get us out of this.

"Is anyone out in the hall?" I asked.

"Just a cleaning lady."

My head popped up at the words. "What does she look like?"

He turned back to me with a questioning face, but before he could say anything, I stood to meet him at the door and looked out of the little window. A smile cracked over my lips when I saw her. I wiped the tears off my cheeks.

"Lorena!" I called through the door. She didn't hear me at first, so I called again. Finally, she looked up.

"Marina?"

I nodded. *"Ayúdanos, Lorena. Por favor."*

o o o

The inside of the Lorena's cleaning cart was definitely not big enough for two people, and yet it was our only option if we wanted to have any chance of making it down to the portals. After much pleading and cajoling in my pathetically broken Spanish, Lorena had agreed to take pity on us. She'd used her master key to get us out of the office and practically shoved us into her cart like overstuffed turkeys in a miniature oven. The metal doors wouldn't close completely, and so Adam had to maneuver the hand that wasn't crammed into my rib cage around the handle, pulling it as close as possible to our hopelessly entangled bodies.

I only prayed that nobody saw his fingers jutting out around the edge of the door as Lorena took us down the freight elevator and through a hallway towards the X10 building.

"*Dime otra vez*," she asked now through the shield of cleaning supplies and rags that separated us as she pushed our cart down the long corridor leading to the other building. "*¿Por qué tienen que regresar a este edificio?*"

"What is she saying?" Adam whispered.

"She wants to know why we're going back to the other building."

"Tell her you forgot something important down there."

"*Dejé algo importante.*"

"*¿Y qué? No vale el riesgo. Ustedes deben irse mientras ya se pueden.*"

Adam grunted into my hair. "What's she saying now?"

"She says it's not worth the risk to go back."

"*¿Y qué dejaste?*" she asked now.

I had to think of an answer quickly, something that would have been worth going back for. "*Mi anillo*," I said, the long-lost Spanish words starting to drift back to my tongue now that I was using them again. I remembered my abuela in the kitchen frying tortillas. The words in my mouth tasted like her cooking oil. She had had a ring on her finger, a small diamond. The only thing my grandfather had left her. She would twirl it around her finger sometimes and talk about him. "*Mi sortija.*"

"What did you tell her?" Adam asked.

"Nothing." I dismissed him. "Just nonsense so she'll take us there."

"I thought you didn't speak Spanish," he teased. But I clenched my mouth shut, a cramp forming in my right leg and something jutting into my other thigh. It was all I could do not to leap out of the cart from the mixture of pain and claustrophobia before we could even get there.

Finally, we came to a stop.

"You can't go in there," a man said.

"*Ellos me enviaron para limpiar,*" Lorena explained.

"No go in," the man repeated in painfully slow speech. "Big disaster. Mess."

"*Sí, hay un lío. Y por eso voy a limpiar.*"

"Oh boy," the man muttered.

Lorena simply sighed, then spoke back to the man in an equally slow cadence. "I clean. Clean mess."

"Oh, I see," the man replied. "They sent you?"

"They send. I clean."

"Mmm."

I couldn't tell if the man believed her story or simply didn't want to deal with the hassle of finding someone to translate, but before I knew it, the cart was rolling again, and whatever was stabbing my thigh doubled down on its determination to pierce into muscle.

Clenching my lips together, I somehow managed to keep the painful grunt from escaping. Before I knew it, Lorena was opening the little door to the cart. Adam and I practically fell out onto the floor, toppling all over each other.

Looking up, I could see that we were shielded from the view of any potential onlookers by a large green army tent. The inside of it was illuminated by two military-grade camping lanterns, hooked on to carabiners latched on to the metal support post at the top of the tent's frame.

At our feet, three parallel three-foot-wide holes had burned their way into the ground like molten lava. They still glowed pink with ooze.

Lorena called from outside the tent flap, "*Apúrense. Les espero aquí.*"

"We're hurrying," I whispered in English, forgetting anything but the abject fear of knowing that the only way home was to chance jumping into the center hole.

Adam took my hand, and I could feel the sweat pooling in his palm. He was just as nervous as I was.

"The portal I made under the lake worked immediately," he assured me.

"I know."

"So, this one will too."

His voice was unsteady. Was he trying to convince me or himself?

"What if it doesn't take us home?"

"When you go to another time period, the Today door always leads home. So long as you have the coin."

"Do you have the coin?"

He reached his other hand into his pocket, pulling out what I assumed to be the last of the supply of flattened pennies he had kept in there.

"I'm scared, Adam."

"It'll work," he whispered.

"I'm so scared. What if—"

But I never got to finish the sentence. Adam squeezed my body to his, and together, we leaped.

CHAPTER FORTY-SIX

The cement floor struck my head with such force, I was temporarily blinded. I shook my head, trying to clear away the stars that overtook my field of vision. Adam had been more fortunate, having crashed on top of me so that my body had shielded him from most of the blow.

I moaned with the encroaching pain as I grabbed my head.

"You okay?" he asked frantically, grabbing my head between his solid hands. He applied a slight pressure as he massaged my temples. "Open your eyes. Can you see?"

"Yes."

"How many fingers am I holding up?"

"Twelve."

He smiled, and a relieved grunt escaped his lips. "Well, you're being a smart-ass, that's a good sign."

He pulled himself up, reaching out a hand for me. As I stood, I could finally make out the scene around us.

We were in the room at the base of the spiral staircase. Behind us, the door to Today was wide open and glowing yellow. As we both turned to stare at it, the yellow began fading to gray. Adam slammed the door closed again.

"We should lock it up," I suggested.

"I don't have any more coins."

"We'll have to do it later then," I conceded, shaking off the last of the stinging pain in my head. Looking around, I could see only that the room looked right, meaning it looked the same as always. But that didn't mean we were really in the right time period. This room hadn't changed much in decades.

But then my eyes landed on something nearby—a small mound of gravel.

"Adam." I smiled.

"What?"

"We're home."

I pointed to the gravel—all that remained of the token Adam and I had used to get back to the lake portal. God, was that only three days ago? That had been first thing Wednesday morning, so today was Saturday. At least no one would be in the school.

Adam leaned down and gingerly picked up the tiny rocks to examine them. Before the last of the glowing light from the Today door died, I could see him looking up at me with a warm expression in his eyes.

"Come on." I turned and walked up the spiral staircase, Adam close on my heels.

Once we made it into the science lab, I saw the familiar markings on the chalkboard—the image that looked like a sun being attacked by its own rays.

"I told you," Adam whispered gently behind my back. "Today always leads home."

I sighed in relief, turning to him with a smile. He was looking at me tenderly all of a sudden. There was something in the expression on his face—something that I could only describe as a fatal knowingness—that scared me half to death.

"Should we head up?" I asked, ignoring the sudden ball in the pit of my stomach telling me that I knew exactly why Adam had that look on his face.

"Marina—"

I shook my head, knowing that whatever he was going to say, I didn't want to hear it. I wasn't strong enough to hear it. But he powered on.

"You know I can't stay, right?"

"No." I refused to even let him speak. "Don't, Adam. Don't say it."

"I have to go."

"We said no more portals," I all but yelled at him. My stomach was suddenly hurting more than my head, and my heart was threatening to burst out of my rib cage. "We promised."

"No portals," he agreed. "Just an airplane. I'll go live in another town for a while."

"Where?"

"I don't know yet. But it has to be this way."

"We'll talk about it later," I said, dismissing him and trying to walk away. But he grabbed my hand, not letting me get far.

"Marina, please. Don't make this harder."

"You can't just go, Adam. What about your job?"

"I'll find another job."

"What about—"

"Marina, be realistic. I'm a teacher here, you're a student."

The ball in my gut now lurched up into my throat. "Don't do this, Adam," I begged. "Please." I was crying now, convulsing with grief.

I couldn't do it. I couldn't lose one more person. I couldn't stand there and let Adam turn into another ghost in my life. "Nobody has to know," I whispered through my tears.

"*We* would know, sweetheart." He held me to his chest, speaking softly into my hair. "We would know. And it would only be a matter of time before other people figured it out."

I stood and cried into his chest for what felt like an eternity.

Was this the way it was always going to go? Was I fooling myself to think it could be any different? What were we going to do, sneak around the school? Duck into broom closets? Meet in his car?

No, that was cheap and dirty. It was beneath us. We made sense underground. But up here—up here we'd probably be breaking the law, even if I was eighteen. Up here, everything that had felt right before turned ugly.

I couldn't ask him to become that for me. I couldn't let myself become that either.

There was only way this could ever end: with Adam becoming one more secret I would have to keep.

He didn't rush me, and I prayed that it was because this was hurting him as much as it was hurting me. I knew he was right, but this still felt impossible. "I don't want to do this alone, Adam. You're the only one who knows me."

He held me even tighter, his arms encasing me completely. I leaned up and kissed him, and though he kissed me back at first, he eventually pushed me away. His hands rested tenderly on my face, keeping me close enough to feel the energy bouncing off his skin. His thumb wiped a tear off my cheek. "Your brother knows you," he whispered.

I struggled to inhale, to let the air fill my lungs.

"Go to Boston, Marina. Start your life."

My body shook violently, and all that was keeping me from

collapsing was Adam's hands on my cheeks, sending me life energy like an umbilical cord. But I knew that somehow I'd have to find the strength to rip myself away from them.

"You head up first, okay?" he whispered. "I'll wait ten minutes and follow so people won't see us together."

"I don't care if they see us together."

"I do," he insisted. "You deserve more than that. We both do."

I nodded reluctantly. I knew I had to turn and walk out of the room, and that he wouldn't be following me.

I knew that when I got upstairs, I would be alone.

"I want to live a life I'm proud of, Marina . . ."

Pushing myself away from him just enough to look into his eyes, I could see the lifetime of regret in his face. His hands fell to my shoulders.

"I *need* to be proud of myself," he repeated now, "so that the next time I see you . . ."

I nodded, trying to find enough strength to encourage him.

". . . you can be proud of me too."

"When?" I asked, swallowing down anything that wasn't the word. "When, Adam?"

He smiled, looking around the science lab, the epicenter of all our secrets. A small laugh escaped his full lips.

"Tomorrow."

CHAPTER FORTY-SEVEN

It was a long walk home, watching the late-afternoon sun begin to set behind the clusters of trees that rimmed the neighborhood between the school and my house. My bike, not surprisingly, had not been waiting for me outside the gym. I hadn't locked it up when I'd left it there, so it was safe to assume I would never see it again.

I instinctively reached for my phone in my back pocket once I started the long, cold walk in the mid-January chill. But of course, that was missing too.

I had left my entire backpack in the pyramid house when I'd chased after Adam. I could only hope it had fared better than the bike. Of course, lots of people knew about that house—even people who knew nothing of the meetings that used to take place there would sometimes use it for parties or just as a place to make out.

I might have to add a new phone to the list of things I'd be digging into my already bleak savings account for.

Thinking of a new phone made me think of Kieren. I would have to tell him I was back. I'd send him a DM when I got home, assuming my father would even let me in the house.

I'd gone missing for three whole days, with only a vague explanation from Kieren to pacify him. I'd also missed school and blown off work, leaving my dad to make an excuse to Mr. Chu for me. At least when I'd snuck off to Portland with Brady in our previous reality, it had been under the pretense of going to summer camp. This time, I'd just taken off. I braced myself for the fact that my relationship with my dad might be permanently altered by this.

How would I make it up to him?

But as I approached my house, I knew that talking to my dad wasn't going to be my immediate concern.

Because Brady's car was parked on the street, waiting for me.

I stopped in my tracks and took a deep breath. I had been hoping to at least have a night to rest before having to do this. But maybe it was for the best this way. I wouldn't have been able to sleep with my guilt hanging over me.

Tell him the truth. Everything else just hurts more . . . in the end.

I walked up to the car and saw that he was asleep inside, his seat reclined all the way back. An assortment of chips and to-go bags littered the floor, and he appeared to have about four days' worth of growth on his cheeks.

Had he been sleeping here the whole time? Why hadn't he gone inside?

I knocked lightly on the passenger-side window, and he bolted up, looking shocked for a moment before realizing where he was. When his head whipped over towards me, I saw a look of extraordinary relief in his red-rimmed eyes.

He pressed a button to unlock the doors, and I took a deep breath and got in.

I had to push a fast-food bag out of the way to sit, and when I closed the door, I could feel how warm it was inside the car. Brady's body heat had filled it up, turning it into a cocoon.

"Hi," I said in a weak voice.

He pulled his seat into an upright position, shaking his head rapidly as though trying to force the sleep out of his brain. He rubbed his eyes. "You scared me half to death," he finally said.

"Sorry, I tried to knock lightly, but—"

"I don't mean by knocking on the damn door, M."

"Right. Sorry."

He finally pulled his hands away from his face and looked at me. His beautiful brown eyes were creased with fine lines I had never noticed before. Had I aged him in the time I'd been gone? Had I really worried him that much?

"Are you okay?" he asked now, a waver barely audible in his rich voice.

I nodded.

"What are you wearing?"

I quickly scanned my own appearance. I was still wearing the overalls from the fort, a fact that would be difficult to explain without telling him everything. "It's—"

"Never mind," he said, dismissing the topic. "It doesn't matter. Did you—did you do what you had to do?"

I nodded again. "I know it seems like it was reckless or . . . I don't know, irresponsible of me to go like that. But I promise I had a good reason."

"I know you did. Or at least, I know that's what you told Kieren."

I cleared my throat when he said Kieren's name. I tried to steel myself for what I had to say next. "Brady, I have to tell you something."

"Kieren told me everything."

354

My eyes popped open suddenly, and my mouth moved to ask what that meant. But I couldn't find the words.

Brady was still looking at me, his face tired and sad. "You don't remember any of it, do you?"

I kept listening, afraid to interrupt.

"The last fifteen months," he continued. "Since the night we got back from the beach behind Sage's hotel?"

I shook my head slightly, enough to affirm that the answer was no: I didn't remember any of it.

"Our first kiss? The first time we said 'I love you'?"

I could only shake my head again.

"Do you still feel anything for me?"

"Yes," I insisted. "Of course I do. I just . . . I just . . . I didn't have time to get used to it. One minute, we were just friends. You were a guy who—"

"Go on, say it."

"You were a guy who I had a crush on when I was fifteen, Brady. That's how I thought of you. And suddenly you were my boyfriend, and I didn't have any time to . . ." The words died in my mouth. I wasn't saying this right. I didn't know if there even *was* a right way to say it.

He nodded, trying to take it in. I could see that his mind was racing, and I could only imagine he was thinking of all the moments he and I had shared in the past fifteen months that only he could remember.

"When I changed what had happened that night, I thought that—" Oh God, how could I tell him this? "I did it because I thought that—"

"You thought you'd be with Kieren when you got back to Today." He finished my sentence for me so that I wouldn't have to. It was a relief, and more than I deserved. "Because you were always in love with Kieren."

My lip was trembling, and I tried desperately to stop it. But it was useless.

"I didn't know it would be like this," I whispered.

"Yeah, sorry to break it to you, but Kieren dumped you as soon as he got to college."

My lip now took on a life of its own, shaking violently.

"And I was there for you."

"I know you were."

"I was your friend when you needed one. And you were mine."

"I'm still your friend, Brady. We can be still be—"

"Stop!" He turned forcefully towards me. "Do not say that word."

We sat in silence for another long, tortured moment. The air was thick in the car, and I didn't know what else I could possibly say, so I was surprised when Brady grabbed my wrist. He rolled it in his hand, a bit too harshly, and pulled up my sleeve to reveal my scars.

"Kieren told me about this too."

"They're the markings—" I began to explain.

"I know what they are," he said, cutting me off, his tone cold. "You let Adam cut you."

I gulped down my guilt, terrified suddenly.

"What else did you let him do?"

But I couldn't say it. I couldn't confirm what he clearly already suspected. How had he known? Or was he just guessing? Because Piper had cheated on him too. Did he just assume that this was what all girls did? That we all just hurt him in the end?

"I'm sorry, Brady," was all I could say. I was crying silently, ashamed of my tears. I had no right to be crying. I wasn't the victim here.

"Get out of my car."

"Please, Brady, please say you'll forgive me. I can't live with knowing that you hate me."

"Sure you can, M. We can live with lots of things."

"Please—"

"Get out of my car!"

With trembling fingers, I reached for the handle. Part of me was still hoping against hope that he'd stop me, that he'd tell me there was some way for us to still be friends. Or at least, that there was a chance he might forgive me someday.

But he didn't stop me.

I opened the door and stepped out, and I stood still as a statue as he started the engine and his car peeled away down my street.

I was still shaking, overwhelmed with grief. I turned to the house, trying to collect myself.

Now it was time to see my dad. I could only pray that he would let me collapse into his arms, despite what I had done to him. Because I couldn't imagine going one more minute without being in the only place in the world that still felt safe.

CHAPTER FORTY-EIGHT

My bike was in the garage.

That was the only positive thing I discovered that night, after my father had reluctantly let me sit at the dinner table despite the fact that he was still furious with me. My stepmother, Laura, had insisted that we should eat something and have a good night's sleep before he could grill me more about any of the details of where I'd been.

It was the longest, most silent meal in history. The lasagna went down like a rock.

Laura tried to make conversation for a while, letting me know that Kieren had found my bike abandoned by the gym and had brought it back for me. "You really owe that boy a thank-you," she added.

No one spoke after that.

Laura loaned me her cell phone for the night when I told her mine was gone, and I used it to let Kieren know I was back.

Then I sat on my bed and called Christy. We'd been friends for so long, even Laura had her number saved in her phone in case of emergencies.

"Where were you?" was all she asked. I had forgotten to ask Kieren to let her know I was safe, and she had spent two days assuming I was sick in bed before swinging by my house, where my father had told her I was missing.

"I had to go help a friend," I said, giving the same vague and ridiculous answer I had asked Kieren to tell my dad.

She didn't say anything for a minute.

"Christy?" I asked.

"Yeah, I'm here. I'm just trying to understand. I don't keep secrets from you."

"I know you don't."

"Sometimes, I just wish . . . I wish I knew you better."

"I know."

There was something else I knew I had to ask her, but I wasn't sure if she would do it. Yet I didn't really have a choice.

"I need a favor," I finally said in a low voice.

"Okay."

"I need you to go to the pharmacy and get me something, please."

She sighed, annoyed. "Why don't you get it yourself?"

"Because . . ." I hesitated, clearing my throat. "I'm grounded, and my dad's watching me like a hawk. But I need it right away. If I don't take it tonight, it'll be too late."

There was silence on the other end of the line. For a minute, I thought maybe she had hung up on me.

"Christy?"

"Why can't Brady go?" she finally asked.

I hesitated, not wanting to tell her any more lies. "It wasn't Brady," I finally admitted.

She was silent again. I sat on my bed, clutching Laura's phone.

"I'll drop it off in an hour," she finally said and then hung up before I could tell her that I would pay her back.

The next four weeks passed in a haze of guilt, depression, and the occasional burst of boredom. I didn't know which was worse. After having spent half a week feeling the extreme stress of fearing for my life and having what I supposed I could officially refer to as my first real love affair, the daily ritual of getting up, getting dressed, brushing my teeth, and trudging through school just didn't seem to be firing off the neurons in my brain in any noticeable way.

I supposed that was the real danger of DW. It didn't take long before you got addicted to the adrenaline. After it was gone, nothing really felt like anything anymore.

My father finally told me that he wasn't mad at the fact that I had left, he was mad because I wouldn't tell him where I had been. "I thought we trusted each other," he said, his voice broken.

I bowed my head, nodding at the floor.

After a week of him giving me the silent treatment, I finally went out to his garage lab one night and helped him reassemble a computer. He didn't speak to me the whole time, except to ask me to hand him some wires at one point. I took that as a positive sign.

At school, it didn't seem to surprise anyone very much that the new AP World History teacher had flown the coop.

"Boy, that didn't take long," Adrian Washington joked when we showed up on Monday morning to find that Principal Farghasian herself was teaching the class.

"Just until I find another sub for you guys," she said from the whiteboard as she furiously tried to scan through Adam's notebook to see what she was supposed to be teaching us.

The only one who seemed truly disappointed was Angela Peirnot, much to Adrian's annoyance.

"I just don't understand it," I heard her whispering to one of her girlfriends behind me. "Who teaches a class for a week and then splits?"

After that, nobody mentioned Adam again. It was like he had never been there.

I finished my MIT application and sent it in, and then I called Mr. Chu and apologized profusely for missing two work shifts without so much as a phone call. After much groveling, I convinced him to forgive me, and he agreed to let me keep my job for the rest of the school year.

Christy wasn't talking to me, and so I was home alone a lot. One night, I was so bored I actually rummaged through Dad's old bookshelf, finding an ancient copy of *Moby Dick*. I fell asleep that night dreaming I was in the middle of the ocean on a churning ship, the ominous presence of a great whale lurking somewhere beneath me.

Somewhere I couldn't quite reach.

o o o

"Marina, come back to Earth." My father's voice woke me one morning a couple weeks later.

"Hmm?" I asked, sitting up quickly. It took a moment to get my bearings. It was the second time in my life my father had woken me early on a Sunday.

He was sitting on the edge of my bed, his mug of coffee in his hands just like old times. And he was talking to me. Did that mean he forgave me? Or did it mean something worse?

"What is it, Dad?"

"You got an email," he said, holding up his phone to me. I still didn't have a phone, since the pyramid house had been empty when I'd swung by after school one day to check it out. And since my dad no longer trusted me, he had insisted on knowing my passwords so he could check all my messages and my social media postings.

Of course, I'd had very few of any of those things since I'd driven away the only people I had ever cared about.

Still, I cleared my eyes and tried to read the message he was holding up. "What does it mean?" I asked, not able to process anything so early in the morning.

"You have an interview." He smiled, seeming to forget that he was mad at me. "A recruiter from MIT. They say you can pick a place nearby for the meeting. A coffee shop or something. I was thinking of that place in town with the rooster on the sign."

I nodded, my heart beginning to race. "Yeah," I agreed. "Yeah, that's perfect." I smiled at my dad and was relieved to see he was smiling back. Then he seemed to remember that we were fighting, and the smile faded temporarily. But I couldn't wait anymore to be forgiven. I threw myself forward into his arms, spilling some of his coffee onto my bed.

"You're gonna be okay, kiddo."

"I love you, Dad."

"You're gonna be great."

CHAPTER FORTY-NINE

The place with the rooster on the sign was called El Gallo, fittingly enough. Even with my pathetic Spanish, I understood that the name meant The Rooster. I cleared my throat nervously before walking in, straightening the blouse and skirt I had picked up at the mall the night before specifically for this purpose. I was about to enter when I suddenly remembered to turn and press the lock button on Laura's keys. It did nothing, so I furiously pressed it again, causing her Toyota to beep repeatedly in protest behind me.

Breathe, Marina. You can do this.

I walked in and scanned the half dozen tables of the cute little café that had admittedly gone a little overboard with the rooster theme, knickknacks and tchotchkes on every surface. I straightened my back, trying to look confident and grown-up. I wished I'd worn jeans. Jeans and my favorite brown sweater would have been perfect. I wished—

"Marina?" a woman asked as she stood. She had been sitting alone at a small table behind a laptop. She was wearing an outfit almost comically similar to my own.

"Yes, that's me."

"Lisa Sanchez. Nice to meet you."

"Nice to meet you too."

We sat down together, and I wondered for a second if I was supposed to get up and get a cup of coffee. Although honestly, coffee was the last thing in the world that I wanted.

"So, tell me," she began, offering me a warm smile with her rich brown eyes, "why do you want to go to MIT?"

I swallowed down a sudden dizziness, like the world was moving too fast and too slow at the same time. It was a simple question. And yet my entire future was tangled up somewhere in the answer. I cleared my throat, nodding a bit too eagerly.

"Well, I love engineering," I began, my voice distorted as it bounced off the high ceiling. "I love robotics. I teach at a computer place. You knew that 'cause it's in my file probably." I wiped my hands, suddenly sweaty, on my skirt. "I love robotics. Wait, I said that already."

"It's okay." She laughed. "Just relax. What do you love about robotics?"

"I love, um . . ." Why could I not think of one sentence in the English language? "I love the idea of how robotics and transportation can intersect. And how, in the future, we could have robots that, you know, do things . . ."

I'm drowning. I'm drowning in the ocean. The whale is going to eat me.

"And I love that—"

"Go on," she encouraged, the warm smile not leaving her face.

"I want— Imagine an airplane," I finally choked out. "An

airplane that could run on its own wind resistance. And it wouldn't need an engine, even, or produce any carbon. It would basically be a big drone. And you could go anywhere in this airplane. And you wouldn't hurt the earth, you wouldn't hurt anything or anybody." I wasn't saying it right.

There's no right way to say it.

I choked down a sudden onslaught of spit, forcing myself to power on. "You could just get from point A to point B without—"

"Yes?"

Adam's face when I told him this story. His bemused smile.

The warmth of his skin.

"You could get from point A to point B—"

"Marina is mine."

Was that the last time I'll ever be happy?

Was it worth it?

"Point A to point B without destroying the—"

Something will go wrong. It always does.

"The earth." I couldn't talk anymore. Because I couldn't stop the tears that were forming. I couldn't stop the fire rushing to my face. "I'm sorry," I whispered.

Now I am become Death. Look at me now, talking about planes that run on wind resistance. Who am I kidding? I am the destroyer of worlds.

I asked Adam if we were good people. He never answered that question.

Lisa Sanchez didn't seem deterred. Her eyes never wavered from my face. In fact, she smiled. She leaned back a bit and examined me, deciding something.

"I'm so sorry," I continued. "I don't know why I'm crying."

She handed me a napkin to wipe my face. "You're crying because you care."

I laughed lightly, trying to dry my face and realizing that I was probably rubbing eyeliner all over my cheeks.

"Can I tell you something?" she asked. "Before my MIT interview, I was so nervous I threw up." She laughed, her eyes darting up to the distant ceiling with the memory, then landing back on me. "I wanted it so badly, and I didn't know if a place like MIT would ever take someone like me."

I nodded, but I was so embarrassed I could barely look at her. "Why wouldn't they take you? You seem really smart."

"I come from nothing. I'd worked so hard. But what if it wasn't enough?"

I nodded, a fresh wash of tears carrying away whatever was left of my mascara.

"What if *I* wasn't enough?" she continued.

"And? Were you?"

She smiled. "Only you can decide that."

"I'm so sorry," I said again.

But she leaned in even closer, like she was telling me a secret. "Never apologize for caring, Marina."

The waitress came and asked if I wanted anything, and Lisa Sanchez ordered us two pieces of coffee cake.

o o o

I decided to walk through town a bit before heading home, letting my feet take me wherever they felt like going. I ended up in front of Groussman's Pharmacy. I couldn't help but lean in to examine the photo of the pinup girl, but it was faded too much to make out anything but the faintest streak of blond hair. Everything else about it had been erased by the decades.

Stepping into the store, I headed up to the glass counter, following the same trajectory I had taken when I had pawned the diamond ring.

There was a young woman behind the counter who bore a striking resemblance to Mimi—the same curly brown hair and ready smile. But she was shorter, and her face was a bit longer.

"Hi," I said awkwardly when I saw her.

"Hello, can I help you?"

"Sorry, it's just . . . you look like a girl I know. Named Mimi."

"Oh, that's funny. That was my great-grandmother's name."

Taken a bit aback, I realized that this was a family business. It had never changed hands, not since it had opened almost eight decades earlier. And since this timeline and the one under the lake were now merged, there was a possibility that something else was the same. "Hey," I asked, "could you tell me, did this place use to be pawnshop?"

"A pawnshop?" she asked, smiling. "I mean, maybe like a million years ago. Why?"

"Do you think . . . do you think anything might be left over from then?"

It took me a couple of minutes of explaining to Mimi's great-granddaughter that I was looking for something that had been in my family once, something that had been lost for decades. I knew this was a long shot. In all the twists and turns of time and space, all the ways this reality and the one under the lake had combined and intersected and broken apart again, maybe that ring was gone forever.

Maybe it had never been here in the first place in this dimension, had never passed from Golda to Sage and finally to me.

But somehow I felt it calling to me. Somehow. Somewhere.

The ring was a promise. And promises never die.

The girl behind the counter was reluctant to leave her post at first, but then she seemed to get into the mood for an adventure. She asked someone to watch the register for her and led me to a back closet.

"My grandpa used to keep all sorts of family stuff back here. It's a real mess, I should warn you."

"That's okay."

"Let's see . . . no, just old paperwork. Cleaning supplies. Some old magazines. Uh, here's a cigar box."

"Wait." I stopped her. "What's in the cigar box?"

She blew about a pound of dust off the top of it and then creaked it open. "Oh my God," she said, smiling.

"What is it?"

She gently reached inside and picked something out. "It's an old ring. That's crazy."

"Can I see it?"

Holding it up for me to see, she twirled it in the overhead light of the closet. The small diamond was dull with age, but otherwise it looked the same. "Oh, wait," she said. "There's a note."

I walked farther into the closet, trying to peer over her shoulder at the note. She held it up enough for us both to read. "It says, 'Do not sell. Owner is coming back.'"

She laughed, trying to put everything back into the box.

"Can I buy it?" I asked her.

She hesitated a moment, her hands not wavering from the box.

"Oh, come on," I teased. "How long has it been back here?"

"Well," she finally agreed, "I guess the owner's not coming back, is she?"

"I'll give you a hundred dollars for it."

She eyed the box one more time, and then her eyes turned to the wallet I was pulling out of my purse. Finally, she opened the box and handed me the ring.

"It's yours."

EPILOGUE

I stood on the platform, waiting for the eastbound train. It would take me as far as New York, where my brother and Piper would pick me up and drive me north to their place—my place, I should start saying—in Boston.

My dad had run into the station to buy me snacks for the trip, and I was flapping my tank top away from my chest to try to relieve myself from the mid-August heat. I checked my new phone, hoping to see a reply from Christy. I had sent her a congratulatory text the night before when she'd posted that she was about to get on a plane for Berklee. In what was perhaps an overeager attempt to rekindle our broken friendship, I had wallpapered the phone with lots of hearts and champagne glasses and fireworks.

She had written me back, *Thank you.*

Nothing else had come in since.

I couldn't be mad at her for drifting away after I'd asked her to go to the pharmacy. I had suspected it would be the last straw for our friendship, not just because she's a Christian and it goes against everything she believes in, but because I wouldn't even tell her where I'd been or who I'd been with. I had asked her anyway. I had asked her because I'd had no one else to ask, and I couldn't risk the alternative. Adam and I hadn't been careful enough the second night.

And I had asked her because, on some level, I suppose I had wanted her to know one true thing about me. Even if that thing was that I had cheated on my boyfriend. Even if it meant I would lose her too.

The fact was, we were doomed from the start. Friendships can't be built on a lie, and my whole life had been a tower of lies since the night I'd lost Robbie, one stacked on top of the other. The tower was always going to fall eventually. Christy and I had been living on borrowed time.

I was so busy looking at the phone, at the blank screen under her last curt little message, that I didn't notice Kieren until he was standing right beside me.

"Hey, you," he said, shocking me almost out of my skin.

"How did you know I'd be here?" I asked, fumbling with my phone and eventually dropping it back into my purse.

"Your stepmom kept posting about how proud she was of you, how you were taking the morning train to school."

"I didn't know you followed Laura online."

He laughed, shaking his head. "She insisted back when you and I were . . . you know."

We stood together for a moment, our eyes instinctively heading down the tracks to where my train would eventually appear.

"I feel like what happened is my fault," he finally said.

"What do you mean?" I asked, nervous suddenly to hear the

answer, or maybe just nervous because he was next to me again. The last time we'd been together on this platform was when I'd seen an alternate present in the Today door—one where we were in love.

"I pushed you towards Adam. I shouldn't have let you stay with him."

I flushed with sudden understanding. "Brady told you?"

"Yes."

I shook away the awkwardness of the moment, but I couldn't quite look at him. "You didn't *push* me anywhere. It was my choice, Kieren."

"I should have protected you, though."

I kept looking down the track, not sure what to say. But then a surge of anger seized me. "It's a bit late for that, don't you think?"

"What do you mean?"

I turned to look at him. "I spent a year and a half learning to live without you. I risked everything to get back to you. Because I loved you."

"M—" He reached for my face, but I backed away.

"And you hurt me."

Kieren looked down at his shoes, nodding slightly. Finally, he opened his mouth to speak. "I know that. I'm sorry, M."

"It's too late for sorry."

He looked at me like I'd slapped him, but after a moment, he leaned in closer. "I guess I always thought," he said, "that someday you and I might find our way back to each other."

The breath forced its way into my lungs. "Yeah." I nodded. "I used to think that too."

My eyes wandered now to the street, to the distant point where the road bent on its way over from the high school.

"And now?" he asked.

"Now I don't know."

He nodded silently. "Maybe I could visit you someday. I mean, I know your brother won't let me in the house, but . . ."

"What about Stephanie?" I asked.

He hesitated, following my gaze to the road. "She would stay behind."

I took a step away from him. What was he even suggesting? That I could be his . . . side chick? That he could keep her and have me too? Is that what he thought of me now? Is that what we had become? Or was it worse than that? Did he mean that we could be just friends? "I don't want that," I said softly. He kept his distance while we continued to stand there. "That's not enough."

Finally, Dad came back from inside the station, his arms laden with candy bars and bags of chips, with one lone apple sitting on top. He froze when he saw Kieren by my side, but then continued to approach us. "Kieren," he greeted him.

"Sir," Kieren said back, years of living with a father in the military having ingrained a rote kind of respect into his tone.

"I'll wait over here while you two say goodbye," my dad offered.

"Thanks, Dad."

After a second, my train approached. The chugging was so silent at first, but soon it overtook us, and speech was impossible. It was a relief when it pulled up close, causing a breeze to whip us in the face.

"Why do you keep looking down the road?" Kieren finally asked.

"No reason," I answered, maybe a bit too quickly. There was no reason to be looking. He wasn't coming for me. He was gone.

Kieren could tell I was lying, but he misinterpreted why. "Is, um . . . is Brady coming?"

I sighed, shaking my head. I had texted Brady several times over the months, asking if we could talk, wanting another chance to apologize. Last night, I had tried again. "He won't respond to my texts. I'll keep trying, though. I'm still hoping he'll forgive me someday."

"Oh."

"I don't expect him to," I admitted. "But you never know."

Kieren took my hand. I didn't want him to at first, but then suddenly I was afraid to let him go. "I hope that happens for you," he said. "I really do."

I squeezed his hand for only a moment, so tight that his fingernails dug into my skin, almost piercing the thick padding of my palms.

And then he was gone. I turned to see him walking away down the platform, and I could still feel the imprint of his hand in mine.

My dad handed me my snacks and walked me to the train door. I closed my eyes when I hugged him, not wanting to see the tears forming in his eyes. "We won't say goodbye," he whispered. "Just till I see you again."'

I nodded, pulling away from him and stepping onto the train. But before I made it all the way on, I turned one last time to look down the long road winding its way into the distance.

The road was empty, as I knew it would be. The journey I was about to take, I'd have to take alone . . . at least for now. I twirled the diamond ring in my pocket, wondering just how long I would be waiting.

Waiting for forgiveness.

Waiting for redemption.

Waiting for Tomorrow to come.

ACKNOWLEDGMENTS

While Marina and Adam's hometown is fictional, it is heavily inspired by Oak Ridge, Tennessee, where a secret town sprang up in the early 1940s to develop the enriched uranium needed for the atomic bombs. Most of my research came from Denise Kiernan's fantastic biography *The Girls of Atomic City*. Find more info about Oak Ridge at atomicheritage.org.

I need to thank the fabulous team at Wattpad Books, especially the brilliant Deanna McFadden, for championing the Down World trilogy from the very beginning. When the first book won the Watty Award for best young adult fiction in 2019, I thought, "What a great ride that was!" I had no idea that the next few years would see my entire trilogy being brought to readers' hands all over the world. It is the great privilege of my life to be able to tell these stories.

A special thanks goes to my editor, Jen Hale, who always asks the right questions, and to my copy editor, Andrea Waters, who changes my "lies" to "lays" whenever necessary. This book is infinitely better as a result.

I'd also like to thank the entire gang over at Wattpad WEBTOON Studios—AKA, my favorite Canadians. I'm especially indebted to all the fantastic reps I've had a chance to work with: I-Yana Tucker, Nina Lopes, Amanda Gosio, and Monica Pacheco.

If there's a recurring theme in the Down World books, it is exploring the murky area between mistakes and second chances; between regret and redemption. The road I took to get here was bumpy at times, but I truly believe it led me home.

Steffen, my life didn't really begin until you "loaned" me a broken computer so I would have to come over and drink wine and eat pizza while you "fixed" it. It's been a hell of a ride since then.

This book, like everything I do, is for our kids. Luna and Levon, you are my everything.

ABOUT THE AUTHOR

Rebecca Phelps started out as an actress and a screenwriter before completing her first novel, *Down World*. She lives in Los Angeles with her husband and two kids. Read more of her work on Wattpad: @geminirosey. For updates on books, writing, and more, follow her on TikTok: @RebeccaPhelpsAuthor or Instagram: @RebeccaPhelpsWriter. Keep an eye out for *Everworld*, coming from Wattpad Books, spring 2023!

Turn the page for a preview of

Available now, wherever books are sold.

01 | BEGIN / END

The last thing I remember is noise.

Images are hazy, and they only come in flashes. Most of them are dark, dripping with night and impossible to make sense of—a glimpse of a tree branch here, a wiry crack in the glass there. Bloodstained fingers. Fragmented pieces of my reflection gazing back at me.

But the noises are vivid, and when I squeeze my eyes shut, I can still hear them. It begins with tires squealing, struggling to gain traction on damp pavement, followed by the devastating crunch of metal connecting with metal. A car door clicks open, and the melodic chime of keys being left in the ignition resonates through the air layered with frantic voices melding together. One of them sounds similar to mine, only warped and laced with pain.

A desperate urge to flee the scene propels me forward, but my limbs fail, and I fall to the ground.

When I wake, I no longer know my own name.

The abrupt shaking of a pill bottle makes the present come back into focus.

Dr. Meyer sits across from me, holding up the bright orange container, and the room is quiet, all eyes trained in my direction. Outside, thick, menacing clouds on the verge of bursting hang low, peering over the canopy of evergreen trees in the distance. There's a garden adjacent to Dr. Meyer's office—a courtyard that must bloom with color later in the year but looks stark and barren against the backdrop of early spring.

After a month of staying here, I've learned that the neurology wing is the nicest place in Pender Falls General Hospital, significantly more inviting than the room I first woke up in—where I was called a name I didn't remember and was surrounded by faces I'd never seen before—or the one in which I spent weeks learning how to use my body again. This meeting is the last checkpoint I have to complete before getting out of here for good.

"Sorry. I lost focus for a second."

"That's all right." Dr. Meyer's smile is gentle, practiced. "This is a lot of information to take in at once, that's why we have your family here with you. The more ears, the better."

Sofia—my mother, though it's far too early to call her that—studiously scrawls notes on the lined paper of the notebook in her lap, while my sister, Audrey, sits on the other side of me, fingers resting on my leg gently in a show of support.

"As I was saying, you'll continue taking these in order to help with your awareness and memory. Over the counter pain meds like acetaminophen and ibuprofen can be taken for headaches and any muscle stiffness you may be feeling."

"How long does she need to take them?" Sofia gestures to the pill bottle. The words are firm, demanding, and I don't know if it's motherly instinct or a desire to be in control of the situation.

"We'll monitor her progress in our follow-up appointments and reassess. For now, she can continue to take them daily before bed."

"Do you think I'm stuck like this?"

The attention shifts back to me, an air of discomfort settling over the room.

"You're not *stuck*, Alina," Dr. Meyer begins, setting his clipboard on his desk. "It's still very early. There's always room for improvement, and it's likely your recovery won't be linear."

A crow lands on a branch near the window, taking cover beneath the overhang as the rain begins to fall. My mother and sister remain silent.

"How does a brain just forget everything it knows, anyway?" My grip tightens around the thick fabric of the sweater I hold in my hands as I watch the bird.

"Your procedural memory is perfectly intact. Once you're back in your normal environment, I'm confident more things from your life, your past, will come back and be familiar." He sets the bottle on his desk then leans back in his seat. "The mind is a wondrous thing. It's not that your brain has forgotten everything it knows, rather, those memories are locked away, and you can no longer find the key. You may find that key again someday, or you may not. My goal is to give you the tools to cope with either outcome."

A wave of nausea builds in my belly, and I don't know if it's an after-effect of smashing my head against a steering wheel, a reaction to his words, or a delightful mixture of both. Waking up to a life that feels brand new and being told you were in a deadly car accident you're lucky to have survived is harrowing. I don't feel lucky. I feel cursed.

The details of the accident were explained to me in simple terms: I was at a party. I left the party. I crashed my car into a tree. I was found by someone out on a run hours later, long after the sun had already risen, though the sounds I remember make it seem as though it all happened in a matter of seconds. Every time I hear it, it feels like nothing more than a story about a stranger, something tragic I might tell someone in passing, not something that belongs to me.

"I think we're finished here," he says. "Unless you have anything else you'd like to discuss."

Despite the fact that there are about a million burning questions on the tip of my tongue, I shake my head, and we all stand, heading for the door. I wander farther down the hall, drifting and ghostlike, while Sofia gets a final word in with Dr. Meyer, speaking in hushed timbres. Audrey stands next to them, shooting me concerned glances every few seconds.

Our physical resemblance reassures me that they truly are my family—we have the same intense brown eyes, dark hair, and tawny skin—but I have no recollection of our life before these hospital corridors and neurology appointments. I don't even know what they think of me.

After several moments of watching the rain fall outside the large windows of the hospital entrance, they join me, and we make our way outside.

A raindrop hits my nose, and Sofia does her best to cover us using her bag as a makeshift umbrella, but it doesn't provide much shelter. My hair is damp by the time we reach the car. As we roll through town, my eyes melt into the landscape of cookie-cutter houses backed by lush mountains and my fingers curl around the strap of my seat belt as I listen to the whir of tires gliding through rainwater. The sun hasn't shone in Pender Falls since I woke up.

Sofia tells me I've lived here all my life. Years of bouncing around British Columbia led her to settle down in a small town in the Interior, somewhere she deemed appropriate to raise a family.

"That's your elementary school," she says as we drive by a blue building with children's artwork pasted to the windows, rain battering the weathered jungle gym.

It continues on like this as she points out the shadowy park I used to frequent as a child and the church next to the cemetery we attend on special occasions. Audrey fills in the gaps from the backseat, accompanying every place with an amusing story. With each one we drive past, it feels like I'm seeing it for the first time. I have no doubt their intention is to help me become familiar with my surroundings, but it only makes me feel like more of an outsider.

After turning onto Seymour Avenue, we pull into the driveway of a house a little ways down the street. It's large, built of red bricks, with sprawling vines creeping up the front and wrapping around the white pillars on the porch like something out of a storybook. Sofia kills the engine and nobody moves for a second.

"This is home," she announces tentatively.

I've been dreading this. Even though Audrey and Sofia were constantly with me in the hospital, it's an entirely different thing to actually live with strangers who are supposed to be family. In reality, they feel about as familiar as the doctors and nurses who milled about the hallways during my stay, coming in and out of my room to bring me medication and rouse me from my sleep.

Sofia pushes open the front door, and I follow her inside.

Immediately as we enter, a barking dog bounds in my direction, and my pulse kicks into gear. The animal, a black and white border collie, jumps onto my legs, growling maliciously, and Audrey scrambles to grab its collar, easing it away.

"I'm sorry!" she exclaims. "Scout isn't your biggest fan but she's usually better than this."

"Audrey." Sofia chastises her. "I told you to take Scout outside before we left."

"Parker must have let her in."

Audrey looks at me apologetically as she struggles to wrangle the animal, expression sincere. She's older by a couple of years, but I've been told we were often mistaken for twins when we were young. Now, I seem to favor our mother more than she does, bearing the same slender nose and defined cheekbones.

Sofia takes hold of Scout's collar and pulls the dog to the French doors, releasing her into the backyard. A boy scrambles into the kitchen, looking flustered. His features are kind, and he has black hair a few shades darker than his skin cropped close to his head.

"This is my boyfriend," Audrey explains. "He's living with us for the time being, until he finds his own place."

He extends a hand toward me. "Parker. My apologies for the dog."

My shoulders melt in relief. He's the first person who hasn't been obviously uncomfortable about having to reintroduce themselves to me. "Nice to meet you," I say, shaking his hand, before adding, "again."

"It's good to have you back," Parker says.

I've heard a lot about him already—he was the subject Audrey gravitated toward to keep the flow of conversation going whenever we hit a lull, but he never came with her to the hospital. Parker watches me for a beat too long, and my face grows hot under his scrutiny.

Sofia touches my shoulder, oblivious to the exchange. "Come, I can show you around."

Leaving them behind, she gives me a brief tour of the house. It's cozy and lived in, family photos adorning the walls, throws draped over couches, and comforting tones of burgundy spread throughout the rooms. In a way, it feels a bit like a cabin, woodsy and warm. She saves my bedroom for last, stopping outside of a door at the end of the hall on the second floor. The short journey up the stairs is enough to make my body feel weary.

Subconsciously, my breath hitches as she twists the doorknob.

A string of fairy lights hangs on the wall above the bed, bright and twinkling, and a diffuser sits on the nightstand, emitting wafts of lavender, making me relax my shoulders. There's a desk in the corner, a surge of intrigue sparking in my chest at the sight of the laptop on the surface, as it's likely to be a treasure trove of valuable information. Across from the bed, a myriad of photos are stuck to the wall, snapshots of someone else's life.

The room is beautiful, but it doesn't feel like it's mine.

Any hope of my memory making a reappearance is rapidly snuffed out, and disappointment presses heavily against the backs of my eyelids. "It's nice."

"I'll let you have some privacy," she offers.

"Thanks, Sofia." It's the first time I've addressed her by name, and I don't realize the magnitude of my mistake until I see the look on her face. "I'm sorry."

"It's all right," she says, her voice wavering. "I'll be downstairs if you need anything."

She leaves the room in a rush. I gravitate to the wall of photos, trying to move past the interaction. The level of awkwardness has apparently been upped now that we're trapped in a house together, and it's hard to imagine a time when it won't feel this way.

There are so many pictures it's hard to focus on one at a time. The majority of them have been taken in crowded living rooms. I've usually got a red Solo cup in hand, surrounded by the same handful of people—a beautiful blond with a dazzling smile, a curly-haired boy most often showing me some form of affection, and a stocky guy wearing a letterman jacket and a goofy grin.

A slew of faces with no memories attached to them. I don't know if I can become the person in the pictures.

A knock sounds on my door, startling me.

"Come in," I call, taking a seat on the bed.

The door clicks open slowly, and Parker pokes his head inside. He sees the look on my face and hovers in the doorway, sticking his hands in his pockets.

"Hey." He greets me.

"Hey," I respond evenly.

He takes my greeting as an invitation to enter the room, then sits on the bed a short distance away. "How are you doing?"

"You know, I've been asked that question so many times, and I don't think I have an answer." A beat of silence hangs between us. "Even if I did, I don't think I'd be able to put it into words."

"I can't even imagine."

"Do we know each other well?"

"We do. You're one of my closest friends."

"Is that really me?" I gesture to the wall of photos with my chin.

"For the most part, yeah," he says. "You were always out. Always. Out with your boyfriend, out with your friends, out doing God knows what. I think you liked being unpredictable." I stare at a photo of me laughing, my arms thrown around the people on either side of me. "But you clashed with your family a fair bit. There were a lot of arguments around here before."

"Wow, I sound *great*," I say sarcastically, causing him to break out in a grin.

"You are," he reassures me.

"At least we get along. It's good to know I wasn't public enemy number one."

He ducks his head, coughing to cover a laugh. I can't explain it, but being around him is the most relaxed I've felt in the short amount of life that I can remember. I believe that we were close before everything happened. It makes him feel more familiar than anyone else. Maybe the relationship with my mother and sister truly was strained.

"What's it like?" he asks suddenly.

"The whole amnesia thing?"

He nods.

"Like I've stepped into somebody's life and now I'm picking up where they left off, except I have no idea what happened before I got here. Everyone is going to expect me to be *that* girl," I say, pointing at the photos on the wall, "but I don't even know her. All I'm going to do is disappoint everyone. I have this constant feeling of guilt—"

"Stop right there." Parker interrupts me, his hand on my arm. "You have absolutely *no* reason to feel guilty. This isn't your fault. You didn't choose this."

It's the first time I've heard the words, and I didn't realize how much I needed them until now. "I don't know why, but I feel like I can trust you. I trust that you'll tell me the truth."

"Of course," he says, reaching out to squeeze my hand. "You can always ask me anything."

"Thanks." I look down at our intertwined fingers.

"I'm so glad you're home," he murmurs, letting go of my hand.

In the next second, he's cupping my face. A jolt runs down my spine as he leans closer and I freeze, but it only takes a second for me to come to my senses.

Placing my hands on his chest, I hurriedly push him away and stand up. "What the hell are you doing?"

Parker looks equally shocked, mouth floundering to come up with an explanation. I wait for him to speak, and he runs a hand over his cropped hair, cursing under his breath. "I'm sorry—that wasn't supposed to happen."

"You're Audrey's boyfriend."

"I am," he confirms, his voice low.

"Then what was that?"

"Something that shouldn't have almost happened again, especially right now." He looks at me remorsefully. "I'm so sorry, Allie. I thought I had more self-control than that."

"*Again?*" The urge to vomit is suddenly sharp. "You've done this before?"

Parker is silent for a few beats. "No," he says finally. "Last time you kissed me. But—"

"This is so messed up!"

"It won't happen again."

"You're right, it won't," I say, gritting my teeth. "You should go."

Without another word, he heads out the door, closing it gently behind him. Once he's gone, my face crumples, and I press my fists against my forehead, mumbling a string of curses like a mantra. What kind of person would do this to their sister, to their boyfriend, to *anyone*?

Minutes ago, it had felt like I had someone in my corner. Now all I feel is the sting of betrayal.

Removing my hands from my face, I stare at the wall of pictures, automatically drawn to a photo of Parker, Audrey, and me. I wonder what other secrets lie behind the multitude of faces and how long it'll take before they all start coming to the surface.